Faults of Understanding

A PRIDE & PREJUDICE
VARIATION

JENNIFER ALTMAN

This is a work of fiction. Names, characters, places, and incidents are products of the author's imagination or are used fictitiously. Any resemblance to actual persons, living or dead, is entirely coincidental and not intended by the author.

Front cover image: *Summer Evening at Skagen* (1892) by Peder Severin Krøyer. Public domain.

Cover by Susan Adriani at CloudCat Design.

ISBN   978-0-578-92155-6

For Jami, who read it first.
In the words of E.B. White:
"It is not often that someone comes along who is a true
friend and a good writer."
Thank you for being both.

"I dare say you will find him very agreeable."

"Heaven forbid! *That* would be the greatest misfortune of all! To find a man agreeable whom one is determined to hate!"

–Jane Austen *Pride and Prejudice*

"...Mr. Darcy has no defect. He owns it himself without disguise."

"No," said Darcy, "I have made no such pretension. I have faults enough, but they are not, I hope, of understanding."

–Jane Austen *Pride and Prejudice*

Prologue

9th December 1811

In the end, Elizabeth blamed Lady Catherine.

Oh, certainly there were any number of others with whom Elizabeth could find fault: Mr. Collins for his lack of discretion; Mr. Bingley for not offering for Jane sooner; her mother for her ceaseless matchmaking. Even her beloved papa for having the temerity to insinuate that accepting Mr. Darcy might be Elizabeth's last chance at matrimony.

Still, it was Lady Catherine who had pushed Elizabeth over the edge.

Sinking into the fine leather squabs of Mr. Darcy's carriage, Elizabeth turned to stare out the window at the hilly terrain—so different from the familiar countryside back home—and the breath left her body in a heavy sigh.

No, it was unfair to condemn Mr. Darcy's aunt. Despite that woman's insolent behavior, Elizabeth had entered into this marriage of her own free will, and the decision had been hers and hers alone. And now, for better or for worse, Mr. Darcy was her husband.

Pulling her gaze away from the passing scenery, Elizabeth shifted her attention to the opposite seat, where the man in question was buried behind his newssheet, much as he had been since the beginning of their journey.

Setting aside the novel she had been attempting to read with little success, Elizabeth cleared her throat.

"Really, Mr. Darcy, I believe we must have some conversation. Even a very little will suffice."

At the sound of her voice, Elizabeth's husband visibly started, slowly lowering his paper to regard her with a rigid expression.

"Forgive me. I had assumed you wished to read your book."

"Not particularly. While I appreciate your consideration, even a great reader such as myself values at least some social interaction during the course of several days spent together within a small compartment."

Elizabeth could see the muscles in Darcy's jaws clench, but he set aside his broadsheet with obvious reluctance.

"Very well. Of what would you wish to speak?"

The lack of emotion in his voice fueled Elizabeth's irritation, and she had to take several calming breaths before trusting herself to reply.

"Perhaps you might tell me a little more about Pemberley. We cannot be more than an hour away, and you have said relatively little about the estate. It might be nice to have some idea of what I can expect when we arrive."

Darcy frowned, turning to observe their surroundings through the frosted glass.

"We are actually quite close. In fact, we should be on Pemberley's lands shortly," he informed her brusquely before directing his attention back to the spot where she sat. "Is there anything in particular you would wish to know?"

Elizabeth was silent, contemplating her response. What she most wanted to know was why her new husband had scarcely said ten words together in the three days they had been in this carriage, and why it seemed to pain him to so much as look in her direction, but she doubted either of those questions would be met with anything beyond Mr. Darcy's usual stony stare.

Clearing her voice, she said instead, "I imagine the house is quite large. How many bedchambers are there?"

"In total, seventeen, however, only twelve of them are currently in use—seven in the family wing, and five guest chambers. There are an additional five chambers on the third floor, as well as the nursery, but those rooms have been closed for many years."

Despite her best efforts to appear indifferent, Elizabeth gaped back at him. *Seventeen bedchambers! Good heavens. That was more than the two inns in Meryton combined!*

"Of course," Darcy continued, "that does not include the servants' quarters."

Swallowing hard, Elizabeth forced a smile.

"Well, that certainly is… large. With a house of that size, I imagine there must also be a good deal of land?" she inquired tentatively, and Darcy nodded.

"There are over four thousand acres. The park itself is ten miles around, so you should have ample space to roam when the weather improves. You are fond of walking, I believe," he added mordantly.

"Yes," Elizabeth murmured.

Darcy's lips tightened, and he briefly looked away. "Good. It is comforting to know there will be one thing you approve of, at least."

Elizabeth opened her mouth to speak, but was saved the

trouble of formulating a reply when her husband once again turned his attention to the view beyond the windowpane.

"Well, you shall not have to wait any longer to have your curiosity satisfied. We have finally arrived."

Chapter 1

D arcy bowed to his partner as the final strains of the quadrille faded into the autumn air. Across from him, Elizabeth offered a slight curtsy and an arch smile, and they parted in silence—she, walking in the direction of her friend, Miss Lucas, and Darcy drifting to a corner of Netherfield's candle-lit ballroom, his mind churning.

How could the dance he had looked forward to all evening—nay, for a fortnight at least, if he were honest with himself—have gone so horribly wrong? That she would take Wickham's part, and paint *him* as the villain! If only she knew the truth. Not that she ever would. To enlighten her would be to put his sister's reputation on the line, and he would take no chances where Georgiana was concerned.

He and Elizabeth had not been separated for long when Darcy became aware of a tall, heavy-looking fellow dressed in an ill-fitting suit advancing upon him at a rapid pace. Narrowing his gaze, Darcy realized it was the bumbling oaf who had danced the first set with Miss Elizabeth. With an inward groan, he turned away, scanning the room for some means of escape, but seconds later, the man drew to a halt before him, bending low at the waist in an exaggerated bow.

"Mr. Darcy," he began, "if I may say so, I have made a remarkable discovery! It has just been brought to my attention that you are the nephew of Lady Catherine de Bourgh of Rosings Park!"

The man continued to speak, but Darcy could scarcely attend to what he was saying. Good God! Was this ridiculous person attempting his own introduction? Darcy could only stare back in total disbelief, and it was a full two minutes before the words "apology" and "Hunsford" penetrated his consciousness, and another moment before he realized that the man who stood before him must be his aunt's new rector.

"What is your name, sir?" Darcy interrupted at the first opportunity.

"Ah! But I should have said so already. Pray forgive me. My name is Collins, sir. William Collins."

Darcy nodded, and the man continued to speak, assuring him of Lady Catherine's good health, and beginning to detail his recent arrival into the neighborhood.

Barely suppressing another groan, Darcy offered the clergyman a shallow bow and was on the cusp of making his excuses, when something Collins said arrested his attention.

"I beg your pardon, did you say you were a relation of the Bennets?" he asked, and even at this slight degree of interest, the parson's face lit with obvious delight.

"Indeed, sir! Mr. Bennet is my cousin, and though I do not like to speak of such things, the Longbourn estate is, in fact, entailed upon me."

Darcy startled slightly at this bit of intelligence, but before he could open his mouth to reply, Collins rushed on, "Oh, but I can see what you are thinking! You are worried for my young cousins. Of course you are! Such feelings do you the greatest credit, sir, although I would expect nothing less from the esteemed nephew of Lady Catherine de Bourgh! But it is now my privilege to inform you that I am very sensible to the hardships and uncertainty that my fair cousins have been forced to endure. Furthermore, you will be relieved to know that I have entered the neighborhood for the sole purpose of healing the breach between our two families and securing the futures of *all* my dear cousins through the joys of matrimony."

Darcy could only gape back at the other man, attempting to parse any relevant information from his rambling speech.

"Are you telling me that you are betrothed to one of the Bennet daughters?" he finally asked incredulously.

Turning red about the ears, Collins began to stammer a reply. "Well, I... that is... I must own that the precise details have not yet been firmly fixed... however, I intend to make my formal addresses on the morrow, and I have every reason to expect a favorable response. Indeed, my dear cousin Elizabeth and I have but one mind and one way of thinking. We seem to have been designed for one another."

At Collins's words, Darcy physically recoiled, the breath seeming to leave his body as he choked out his response.

"You intend to marry Miss Elizabeth?"

Collins beamed back at him. "Am I not the most fortunate of men? My dear cousin is uniformly charming! From almost the moment of my arrival, I singled her out as the companion of my future life, and I am assured by her honored mother that my suit will be most welcome. Indeed, if you call tomorrow, I am certain you will have occasion to wish us joy!"

Darcy stiffened, his heart leaping into his throat. Elizabeth, married to this cretin? It was insupportable! Luckily, he was saved from formulating a reply as the parson was not silent for long.

"Ah! But I can see your concern, and I perfectly comprehend your feelings. You are, naturally, thinking of your aunt. Once again, I am in a position to put your mind at ease. Rest assured, Lady Catherine has sanctioned the match with the greatest degree of condescension. Twice has she given me her opinion on this subject. Indeed, it was right before I left Hunsford that she said, 'Mr. Collins, you must marry. A clergyman like you must marry. Choose properly, choose a gentlewoman for my sake'. And when I wrote to her of my plans for my dearest cousin Elizabeth, she penned her reply with the greatest alacrity. 'Marry the girl, Mr. Collins', said she. 'Bring her to Hunsford as soon as may be, and I will visit her'."

Collins finally paused long enough to draw breath, and Darcy cut him off with the briefest of bows.

"You will excuse me."

Turning on his heel, Darcy beat a hasty retreat, striding towards the center staircase without a backwards glance. Reaching his rooms, he stalked across the threshold, struggling to remove his too-tight jacket and tossing it unceremoniously over the back of a nearby chair. Making his way to the decanter that sat on a low table, he poured himself a generous portion of brandy before pacing to the window and staring out at the lit torches that lined the gravel drive.

It could not be true. Elizabeth Bennet—his Elizabeth!—married to such a man?

Of course, the clergyman had not yet offered for her... but clearly Collins had no doubt of receiving a positive response when he eventually made his addresses.

Was such a thing possible? Darcy could anticipate Mrs. Bennet's endorsement of the match, but surely Elizabeth would not welcome her cousin's attentions?

Darcy set down his glass with a bang before continuing to pace his chambers. He could not believe she would go along with such a scheme. She was too intelligent, too lively and witty and bold to ever attach herself to such an imbecile as her cousin.

Still, Darcy had every reason to believe that she was an obedient daughter. He had witnessed her loyalty firsthand when she had walked three miles to Netherfield to nurse her sister Jane. If she would go to such lengths for a trifling cold, would she not do everything in her power to secure the future of her entire family, even if it meant sacrificing her own happiness in the process?

A sick feeling settled in the pit of Darcy's stomach. She would marry Collins. She would see it as her duty. And worse yet, she would go with him to live at Hunsford, where Darcy would be forced to witness her misery—or, heaven forbid, her felicity—each and every spring when he visited his aunt's estate.

No! He could not leave her to such a fate. Something must be done, and soon, as Collins intended to make his offer the very next day.

Sinking into a chair, Darcy rubbed his temples. Perhaps

if he spoke to Mr. Bennet… but what incentive would that gentleman have to do as Darcy asked? Why should he not wish to see his favorite daughter married to the heir to his estate? Even if Darcy could convince him that such a match would not be in Elizabeth's best interest, understanding and agreeing were two different things. No, the only way Mr. Bennet might concede is if there were another offer on the table. A better offer. Someone who was able to provide his second daughter with far more than William Collins ever could.

Darcy's head snapped up and he immediately sat straighter in his chair. No. It was impossible! He could never form such an attachment. It would be a degradation to the Darcy name! Her family was inferior to his own in every respect. Such an alliance went against all that he stood for.

But you want her, a small voice whispered inside his head. *Though it goes against your will, against your reason, and even against your character, you want her still.*

The hours that followed were some of the longest and most agonizing of Darcy's life, but by the time the sun peeked over the horizon, he knew what must be done.

As was often the case, Elizabeth was the first one of her sisters to leave her bedchamber the morning following the ball. Although she had slept far later than was her custom, she had no doubt that most of her family would likely be abed until midday.

Elizabeth sighed. Today was the day Mr. Collins intended to pay his addresses—he had all but said so last evening in the carriage while her sisters tittered and her mother beamed—and she was dreading the conversation as well as her mother's vitriol which would surely follow her inevitable refusal.

Knowing his habits, she doubted her cousin would be about at such an hour, nevertheless, she crept down the back staircase, intending to go to the kitchens for a bite to eat before taking her usual morning ramble. She would need all the strength and serenity she could muster to deal with the interview that would likely take place upon her return.

But she had scarcely made it into the lower passageway when she heard her name called in her father's familiar tones. Poking her head into his book room, she found him seated in his usual spot, a cup of tea cooling on the perpetually cluttered surface of his desk.

He beckoned her in, and she grinned back at him, crossing the floor and taking her usual seat in one of the overstuffed chairs across from him.

"Good morning, Papa. I see you have also decided to forgo sleeping the day away," she teased.

"Indeed," he answered, though the half smile he offered was soon replaced by a more somber expression as he continued, "As a matter of fact, I have already had the dubious honor of receiving a visitor."

Elizabeth's smile instantly faded. "Not Mr. Collins? I was certain I would be spared having to face him until after breakfast, at least!"

"No, no. I have not yet had the pleasure of your cousin's company. Though I suspect that reprieve should not last much longer." After a slight hesitation, he continued, "You plan to refuse him, then?"

"Were you in any doubt? I am sorry, Papa. I know it will break Mamma's heart, but I simply cannot marry a man I do not respect, not even for Longbourn. I hope you can understand."

"I see. And is this the only reason? Your decision would have nothing to do with your preference for another gentleman, perhaps?"

"Another gentleman?" Elizabeth repeated, her brow furrowed in confusion.

Mr. Bennet leaned back in his chair, peering at her over the tops of his spectacles. "You appear surprised. I wonder, Lizzy, how you would feel to learn that my early morning caller was none other than Mr. Darcy?"

"Mr. Darcy!" Elizabeth's shock was absolute. Whatever would bring Mr. Darcy to Longbourn, and at such an unacceptable hour? Unless... "It is not Mr. Bingley, is it? Has something happened at Netherfield?"

Mr. Bennet was quick to put her mind at ease with a shake of his head. "No, no. This has nothing to do with Mr. Bingley or your sister. In point of fact, Mr. Darcy came here to make his own offer of marriage. For you."

Elizabeth choked out a laugh. "An offer of marriage, from Mr. Darcy! Surely you are joking?" she began, but one look at her father's expression caused her to sober, and her mouth dropped open as a strange buzzing filled her ears.

"Ah. So you *are* surprised," Mr. Bennet replied.

"Nay! I am astounded! Mr. Darcy despises me. You must have misunderstood."

"I assure you, I did not. The gentleman made his intentions quite clear."

"But... I do not understand. It is impossible! Besides

the fact that Mr. Darcy has never so much as looked at me unless it was to find fault, Mr. Wickham claims that he is promised to Lady Catherine's daughter."

"Your cousin's patroness?" When Elizabeth nodded, her father frowned. "And who is Mr. Wickham to be acquainted with the personal affairs of these people?"

Reflexively, Elizabeth waved her hand in an agitated manner. "His family has a connection to the Darcys. Mr. Wickham's father was the late Mr. Darcy's steward."

"Hmm... Well, clearly Mr. Wickham is mistaken. If the present Mr. Darcy was indeed betrothed to Miss de Bourgh, he certainly would not have been on my doorstep this morning, speaking of making an offer to you."

Filled with a sudden restless irritation, Elizabeth climbed to her feet, pacing to the window and staring out into the garden. *This could not be happening!* Surely her beloved papa would never force her to marry Mr. Darcy!

"You did not give him your consent?" she cried, turning once again in her father's direction. "Oh, pray, tell me you did not!"

Mr. Bennet's eyebrows rose at the fervor in his daughter's voice. "Lizzy, we both know Mr. Darcy to be a man of consequence. Indeed, he is the kind of man to whom I should never dare to refuse anything which he has condescended to ask." Elizabeth blanched, but her father continued, "However, as Mr. Collins had already made his intentions towards you abundantly clear, I felt I owed it to your cousin to hold off on giving Mr. Darcy my approbation. I also thought it prudent to ascertain your feelings in the matter."

Elizabeth groaned. First Mr. Collins and now Mr. Darcy! How was it possible for her to have attracted the notice of the two most loathsome gentlemen in the entire kingdom!

"My feelings, I assure you, are quite fixed. I cannot think what would have possessed Mr. Darcy to believe I would welcome his addresses. From the very beginning—practically from the first moment of our acquaintance—he has impressed me with his arrogance, his conceit, and his selfish disdain for the feelings of others. He is, without a doubt, the last gentleman in the world I could ever be prevailed on to marry!"

An amused glimmer shone in Mr. Bennet's eyes as he answered, "I thought surely that distinction went to Mr. Collins."

Her anger spent, Elizabeth returned to her seat, staring coolly back at her father. "At least Mr. Collins had the decency to request a private audience with the object of his interest. Tell me, has Mr. Darcy any idea of proposing to me in person, or is all of this to be worked out through intermediaries? Am I to meet him next at the altar?"

Mr. Bennet smirked. "I believe it is Mr. Darcy's intention to call on you this afternoon. Somehow, he seems to have got wind of your cousin's motives and thought to preempt a betrothal in that quarter. I believe he wanted to make certain I knew you had other, shall we say, *more lucrative* options, at your disposal."

Elizabeth studied her father, and a sliver of unease took hold inside her stomach. "Papa, I hardly know what to say. I cannot possibly accept Mr. Darcy *or* my cousin. If I were to wed either, I should be miserable every day of my life. Pray, tell me you shall not make me choose between them!"

Across from her, Mr. Bennet sighed, removing his spectacles and polishing the lenses with his handkerchief before replacing them upon his nose.

"I am not proud of this, Lizzy, but I will admit that when I first realized Mr. Collins would offer for you, I did think to coerce you to accept him. However, I can assure you the thought was gone in an instant. I know my cousin could never make you happy. He is not a gentleman you could respect, and your lively intelligence would die a slow death under his negligent care. But for a moment, it gave me great comfort to think of you always at Longbourn. Of all my children, you are the one who has been most like a son to me. The one I have groomed in the management of the estate. Longbourn is in your blood, in a way that it never has been for any of your sisters. You care more about the tenants, the land, and the health of the estate than the rest of them combined—indeed though I am loath to say it, more even than myself—and it would have been a fine thing to have one day seen you as its mistress. To think that you might have had a son to continue that legacy…"

Feeling like the worst sort of ingrate, Elizabeth opened her mouth to speak, but her father stopped her with a raised palm.

"Do not make yourself uneasy, my dear; the feeling did not last long. Perhaps if Collins had been a different sort of man… But no. I could not see you trapped in such a marriage. You could never be happy unless you could respect your husband—unless you looked up to him as a superior."

"Thank you, Papa," Elizabeth whispered.

But her gratitude was short lived as her father continued, "However, now you have been given another choice."

"You cannot be serious! Mr. Darcy is every bit as

horrible as Mr. Collins! I do not know what misguided notion has compelled him to make me an offer of marriage, but he does not love me, and I know that I could never love him. I care nothing for his ten thousand a year or his grand estate. I will not marry without affection."

Across from her, Mr. Bennet's eyes narrowed. "Is that truly how you feel?" At Elizabeth's nod, he continued, "I am sorry, Lizzy, but I must ask you to think carefully on this, for if you reject both Mr. Collins and Mr. Darcy, there is a very real possibility that you shall never be any man's wife."

"But that is… You cannot honestly think…" Elizabeth's voice trailed off and Mr. Bennet sighed.

"What I think is that you must be realistic, my child. If it is widely known that you have refused two extremely advantageous offers of marriage, then yes, I do believe that it will materially damage your prospects."

"But that is nonsensical, not to mention grossly unfair!"

"Perhaps. But it is the way of the world. Gossip is easily spread; it will be talked about. People will say you believe yourself to be above your company. They will call you proud and self-important, and it is likely that other gentlemen will fear encountering a similar rebuff."

"But why should anyone ever find out?" Elizabeth cried, surprised by her father's answering chuckle.

"Do you really need ask? I think it likely that Mr. Collins has already made half the neighborhood aware of his intentions, and your mother has no doubt told the rest. I do not know who Mr. Darcy has spoken to, besides myself, but it would not be unreasonable to assume he has made mention of it to his friend. I do not believe I need to tell you how quickly rumors will begin to circulate."

Elizabeth opened her mouth to speak, but again, Mr. Bennet held up his hand.

"Now, I know what you are going to say, but pray, hear me out. Besides the fact that you would be risking spinsterhood by refusing both of these gentlemen, I still maintain that Mr. Darcy may be a good match for you. I know you claim not to like him, and he did make that unfortunate comment about you at the local assembly—"

"I do not merely claim not to like him! I cannot abide the sight of him, and his feelings for me are hardly any better."

Mr. Bennet lifted his brow, but continued speaking, "—however, he is a man of intelligence and good principles. I believe he is a gentleman you could look up to and esteem. You would be well provided for, and I trust that he would treat you with respect. Besides, I observed him last night, during your dance, and no matter what you say, I do not think he looks at you without affection."

"I cannot agree with you, but regardless of his feelings, would you discount my own? As I have already stated, I could never love him."

"Ah, love." Mr. Bennet sighed. "Oh, my Lizzy. You are full young, and still see the world in shades of black and white. But take it from one who knows: Marrying for love does not guarantee happiness."

"You speak of you and Mamma?" Elizabeth said softly, and her father nodded.

"I know what you think of our union, and I know I am to blame for not treating your mother with more regard, but I can assure you that I had the deepest affection for her when we married. But love fades quickly if it is not accompanied by mutual respect."

"Will you force me to marry him?" Elizabeth whispered.

"No, my dear, I will not. But I would ask you to allow him to make his offer. Furthermore, I would ask that you do not tender your reply without giving the matter ample consideration. Twenty-four hours. I will ask you to think on it for the span of one full day. If you still maintain that you do not wish to have him for your husband, we shall not speak of this again."

Slowly, Elizabeth nodded. It seemed unnecessarily cruel to give any gentleman false hope—even Mr. Darcy—but Elizabeth could live with her father's request.

"Very well. I shall hear Mr. Darcy out, and I promise to do my best to keep an open mind."

Mr. Bennet nodded his approval. He had just begun to make his reply when the slight creaking of one of the floorboards in the outer corridor briefly halted their discourse, and both father and daughter turned towards the door.

When their gazes met again, Elizabeth's eyes were wide, but Mr. Bennet only waved off her obvious apprehension.

"Be easy. No doubt it is only Hill, gone to bring your Mamma her tea. I daresay it is still far too early for any of the family to be up and about on the morning following a ball."

Elizabeth nodded, but it was not her mother or her sisters she was worrying about. Coming to her feet, she slowly padded to the door, gently lifting the latch before throwing it ajar.

The passageway was empty.

Behind her she could hear her father's soft chuckle.

"I imagine I know what you are thinking, but I doubt

even Collins would stoop so low as to go listening at doors. Now, come. There is something I wish for you to see before you meet with Mr. Darcy."

Elizabeth closed the door, retracing her steps as her father opened the top drawer of his desk, extracting a heavy sheet of parchment and passing it into her hands.

Resuming her seat, Elizabeth scanned the page that was written through in a very close hand, which she soon realized was Mr. Darcy's.

"It is not the formal marriage articles, of course," her father continued, "but he wanted me to have a general idea of what he would settle on you, should you consent to become his wife."

Elizabeth began to read, her eyes growing round as the clock ticked off the seconds.

Twenty-five thousand pounds to be immediately settled on her at the time of their marriage, to do with as she pleased... Five hundred pounds per annum in pin money (and more should she require it)... a horse and carriage dedicated to her own personal use... A generous clothing allowance... Free rein in the running of the households at all his properties, including an unlimited allowance to redecorate those abodes as she saw fit... Five thousand pounds settled upon each of her sisters, and an equal sum to be settled upon her mother at the time of her father's death... large portions set aside for any daughters the marriage might produce...

Elizabeth stopped reading. Lifting her gaze, she stared into the near distance, her pulse pounding in her ears. *Good heavens!* No wonder her father was insisting that she carefully consider Mr. Darcy's offer.

"I hardly know what to say," she finally stammered,

turning back to face her father. "Mr. Darcy certainly intends to be exceedingly generous."

"He does indeed," agreed Mr. Bennet, taking the document back and returning it to his desk.

"Did he ask you to show that to me?"

"He did. Said he believed that as one of the parties involved, you had a right to know the specifics of the marriage contract."

More like flaunting his wealth in an attempt to coerce me to accept him, Elizabeth inwardly grumbled, but she only smiled tightly before once again coming to her feet.

"If there is nothing else, may I go now?" Elizabeth asked, and her father nodded his consent.

Murmuring a hurried farewell, she slipped out into the corridor, her feet automatically carrying her towards the door to the gardens. She needed to be out of doors. To breathe the fresh, cool air. To walk as far as her feet would carry her. Perhaps then she would be able to sort through this tangle and settle upon a course of action. But no sooner had she reached for the latch, when a sudden thought arrested her movement. What if Mr. Darcy should be out there? Perhaps he had gone for a walk, or a ride, to pass the time before returning to pay his addresses.

Slowly she withdrew her hand. No, she could not risk it. She would go above stairs. Perhaps Jane was now awake and would be able to help her make sense of this astounding turn of events.

Chapter 2

A quarter of an hour later, Jane gaped back at her from the window seat, her astonishment at Elizabeth's news clearly reflected in her gaze.

"Mr. Darcy wishes to marry you? Lizzy, are you certain?"

Elizabeth regarded her sister with a lifted brow, and Jane continued, "Forgive me, that was a silly thing to say. It is only that I can hardly comprehend it! Had you any indication he held you in such esteem?"

"I assure you, I am as shocked as anyone! Shocked. Grieved. Baffled. Oh, Jane! What am I to do? I cannot marry him! You of all people know how I feel about Mr. Darcy. He is absolutely the last man in the world I should ever wish to marry!"

Jane frowned. "I do not think he is as bad as you make him out to be. But if these are your true feelings, then of course you must refuse him."

"Yes. Yes, you are correct. I must refuse him. To marry such a man is unthinkable. He is every bit as bad as Mr. Collins. I should rather end up an old maid than tie myself to either one of them. I shall simply content myself with being a devoted aunt to your children, and perhaps your Mr.

Bingley will take pity on me and allow me to live with you when I have nowhere else to go."

Jane flushed crimson. "He is not *my* Mr. Bingley. You know that things between us are by no means settled."

"No, but they will be soon enough."

Jane sighed before deftly changing the subject.

"I do feel rather sorry for Mr. Darcy though. I believe he must love you a great deal."

Unable to hide her surprise, Elizabeth stared back at her sister with wide eyes. "Do not be ridiculous! Mr. Darcy does not love me. I dare say he does not even like me. Have you forgotten so quickly that I was not even tolerable enough to tempt him to dance?"

"Yes," Jane answered with a knitted brow, "that was a terrible thing to say, and in company, too. But people do not always say what they mean. And since then, I have begun to suspect he is not so indifferent as you believe. I could not help but notice the way he looked at you when we were guests at Netherfield. And he did ask you to dance last night. You were the only one he singled out in such a way. He danced with no one else, save Mr. Bingley's sisters."

Elizabeth gave an exasperated huff. "Now you sound like Charlotte. If he stared at me at Netherfield, it was only to find fault. And he likely asked me to dance because he knew it would vex me."

"Lizzy, gentlemen do not offer for ladies simply to aggravate them. If you accept him, he will be pledging himself to you for all eternity."

Elizabeth groaned. Yes, Mr. Darcy would be pledging himself to her, just as she would be pledging herself to him.

"Likely he did not even think it through. It is only some

misguided attempt to keep me from marrying his aunt's rector. Domineering, overbearing, insufferable man!"

Jane had just opened her mouth to speak, when a light tapping on the door silenced the sisters' conversation.

"Enter," Jane called, as Elizabeth held her breath, prepared for her mother to sweep in, demanding that Elizabeth ready herself to meet with her cousin. But when the door opened, it was not Mrs. Bennet who entered, but Hill. Fixing her attention on Jane, the housekeeper stepped into their chambers carrying a folded sheet of parchment.

"Forgive the disruption, Miss, but a letter just come from Netherfield."

"Thank you, Hill," Jane answered, reaching out to take the proffered note.

Her expression was serene, as always, but Elizabeth thought she was likely relieved to be receiving the letter in the privacy of her chambers rather than in the parlor where her mother would no doubt find out about it and interrogate Jane on its contents.

Hill curtsied and left the room, closing the door behind her, and Jane turned her attention to the elegant hot-pressed paper, gingerly breaking the seal. Elizabeth watched her sister's countenance as she read, noting the distress that soon furrowed Jane's brow.

"It is from Caroline Bingley," Jane said softly. "The whole party, save Mr. Darcy, have left Netherfield by this time, and are on their way to Town—and without any intention of coming back again. Here, you may read it for yourself." She passed the letter to Elizabeth, who quickly scanned the page, pressing her lips together tightly as she read. When she had finished, she handed the missive back to her sister.

"He will return no more this winter," said Jane morosely. "He will forget about me."

"Nonsense," Elizabeth scoffed. "This letter only asserts that Miss Bingley does not mean for him to return. These are her intentions, not his."

"Perhaps. But Mr. Bingley will stay if his sisters wish it. And once you reject Mr. Darcy—as I know you must—he will warn his friend against us. They will all work to keep Mr. Bingley in Town. I shall never see him again."

Elizabeth once more began to protest, but the look on Jane's face caused the words to die on her lips. In truth, who was she to say that her sister was not correct? Mr. Darcy did seem to hold a great deal of influence over his friend, and if—nay, *when*—Elizabeth rejected him, there was little doubt that he would do everything in his power to sever any connection between Mr. Bingley and their family.

Jane looked away and Elizabeth stood, moving to gather her pelisse and bonnet.

"I can see you wish to be alone, so I will leave you now, my dearest sister, but we are by no means finished with this discussion. I believe with all my heart that Mr. Bingley is your destiny, and if it is at all within my power to bring him back to you, pray, know that it shall be done."

Deciding that an outing was imperative, whatever the risks, Elizabeth once again made her way down the back stairs, happy to find no one but the housekeeper when she reached the floor below.

"Hill, I am going for a short walk. I am not certain if

Jane will wish to come down for breakfast, but perhaps you might bring her some tea?"

The housekeeper readily agreed, and Elizabeth moved towards the door to the gardens before turning back around.

"Oh, and Hill, have you seen our cousin yet this morning?"

"Aye, Miss. He went out about ten minutes before you come down. Said he had some business in the village that could not be delayed."

"In Meryton? Did he ask for the carriage?"

"No, Miss. Said he was of a mind to walk."

Elizabeth nodded. "I see. Thank you."

Making her way along the corridor that led to the side door, Elizabeth's thoughts raced. Why would Mr. Collins have gone to Meryton? She could not remember him expressing a need to visit any of the shops, and it was even more unusual that he should choose to go on foot, as Mr. Collins was not fond of walking.

An hour later, Elizabeth was no closer to answering any of these questions—nor to a solution to her conundrum about Mr. Darcy—when she made her reluctant return to Longbourn. This was an unfortunate occurrence, as she had no sooner entered the lane that led to the house when she became aware of a tall black stallion approaching from the opposite direction. Dread twisted her stomach as she recognized the rider, but she grudgingly halted her steps, waiting as the horse drew near.

When he gained the drive, Mr. Darcy neatly dismounted, leading his horse the remainder of the way before removing his hat and offering her a formal bow.

"Mr. Darcy," Elizabeth murmured.

"Miss Elizabeth."

The two stood in silence for several minutes before Darcy continued, "I trust your father has spoken with you?"

"He has, sir."

Darcy nodded, and Elizabeth watched as he shifted his hat from one hand to another.

"I had thought we might take some time to discuss my proposition. Shall we return to the house? Or a walk, perhaps?"

Elizabeth hesitated. She would greatly prefer to speak with Mr. Darcy outside, where they might be assured of more privacy, but she had already been gone for some time. Besides, she was confident that Mr. Darcy would also prefer to speak outside the house, and a certain perverseness made her not want to make things any easier on him.

"You may accompany me back to Longbourn if you wish. I am sure my father will not object to our making use of his book room."

Darcy nodded, his expression pained, and they moved into the yard. One of the grooms approached to take the horse, and Elizabeth led Mr. Darcy through the gardens to the side entrance she had used earlier. She was not surprised when her father met them in the corridor, having seen them approaching from the window. After briefly informing Elizabeth that her mother and sisters remained above stairs, and that Mr. Collins was still out, he ushered them into his library with a wry smile before quitting the room, leaving the door slightly ajar.

Elizabeth took a seat by the window, folding her hands demurely in her lap and watching as Mr. Darcy paced about the room, finally coming to stand several feet away.

"Your father has shown you the papers I drew up?" he inquired abruptly.

"He has, sir," Elizabeth answered before adding, "I suppose I should thank you. The settlement you proposed was very generous."

Darcy dismissed her words with a wave of his hand. "It is no more than you deserve. There is very little I would be unable or unwilling to provide you with, once we are married, but if there is anything in particular you would like outlined in the articles, you need only ask."

Elizabeth murmured her thanks, and the room grew quiet.

"No doubt you were surprised by my intentions," Darcy eventually stated.

"Indeed. I was quite astounded."

"Yes. I must beg your pardon for taking you unawares. Given the disparity in our stations, I can see that this must come as a shock. In truth, I had not made up my mind to offer for you until last night."

Elizabeth could feel the heat building in her cheeks, but she somehow managed to answer serenely, "Disparity? Forgive me, I do not understand. You are a gentleman, and I am a gentleman's daughter. So far as I can see, we are equal."

Across from her, Darcy's eyebrows lifted. He opened his mouth and closed it again several times, before finally saying, "I beg your pardon. What I meant to say is that it would not have been appropriate to give rise to expectations by showing any partiality to you before such a time as I had determined to pay my addresses. However, when I came to understand that an offer of marriage was soon to be made to you by Mr. Collins, I knew I must act with all due haste."

"I see. And pray, tell me, Mr. Darcy, what concern is it

of yours whether I should marry my cousin, or any other gentleman for that matter?"

Elizabeth watched as Darcy's entire body stiffened. "I had the misfortune of spending almost twenty minutes in conversation with Collins last evening, and it took less than five of those minutes to know that it would be a degradation for you to wed such a man! He is not your equal in intelligence or wit, and I must add that his lack of decorum was truly shocking. You are his superior in every way. I do not believe your cousin could ever make you happy, nor give you the life you deserve. Marriage to him would be a misery for you!"

Despite her intention to remain detached, Elizabeth's eyes grew wide at Darcy's impassioned speech. Could it be that the gentleman had formed some sort of attachment to her after all? Elizabeth flushed at the thought. To keep herself from dwelling on such a notion, she responded in a way she knew must provoke him further.

"Nevertheless, he would be a prudent match for me."

For a moment, Mr. Darcy looked physically ill, before his expression softened and he leaned forward, addressing her earnestly, "Aye. And that is why I knew I must speak. I am aware that your father's estate is entailed upon your cousin, and as such, you may feel it would be pragmatic to accept him, for the sake of all your family. But now you see, you have another way. I know I cannot give you Longbourn, but should you agree to marry me, your family will always be provided for. On this, I give you my word."

Elizabeth shifted uncomfortably in her seat. She had promised her father she would not make any hasty decisions regarding Mr. Darcy's offer, but she could not in good conscience allow him to continue if his sole motive was to save her from a marriage to her cousin.

"Mr. Darcy, I thank you for your concern for my welfare, however, you may rest easy, sir. I have already decided I will not be accepting my cousin's proposal of marriage, should he see fit to make one. So you need not worry for my future, and as such, you should feel under no further obligation to me. You have made me no formal offer, and I understand that you will have no wish to make your addresses now. We may both continue on as we were before."

Darcy's thick brows drew together, and he studied her for a moment before he spoke.

"While I am gratified to know you have decided against attaching yourself to your cousin, pray, allow me to correct your misapprehension as to my desires. I have no wish to withdraw my offer. I have made my intentions known to your father, and it would be dishonorable to back out now. However, you are correct that no formal address has been made. I hope you will allow me to correct this oversight."

To Elizabeth's horror, he dropped to one knee, taking up her hand. "Miss Elizabeth, will you do me the courtesy of becoming my wife?"

An unexpected jolt traveled up Elizabeth's arm at the warmth of Mr. Darcy's fingers on her ungloved hand. Quickly, she stood, breaking their connection and forcing Mr. Darcy to rise. Pacing several steps away, Elizabeth stared through the mullioned glass before turning back to face her unexpected suitor.

"Mr. Darcy, I hope you do not think I spoke in such a way to entreat you to make your proposal. I was in earnest when I offered to forget the entire situation."

"I am well aware of your intentions."

"Then you are saying you still wish to marry me?"

"I do."

Exasperated, Elizabeth threw up her hands. "But why? I have already told you I do not intend to marry my cousin and that I have no expectations of you!"

Mr. Darcy's eyes widened, clearly taken aback by her outburst.

"Is it so surprising that I would wish to marry you?"

At such a remarkable question, Elizabeth could not help quirking one eyebrow in surprise. "I believe I have already stated as much. And as you can no longer claim Mr. Collins as your motive, I should like to know why you would wish to make me your wife. We have scarcely known each other a month, and as you have so helpfully stated, we are not of the same circles."

"Yes, of course you are correct. And while I realize our acquaintance has been of a brief duration, I assure you, I have given this matter a great deal of thought. We get on satisfactorily. We are well matched in intelligence, if not in temperament. I believe you would be an admirable mistress for my estate, and a worthy example to my sister. Are these not all respectable reasons to marry?"

Elizabeth released a frustrated sigh. This was not going at all as she had planned.

"Yes, I suppose they are. But you must wish for something beyond all that? Certainly, you could find someone more... more..." Her voice faltered and she drew a breath before changing tactics. "In any case, I was under the impression that you were already promised. Are you not betrothed to your own cousin?" she asked archly.

"My cousin?" Darcy repeated.

"Yes, Miss de Bourgh. I believe she will have a very large fortune, and that it is the wish of both your families that you unite your two estates."

Inexplicably, Darcy's lips tightened as he ground out, "I am not engaged to Anne. And you would do well to avoid listening to idle gossip."

Elizabeth looked away in embarrassment. He was right, of course. But before she could formulate an adequate apology, Mr. Darcy continued in a gentler tone, "It is true that when my cousin and I were children, our mothers spoke of our one day growing up to marry, but it was merely an idle wish. It was never anything more than that. Had my matrimonial interest veered in that direction, I assure you, Anne and I would have wed some time ago."

Elizabeth nodded. "Very well. I accept your assertion that you are not promised to Miss de Bourgh; however, I am still not convinced I would make you a good wife."

Darcy looked momentarily startled, but answered smoothly, "Is this your only objection? If it is my feelings you are worried for, I have already told you it is my belief that you would suit me quite well. However, if I can say anything further to put your mind at ease, I am happy to do so."

Elizabeth paced to the window, drawing back the curtain. Once again gazing out into the garden, she attempted to bring order to her jumbled thoughts. She did not know how long she stood there before she felt the light press of a hand upon her shoulder and heard Mr. Darcy's deep baritone speaking softly in her ear.

"You must know that I will treat you with kindness, Miss Elizabeth. I realize I am asking you to take a leap of faith, but I promise you will want for nothing. Whatever is in my power to give, you shall have."

Elizabeth turned away from the glass and gazed up into Mr. Darcy's warm brown eyes. He stared back at her, and Elizabeth saw a host of emotions written across his features. Without conscious thought, her eyes dropped to his lips, which were full and looked surprisingly soft. Before she knew what she was about, she heard herself speaking the question that was at the forefront of her mind.

"You would want a child, I imagine. A son and heir for your estate."

She could see him start, but after a brief hesitation, he answered carefully, "Pemberley is not entailed, so if we do not have a son, a daughter may inherit. And if for some reason we are not blessed with children, the estate would pass to my sister's offspring. But to answer your question: Yes, I do want children. Not for the purposes of the estate, but because I would wish to have a family one day."

Elizabeth turned away, surprised by how strongly both his words and the tenderness of his gaze had affected her. At her back, she heard Darcy clear his throat.

"Do you not... that is... are you not fond of children?"

"Oh, no. I am very fond of children," she answered, shifting to face him again.

Darcy nodded, appearing somewhat uncertain. "Good. That is... good. I am glad to hear it."

Elizabeth stepped away, crossing to the far side of the room. If she was going to maintain her composure, she needed to put some distance between them. Darcy followed her with his eyes, but remained standing where he was.

Clearing her throat, Elizabeth began, "There is one

more matter I think it imperative that we discuss. What have you to say of Mr. Wickham?"

At the mention of Wickham's name, Mr. Darcy's spine stiffened and his countenance, which had been so animated only a moment ago, turned cold.

"I have nothing whatsoever to say on the subject of that gentleman. What has he to do with this?"

Elizabeth lifted her chin. "I believe he has everything to do with this. Your ill treatment of him speaks to your character."

"*My* ill treatment?" Darcy virtually spat, crossing the floor in quick steps before turning back and pacing in the opposite direction. When he finally stopped in front of her, his eyes were hard and his voice when he spoke had a frosty edge. "As I have already stated once, you would do well not to believe everything you hear. There are, after all, two sides to every story."

"Very well. Then I am willing to listen to yours."

Darcy was silent, but Elizabeth could see the tic of a muscle in his jaw.

"I see," Elizabeth eventually answered.

"If you are hoping for a proposal from him," Mr. Darcy said darkly, "you are bound to be disappointed. Wickham will marry a woman of means, if he marries at all."

"And whose fault is that?" Elizabeth cried. "You are the one who has reduced him to his present circumstances. Had you provided him with the living promised in your father's will, he would not be forced to live in comparable poverty even now. It is because of you that Mr. Wickham cannot marry where he chooses."

"Is that what he told you?" Darcy turned away, muttering under his breath, "Good God. The man will stop at nothing to blacken my name." When he moved to face her again, Elizabeth could see him struggling to regain control of his emotions.

"I cannot divulge all of my dealings with Wickham, as there are others who would be harmed by my disclosures. However, I can tell you that Mr. Wickham lies as easily as he breathes. The living in question was rejected by him. Instead, he requested monetary compensation, as he did not think himself suited to the church—a sentiment with which I whole-heartedly agreed—and instead I paid him three thousand pounds, in lieu of the living. This was in addition to the one thousand pounds left him by my father. So, if Mr. Wickham currently finds himself in precarious financial circumstances, you might ask yourself why that is."

Elizabeth stared back at Mr. Darcy, fully feeling the shock of his declaration and the humiliation of her misplaced conviction. When she did not speak, Darcy continued, "If you doubt my words, I can summon more than one witness to speak to their veracity. I assure you, Mr. Wickham cannot say the same."

"No," she murmured, a flush warming her cheeks, "that will not be necessary. I believe you."

In an instant, Darcy's expression softened, and his anger seemed to dissipate as quickly as it had come.

"I beg your pardon. It was not my intention to cause you distress. But I am glad to have had an opportunity to speak to you on this matter. I hope you will heed my warning and stay far away from Mr. Wickham. He is not an honorable man."

Elizabeth offered him a shaky nod before saying, "You have given me much to think about, Mr. Darcy, and I hope you understand that I can give you no answer today. I must first speak to my cousin, and then I would like some time to consider the matter. This has all been rather… sudden."

"Of course," Darcy answered quickly. "I will importune you no further. But I hope you will permit me to call on you tomorrow?"

Elizabeth nodded, and Darcy bowed slightly at the waist before turning towards the door, but Elizabeth's voice halted his progress.

"You will remain at Netherfield, then?" she asked.

Darcy turned. "I will. Bingley has been kind enough to allow me the use of the house for as long as I should require it."

"Then it is true… that he has left the neighborhood? My sister had a letter from Miss Bingley earlier today."

"Yes, I believe he had some business in Town."

"And… will he return? When his business is concluded?"

Darcy shrugged. "With Bingley, it is hard to say. His sisters, I know, would prefer to remain in London, and Bingley is always happiest wherever he is—as I think he remarked once when we were together at Netherfield."

Elizabeth nodded slowly, and with another bow, Darcy quit the room, leaving her with much to ponder about the man she was so certain she despised.

If Elizabeth thought her day could not get any worse, she was soon to be corrected. For no sooner had Mr. Darcy departed, than Mr. Collins returned, sweeping into the front parlor and demanding a private audience with his cousin Elizabeth.

Elizabeth reluctantly stood, relieved that at least her mother was not present. As luck would have it, the revelry of the night before had kept Mrs. Bennet and her two youngest daughters above stairs; and Jane, as well, remained in her chambers, so it was only Mary and Mr. Bennet on hand to witness Elizabeth's summons.

Shooting his second daughter a sardonic smile, Mr. Bennet nodded his consent, and she and her cousin made their way to the empty breakfast room.

Perching gingerly on the edge of a chair, Elizabeth opened her mouth, searching for a way to let her cousin down as gently as possible, but it was he who spoke first.

Bowing obsequiously, he began, "Forgive me, madam, for what I am about to say. I know it will be distressing to you, but it cannot be helped. After careful consideration, I have determined that I must look elsewhere for the companion of my future life. While it is true that I entered the neighborhood with the intention of choosing a wife from amongst the ladies of this household, I now realize that despite your amiable qualifications, I must think carefully about my responsibility both to my congregation, as well as to my esteemed patroness. Additionally, as a man who naturally seeks happiness in the marriage state, I believe it incumbent upon myself to select a bride who will contribute to my own felicity. Thus, I must humbly withdraw my pretentions to your hand."

Mr. Collins stared at Elizabeth expectantly, but she could only blink back at him, so great was her astonishment.

"You are abandoning your suit?" she asked, incredulously.

"Indeed; I believe I must. I realize this will come as a great disappointment to you, but we are all liable to error."

Not certain if she was more of a mind to laugh or scream, Elizabeth pressed her lips together before saying, "Very well. I accept your reasons, sir, and release you from any perceived expectations."

Mr. Collins nodded somberly. "I should also add that due to these…ah…unforeseen developments, I have decided it might be best for me to return to Kent on the morrow. In the meantime, I have accepted an invitation to dine at Lucas Lodge, and will repair there forthwith. However, before I go, I thought it incumbent upon myself to issue you a warning, my dear cousin: Not everyone will turn a kind eye upon those who seek an alliance with their betters. I hope you will give serious consideration to this fact before consenting to enter into a union that has not been properly sanctioned."

Elizabeth's eyes grew round, but her cousin quickly pressed a finger to his lips.

"Ah, but I have said too much. From this moment forward, let us be forever silent on this point."

And with that, Mr. Collins bowed low at the waist and quit the room, leaving Elizabeth to wonder what her cousin knew, and exactly where he had gone when he had left Longbourn earlier that day.

Chapter 3

E lizabeth awoke the following morning after a restless slumber. Today she was to meet with Mr. Darcy, and she was no closer to knowing what she should do. Glancing out her bedroom window, she could see the sun shining brightly on the autumn leaves, and she instantly felt an almost painful need to be out of doors. Quickly donning a simple morning dress, she gathered her pelisse and bonnet, hoping a long walk in the cool air would help her to sort her jumbled emotions.

As was often her habit, her footsteps carried her to Oakham Mount, to a favorite spot where a fallen log rested in the shade of a great oak. Taking a seat upon the rough wood, she untied the ribbons of her bonnet, setting it beside her and allowing the breeze to lift the curls at the back of her neck.

She should have refused him immediately. Why, oh why, had she agreed to her father's demand to wait before giving Mr. Darcy her answer? Her mind had been quite made up on the matter, and surely giving any man false hope was unnecessarily cruel… On the other hand, if Mr. Darcy had only proposed to save her from Mr. Collins, why had he not withdrawn his offer once she had made it clear that she had no intention of marrying her cousin?

Suddenly restless, Elizabeth stood from her seat, beginning to pace the small clearing with rapid, urgent steps. Surely she was not actually considering marrying Mr. Darcy? It was unthinkable! Taking a calming breath, she attempted to order her tangled emotions. She needed to approach this in a rational manner. She would make a list! Yes, that was the way to go about it. She would catalogue all the reasons for and against marrying Mr. Darcy. Certainly, if she did that, she would see the overwhelming evidence supporting a refusal.

She looked around the small clearing, as if expecting a writing desk complete with parchment, pen, and ink to appear before her, then laughed at her own fanciful imagination. Well, no matter, the list would just have to remain in her head for now. She could commit it to paper once she returned to the house.

Making her way back to her log, Elizabeth sat. She would start with the "against" column. That would be easier.

Reason number one: Obviously, she despised the man. Elizabeth chewed her lip. Well, perhaps "despised" was a strong term. She definitely did not like him. He was proud and arrogant and overbearing.

Still… there were times when his behavior could be… almost agreeable.

Unbidden, a smile pulled at her lips as she remembered the way he had set down Caroline Bingley when she had asked him to pen her respects to his sister. He had been almost rude in his terse responses to Miss Bingley's fawning, but the woman had been too insensible to notice.

And then there had been the way he had spoken to her

during his proposal, his hand warm on her shoulder, his deep voice murmuring softly in her ear.

"You must know that I will treat you with kindness. I realize I am asking you to take a leap of faith, but I promise you will want for nothing. Whatever is in my power to give, you shall have."

Elizabeth unbuttoned her pelisse as an unexpected rush of heat crept up her neck. She should not have dressed so warmly. The weather was clearly far more temperate than she had expected.

Right. Reason number two.

Elizabeth pondered. Surely there were any number of other reasons to support the fact that Mr. Darcy would make her a terrible husband! He was... he was... rude! Yes, that was it. He had insulted her on the day of their very first meeting in a most grievous manner, within earshot of not only herself but a whole roomful of her neighbors! Despicable!

Her brow furrowed as she remembered how she had paraded past him after his ill-timed comment, deliberately making eye contact so he could be in no doubt that she had overheard his cutting remark. Their gazes had only met for a second, but in that time, she had detected a look on his face that could only be described as profound regret and the deepest mortification.

Elizabeth shook her head, attempting to rid herself of the memory.

Well. Never mind about that now. Reason number three.

Elizabeth stared out at the horizon. Reason number three...

Oh, this was too difficult! Naturally, there were far too many negatives for her to sort through them all right this moment. Perhaps she should have started with the "for" column instead. Yes, that would be easier. Surely there were hardly any positives when it came to a match with Mr. Darcy.

Very well. For.

Reason number one: He was rich. Not that money had ever been much of an inducement for Elizabeth. She would much rather have affection. Still, money purchased peace of mind. Security. And not just for herself, but for her entire family. If she married Mr. Darcy, they would be well provided for, even if something happened to her beloved father. Mr. Darcy had been very clear on that. He even planned to have it written into the marriage articles. And as for herself, she would want for nothing. Never again would she have to make over last season's gown because her younger sisters were still growing and had the greater need for a new wardrobe. Or gaze longingly at the latest novel that had come into the bookshop, knowing her remaining pin money was not enough to purchase it. Elizabeth sighed. As much as she hated to admit it, it would be a vast relief to be free of her mother's constant wailing about their circumstances and her non-stop machinations to marry her daughters off to the highest bidder. Perhaps if her mother could be assured of their protection, she would cease her worrying and allow Elizabeth's sisters to marry where they pleased...

Which immediately brought her to reason number two: Jane. If ever there was a soul who deserved to marry for affection, it was her beloved sister. Never had Elizabeth seen Jane look on any gentleman as she did Mr. Bingley, and although her sister did not put her emotions on display for all and sundry, knowing her as Elizabeth did, she was convinced that Jane was deeply and profoundly in love. But now Mr. Bingley had gone away. What would happen if Elizabeth refused Mr. Darcy? He too would go away, and likely persuade his friend to steer clear of Hertfordshire and those detestable Bennets. Perhaps Mr. Bingley would give up the lease on Netherfield, and Jane would never lay eyes on him again! For while she believed Mr. Bingley to be partial to her eldest sister, she had also noticed a certain laxity in his character. Even Mr. Darcy, one of his closest friends, had admitted that Mr. Bingley could be easily led. Would Mr. Bingley's nascent feelings for Jane be enough for him to stand up to his sisters and his friend if they conspired to keep him away?

Elizabeth blew out a weighty sigh. Very well… reason number three: Her future marital prospects. Her father seemed to feel that refusing both Mr. Collins and Mr. Darcy would materially damage her chances of receiving another proposal of marriage. And as much as she hated to admit it, it was possible he was correct. Hertfordshire was not exactly teeming with eligible bachelors as it was, and her portion was practically non-existent. Not to mention the fact that she already had a reputation for being impertinent and outspoken.

Of course, Mr. Collins had not actually proposed, but he had certainly been vocal about his intentions. If word got out that she had refused both her cousin and Mr. Darcy, would she be setting herself up to a life lived on her own, forever dependent on her father, and when he was gone, on her sisters' husbands… assuming her sisters were able to marry men with the inclination and means to care for her?

Elizabeth grimaced. Reason number four. Well, as much as she was loath to admit it—and she absolutely would *not* admit it to anyone, not even her beloved Jane— Mr. Darcy was quite pleasing to the eye, especially when he was not frowning. He was tall, with a full head of curly hair, and a noble mien. And dark intense eyes, that seemed to look right into your soul when he spoke to you.

Suddenly, Elizabeth's entire body grew warmer still, and she unfastened the remainder of the buttons on her pelisse.

Harumph. Reason number five. While she had not dwelt upon it overmuch, it was clear that Mr. Darcy was intelligent. He was well-educated. He liked books, and was no doubt well-read. She had heard him speak rationally on any number of topics. And unlike most gentlemen of her acquaintance, he did not seem to think it unusual for a woman to have thoughts and opinions of her own. In fact, he had seemed almost eager to engage her in philosophical discourse during the time they had spent together at Nether- field. How many men would welcome such conversations with their wives?

Elizabeth jumped to her feet, snatching up her bonnet and jamming it back on her head. This was ridiculous! She was making no progress at all. It had been silly to try to conjure up a list in her head. She would do much better to return to Longbourn and seek out pen and paper. Yes, if she had the correct materials at hand, surely she would be able to see that the reasons against marrying Mr. Darcy far outweighed those in favor.

She would return to Longbourn directly and commit everything to paper. Then she would have irrefutable proof that to wed that gentleman would be a frightfully bad idea.

∼

Elizabeth turned into the lane that led to Longbourn, noticing with some trepidation that there was a carriage parked in the drive. Her apprehension grew as she neared the house, noting that the equipage was one of the stateliest conveyances she had ever seen, and certainly did not belong to any of her neighbors. Stopping to stare at her reflection in the gleaming black lacquer, her stomach sank in comprehension. The carriage must belong to Mr. Darcy. He had come for her answer even sooner than she had expected, and she still had no clear idea what she should tell him. But why had he chosen to use his carriage for the three-mile journey, rather than ride his mount, as was his usual custom? Was he endeavoring to demonstrate his wealth and consequence in an attempt to sway her decision? Or did he intend to marry her on the spot and carry her away to London or Pemberley this very day? Her heart pounded at the thought, even as her mind contradicted such wild speculation. How preposterous! Certainly, he could not expect her to marry him today. There were still the marriage articles to address and the banns to be read… unless he had already ridden to Town to obtain a common license. She shook her head at her own foolishness. No, he would not have done so prior to her acceptance. Would he? No. More likely he intended to return to Town after speaking with her—either to begin the process of drawing up the marriage contract, or, in the event of her refusal, to carry on with his life…

Elizabeth froze, and for a brief moment, the impulse to turn and flee was strong. She darted a glance at the front windows, but could see no one within the morning room. Perhaps she had not been seen. She could turn back and ramble for a few more hours, returning after Mr. Darcy had gone...

Elizabeth sighed. No, she would have to face him eventually. It may as well be now. Deciding that she would at least go to her room to make herself presentable before confronting him, she walked around to the side of the house, but she had no sooner reached out her hand when the door was thrown open to reveal her sister Kitty on the opposite side.

"Oh, Lizzy! Thank heavens you have come! There is a visitor in the parlor, and Mamma is in a state! We were just about to send someone out to search for you."

Her sister's agitation was palpable, and Elizabeth could only imagine her mother's vexation at having to play hostess to Mr. Darcy.

Stepping into the corridor she untied the strings of her bonnet, hanging it on one of the wooden pegs near the door before slipping out of her pelisse.

"Very well. I just need to change my dress. Pray, tell Mr. Darcy I shall be down directly."

She started to move towards the stairs, but Kitty's expression halted her in her tracks.

"Mr. Darcy? But Mr. Darcy is not here. It is Mr. Collins's patroness, that woman he is always going on about. Lady Catherine de Bourgh."

Elizabeth's mouth dropped open, but Kitty was still speaking.

"She arrived more than half an hour ago, and Mr. Collins has gone off to Lucas Lodge to make his farewells. Mamma sent for our cousin straight away, but he has not yet arrived, and in any case, Lady Catherine says she is here to see you!"

"Me? I do not understand. Why should our cousin's patroness wish to see me? We are in no way acquainted."

Kitty seemed about to answer, but just then a door opened at the far end of the corridor and Mrs. Bennet rushed forward.

"Lizzy, where on earth have you been? Is it not bad enough that you have somehow managed to drive Mr. Collins away, without you disappearing for hours on end when you are needed at home? You must come to the drawing room at once! Her ladyship has been waiting more than half an hour already!"

Still trying to make sense of it all, Elizabeth once again expressed the need to change her clothing, but her mother was already pushing her down the passageway.

"There is no time for that now!"

Mere seconds later, Elizabeth entered the parlor, blinking at the scene in front of her. The woman who must be Lady Catherine sat in a high-backed chair in the center of the room, with all of Elizabeth's family arranged in a circle around her. Upon their entrance, her ladyship's gaze swept up Elizabeth's body, from the muddy hem of her gown to her tousled hair, and her lips turned down at the edges. After a moment, she shifted in her seat, addressing her remarks to Mrs. Bennet.

"And this, I suppose, is your second eldest daughter?"

Mrs. Bennet agreed that it was, and Lady Catherine narrowed her gaze. Continuing to speak to Elizabeth's mother, she said, "You have a very small park here, though I noticed a moderately attractive little wilderness on one side of your lawn. Perhaps your daughter would take a turn in it with me."

It was not lost on Elizabeth that the remark had been a

statement and not a question, but she could hardly spare a thought for anything beyond the fact that the lady had yet to address her directly, nor seek a proper introduction. But her mother was already nodding her consent, babbling about the hermitage and the various walks Elizabeth might show her ladyship. Before she knew it, she was once again donning her pelisse and bonnet, and following the imperious woman out the door.

The two walked in silence until they were some distance from the house. Once they had entered the copse, Lady Catherine finally turned, fixing Elizabeth with a penetrating gaze.

"I suppose, Miss Elizabeth Bennet, that you can be at no loss to understand the reason for my journey hither."

"Indeed," Elizabeth replied, "you are mistaken, madam. I am completely unable to account for it."

Lady Catherine's eyes narrowed. "You ought to know that I am not to be trifled with. Do you truly claim ignorance in this matter?"

"I am afraid so, your ladyship. I can think of no reason that would bring such an esteemed person as yourself into Hertfordshire to call upon someone with whom you are unacquainted."

Lady Catherine harrumphed, before continuing to speak. "A report of a most alarming nature reached me at my brother's house in Town yesterday afternoon. Indeed, it was only by a stroke of luck that my rector knew where to find me. You can no doubt imagine my surprise when Mr. Collins saw fit to send me a letter by express, informing me that my own nephew, Mr. Fitzwilliam Darcy, had made you an offer of marriage."

A hot flush warmed Elizabeth's cheeks and her stomach

sank as understanding dawned. Of course. Now everything began to make sense. Mr. Collins *had* overheard her speaking with her father yesterday morning, and he had wasted no time in notifying his patroness. No wonder her cousin had withdrawn his suit. He could not risk any association with the woman Lady Catherine would blame for usurping the role intended for Miss de Bourgh.

"Well? What have you to say for yourself?" Lady Catherine barked, pulling Elizabeth from her thoughts. "Do you deny it?"

"No, ma'am. That is, yes, Mr. Darcy has made me an offer of marriage."

"And have you accepted him?" Lady Catherine demanded.

Elizabeth felt her eyes widen in surprise. "I beg your pardon, but I believe that is between Mr. Darcy and myself. I am not in the habit of discussing my private affairs with strangers."

"Strangers! Impudent girl! I am almost the nearest relation he has in the world. And as such, I am entitled to know all his dearest concerns."

"Perhaps. But you are not entitled to know mine."

At Elizabeth's response, Lady Catherine's face grew purple with rage. Slamming the tip of her walking stick into the ground, she launched into a diatribe the likes of which Elizabeth had never been subjected to in her entire life. She began by informing Elizabeth of Mr. Darcy's prior betrothal to her own daughter, but when Elizabeth spoke up to repeat Mr. Darcy's claim that no such offer had been made, she went on to describe the proposed union as being "of a peculiar kind," confirming Mr. Darcy's account of the marriage being merely the favorite wish of their mothers, planned when the two children were in their cradles. However, when it became clear that this argument was not working, she quickly switched tactics, assailing Elizabeth in the most vehement manner. She spoke at length about the inferiority of Elizabeth's connections, and the degradation that an alliance with her family would be to the Darcy name.

She then sprang into a lengthy tirade, accusing Elizabeth of trapping Mr. Darcy with her "arts and allurements." At first, it was all Elizabeth could do to keep from laughing aloud. To think that this woman believed her either capable of or in any way inclined to entrap Mr. Darcy! If only she knew the truth!

But her humor died when Mr. Darcy's aunt crossed the line from insult to infamy. Sweeping a contemptuous gaze over Elizabeth's person, she said, "Do not think me unfamiliar with this sordid method of trickery. I know your kind all too well. You would not be the first woman to attempt to ensnare one of your betters with a full belly."

Elizabeth gasped, mortification and fury creating a white-hot fire at the core of her being.

"How dare you speak to me in such a vile manner! You have now insulted me in every possible way, and this conversation is at an end." She pivoted on her heel, but Lady Catherine's voice arrested her steps.

"You will go nowhere until you answer my question!" she cried. "Indeed, I will not move from this spot until I know your intentions. Do you mean to marry my nephew?"

Elizabeth whirled around, and before she had time to contemplate what she was about to say, the words flew from her lips in a torrent of emotion.

"Yes, I do intend to marry him! And there is nothing you can do to stop me!"

Lady Catherine visibly startled, but seconds later, her expression hardened.

"Very well, Miss Elizabeth Bennet. Then I shall know how to act. Do not imagine that your ambition will ever be gratified." Her lips pulled into a sneer as her eyes drifted to Elizabeth's stomach. "I doubt the child you carry is even his. And you are quite mistaken if you believe you will ever pass off some other man's bastard as the heir to Pemberley."

"Enough!" a deep voice thundered, and Elizabeth looked up to see Mr. Darcy advancing on them with ground-eating strides.

Looking more relieved than intimidated, Lady Catherine drew herself up to her full height. "Darcy! There you are. I was just telling this—"

"Pray, cease speaking, madam!" Darcy snapped over his aunt's authoritative tones. "I have heard quite enough already."

Lady Catherine's face grew pink, but before she could respond, Darcy turned to Elizabeth and his voice gentled.

"Pray, accept my deepest apologies, Miss Elizabeth. If you would not mind, I should like a moment alone with my aunt. I will join you in the house shortly."

Elizabeth nodded numbly, and without a backwards glance at Mr. Darcy or his noble relation, she fled the garden.

Elizabeth did not return to the house. Still mortified and restive from her bout with Lady Catherine, she made her way to a small clearing near the side entrance, where a curved bench sat beneath a small gazebo. It was there that Mr. Darcy found her some ten minutes later, staring vacantly at the dormant rose bushes in the near distance. He approached slowly, taking a seat on the opposite end of the bench.

"She is gone," he said quietly.

Elizabeth nodded. She had heard the slam of a carriage door and the crunch of wheels and hooves on gravel some moments past.

Sliding closer to where she sat, Darcy regarded her with a somber expression before saying, "Elizabeth, I am profoundly sorry. My aunt had no call to speak to you in such a way."

Elizabeth started at his use of her Christian name, but she nodded her appreciation. "It is of no importance," she murmured.

"On the contrary, it is of the utmost importance. I hope you know such contemptible behavior is abhorrent to me, and is something I will not condone. I have told my aunt as much."

"Thank you. I am sorry you had to witness such a scene, but I appreciate your defense of my character."

"There is no need to thank me. No one should have to suffer that nature of abuse, but I would certainly never tolerate such conduct towards my future wife." His lips tipped up into a smile as he said softly, "Besides, it is I who should be thanking you. I promise I will give you no reason to regret your decision."

Elizabeth's head snapped up at Mr. Darcy's declaration,

her breath catching in her throat. Good heavens! Her words, which had merely been a retort thrown back at Lady Catherine in defiance and anger had been overheard by Mr. Darcy, and he had taken them as fact. She gazed back at him, her thoughts swirling.

She had not conclusively determined to refuse him— but she had not made up her mind to accept him either. However, her rash words seemed to have sealed her fate. She opened her mouth to attempt to explain. She needed more time. She needed to be absolutely certain before embarking on such a drastic course, one that would affect her entire future. But before she could order her thoughts, Mr. Darcy lifted her hand, pressing a soft kiss upon her knuckles.

"You have done me a great honor in accepting my offer, and I will do everything in my power to make you happy."

Elizabeth stared back at him. The intense emotion reflected in his gaze sent a shiver down her spine and it was all she could do to slowly nod in his direction.

And just like that, the die was cast.

The following se'nnight passed in a blur. Mr. Darcy did not wish to wait to marry. There was some business at Pemberley which required his attention, and he did not want to risk traveling too late in the season, when the roads would be at their worst. And so, he departed for London to acquire a common license, and Elizabeth was married in the Longbourn chapel a mere eight days after accepting Mr. Darcy's offer.

Later, when she reflected on her wedding day, Elizabeth

would remember it as a myriad of images—the feel of her father's wool coat beneath her damp palm as he walked her down the aisle, the brief look of unguarded reverence in Mr. Darcy's eyes when he beheld her at the altar, the fluttering in her belly when her new husband took her hand for the first time—but on that day, a strange sort of numbness took over, as if she was merely playing a part, dutifully standing where she was told and reciting her lines, but knowing that when it was all over, she would go back to her real life, back to being Miss Elizabeth Bennet of Longbourn.

She remembered, however, with great clarity, standing in the crowded vestibule, and how proud she was that her fingers only trembled slightly when she leaned over the marriage lines to sign her name before passing the pen to Mr. Darcy. She watched him as he signed, and in that instant, it all became terrifyingly real. She belonged to him now. This stranger whom she did not understand and hardly knew was now her husband. She was his property—just as surely as his fine carriages, or his fancy townhouse, or even the clothing on his back—to do with as he pleased. She had promised to love him, to honor him, and to obey him. Every possession of hers, too, in essence belonged to him. And every decision she made from this day forward must be made with his blessing.

And so, when Mr. Darcy gently took her arm to lead her to the waiting carriage, an expression that Elizabeth would later recall as pure adoration transforming his features, the only thought running through her mind was this: *What have I done?*

The wedding breakfast was held at Netherfield. Mr. Bingley had returned—alone—the day before the ceremony, stating only that his sisters and Mr. Hurst remained in Town due to a prior engagement.

At first, Mrs. Bennet was loath to give over the opportunity to host the breakfast herself, but upon hearing that Mr. Darcy's cousin—a colonel in his majesty's army and the son of an earl—would stand up with him, and that the earl and countess themselves might be in attendance, she saw the sense of having the breakfast in a more stately setting.

In the end, Mr. Darcy's cousin could not get away from his regiment, and the Earl and Countess of Matlock were likewise unavailable, and so it was Mr. Bingley who stood up with his friend.

Mrs. Bennet made the best of the situation, focusing her attention on the fact that Mr. Bingley had returned to the neighborhood, and using all her energy to contrive a way for the gentleman to be alone with her eldest daughter. Indeed, to prevent any further embarrassment to her dearest sister, Elizabeth did her best to keep Jane by her side during the wedding breakfast—although in truth, her desire for Jane's company may have been equally due to a powerful disinclination to be left alone with her new husband.

But before long, the breakfast was winding to a close— the minutes Elizabeth would be in familiar surroundings amongst her loved ones slowly ticking away. She glanced across the room to see Mr. Darcy in conversation with Mr. Bingley and Sir William Lucas, but as if sensing her gaze, he shifted his attention to where she stood, and her cheeks burned at the smile that brightened his features when his eyes met hers. Turning back to say something to his friend, she watched as he shook hands with both gentlemen before making his way to her side. He bowed slightly to Jane, who once again wished him joy before slipping away, leaving the two of them alone within the crowd.

To Elizabeth's amazement, Mr. Darcy lifted her hand, turning it over and placing a gentle kiss upon the inside of her wrist. A sharp gasp caught in her throat as he straightened, holding fast to her hand, his thumb tracing lazy circles along her palm.

"Will you be ready to leave shortly?" he murmured. "I had hoped to travel for at least a few hours before we lose the light."

Elizabeth stared back at him, amazed once again by the tenderness she saw reflected in his gaze. Offering him a jerky nod, she answered, "Yes, of course. I will go upstairs and change. We may depart within the hour if you would like."

Darcy nodded. "Good. That is... thank you. I will call for the carriage and make sure everything is loaded properly. Perhaps we may meet back here in thirty minutes or so, to say our goodbyes?"

Elizabeth agreed, scanning the crowd for her sister and then summoning a maid to take them to the bedchamber that had been set aside for their use.

Crossing the threshold, Elizabeth made her way to the wardrobe, removing the traveling gown her maid had hung there earlier and draping it over the back of a chair. A small fire crackled in the hearth, but instead of making the room feel cozy and snug, sweat prickled on Elizabeth's brow, and she suddenly felt overwhelmed by the stuffiness in the room.

"Jane," she called to her sister, who was busily pouring

water into a nearby washbasin, "pray, open a window. It is far too warm in here. I feel as though I shall faint if I do not have some fresh air."

Jane smiled. Setting down the pitcher, she moved to the tall French windows that led to a small balcony, throwing them open.

"Better?" she asked, and Elizabeth nodded.

"Much."

Jane came up behind her, beginning to work the buttons that ran down the back of Elizabeth's gown. Peeling off the fine muslin, Elizabeth stepped into her simple traveling dress, easily fastening the hooks that were conveniently located at the front of the bodice. At least she would not need a maid to help her remove it this evening when she and Mr. Darcy stopped for the night. Elizabeth's cheeks grew warm at the thought, and she turned away from her sister. Best not to dwell too much on what would occur between herself and Mr. Darcy at the inn. She had gone into this marriage with her eyes wide open, and she knew what was expected of her. She had no intention of putting Mr. Darcy off, or of denying him his conjugal rights. But she would cross that particular bridge when she came to it.

She glanced over at her sister, who was staring back at her, a melancholy expression in her usually clear blue eyes. Forcing a smile, Elizabeth took Jane's hands, squeezing them gently and leading her to a small settee near the open windows.

"Jane, pray do not look at me like that. You know I shall miss you terribly, but if you begin to cry, then I will too, and it would not do for me to join Mr. Darcy with red-rimmed eyes on our wedding day. He might imagine I am unhappy with my choice."

Jane choked back a sound that was half laugh, half sob.

"How can you jest about something like this? I know better than anyone how you feel about Mr. Darcy. You have made your aversion plain from the moment you were introduced. You can scarcely tolerate the gentleman's company, and now you have pledged yourself to him for all eternity. Oh, Lizzy, why did you do it? I know it was not for his money or his social standing. I do not understand."

Elizabeth sighed, turning to stare out the open window at the lead-gray sky. "You must not speak so, Jane. Whatever my reasons, it is done now. Besides, many people marry without affection." Smiling at her sister, she added, "Not everyone can be as blissfully happy as you and Mr. Bingley."

Jane flushed. "But you have not simply married without affection; you have married a man you vehemently dislike. You, who always said you would only marry for love." After a slight pause, she continued, "And I am not certain Mr. Bingley holds me in any special regard. The only reason he returned was for your wedding. He is leaving tomorrow."

A sudden gust of wind rattled the shutters and a door banged closed in some other part of the house.

"The wind is picking up," Elizabeth said, moving to latch the windows before returning to her sister. Ignoring Jane's words about Mr. Darcy, she continued, "Mr. Bingley is only going north for the festive season. He will be back; I am certain of it." She did not add that now that she was married to Mr. Darcy, she would do everything in her power to ensure that her husband used his influence to steer Mr. Bingley towards Jane and not away from her. After a moment she added, "But perhaps there is something to

Charlotte's advice. Perhaps it would be to your benefit to leave Mr. Bingley in no doubt of your true feelings before he goes. You do love him," she asked gently, "do you not?"

Jane's lip trembled and she gave her sister a shaky nod. "I do," she whispered. And then, with more feeling, "Oh, Lizzy! I love him so dearly. I know how Mamma goes on about his five thousand a year, but that means nothing to me. Even if he had not a shilling to his name, I would still wish to be his wife."

Elizabeth reached out her arms drawing her beloved sister into a tight embrace. "And so you shall be," she whispered. If it was the last thing she did, Elizabeth would see Jane marry for love. Even if binding herself to the arrogant Mr. Darcy was the price she was forced to pay.

Numbly, Darcy stepped from the balcony into the dimly lit bedchamber. Staggering to a nearby chair, he sank into the cushions, his mind reeling from all he had heard. Elizabeth had married him against her will. She did not love him. No, it was worse than that. If her sister's words were to be believed, Elizabeth detested him.

A wave of nausea twisted Darcy's stomach, and he was certain he would be ill. How had this happened? Why would she have accepted his offer if her sentiments were so decidedly against him? And how could he have been so blind as to have had no notion of her true feelings?

His thoughts careened back to all the times they had been in one another's company, when she had come to tend to her sister at Netherfield. Could what he had taken as flirtatious banter have actually been genuine ire?

Suddenly he remembered the expression on her face when he had asked her to dance at the Netherfield ball. Had the fleeting look in her eyes that he had taken as surprise actually have been distaste?

Leaping from his seat, he paced to the fireplace, raking his fingers through his hair. But then why had she agreed to be his wife? One of the two of them—either Elizabeth or her sister—had shut the window before they had finished their conversation, but Darcy was inclined to believe Miss Bennet's assertion that Elizabeth had not married him for material gain. Sinking back into his chair, Darcy groaned. What did it matter why she had done it? The fact remained that he was now bound in perpetuity to a woman who loathed the very sight of him.

And there was not a single thing he could do about it.

Chapter 4

9th December 1811

The carriage clattered to a halt in Pemberley's circular drive. Without waiting for a footman, Mr. Darcy unlatched the door, and Elizabeth allowed him to hand her to the ground. As her husband addressed one of the waiting footmen, her gaze took in the massive stone edifice before her, and her pulse instantly quickened.

The house was enormous, but somehow the Palladian architecture made it feel warmer and less austere than depictions she had seen of other grand houses of its caliber. Still, it was enormous. Stepping closer to the portico, Elizabeth tipped up her chin, silently counting row upon row of windows, all of them glittering like jewels in the late-afternoon sun.

Goodness, how many rooms must there be? And how many servants to keep all those windows sparkling...

For the first time, the gravity of what she had undertaken in marrying a man like Mr. Darcy settled like a weight in the pit of her stomach. But before she could dwell on it any further, she felt the slight pressure of her husband's palm at the small of her back as he steered her towards the stone steps.

There, standing in perfect formation, nearly two dozen servants were waiting to greet them. Her husband briefly met her gaze before beginning to take her down the line, and Elizabeth forced a shallow smile. She was introduced to Mrs. Reynolds, the housekeeper, and Mr. Lawson, the butler. She had already met Mr. Darcy's valet, a man called Harris, but Mrs. Reynolds introduced her to a young woman by the name of Miss Cassidy, who would be acting as her lady's maid. Elizabeth thought she looked affable, but did not have long to form more of an impression before she was shuttled along to meet a row of footmen—all tall and broad shouldered—dressed in immaculate dark-green livery, followed by an equal number of perfectly turned-out housemaids.

With each new person, Elizabeth smiled and murmured words of greeting, knowing that everything from her clothing to the expression on her face was being carefully recorded and judged. At Longbourn, there had only been Mr. and Mrs. Hill plus one housemaid, a cook, and two additional kitchen maids who worked below stairs. How she would remember all the servants here at Pemberley, she could not begin to comprehend.

After what seemed like an eternity—although it was likely no more than a quarter of an hour—they had reached the end of the line, and Mr. Darcy took her elbow, leading her up the stone steps and into a cavernous entrance hall. Peeling off her gloves, Elizabeth relinquished her pelisse to the butler who had followed them inside, before turning to take in her surroundings. Everything was marble, from the polished floors, to the vaulted ceiling, to the majestic pillars at each of the room's four corners. And although the room was not in any way gaudy or ostentatious—if anything, it was stunning in its simplicity—it was easily the grandest entryway Elizabeth had ever seen, and it spoke volumes about the status of the house and its owners.

Elizabeth swallowed, noticing that Mr. Darcy was staring at her with a quiet intensity that made her stomach tighten. But when his eyes met hers, his expression shuttered as he took a step in her direction.

"You are not displeased, I hope?" he asked, a note of what Elizabeth could only describe as sarcasm in his voice.

"No, of course not," she answered, her cheeks heating at being caught staring like some sort of country bumpkin. "Just a little overwhelmed, perhaps. I had not anticipated being introduced to the entire household upon arrival."

Darcy frowned. "It is a mark of respect that they wished to greet you. You are the new mistress, after all. Besides, that was hardly the entire household. Only those who work above stairs."

Elizabeth's eyes widened, but before she could open her mouth to say anything further, Mr. Darcy had turned his back, leading her towards a curved staircase at the far end of the hall.

"Come, I will show you to your chambers. No doubt you will wish to settle in and rest for a time before dinner."

Hurrying to catch up with her husband's long strides, Elizabeth lifted her skirts, following him until they reached the upper landing. Darcy led her down a long corridor and then up another flight of stairs. When they reached the top, he turned left, stopping about halfway down the passageway. Opening a heavy wooden door, Mr. Darcy stepped back, and Elizabeth entered an expansive bedchamber. Sunlight filtered in through the tall windows, reflecting off the yellow damask wallpaper, giving the entire room a cheerful glow. And although the chamber was large—in fact it was quite the largest bedchamber Elizabeth had ever seen—the way the furniture was arranged rendered it somehow intimate, while the abundance of windows made it bright and airy.

Following her across the threshold, Darcy gestured towards the far corner. "There is a dressing room and bathing chamber there, behind that screen, and the doorway near the fireplace leads to a sitting room that is shared with the master's chambers on the other side. I believe you will find everything you require, but if not, Mrs. Reynolds will be happy to assist you in procuring whatever you need."

Elizabeth nodded, her eyes still sweeping the room. "This is lovely. I had expected something quite different after seeing your front hall, but I will admit to being rather relieved."

Darcy's brow furrowed, but when he spoke, his tone was civil, if not particularly warm. "Good. I am glad you approve. The apartment has been redone twice since my mother was in residence. The first time about a year after her passing, and then again two years ago when my sister's apartment was redecorated. Mrs. Reynolds oversaw the arrangements."

"Your housekeeper has done a remarkable job. As it happens, yellow is one of my favorite colors."

"That is a stroke of luck, then. Of course, you may feel free to change whatever you wish. If any of the furnishings are not to your taste..."

"Oh, no! I like everything very much."

Inexplicably, Darcy looked away, however Elizabeth was spared any explanation of his displeasure by the appearance of four footmen bearing her trunks, followed by the housekeeper and Elizabeth's new maid.

Stepping aside to make way for the servants, Darcy cleared his throat before saying, "Well, I shall leave you now to settle in." Turning to Mrs. Reynolds, he added, "Please see to it that Mrs. Darcy has everything she requires. We shall dine at half past six."

The housekeeper nodded her assent, and with a brief bow in Elizabeth's direction, Mr. Darcy quit the room.

Several hours later, Elizabeth stood in her newly appointed bedchamber while Cassidy fastened the buttons at the back of her gown. It was a modest frock, and one Mr. Darcy had seen before, but she had not had time to acquire a new wardrobe before leaving Longbourn. No doubt it was not up to the standards of her new station, but there was nothing for it. Short of wearing a ball gown—and even then, she had only two, both of them several years old—this was the nicest dress in her wardrobe. Hopefully it would be suitable for a simple dinner at home.

When the maid had placed the last hairpin in her dark curls, Elizabeth stepped back, admiring her reflection in the mirrored glass. Despite the dress, she felt she was in decent looks, having had the opportunity to rest and refresh herself before bathing in the largest copper tub she had ever beheld.

Turning to thank Cassidy for her expert care, she was on the brink of enquiring as to the direction of the dining room, when a knock sounded from the corridor. The maid went to answer, opening the door to admit Mr. Darcy, who was elegantly attired in black dress.

"Elizabeth," he said succinctly, halting as soon as he had crossed the threshold.

"Mr. Darcy," Elizabeth answered, a touch more tartly than she had intended.

Her husband's lips turned down at the corners, and Elizabeth lifted her chin. She would not apologize for her attire. If Mr. Darcy had wanted a wife of fashion, he should have married Caroline Bingley and not her.

Dismissing the maid with another murmur of thanks, she reached for her gloves. The latch clicked as Cassidy hurried out, closing the door behind her, and Elizabeth turned to see her husband regarding her with a grim expression.

"Must you do that?" he asked.

"I beg your pardon?"

"We have been married above three days, and yet you are still addressing me as 'Mr. Darcy'. I am your husband, not some passing acquaintance. Do you not think it time that you began calling me by my given name?"

Elizabeth's cheeks grew warm at her husband's forbidding tone, and she swiftly averted her gaze, fiddling with her gloves. "My parents address one another in a similar manner. It is not so unusual."

Mr. Darcy's frown deepened. "Do they never use one another's Christian names? Even when they are alone?"

"I should have no notion of what they do when they are alone," Elizabeth answered evasively, "but even in a private family setting, they generally do not."

"I see. And this is your preference?"

"I…"

"Would you have me call you 'Mrs. Darcy'?"

"No," she answered. "I have no objection to you calling me Elizabeth."

"But you will not call me Fitzwilliam."

Elizabeth lowered her lashes, struggling to maintain her equanimity. "It is not the same."

"Forgive me, but I do not understand. How is it acceptable for me to call you by your given name, but not for you to do likewise?"

Elizabeth released a breath, meeting his gaze and wondering how she could explain.

"It is just that, the circumstances are not equal. You are accustomed to being called Mr. Darcy, and I am accustomed to referring to you in that manner. I am not yet comfortable being addressed as Mrs. Darcy. I... I mean no disrespect, but I do not *feel* like Mrs. Darcy. And, for me, you do not feel like..."

Her voice trailed off and Darcy visibly stiffened. "Can you not even say it? Fitzwilliam. Fitzwilliam is my given name."

"Yes. I know."

Darcy looked away. After a moment he said, "We should go down. We are already late."

Elizabeth was tempted to ask how they could be late to a dinner that included no others, but she was too relieved to have the conversation at an end.

Pulling on her gloves, she nodded, and after a brief hesitation, Darcy offered his arm. Resting her fingers lightly against his sleeve, she allowed him to escort her down the sweeping staircase, and across the entryway, their footsteps echoing in the silent hall.

A short while later, they entered a large dining parlor.

Elizabeth's eyes grew round at the elegance of the room, but she managed to quickly school her features as her husband guided her to her place at the head of the table. The embroidered linen tablecloth only held place settings for two, but an elaborate floral centerpiece and several silver candelabras filled the remainder of the space.

Slipping into her seat, Elizabeth noted that the second place setting was to her left, as opposed to at the opposite end of the table. She watched as Mr. Darcy took that seat, unfolding his napkin and gesturing to a waiting footman who came forward with the wine.

Catching her looking in his direction, Darcy fixed her with an inscrutable expression.

"I hope you will forgive the unorthodox seating arrangements. When my sister is at home, I always take the place beside her. The table is too large for two people to converse easily when seated at such a distance from one another."

"Of course," Elizabeth murmured, still somewhat surprised that the proper Mr. Darcy would stray so far from formality. But she ceased thinking about it as a jib door at the back of the room opened, and a string of footmen appeared, carrying a variety of serving trays. A soup tureen was set down closest to Elizabeth, while platters with meat, vegetables, and an assortment of other dishes were spread out along the table.

Elizabeth blinked, staring at the bounty before her in amazement. *Goodness, who could be expected to eat so much food?* There was enough to feed at least a dozen people.

Realizing that Mr. Darcy was regarding her expectantly, she quickly reached for the tureen.

"Shall I serve the soup?" she asked brightly, as all the footmen save one exited the room.

"Please." Darcy reached for his glass, taking a swallow of the deep red claret as Elizabeth raised the lid of the tureen. A rich aroma filled the air, and her eyebrows lifted.

"Turtle?"

Darcy nodded stiffly. "A little extravagant for a simple family dinner, perhaps, but I thought you would enjoy it."

Although the words themselves were considerate, his tone was brusque.

Looking away, Elizabeth murmured her thanks before serving Mr. Darcy and then herself.

Dipping her spoon into the creamy broth, she could feel her husband watching her; luckily, she did not have to dissemble as the soup was delicious.

She made a point to tell him so, adding, "You must give my compliments to your cook."

Darcy offered her a curt nod before beginning on his own portion. "You may give them to her yourself. I will introduce you to Mrs. Webb in the morning. I hope you will find her satisfactory. She is not classically trained, but her fare, as I hope you will find, is excellent."

"If this is any indication, I am certain I will enjoy her cooking very much. Has she been with the family for some time?"

"Yes, for several years. I hired her just after my father's death."

Elizabeth returned her eyes to her plate, feeling somehow guilty for inadvertently bringing up what must be unhappy memories.

The two ate the remainder of the course in relative silence. In between bites, Elizabeth surreptitiously studied the rest of the dishes laid out along the table. Besides the soup, there were partridges with bread sauce, an herb pie, roast loin of pork, pickled vegetables, and a ragout of venison braised in red wine.

Although the quantity was out of all proportion to the number of diners, everything was beautifully presented, and the mingled aromas that filled the room caused Elizabeth's stomach to rumble in appreciation.

When they had finished the soup, a footman instantly appeared, clearing their bowls, while another replaced the tureen with a silver dish, lifting the domed cover with an extravagant flourish.

Elizabeth gazed at the exquisite *gelée* set in an elegant mold and served on a bed of wilted lettuce, before turning to her husband with an expectant expression.

"Ah. I hope you will enjoy this," he offered, "it is one of Mrs. Webb's specialties."

Elizabeth's gaze shifted back to the dish in front of her, her fingers automatically tightening around her fork.

"It is... lobster?" she asked, as Mr. Darcy carved off a thick slice, neatly sliding it onto her plate.

"Aye, in aspic. It is a favorite of my sister's."

Elizabeth lifted her glass, taking a large swallow of her wine. "Indeed... it looks... lovely. Almost too lovely to eat," she added, forcing a laugh.

Darcy regarded her strangely before composing his features. "Yes. It is quite a work of art. But I assure you it tastes even better than it looks." As if to demonstrate, he plunged his knife into his own serving, layering a large bite onto the back of his fork and raising it to his lips. Elizabeth toyed with her napkin beneath the table, finally picking up her own fork and slicing off a small corner.

"Is something the matter?"

"No! Not at all," Elizabeth answered, but she set the morsel down untasted, taking another sip of her wine.

Beside her, Darcy frowned. "Do you not care for lobster?" he asked.

Elizabeth sighed, finally lifting her eyes to meet his penetrating gaze. "Forgive me, it is not that I do not care for lobster, but rather that lobster does not care for me."

"I beg your pardon? Do you mean to tell me it makes you ill?"

Elizabeth nodded sheepishly. "Yes, I am afraid so."

Deliberately, Darcy set down his fork, pushing his plate towards the center of the table. "You should have said something."

Elizabeth opened her mouth, but before she could speak, Darcy motioned to the footman standing at the corner of the room.

"Peter, take this back to the kitchens. See if Mrs. Webb has any fish she can send instead."

The footman nodded as Elizabeth blanched. "Mr. Darcy, truly that is not necessary. There is more than enough food on the table without an additional dish. Indeed, I do not think I will be able to eat half of what is here. And there is certainly no need for you to send your own dish back, when you were clearly enjoying it."

The footman glanced from Elizabeth to her husband before Mr. Darcy waved him off with a flick of his wrist. When Peter had gone, he replied, "I would no longer find any pleasure in it."

Gesturing to the other dishes laid out before them, his mouth curved up into a mocking smile as he added, "May I serve you something else? Some venison perhaps? Or a slice of the herb pie? Unless those items make you ill as well?"

Elizabeth folded her arms, anger quickly replacing any sense of remorse. Glad the footman had not yet returned, she answered coolly, "That was uncalled for."

"I beg your pardon? It was a simple question. I think it would be helpful for me to know if there are other foods you cannot tolerate."

"Nothing that is on this table."

Darcy sent her a withering glance, and once again, Elizabeth released a heavy sigh.

"If you must know, it is mostly shellfish. Lobster especially, but also shrimp and crayfish."

Darcy's eyes flashed, but he did not say anything further. A moment later, the footman returned, and Darcy lifted Elizabeth's plate, filling it with hefty portions of the dishes remaining on the table.

The rest of the meal passed in strained silence. When the last dish had been cleared away, Elizabeth stood, Darcy immediately following suit.

Taking a steadying breath, Elizabeth squared her shoulders. "If I may, I should like to go to the kitchens. I wish to speak to Mrs. Webb."

"That will not be necessary. You will see her in the morning."

Elizabeth instantly bristled at her husband's commanding tone. "Necessary or not, I intend to go. Will you take me, or shall I ask one of the footmen?"

Darcy's jaw tightened, and their gazes locked in a silent battle of wills. Finally, Darcy looked away, saying in a strained voice, "Very well. If you are that determined, I will escort you."

The footman, Peter, sprang to attention, hurriedly opening the door at the back of the room, and Elizabeth followed Darcy down a narrow corridor and then several flights of stairs. At the bottom of the steps, he turned left, leading her along another passageway and through a series of rooms that Elizabeth soon realized were all part of Pemberley's kitchens. Her head swiveled left and right as she took in pantries and larders, all while hurrying to keep up with Mr. Darcy, who moved at a brisk pace.

As they continued through the labyrinth of rooms, Elizabeth was once again reminded of the size of the manor of which she was now mistress, and her pulse quickened. At Longbourn, the kitchens consisted of one good-sized chamber with a small stillroom and pantry attached. But here at Pemberley, the space was at least triple the size. Elizabeth noticed in passing that every chamber they walked through was immaculately clean, the shelves neatly stocked, and the floors gleaming.

Darcy continued to weave his way through a maze of corridors, several startled footmen leaping out of the way with a hasty bow as they passed. Finally, they entered a vast room with several long tables running down its center and an enormous hearth where multiple pots were hung above a crackling blaze. The air filled with the scrape of chairs being hastily pushed back as several maids and footmen sprang to their feet, one young girl actually emitting a frightened squeak.

A plump woman of middle years with graying curls escaping the confines of her starched cap stepped quickly in their direction, dropping a deep curtsy, to which Mr. Darcy responded with a deferential bow. To Elizabeth's surprise, his expression instantly altered, an amiable smile gracing his features as he regarded the cook who still looked excessively ill at ease.

"Mr. Darcy, sir! I hope nothing was amiss with the dinner?"

"No, not at all, Mrs. Webb," he answered warmly. "The meal was delicious, as always." Cupping Elizabeth's elbow he continued, "Pray, forgive our intrusion. If you would allow me to introduce my wife, I believe Mrs. Darcy wished to have a word."

The cook turned to Elizabeth, dropping another curtsy, before saying, "It is an honor, ma'am. I hope you will forgive me for not being on hand to greet you when you arrived. Unfortunately, I was detained by a delivery from one of the shops, and I did not—"

Elizabeth held up her hand, stopping the flow of words with a heartfelt smile.

"Pray, do not make yourself uneasy; I was hardly expecting the entire household to be on hand at my arrival," she said with a laugh. "I only wished to stop down now to thank you for the superb meal. I cannot remember when I have enjoyed a dinner more. The turtle soup, especially. It was quite the best I have ever tasted." Leaning forward she added in a conspiratorial whisper, "But do not tell my mother. She is very proud of the recipe she has passed along to our own cook, though it does not hold a candle to yours."

The older woman flushed scarlet, murmuring her thanks before a shadow crossed her features.

"I am glad you enjoyed it, ma'am. And I hope you will allow me to apologize about the lobster. If I had known it was not to your liking, I never would have included it on the menu."

Elizabeth opened her mouth, but before she could speak, her husband stepped forward.

"You have nothing to apologize for, Mrs. Webb. The fault is entirely mine. I suggested the dish, as I know it is one of your specialties. I should have consulted my wife on her preferences before so doing."

The cook shifted her weight, twisting a dish cloth between her fingers, and Elizabeth smiled, attempting to put the woman at ease before looking to her husband.

"Nonsense, it was no one's fault. But I did wish to explain. It is not that I disliked the dish. The presentation was beautiful, and I am certain it was delicious. However, I am afraid I seem to have an intolerance to some seafood, most especially lobster. I do not know why, as no one else in my family has this difficulty, but after several unfortunate instances, I try to avoid eating it. Please know I meant no offence."

The cook seemed to visibly relax at Elizabeth's words, and she clucked her tongue in sympathy, explaining that one of her nephews had a similar issue with certain nuts. After a slight pause, she added, "I will see to it that we do not serve it in future," to which Elizabeth answered, "Not at all! No, you must continue to prepare it, as I could see how much my husband was enjoying the dish. And I would certainly never wish to suspend any pleasure of his."

She cast a sidelong glance at Mr. Darcy, who did not appear amused, but merely thanked Mrs. Webb for her time before escorting Elizabeth from the room.

After they left the kitchens, Darcy and Elizabeth repaired to the withdrawing room. Neither spoke, and Elizabeth could almost feel the tension radiating from her husband's person as they crossed the front hall. When they reached the parlor, Darcy closed the heavy oak doors, and Elizabeth made her way to a nearby settee, perching primly on its edge. Darcy moved to the sideboard, reaching for a decanter and removing the stopper.

"May I get you anything?" he asked curtly over his shoulder.

"No, thank you."

Offering her a single nod, he proceeded to pour himself a generous drink before taking a seat in one of the wing-back chairs across from her.

Elizabeth turned away, staring into the fire. The hissing and snapping of the flames seemed to match her mood, and she found herself growing angrier and angrier as Darcy sat opposite her, sipping his drink as if nothing was amiss. She knew she should hold her tongue, but after several minutes, the tension became unbearable, and she turned to face her husband.

"That was badly done."

"I beg your pardon? To what, exactly, are you referring?"

"You know perfectly well of what I speak. Making a scene, at dinner. Sending the food back. Making me feel as if I had done something wrong; as if my inability to tolerate the lobster was a personal affront. I do not know what you have been accustomed to up until now, but I will not be bullied, nor will I be made to feel humiliated in my own home."

Darcy stared back at her, his expression rigid. "*You*

were made to feel humiliated? How do you think I felt when you announced in front of the servants that you would not eat the dinner that I had specially asked to be prepared for you? How do you suppose Mrs. Webb felt when you marched into her kitchen without prior warning?"

"I went down there to set things to rights! If you had not insisted on sending back the food, she need never have known I did not eat it. As it was, I felt it incumbent upon me to explain, so that her feelings were not injured."

"Did you ever stop to think that invading Mrs. Webb's personal domain might not have been the best way to accomplish that? Did you fail to notice how uncomfortable everyone was? The servants have a right to their privacy, just as we have a right to ours. Having the new mistress arrive unannounced in the servants' hall was ill-mannered, at best."

Ill-mannered! Oh, that was rich, coming from him. Elizabeth bit her lip to keep from saying something she would likely regret, but a small voice inside her head whispered that what he said was not entirely without merit. Had she made Mrs. Webb uncomfortable with her visit? It had never occurred to her that her presence in the kitchens would be unwelcome. At Longbourn, she would think nothing of going below stairs whenever she pleased, and she had never felt that her presence had caused the kitchen staff any distress. Still, perhaps it would have been a kindness to have announced her intentions beforehand... she had simply never thought to do so. Elizabeth frowned. She needed to remember that she was no longer Miss Elizabeth Bennet of Longbourn, but a married lady of elevated society and the mistress of a great house.

Forcing a sense of calm she did not feel, Elizabeth turned to her husband.

"Be that as it may, I would have had no cause to go down to the kitchens in the first place if you had not made a scene in the dining room." She rose to her feet, and Mr. Darcy immediately set down his glass and stood.

"If you will excuse me," she said crisply, "I find that I am rather tired from today's journey. I will retire, if you have no objections?"

"Of course," Darcy answered. "I will escort you to your chambers."

"No, pray, do not trouble yourself. I can find my own way." And without waiting for a reply, Elizabeth swept from the room.

Darcy strode across the threshold of his chambers, slamming the door behind him with such force that it rattled on its hinges. Tugging off his coat, he tossed it onto a nearby chair before pulling at the folds of his cravat and flinging it in the same general direction.

Just then, the door to the adjoining dressing room opened and Harris, his valet, appeared, his eyes immediately going to Darcy's discarded clothing.

"Good evening, sir."

Although Harris's face remained impassive, Darcy could sense the valet's displeasure. Offering his man a brief nod, he crossed to a table on the far side of the room to pour himself another brandy. He knew he should not—he was already feeling the effects of the one he had consumed downstairs, and he was sure to wake up with a raging headache—but he poured it anyway. Out of the corner of his eye, he could see Harris heading for the dressing room with his coat and neck cloth. When the man returned, Darcy snapped, "Have some water sent up, I would like a bath."

At his master's words, the valet's eyebrows lifted. Darcy always bathed before changing for dinner, and had, as usual, done so earlier this evening, and it was evident that the unusual request—as well as Darcy's savage tone—had caught his man off guard. For a moment, the valet's composure slipped, and Darcy could just make out a slight widening of his eyes, before the man's usual mask of serenity slid back into place.

"Very good, sir. I will have it sent as soon as may be, though it will take some time to heat the water."

Harris turned to go, but Darcy's gruff reply held him in place. "No. Not heated. Send it cold."

"Cold, sir?"

"Yes. Cold. And then you may be excused."

Harris gaped at him like a scalded kitten before offering a brief nod and scurrying through the doorway.

Taking his drink, Darcy crossed to the armchair by the fire, sinking into the deep cushions. The entire evening had been a fiasco. After all his careful planning—sending an express to his housekeeper, asking Mrs. Webb to prepare a feast fit for a queen—it had all been ruined. Elizabeth had scarcely reacted to the elegantly laid table or the wide variety of gourmet fare. Instead, she had stared at the first course with revulsion, claiming that to take even a bite of the *Lobster en Gelée* would make her ill. And then she had proceeded to take *him* to task for *his* behavior? To say that she felt bullied and to intimate that it had been his intention to humiliate her! As though he were no better than some common ruffian.

Raking his fingers through his hair, Darcy took a long swallow of his drink. In truth, it was not just the evening that had been a debacle. *That*, he might have recovered from. No, his descent into hell had begun the minute he stepped out onto that balcony at Netherfield to hear Elizabeth speaking with her sister. How he had managed to go back down the stairs and greet her in the entrance hall with any degree of equanimity, he still could scarcely fathom. He had wanted to scream at the top of his lungs, to rail against his fate. How dare she stand before him with that pert expression, that half-smile pulling at her lips, after the things she had said? She had married him under false pretenses, acting the part of the joyful bride, when all the while there was nothing but hatred in her heart.

From that moment on, the entire journey north had been a misery. He had scarcely been able to look at his new wife. Every time he had so much as glanced in Elizabeth's direction, the conversation he had overheard played out again and again inside his head.

"I know better than anyone how you feel about Mr. Darcy. You have made your aversion plain from the moment you were introduced. You can scarcely tolerate the gentleman's company, and now you have pledged yourself to him for all eternity."

It had been Miss Bennet who had voiced those words, but his wife had said nothing in protest. Darcy remembered how he had held his breath, waiting for Elizabeth to contradict her sister. To say that Jane had misunderstood. That of course she did not despise the man she had just married.

But no such reassurances fell from Elizabeth's lips.

Instead, Darcy had heard her sad sigh. *"You must not speak so, Jane... It is done now. Besides, many people marry without affection."*

And then, Jane's soft reply, *"But you have not simply married without affection; you have married a man you vehemently dislike."*

Darcy reached for his glass, draining the remainder of the amber liquid and reveling in the pain he felt as it scorched a path down his throat.

It was no more than he deserved. If his life was ruined, he had only himself to blame. She had given him a way out, and he had refused to take it. What had possessed him to insist on standing by his offer of marriage after Elizabeth had made it clear that she had no intention of accepting her cousin?

Damn fool! You should have run like hell when you had the chance.

But no, he had been too stupid to see the truth. He had been living in a dream world—picturing intimate dinners and romantic interludes, while Elizabeth saw their union as no more than a marriage of convenience. A pact she made with the devil for the sake of her family, just as she would have done with Collins. She had merely sold herself to the highest bidder.

Slamming his glass down upon a nearby table, he lurched to his feet, staggering to the fireplace before slowly shifting his gaze to the door at the opposite end of the room. The door that led to the sitting room that connected his apartment to his wife's.

Well, that was one good thing to have come out of this disaster of an evening. At least Elizabeth would not be expecting him in her bedchamber, which would save him from having to make excuses for his lack of interest in the physical aspect of their marriage.

Returning to his chair, Darcy dropped his head in his hands. God help him, as much as he was loath to admit it, a lack of desire was certainly not the problem. Were that the case, he would not be ordering cold baths. But there would be no intimacy, no children. On that he was resolved.

For although the women he had taken to his bed had been few and far between, they all had one thing in common: they had come to him willingly. Never in his wildest imaginings had he contemplated forcing his attentions on any woman, and he was certainly not about to start with his own wife.

Not that he thought Elizabeth would rebuff his overtures. She had made her readiness plain the night of their wedding. He could still see her standing outside the door to her bedchamber at the inn, looking up at him with questioning eyes...

Luckily, it had been easy enough to put her off, as he had not intended to share her bed at a coaching inn in any case. But now that they were settled at Pemberley, she would no doubt wonder at his reluctance to consummate their union.

Darcy groaned. How had this happened? Was it less than a se'nnight ago that he had lain awake, imagining their first coupling and dreaming about all the ways he would please her? Now they were man and wife, and it was not to be.

Darcy shook his head and a bitter laugh rumbled in his throat. Oh, how the lecherous men at his clubs would ridicule him if he were to share his thoughts. He could almost see them now, looking down their noses and mocking him for his sanctimonious code of honor and his precious principles. Even his cousin, Richard, who was like a brother to him, would rib him mercilessly. Indeed, no one of his acquaintance would eschew lying with his own wife simply because he realized she did not love him. Good God, if that were the case, half the gentry would find themselves without an heir.

But Darcy could not do it. He would never be able to lie with Elizabeth knowing that the marriage bed would be a chore for her. He would simply have to find a way to make it clear to her that theirs would be a marriage in name only. He would not be able to look himself in the mirror otherwise.

Lifting his gaze, his eyes came to rest on the writing desk in the corner of his chamber. A lone letter sat on its surface, awaiting his reply. Crossing to the desk, he unfolded the thick vellum, staring down at Bingley's unruly scrawl.

Well, this was one thing he could remedy. He had not been able to save himself, but he could save his friend.

Slowly, he sat, listening to the scratching noises his pen made against the parchment as he poured out his thoughts in wrathful strokes.

Bingley,

You write seeking advice, and so I shall give it. Although it pains me to say this, I must agree with your sisters. While Miss Bennet is clearly an amiable young lady, her serene disposition and mild manners have led me to believe that she does not possess a heart that will be easily touched. Like-

wise, in my observations of her behavior towards you, I have noticed no evidence of any peculiar regard. It is therefore my estimation that should she accept your offer, it would merely be for the betterment of her family and nothing more. Pray, forgive my candor. My sole object is your happiness. However, to that end, I must persuade you against returning to Hertfordshire at the present time. Doing so would only give rise to expectations that it would not be in your best interest to fulfill. You would do well to remain in Town—or better yet, at your relations' in Scarborough—until such a time as you have mastered your feelings in this matter.

I remain, as always, your servant and friend,
Fitzwilliam Darcy

Darcy watched as the deep red wax spread across the parchment, like a pool of blood seeping from an open wound. No, he would not see Bingley trapped as he had been. Better for his friend to form an alliance based on fortune and connections than to find himself married to a wife who could scarcely tolerate his company. The pain of loving a woman who did not return those feelings was a curse no man should have to bear.

Not that he loved Elizabeth. Heaven forbid.

For should he ever succumb to such a sentiment, he would be well and truly damned.

∾

Elizabeth could not sleep. Although her chambers were snug and warm, and her new bed soft and comfortable, her mind could not be easy after her argument with Mr. Darcy.

When she first returned to her apartment, she had rung for Cassidy. The maid appeared almost immediately, helping her to undress and preparing her for bed. But once she had gone, Elizabeth found she was not at all tired. Her mind raced, and she paced the expansive chamber, her agitation growing with each step across the Aubusson carpet.

Although Mr. Darcy had made a valid point about her imprudent decision to go down to the kitchens, that did not excuse his behavior at dinner. He must have known she would be on edge on this, her first evening in her new home. And yet, instead of making an effort to see that she was comfortable, he had put on an ostentatious display, serving a feast better suited to a dinner party for the upper-most circles of society. Clearly, it had been a meal arranged to impress, to show his status, and perhaps to underscore the disparity between his social circle and her own. And if that were not bad enough, he barely took the trouble to speak to her, unless it was to reprimand her for daring not to eat one of the dishes his cook had prepared. As if it was her fault lobster made her ill!

Despite her ire, a small smile pulled at the edges of her lips. *It would have served him right if I had eaten it. I doubt he would have been amused when I cast up my accounts all over his fine linen tablecloth!*

Worn out from pacing, Elizabeth dropped into one of the silk slipper chairs in front of the fire. While all of that was true, she still should not have provoked him as she had in the withdrawing room. For better or for worse, he was her husband, and as such, he was entitled to her respect. She should have suppressed her desire to lash out and offered to play the pianoforte, or at least attempted to engage him in civil discourse, as a good wife would do.

Elizabeth sighed. In a household with four sisters, an anxious and overbearing mother, and a disinterested father, she had grown too accustomed to speaking her mind. But things were different now. She was no longer a carefree miss. Only three short days ago, she had stood before God and all those assembled, and promised to honor and obey her husband. She was all too aware of what the married state meant for women—Mr. Darcy owned her, in every sense of the word. And while he had never struck her as a cruel man—she would not have married him if he had—by his own admission, he possessed a resentful disposition. If there was any chance of felicity in her new life, she would do well not to ruffle his feathers.

Tucking her feet up under her, she glanced at the door that connected her room to the parlor that adjoined her husband's chambers. Would he come to her tonight? When they had arrived at Pemberley earlier today, she was almost certain that he would. He had not made any demands on her during their three-day journey from Hertfordshire, but Elizabeth had assumed that was due to the fact that they had been staying in small coaching inns, and she suspected the fastidious Mr. Darcy would wish for more privacy when taking his wife to the marriage bed for the first time.

But since their argument, she could not imagine he would come.

In truth, Mr. Darcy's behavior since their betrothal had puzzled her exceedingly. There had been times she had caught him staring at her in a way that did not seem to be entirely about finding fault. And there were one or two instances—most notably when she faced him at the altar and during the wedding breakfast—that she could have sworn she had seen genuine admiration and affection in his gaze. It had given her a reason to hope that her marriage might be a happy one after all, despite its bad beginnings.

But ever since they departed Netherfield, she had the growing inclination that something had changed. Although Mr. Darcy had never been gregarious, he was even more distant and withdrawn than usual on the journey north, barely speaking to her unless it was strictly required. He had booked separate chambers at each of the inns where they had stayed the night, and meals had been sent to her private sitting room. The only occasions they had spent together, apart from their hours in the carriage, had been to take tea, or a quick bite, when they had stopped to change horses.

Since arriving at Pemberley that afternoon, it had been more of the same, and Elizabeth was beginning to worry. What could have occurred to cause such a shift in her husband's disposition? Had her mother or one of her younger sisters said or done something to make him regret his decision to take Elizabeth as his wife? Or had she herself unknowingly caused him some offence?

Perhaps he had found her intimating that they would share a bed on their wedding night too forward...

Releasing a frustrated sigh, Elizabeth paced to the window, staring through the darkened glass. Well, there was no sense in upsetting herself unnecessarily; goodness knows she had never had much success at sketching Mr. Darcy's character. She would simply have to hope that whatever had caused his current fit of pique would soon be forgot, and that their married life would settle into a more calm and steady rhythm.

Eventually the candles burned down to tiny nubs, and Elizabeth took herself to bed, no closer to understanding the enigmatic man she had married.

Chapter 5

Dear Jane,

Mr. Darcy and I arrived at Pemberley yesterday afternoon after an uneventful journey. The house is amongst the grandest I have ever beheld, and the number of servants could easily staff Netherfield twice over. Dinner last night was an impressive affair-- oh, how I wish Mamma had been there to see it! Today I shall explore my new home, and hope not to get too horribly lost in the process.

I miss you already.

Your loving sister,
Elizabeth

E lizabeth awoke early after a restless night. As she was not yet familiar with the customs of the house, she kept herself busy writing letters at the small escritoire in her bedchamber. When she finally determined enough time had passed, she rang the bell, and in a matter of minutes, Cassidy appeared, followed by a housemaid bearing a tray with tea, freshly baked bread, strawberry jam and thick, creamy butter. Struck by the thoughtfulness of the housekeeper, Elizabeth enjoyed her breakfast as Cassidy moved around her chambers, laying out Elizabeth's clothing and humming a merry tune.

Watching the young woman go about her business, Elizabeth could not keep a small smile from forming on her lips. Although the idea of having her very own maid still seemed like an unnecessary luxury, she already found herself quite pleased with Miss Cassidy. The maid was young, but had already shown herself to be efficient, enthusiastic, and cheerful—qualities Elizabeth greatly esteemed.

When Elizabeth had finished her breakfast, Cassidy helped her to dress in a simple morning gown before setting to work on her hair. For some time, Elizabeth merely watched the maid in the mirrored glass, until it eventually occurred to her that she might do well to engage the voluble young woman in conversation. After all, if anyone would be able to give her a true sense of what life on the estate was like, it would be one of the servants.

Catching the girl's eye, Elizabeth offered an encouraging smile before saying brightly, "That looks very well, indeed—you seem to have quite a knack with hair."

Cassidy murmured her thanks and Elizabeth continued, "I suppose working in such a large house, you have had a good deal of practice. Have you been at Pemberley long?"

"Oh, yes, ma'am. All my life," the young girl answered, flushing at Elizabeth's praise. "My father has a farm on the estate, and all my brothers and sisters have worked for the family at one time or another. I started here in the kitchens when I was fifteen, but Mrs. Reynolds made me housemaid a couple of years later. My mum used to be a lady's maid up in Yorkshire before she and my father married, and she taught all us girls to sew and do hair and all that. That's how I come to start looking after Miss Darcy when she was up from school."

At the mention of Mr. Darcy's sister, Elizabeth was instantly intrigued. She remembered that Mr. Wickham had described her as exceedingly proud, but after what Mr. Darcy had told her before they married, she was beginning to doubt the veracity of anything Wickham had divulged about the family.

"And, did you enjoy that?" she asked casually. "Tending to Miss Darcy?"

"Oh, aye! I never met a person with a sweeter temper. I'd be with her still if Mr. Darcy hadn't sent her to Town."

"You did not wish to go with her?"

Cassidy shook her head. "Mrs. Reynolds said I might go if I liked, but I could never leave Pemberley. And Miss Darcy is always up for the summer months. She never travels with a maid, so I always wait on her when she comes. Or... at least I did..." she stammered, meeting Elizabeth's eyes with an uneasy expression.

"And so you shall continue," Elizabeth replied. "At home, I shared one maid with four sisters, so I see no difficulty in sharing with Miss Darcy when she is in residence."

Cassidy looked suitably relieved at this intelligence, and after a slight pause, Elizabeth continued, "You are happy here, then?"

"Oh, yes, ma'am! Pemberley is the finest estate in all of England! Of course I've never worked anywhere else, but lots of the maids and footmen have been in service in other places, and they all say the same."

"And Mr. Darcy," she began tentatively, "is he very particular? About the running of the household?"

Cassidy's brow crinkled in confusion as her eyes once again met Elizabeth's in the mirror. "Particular, madam?"

"Yes, that is, is he very exacting in his requirements... for the servants?"

The maid paused, appearing to consider the matter. "Well, he does like things orderly, to be sure. But he's not one of those sorts who thinks of nothing besides themselves. He always has a kind word to say when he meets with anyone in the household. Mrs. Reynolds has been with the family since Mr. Darcy was a boy, and she says he was as good-natured a child as ever lived."

Elizabeth had to admit that she was somewhat taken aback by the lavishness of Cassidy's praise. Of course, she did not expect any of the servants would speak ill of their master—especially to the new mistress—but the genuine warmth and enthusiasm with which the maid professed her opinions, both about Mr. Darcy and his sister, went a good deal above the polite deference Elizabeth had anticipated.

She was so deep in her own thoughts, she hardly noticed when Cassidy finished with her hair and moved to stand expectantly beside the dressing table.

Looking up with a start, Elizabeth flushed. "Forgive me, Cassidy, I was woolgathering. Was there something else you wished to say?"

"Aye. Mrs. Reynolds said I should tell you she would be pleased to wait upon you in the morning room, whenever you were ready, Mrs. Darcy."

Nodding her agreement, Elizabeth rose to follow the maid down the stairs and into a large sunny parlor where a cozy fire danced in the hearth. Cassidy dropped a brief curtsy before taking her leave, and soon afterwards, the housekeeper appeared. Turning away from the window where she had gone to observe the prospect of Pemberley's gardens, Elizabeth greeted the older woman with a warm smile.

"Mrs. Reynolds, I must thank you for your kindness in sending breakfast to my chambers. I confess I was somewhat worried about finding the dining parlor again, and in any case, I did not know at what time the morning meal was generally served. So, it was quite a relief not to have to concern myself with such matters."

The housekeeper's brow momentarily furrowed, and Elizabeth wondered if she had gone too far in divulging that her husband had not bothered to inform her of any of these particulars himself, but Mrs Reynolds soon allayed those reservations.

"It was the master's wish that breakfast be brought to your apartment, madam. Mr. Darcy thought you might find it more relaxing on your first morning here."

"Oh, I see," Elizabeth murmured. "And, has my husband already breakfasted, then?"

"Yes, madam. Mr. Darcy always rises at daybreak. Breakfast is usually set out in the small dining parlor at eight and cleared by ten, but of course we will adapt our schedule to suit your preferences. We do keep the service going longer when Miss Darcy or other guests are in residence."

"I thank you," Elizabeth answered, "but your usual schedule will do very well for me. I am also an early riser."

Mrs. Reynolds nodded her approval. "Very good, madam. As we are speaking of it, the master also bid me to make his apologies for not joining you before now, but he had an early meeting with Mr. Boyle, the steward."

The housekeeper sniffed, and Elizabeth could not miss

the look of distaste that flickered across her countenance before she continued, "However, he wished for you to be informed that he would join you as soon as his business was concluded. In the meantime, he asked if I might take you through the upper stories, so that you could become better acquainted with the house, if you would find that agreeable?"

Elizabeth was quick to indicate that she would, inwardly breathing a sigh of relief at this further reprieve from having to face Mr. Darcy after last night's quarrel.

Following at the housekeeper's heels, the pair retraced Elizabeth's steps to the family wing where Mrs. Reynolds opened each door in succession to reveal numerous bedchambers, all spacious and tastefully furnished. The same was done with the guest wing opposite, until Elizabeth became dizzy at the number of rooms. She said as much to the housekeeper who laughed, echoing what Mr. Darcy had told her in the carriage about the additional chambers and nursery on the floor above, which were not currently in use.

The tour of the upper floors ended in Elizabeth's own apartment, as Mrs. Reynolds hoped to take note of any changes her new mistress wished to make to the décor.

After once again surveying the expansive space, Elizabeth attempted to demur, but the housekeeper continued to look dubious, furrowing her brow in obvious uncertainty.

"Truly, Mrs. Reynolds," Elizabeth said at length, "I find the apartment exceedingly comfortable. I understand from my husband that I have you to thank for that. He mentioned that the rooms were redone only a year or two ago, at your direction."

"Aye, and time it was, too. I am glad you find the

furnishings to your liking, but there must be something that you would wish to change, to make the space feel more your own. Mr. Darcy was very clear that you should have whatever you desired."

Elizabeth lifted her brow, pleased despite herself that her husband would have extended such a courtesy. Casting her eyes about the space, she took in the soft-yellow wall-coverings and the elegant yet comfortable furnishings. In truth, it was all very much as she would have chosen if given a blank canvas, but she could see that the house-keeper would not be satisfied unless she agreed to some slight alteration.

"Well, if it is not too much trouble... I am very fond of books. Might we set up some shelves, and possibly a comfortable chair for reading? Perhaps in that alcove over there, near the fireplace?"

"I think that a lovely idea," the housekeeper answered, her expression brightening. "We might even move the desk closer to the windows, where the light is better, to give you a little more room..."

"Oh, yes, I should like that very much," replied Elizabeth.

They spoke for a few minutes more, agreeing to meet later in the day to go over some household business, before Mrs. Reynolds turned to go. She had almost reached the door when she stopped, once again facing in Elizabeth's direction.

"If I may be so bold, madam, I hope you will allow me to say how very happy we all are to have you here. Pemberley has known a great deal of sorrow, and there is no one in the kingdom who deserves happiness more than the master. It is wonderful to see some sunshine about the place again."

Elizabeth murmured her thanks, but inside her feelings were far from easy. If only the housekeeper knew that she and Mr. Darcy were barely on speaking terms!

Mrs. Reynolds soon quit the room, and Elizabeth retrieved her sewing basket, hoping to give herself something to occupy her mind while she awaited Mr. Darcy in the morning room. Typically, embroidery was not her first choice of amusement, but her thoughts were in too much of a tangle for reading, and she felt the sudden desire to keep her hands busy.

Descending the main stairs, she had just reached the lower floor when the sound of raised voices coming from the opposite side of the corridor arrested her steps. Recognizing the present speaker as her husband, Elizabeth inched closer to the sound.

"I will remind you that you are here at my pleasure," Darcy said coldly. "You will do things my way, or seek employment elsewhere."

Beyond the sheer volume of his words, there could be no mistaking the hostility in his tone, and she could not help but feel sorry for the unfortunate soul who had incurred his wrath.

The voice that replied was deep and masculine, but the words were too muffled to make out.

"We are through here. I have nothing more to say on this subject." Again, her husband's voice, followed by the sound of a door opening.

Elizabeth jumped back, hastily retreating before she was caught in the act of eavesdropping on a private conversation. Stealing into the morning room, she breathed a sigh of relief at not having been discovered, but she could not so quickly forget the barely suppressed rage in her husband's voice, wondering if that same fury would soon be turned loose upon herself.

Closing the door of his study with a bang, Darcy paced back to his desk, dropping into the chair he had recently vacated. Having risen well before sunrise after very little sleep, he was already at the end of his tether, and his meeting with Boyle had done little to improve his sour disposition.

After penning his letter to Bingley, he had sat up late into the night, trying to calm his fractured emotions. He had allowed his temper to get the best of him the night before, but he could not permit that to happen again. While his friend might still be able to avoid being ensnared in a loveless marriage, it was too late for him. Elizabeth was his wife, for better or for worse. They were bound together by God and the law, and if there was any hope for them to escape a lifetime of misery, he would have to do better. Punishing Elizabeth was not the answer. He knew that now. He had not been brought up to treat any woman with the disdain he had demonstrated to his wife last evening, and he would not abandon his principles now. He was her husband, and it was his duty to see her taken care of. No matter his feelings, he *would* behave as a gentleman and treat her with respect.

Glancing at the clock on the mantlepiece, he released a heavy sigh. Mrs. Reynolds must be finished showing Elizabeth around the upper floors by now. He should seek her out and offer his apologies. Then, he would take her through the rest of the house. Once she knew her way around, and was more comfortable in her environment, he was certain she would find plenty to occupy her time, and heaven knew he had his hands full with Boyle. Like any number of couples of his station, he and Elizabeth would live their own lives, coming together at dinner and for a few hours in the evening for civil discourse, but otherwise, content to go their separate ways. Theirs would never be a marriage of affection, but there could be peace. Contentment.

And in order to make it so, he would need to put that horrible moment at Netherfield out of his mind. To lock it away, as he had done with every other crippling disappointment he had been dealt over the last eighteen years.

No, he would never have the marriage he envisioned, but at least there could be tranquility.

And that would have to be enough.

A quarter of an hour later, Elizabeth sat in a comfortable chair in an expansive parlor. Too anxious to attend to her sewing, she sat idly by the fire, listening to the hiss and crackle of the flames and staring out a nearby window, her embroidery frame resting forgotten in her lap. When at last the door opened, Elizabeth set her needlework aside, quickly climbing to her feet as Mr. Darcy entered, appearing customarily grave.

Elizabeth smoothed her skirts as Mr. Darcy sketched a shallow bow.

"Good morning."

"Good morning," Elizabeth murmured.

"I hope I do not intrude?"

"Not at all. Mrs. Reynolds told me I might expect you when your business was concluded."

Mr. Darcy nodded stiffly before saying, "Yes. Forgive me for not joining you for breakfast."

"Of course. I appreciated the tray you had sent to my rooms."

Conversation lapsed and Elizabeth turned to once again gaze out a nearby window.

After a brief hesitation, Darcy cleared his throat.

"I trust Mrs. Reynolds took you through the guest chambers and the family wing as I suggested?"

Elizabeth redirected her gaze, forcing a tight smile. "Yes. She was good enough to show me through most of the second floor. She seemed quite eager for me to redecorate my own apartment. I tried to tell her I was very happy with the rooms, but we eventually decided upon a few small alterations. I hope you do not mind."

"On the contrary. I instructed Mrs. Reynolds to see that you had free rein over all the furnishings in the house. Change whatever you wish."

"Thank you."

Once again, Darcy made a sound in the back of his throat. "I thought I might show you the principal rooms myself, if you have no objection. We might go now, unless there was something else you needed to attend to?"

Elizabeth suppressed a smile. She hardly had any pressing engagements at the moment.

"No, not at all. I would like that," she answered.

Elizabeth began moving towards the door, but her husband seemed in no hurry to follow. Instead, he shifted his weight, running his fingers through his hair and staring down at the carpet.

Elizabeth stopped, turning back in his direction.

Finally, Darcy spoke.

"I... before we begin, I wished to have a word... about last night."

Elizabeth stiffened, preparing herself for his chastisement, however, when her husband seemed disinclined to say anything further, she decided to begin herself.

"Yes, I wished to speak with you as well. Pray, forgive me for my behavior... I had not—"

"No!" he interrupted, his tone more vehement than Elizabeth would have expected. "It is I who should apologize. I am afraid I was overly fatigued. I should not have spoken to you as I did."

Surprised, Elizabeth nodded slowly before saying, "I suppose neither of us were at our best last evening. But when I reflected on it later, I realized you made a valid point about going down to the kitchens unannounced."

Once again, Darcy shifted uncomfortably. "Yes. Well. I could have been more forgiving in the way I expressed myself. Perhaps we can put the incident behind us?"

Elizabeth forced her lips into a light smile. "Consider it forgotten."

At her words, Mr. Darcy seemed to relax slightly, and with a brief nod, he stepped back, gesturing for her to precede him from the room.

Together, they traversed the wide entrance hall, and Darcy pushed open a heavy mahogany door before stepping back so Elizabeth could enter.

Crossing the threshold, her eyes grew round as she took

in her surroundings. The room they had entered—a parlor —was easily the grandest of its type Elizabeth had ever seen. From the French rococo and Louis XV style furnishings, to the silk damask wall hangings and gilded girandoles, the entire chamber fairly glowed in a golden haze of lavish sophistication.

Attempting to compose her features, she turned to Mr. Darcy, who looked suddenly discomfited—as if he were able to read her thoughts, despite her efforts to appear unaffected.

"This is the main salon," he offered, "however it is not generally used by the family. We only occupy this room on special occasions, or when we are entertaining large parties."

"I see," Elizabeth murmured, her eyes lifting from the Axminster carpet to the fresco painted on the vaulted ceiling. "It is quite... dazzling."

Darcy turned to take in his surroundings, glancing around the space as if seeing it for the first time. "Yes. The décor is not necessarily to my taste, but it is one of the rooms on the tour, so Mrs. Reynolds has always felt it important to keep it looking somewhat impressive. Visitors expect a certain amount of opulence, I suppose."

Tearing her gaze away from the marble chimney-piece, Elizabeth blinked back at him. "The tour? Do you mean to say that the house is open to the public?"

Darcy seemed to visibly start and then colored before saying, "Yes. Forgive me, I should have mentioned that. But you will not be too much inconvenienced. We do not get nearly so many visitors as Chatsworth or Blenheim, and most people only come in the summer months, so you will not have to think about it for some time."

"I see," Elizabeth repeated.

Once again, Darcy cleared his throat. "I imagine it must seem strange," he finally offered, "to one who is not accustomed to it. However, there is nothing you need do. Mrs. Reynolds handles the tours, and a footman will always be sent to notify the family when there are visitors in the house, so we know to stay out of the public spaces. And it is only the state rooms that are open for viewing, which would be this salon, the large dining parlor, the library, the portrait gallery, and two or three of the principal bedchambers on the guest wing. Visitors may also tour the gardens in the spring and summer, but those excursions are conducted by the chief gardener, or a member of his staff. So you see, you shall hardly be disturbed at all."

Attempting to school her features, Elizabeth nodded mutely, slowly coming to terms with the fact that she now lived in a house so grand it was a curiosity, open to the public. How very odd! It took her a minute to realize that Mr. Darcy was speaking to suggest that they carry on to the formal dining parlor, which could be accessed through a large double doorway at the rear of the room.

Darcy led the way, and Elizabeth followed, once again drawing a sharp breath as she crossed the threshold.

The dining parlor was enormous. It was twice the size of the smaller dining room they had eaten in last evening— which she now realized must be reserved for family dinners —and three times as grandiose. The massive fireplace boasted a chimney-piece of Carrera marble, and a magnificent crystal chandelier hung over the polished mahogany table which was laid with silver candelabras and a stunning service of Wedgewood bone china.

She turned wide eyes on Mr. Darcy, who she realized was speaking again.

"We keep the table set for visitors and change the service once each month. Like the main salon, we use the room ourselves but rarely. The table you see here seats twenty-six comfortably, but we can accommodate more by putting up several smaller tables in the corners of the room, as my parents used to do for ball suppers. Since my father's passing, we rarely entertain on any great scale, however, and use the small dining parlor for most of our meals."

Elizabeth was quiet as Darcy guided her out another door on the opposite wall and back across the entrance hall. They passed into several other rooms: the morning room she had been in previously, the small dining parlor, and the withdrawing room they had retired to last evening, as well as a music room, a billiards room, and two other parlors. As they went, Elizabeth noted that these chambers were all lofty and handsome, but without the grandeur on display in the main salon or the large dining parlor. She was also pleased to see that each room featured tall windows, and through every one there were beauties to be appreciated. Even in winter, the prospects in all directions were incredibly fine, and she looked on each one with growing delight.

When they had exhausted the rooms on the ground floor, Darcy escorted her up the main staircase, and, upon reaching the spacious first floor mezzanine, took them down another corridor where they entered a very pretty sitting room. Her husband explained that it had been recently fitted up for his sister's personal use, as she had taken a liking to it, but as Miss Darcy was now mostly in

Town, Elizabeth was, of course, welcome to use it if she found it agreeable.

"Very much so," Elizabeth answered, and her husband nodded his approval before leading her back out the way they had come.

Upon reaching the passageway, Darcy seemed to hesitate before gesturing to the right.

"If we go this way, we will come to my study and the library. I hope you will find it to your liking. I know you are fond of books, and the collection is extensive."

Elizabeth brightened at his mention of the library, but she could not help but notice that there was still a portion of the corridor they had yet to explore.

"I am eager to see it," she answered, but instead of following his lead, she nodded to the left. "And what is down this way? Does the corridor not connect on the other side?"

Darcy's eyes darted in the direction she indicated, and he paused before answering slowly, "It does; however, there is not much of interest down that way. Only the ballroom, which has been closed up for some years... and the picture gallery."

"Oh!" Elizabeth cried, her eyes instantly lighting. "Might we go that way instead? You need not take me through the ballroom, but I should like very much to see the gallery." She knew so little of her husband's family, that the idea of viewing the likenesses of his ancestors intrigued her a great deal.

The ghost of a frown wrinkled Darcy's brow, his eyes once again darting down the passageway as Elizabeth observed him with interest. He was clearly not disposed to take her there, and Elizabeth found herself puzzled as to the reason. *'Tis very strange. He has shown no trepidation in showing me any of the other rooms.*

Several more seconds ticked by before Darcy finally nodded. "Of course," he murmured, and Elizabeth was left to wonder if she had only imagined his reluctance. *Perhaps there is a very embarrassing portrait of him in his christening gown,* she thought, smothering a smile as she followed her husband along the polished floor.

Entering the gallery, Elizabeth was immediately arrested by the sheer size of the space, for to even call it a room was not entirely accurate—it was more along the lines of a colonnade, connecting one wing of the house with the other. Upon one side, paintings of varying sizes were spread along the high wall.

Now that they were inside, Darcy seemed more at ease, pointing out various ancestral relations as they strolled along. Elizabeth looked on them with interest, but her attention was not truly captured until they reached the midway point in the landing, and Darcy stopped.

"My parents," he said quietly, indicating the portrait before them.

Elizabeth's gaze shifted from her husband's serious mien to the handsome young couple smiling down at them with bright eyes and warm expressions. Beneath the painting, a bronze plaque read: Mr. Robert George Darcy and Lady Anne Fitzwilliam Darcy, 1779.

Elizabeth studied the portrait. She could immediately see the resemblance between Mr. Darcy and his father, though he had his mother's eyes.

"Your mother was very beautiful," Elizabeth murmured.

"Yes. She was."

"And your father handsome. You look like him."

Instead of appearing pleased by the compliment, Darcy frowned. "They were very young. This was painted directly following their marriage."

"They look happy."

"Yes."

They stood in silence for a moment more before Elizabeth turned to study the painting hanging directly to the right of the portrait of the senior Mr. Darcy and Lady Anne. This one showed a young girl of approximately fifteen or sixteen years of age. There was a distinct resemblance to Lady Anne, though from the style of dress, Elizabeth could tell that it was painted much more recently.

"Your sister?" she asked, and Darcy nodded.

"This was done only last year. Georgiana did not wish it, but I thought it was time. She looks very like our mother, I think."

"She does. I noticed the resemblance immediately." Elizabeth regarded her husband, who was staring at the painting with such a clear expression of affection that it stole her breath. "You must miss her a great deal," she said softly.

"I do. I always miss her when she is away. But she will be home at Christmas. That is, if you have no objection?"

Elizabeth knitted her brow. Did he truly think that she would prevent his sister from returning to her home during the festive season?

"None at all," she answered. "I am looking forward to meeting her. Will you travel to Town to collect her?"

"No. My cousin, Colonel Fitzwilliam, has offered to escort her here on his way to Briarwood, Lord and Lady Matlock's estate. It is but two hours to the north."

"Ah. I see."

Elizabeth paused, but her husband did not seem to have any more to say on the subject, so she turned to continue exploring the remainder of the gallery.

On the opposite side of Miss Darcy's portrait hung another painting of the former Mr. Darcy and Lady Anne in later years, but it was the painting next to it that caused her footsteps to grind to a halt as she stared up into the face of her husband. Although she could tell the likeness was taken some years ago—perhaps five or six—the resemblance to the man himself was striking, though he appeared more relaxed and easier than she had ever known him to look in person. But while his lips turned up at the corners, there was still a trace of sadness in his eyes. Elizabeth gazed at the portrait, transfixed, for a long time, until Mr. Darcy cleared his voice self-consciously.

"That was painted right after I left university. My father commissioned it the summer after I graduated, but he did not live to see its completion."

Elizabeth nodded, surprised that a lump appeared to have formed at the back of her throat, making speech seem quite impossible.

No wonder he did not wish to show me the gallery, she thought. No doubt all these paintings awakened memories that must cause him a great deal of pain.

Struggling for something to lighten the mood, she continued on, thinking to find a new painting to distract his attention, but to her surprise, the place beside her husband's portrait was empty, though it was clear from the markings on the wall that a painting had once hung in that spot.

"Have you sent this one out for restoration?" she asked,

wondering at the fact that no other paintings in the gallery appeared to be missing.

Slowly, Darcy stepped up to her side, gazing at the faded paper on the wall.

"No. I had it taken down and put into storage. I... I thought perhaps we might hang your portrait there."

"Mine?" Elizabeth gasped, her head snapping in his direction.

At her obvious surprise, Darcy offered her a slight smile, the first warm expression she had seen from him since the day of their wedding, and a sudden jolt shot down Elizabeth's spine.

"Yes, yours. And why not? You are a Darcy now. Your portrait should hang here with all the rest."

"Yes, but... I..."

"Have you never had your likeness taken?" he asked curiously.

"No. Never."

Darcy's eyebrows lifted. "Not even a miniature?"

Elizabeth shook her head.

"Well, then it is high time we corrected that. You have a face that was made for painting."

Elizabeth's eyes grew round, and Darcy's expression instantly altered, as if only now realizing what he had said.

"I shall make inquiries," he continued brusquely. "Perhaps a local artist, so we do not need to have anyone travel from Town."

Elizabeth nodded, numbly.

Seeming to recover his equanimity, Darcy took her elbow, leading her towards the outer corridor. "Come, let us finish the tour."

Upon exiting the gallery, they passed the sitting room

and another small parlor before coming to the door Elizabeth knew led to Mr. Darcy's study. He stepped inside to show her the room—it was of a good size, though smaller than she might have expected, and fitted up with a large mahogany desk, two wingback chairs, and a shelf of books —but they did not tarry there. Instead, they continued down the passageway until they reached a set of carved double doors. Darcy stopped, and, with great ceremony, pushed them open, allowing her to enter.

Crossing the threshold, Elizabeth could not contain the gasp that escaped her throat upon entering the largest and grandest library she had ever beheld. The space was two stories tall, with shelves from ceiling to floor and a staircase in the center that led to a balcony which ran the entire circumference of the room. There was a stunning fresco on one wall, and two enormous marble fireplaces on either end. Although the space was vast, the furniture was arranged in small groupings, making it feel intimate and welcoming, and there was no shortage of cozy places to curl up and read.

"It is magnificent," she breathed, as Darcy closed the doors behind them.

"I am glad you approve."

"I think you knew I would. No one who loves books could find anything wanting in a library such as this."

"Indeed. It is one of my favorite rooms in the house, however I cannot take all of the credit. It is the work of many generations."

Elizabeth walked slowly around the perimeter of the room, running her fingers reverently over the gilded spines, stopping now and then to pull an item from the stacks when she recognized one of her favorites.

She had only made it halfway down one wall when a soft snort broke the silence. Glancing in the direction of the closest fireplace, she noticed for the first time that she and Mr. Darcy were not alone. A sleek brown ball of fur lay curled upon the hearth rug before a crackling blaze.

The animal let out another deep snore, slowly rolling onto its back, and Elizabeth's lips quirked up at the corners.

"I did not realize we had company," she said, turning to face her husband. "I confess that while I assumed you kept hounds, I did not take you for the type to allow them full-run of the house."

"Generally speaking, I do not. This one is an exception," Darcy answered. "However, there is no cause for alarm. She is well behaved, and keeps mostly to my study or the library." After a pause, he added, "I hope you do not dislike dogs?"

Elizabeth moved closer to the animal who continued to doze, speaking to Mr. Darcy over her shoulder. "Oh, no, I was only teasing. I am very fond of dogs. I would have dearly loved to have one for a pet if my father had allowed it." She was only a few feet from the fireplace when the animal's nose twitched, and a moment later, the dog's soft brown eyes opened. Fixing Elizabeth with an attentive stare, the hound clambered to her feet, loping to Elizabeth's side and nosing the fabric of her gown.

Elizabeth laughed, running her fingers along the top of the animal's head.

"And what is your name?" she asked, continuing to stroke the dog's silky fur. Her tail wagged furiously, but she kept her nose buried in Elizabeth's skirts.

"Her name is Harpocrates. Harp, for short." Before Elizabeth could comment, Darcy brought the sole of his

boot down hard on the wooden floor, and the animal immediately raced to her master's side.

Elizabeth frowned. "Is that how you summon her? Are
you in the habit of stomping your feet to get her attention?"

Despite the irritation in her tone, Darcy smiled. "Yes. I
have found it to be the best way."

Once again, Elizabeth felt a surge of annoyance. She
had always known her husband was overbearing and offi-
cious, but this was beyond the pale! Would he soon be
snapping his fingers to draw *her* notice? She opened her
mouth to voice her outrage, but before Elizabeth could
speak, Mr. Darcy continued calmly, "She is deaf. But she
can feel the vibration in the floorboards. And she is very
obedient. She always comes when called."

Elizabeth's mouth snapped shut as her cheeks heated
with mortification in realizing her error.

"Harpocrates," she murmured. "The Greek god of
silence."

Darcy's smile deepened. "Yes. I thought it rather clever
when I came up with it. But the name is a mouthful. And it
is not as though she answers to it. Harp is simpler."

Without looking back, Darcy walked to the French
windows at the far side of the room, Harpocrates happily
trotting at his side. Opening the doors to the garden, he
gave the animal a light slap on her withers and she raced
out into the winter sunshine. Closing the window against a
gust of frigid air, he came back to where Elizabeth was
standing.

"She is able to go out on her own?" Elizabeth asked and
Darcy nodded.

"She knows the gardens and will stay close to the
house." After a moment, he added, "She gets plenty of

exercise, as I often take her with me when I walk the estate, but she enjoys her independence, too. I would not be doing her any favors by coddling her."

The two took seats by the fire, and Elizabeth stared into the flames, lost in thought.

"You are quiet," Darcy said after a while. "I hope the prospect of having Harpocrates in the house does not distress you."

"Oh, no! Not at all. As I have already said, I am fond of dogs. I was just wondering how you came to be in possession of a deaf hunting dog. She is a hunter, is she not?"

"By breeding, yes, though she is not used in that capacity. Mostly because I rarely hunt, but also because it would not be safe for her."

Darcy stood, using a nearby fire iron to stir the flames. "It is a shame, as she has a remarkable sense of smell. I have often heard it said that when one area of perception is missing, the other senses are strengthened, and Harp certainly seems to prove that theory. But she would not be able to hear the sounds of gunshots or the pounding of the horse's hooves. And we could not call to her if she were in danger."

Elizabeth murmured her understanding before asking, "So, has she always been deaf? Was she born that way?"

"Yes," Darcy answered, returning the fire iron to its place and resuming his seat. "I purchased her when she was only a few months old. I was at a house party a few summers ago, and one of our host's hunters had recently delivered a litter. My friend mentioned that they had noticed one of the pups appeared to be deaf; the kennel master was going to put her down. I was curious, so I asked if I might take a look, and I was smitten the moment I saw her. Not only was she a beautiful animal, but it was immediately evident that she was smart as a whip. I offered to purchase her on the spot."

"That was kind of you. But... why would you ask to purchase her? I am certain your friend would have been happy to give you the pup if they were only planning to put her down."

Darcy stared back at her, an inscrutable expression in his dark eyes.

"I have always been taught that when one receives something of value, the bearer should be fairly compensated. I paid for the dog because, to me, her life had value."

A warm flush crept up Elizabeth's neck at the implied reprimand, and she quickly looked away. "Forgive me. I... I suppose I never thought of it that way..."

The clock on the mantel struck the hour, and Elizabeth jumped to her feet, smoothing her skirts.

"Well, I should not take up any more of your time; I am certain you have matters of business to attend to."

Darcy stood when she did, though his brows were drawn together in confusion. "As you wish. I will see you at dinner, then?"

Elizabeth nodded before turning on her heel and hastening from the room, feeling all the indignity of being set down by one she had always regarded as her inferior in both compassion and comportment.

Chapter 6

After Elizabeth's cowardly retreat from the library, she sought out Mrs. Reynolds, meeting with the housekeeper in the upstairs sitting room to discuss menus for the week. She learned that Mr. Darcy, despite last evening's dinner, preferred simple fare, and generally only ate breakfast and an early supper of one course. He never indulged in rich desserts, so they were generally only served when there were guests in the house. He often took tea in the afternoons, but avoided biscuits and cakes, preferring finger-sandwiches or fresh fruit.

Elizabeth listened to all of this with increasing interest, realizing how little she truly knew her husband. She was also pleased to learn that their tastes coincided in many ways, as she also preferred simple food, and while she did have a fondness for sweets, she generally only indulged in them on special occasions.

After approving of the cook's suggestions for that evening's meal and finalizing the menus for the remainder of the week, Mrs. Reynolds departed and Elizabeth returned to her chambers. She penned another brief letter to Jane and then curled up in the window seat to read, but soon grew restless. It was still an hour until tea time, and although she would have dearly loved a walk in the gardens, a steady rain had begun to fall, preventing her from venturing out of doors. To keep herself occupied, she decided to have another wander around the house, hoping to become more familiar with its layout.

Crossing the vast entrance hall, she made her way into the formal salon, and her breath caught anew as she took in the elegant space. The room rivaled any she had seen for stylish sophistication and made even Netherfield—one of the finest manor houses in all of Hertfordshire—look like a humble cottage by comparison.

Settling onto one of the silk jacquard settees, Elizabeth's thoughts once again turned to the man she had married. What must it have been like to grow up surrounded by such opulence? To know, practically from the cradle, that you would one day be master of all you surveyed?

There was no question that from their first meeting, she had considered Mr. Darcy to be proud and above his company, but now, after getting only a small glimpse of the world in which he was raised, was that so surprising? How could one be brought up amongst all of this, as son and heir, and not feel some sense of pride? Were such feelings not reasonable and justified?

She suddenly recalled a conversation she had once had with her sister Mary about the distinction between vanity and pride. It had been Mary's assertion that the two were different things, and that a person may be proud without being vain. That pride related more to our opinions of ourselves, whereas vanity reflected what we would have others think of us.

Turning to gaze out the rain-spattered window, Elizabeth pondered this seriously for the first time. As much as it pained her, she had to admit that Mr. Darcy was not vain. He had no wish to be thought well of by others. If anything, he seemed distinctly uncomfortable with any sort of public approbation, as clearly evidenced by his obvious aversion to Caroline Bingley's fawning.

Leaning back against the tufted cushions, Elizabeth once again recalled her first meeting with her husband at the Meryton assembly. It was true he had been rude—standing at the edge of the room for most of the evening and not deigning to dance with anyone beyond the two ladies in his own party—and that comment he had made about her had been unpardonable.

However, for the first time, she put herself in his shoes.

What had it been like to hear the whispers her neighbors had scarcely taken the trouble to conceal regarding his wealth and matrimonial eligibility? To feel the curious stares of a room full of strangers, and to know their interest stemmed from nothing more than his value as the proverbial golden goose? What would it be like to constantly live with that type of scrutiny, especially for a man who was clearly uncomfortable with being the center of attention?

She could not help but wonder how their behavior had shaped his, and whether the man she had met at that assembly bore any resemblance to the real Mr. Darcy.

Elizabeth sat with her reflections until Mr. Lawson came and offered to have the tea service brought in. Climbing quickly to her feet, Elizabeth accepted the proposition of refreshment, but chose to have it served instead in the more comfortable sitting room upstairs.

Her husband did not join her. The butler indicated that Mr. Darcy was attending to matters of business, though when she passed the door to his study, the room was empty.

And although Elizabeth appreciated the attentiveness of everyone in the household, the solitude was already beginning to wear on her. Was this what her new life was to be? Mr. Darcy hiding away somewhere working, while she rattled around this enormous house, all on her own? The thought was both alarming and dispiriting. She could not imagine going on in such a way. She needed people, and she needed employment. She missed her sisters' incessant chatter, her father's sardonic wit, and even her mother's nervous lamentations. She missed being able to walk into Meryton to call on her Aunt Philips. And while she had known that marrying Mr. Darcy would mean a different way of life, she was not prepared to become one of those women who did nothing but embroider cushions and pay social calls on their neighbors.

Eventually, Elizabeth returned to her chambers, and Cassidy soon arrived to assist her with changing for dinner. Tonight, Elizabeth wore one of her newer gowns, though she was aware that it was still at least a year out of fashion, and had not been of the highest quality even when it was first purchased. And while Cassidy pronounced it "very pretty," Elizabeth could sense the maid's disquiet as she looked through her mistress's meager wardrobe.

Elizabeth smothered a sigh. She would have to go shopping. She knew Mr. Darcy would not mind. He had already told her—several times—that she should purchase anything she deemed necessary as there had been no chance to procure a proper trousseau before their hasty nuptials. And while she knew most women would leap at such an opportunity, somehow the thought of setting aside all that was familiar—shedding the very clothes from her body to transform into some new version of herself she would scarcely recognize—was more difficult than she had anticipated.

Catching Cassidy's eyes in the mirrored glass, she realized the maid had been speaking to her, and Elizabeth flushed at being caught out for the second time in as many days. *Goodness, she must think me utterly self-absorbed to be daydreaming all the time.*

"Forgive me, Cassidy, I am afraid I was not attending," she offered sheepishly. "What were you saying?"

"Oh, I was just asking if you might like me to do something special with your hair. A ribbon, mayhap? Or some jeweled pins? Have you any of those?"

Elizabeth shook her head, feeling suddenly lacking. "I am afraid not."

Cassidy looked so dejected that Elizabeth turned to scan her surroundings, hoping for inspiration. Her gaze landed on a vase of winter heather sitting on a low table near the window and she quickly stood, walking in that direction.

"Perhaps a sprig of heather?" she suggested, and the maid's face instantly brightened.

Plucking one of the stems, Cassidy pinned the purple bloom into Elizabeth's dark curls. The effect was lovely, and Elizabeth smiled, suddenly feeling a little more like her old self. She had just offered her thanks when a knock sounded at the door, and the maid went to answer, stepping back as Mr. Darcy entered the room.

Cassidy dropped a brief curtsy, and Elizabeth nodded to indicate she may leave. When she lifted her eyes to meet her husband's, she noted that he was staring at her with his usual quiet intensity, but when he finally spoke, his voice was unaffected.

"Shall we go down?" he asked impassively, and Elizabeth nodded her agreement.

The two made their way to the floor below without speaking.

When they reached the dining parlor, he pulled out her chair, seating himself once again at her side. Peter, the first footman, approached to pour the wine, and soon afterwards, several others appeared with their dinner, which consisted of brown onion soup, beef steaks, and finally, a roast chicken with egg sauce. When the last dish was revealed, Elizabeth could see a look of surprise cross her husband's features.

Glancing nervously in his direction, she carefully unfolded her napkin.

"I hope you are not disappointed. Your housekeeper said you had a preference for simple dishes. I thought to request a ragout or a fricassee, but Mrs. Reynolds mentioned roast chicken was a favorite of yours."

"Indeed, it is, and I have not had it in quite some time. Although it is Mrs. Webb's egg sauce that makes the dish truly exceptional." After a moment, he added, "Thank you for arranging it."

Elizabeth flushed, offering him a slight nod. She was surprised at the sense of gratification she felt at having pleased her husband in this small way, and yet it puzzled her that she should feel such an emotion. After all, she had not cooked the chicken, nor even thought to suggest it. She had merely agreed to the scheme when Mrs. Reynolds had cited her husband's preference for the dish. Still, it cheered her to see him enjoying his dinner, and she had to agree that the egg sauce was quite delicious.

They ate for a time in silence, before Elizabeth began, "You mentioned that Miss Darcy would be joining us soon. Should I expect any of your other relations for the festive season? I had not thought to ask how you generally spend that time of year."

Darcy lifted his glass, taking a swallow of his wine. "No, only my sister. And perhaps Richard—that is, my cousin, Colonel Fitzwilliam—may stay for a few days, though he will continue on to Briarwood for the holiday."

"Is that usual? Do you never spend Christmas with your aunt and uncle? Their estate is quite close, is it not?"

"It is." He was quiet for a minute before continuing, "Georgiana and I have spent the winter in Town these last few years, since my father's passing. I thought it would be easier for her... not to be reminded of past Christmases, when we were all together, here at Pemberley. But as that is not possible this year..." He took another sip of wine. "In any event, I thought you would prefer a quiet celebration."

Elizabeth nodded. While it would be strange to be away from her own family and the traditions she was accustomed to, she could see where a small family Christmas would be preferable to traveling or playing hostess to an assortment of relations she did not know so soon after her marriage.

"I am looking forward to meeting the colonel, and your sister, of course. I remember Miss Bingley speaking quite highly of her."

To Elizabeth's surprise, Darcy scowled, helping himself to another serving of chicken. "Miss Bingley knows my sister but little. I hope you will form your own opinion and not use her depiction as your guide."

"Very well. Might you tell me a little about Miss Darcy, then? I should be happy to hear your description, as I am certain you know her better than any other."

In fact, Elizabeth was quite curious on this point. To hear Miss Bingley tell it, Georgiana Darcy was a musical prodigy, a renowned beauty, and the darling of high society all rolled into one. However, Mr. Wickham, who had known her since birth told a different story. Who was the real Miss Darcy? The accomplished, elegant heiress Miss Bingley had described, or the handsome but extraordinarily proud young woman of Mr. Wickham's acquaintance?

Darcy seemed to ponder the question before answering, "My sister is a kind and gentle soul. She has a natural reticence about her, which I am trying to help her overcome. I felt we had been making some progress, but she has had a difficult time of late. I had hoped..."

Elizabeth set down her fork, looking back at Darcy expectantly. He seemed pained as he continued, "I had hoped she might find a friend in you. I believe she could benefit from both your lively disposition and your good sense."

Elizabeth stared back at him, startled by this unexpected compliment. "I would be very pleased to assist her in any way I can. It must have been difficult, growing up without a mother's guidance and affection."

Mr. Darcy frowned, and Elizabeth felt her cheeks grow warm, realizing he must be considering her own mother's lack of good breeding and perhaps questioning his earlier assertion that Elizabeth would be a lady worth emulating. Tipping her chin up a notch, she said defiantly, "While my mother may not always have been a model of decorum, at least there was love. And I was lucky to have had my Aunt Gardiner and the best possible older sister."

Darcy nodded distractedly. "Yes, Georgiana has had our aunt, at least. Not Lady Catherine," he hurried to add. "I speak of Richard's mother, Lady Matlock. But my sister has been mostly at school, and then…" Darcy's cheeks grew red, and he quickly took another swallow of his wine. "In any case, she has a reliable companion now—an older widow. Mrs. Annesley has made a good beginning, however I believe my sister would benefit greatly from the affection of one closer to her own age."

Elizabeth attempted what she hoped was a winning smile. "Well, I can make you no guarantees, but I shall promise to do my best. You may rely upon it."

After dinner, the pair retired to the withdrawing room and Elizabeth offered to play the pianoforte, which seemed to please her husband. She was resolved to work harder to keep the peace and not to allow her usual impertinence to rise to the fore. While he had been in no way warm or affectionate—that was simply not his nature—Mr. Darcy had at least treated her with civility since offering his apology for last night's argument, and she was not in any hurry to start another one.

When she had played and sung for nearly three quarters of an hour, she pushed back the bench and stood from the instrument. Darcy complimented her on her performance and Elizabeth thanked him, taking a seat on a small sofa near the fire. The two sat in silence for several long moments, until Darcy finally cleared his throat.

"Perhaps you would like to select a book from the library?"

Slowly, Elizabeth shook her head. "I appreciate the offer, but I find I am not in the humor for reading."

"Some refreshment, then? Coffee? Or tea? Or perhaps a glass of wine?"

"I thank you, but no."

Darcy stood. "Well, I believe I will have a brandy. That is, if you have no objection?"

Elizabeth lifted her brow, surprised that he should be seeking her approbation. When she murmured that she did not, Darcy walked in the direction of the drinks table. She wondered if this was a common occurrence or if her husband felt the awkwardness of their situation as much as she did. She had never seen him imbibe at Netherfield, at least no more than a glass or two of wine at dinner. She sighed as he came back to where she sat, lowering himself into an armchair nearby.

Outside, a gust of air rattled the windowpanes, mingling with the ticking of the clock on the mantel and the crackle and pop of logs in the grate.

"I was wondering," Elizabeth began tentatively, "if you might show me around the park tomorrow? I am accustomed to walking out most days, and I should like to become acquainted with the gardens."

Darcy's gaze flicked from her face to the darkened windowpanes and back again. "If you wish, and if the weather holds."

Elizabeth smiled, murmuring her thanks. "So long as it is not wet, I will be happy to go. I do not mind the cold."

"You will mind it in another month or so. The weather

can be severe in this part of the country. It is not so temperate as Hertfordshire."

Elizabeth tilted her head. "Will there be much snow?"

"Yes, we usually see a fair amount. Hopefully the roads will still be passable for the next few weeks. I would hate for anything to delay my sister's visit."

"When does she come?"

"On the twenty-first. She will stay a fortnight."

"Does she bring her companion?"

"No. Mrs. Annesley will go to her son, in Gloucester. She will rejoin my sister in Town after the New Year."

"I see. It is good of you to allow her time to be with her family. I am certain she is appreciative."

Darcy did not reply, merely taking another swallow of his drink.

A few minutes passed before Elizabeth stood. "Well, it is getting late. Perhaps... we should retire?" She looked up at her husband expectantly, a challenge in her gaze. If they were ever going to consummate their marriage, she would just as soon get it over with.

"Yes, of course," Darcy replied, setting down his glass. "Allow me to escort you to your chambers."

This time, Elizabeth nodded, and the two walked up the stairs together. However, when they reached the door to her rooms, Darcy merely bowed over her hand, wishing her a good evening before turning in the direction of his own apartment, leaving Elizabeth to stare silently after him.

The following morning, Cassidy arrived at Elizabeth's summons bearing a note, which she handed to her mistress with a slight blush before retreating into the adjoining dressing room.

With some trepidation, Elizabeth unfolded the single sheet of parchment to see her husband's precise hand.

Elizabeth,

If it is not too early, I would be pleased to have you join me for breakfast in the small dining parlor at nine o'clock.

FD

Elizabeth's gaze shifted to the dressing room where she could hear Cassidy humming a simple tune, and she released a muffled sigh. Did the maid think it odd that her husband was sending her missives by way of the servants rather than coming to speak to her in person? Was the entire household aware that Mr. Darcy kept to his own rooms and she to hers? Elizabeth flushed at the thought. She knew how easily gossip flowed between the household servants. But then, what did she know of great houses or the upper echelons of society? Perhaps it was perfectly natural for gentlemen of the first circles to scarcely see their wives and to communicate via letter, even within the same household.

Turning her mind from gossiping servants, Elizabeth allowed herself to focus on her husband's request. Was the note meant to be an olive branch, of sorts? Mr. Darcy had certainly been more courteous in the past twenty-four hours than he had been since their wedding day, although he continued to show her no more affection than he did for his butler or his valet.

Which Mr. Darcy would greet her at breakfast? The

kind, caring gentleman she had caught mere glimpses of in the short days of their betrothal, or the cold, aloof aristocrat he had reverted into as soon as they were married? Perhaps he merely needed time to become accustomed to the change in their relationship, and what she had seen as resentment and hostility had merely been anxiety and apprehension...

Glancing at the clock, Elizabeth refolded her husband's letter. There was no use speculating. She would have her answer soon enough.

Elizabeth entered the dining parlor to find Mr. Darcy already there. As she crossed the threshold, he stood, setting aside the news sheet he had been reading. When he spoke, his manner was polite, yet formal, but Elizabeth thought with some relief that he appeared more ill at ease than anything else.

"Good morning," he offered as Elizabeth stepped farther into the room. "You slept well, I hope?"

"I did; thank you. And you?"

Darcy stated that he had, and Elizabeth crossed to take the seat he offered. Gesturing towards the sideboard, he continued, "What may I bring you?"

"Oh. Perhaps just some bread and butter? Or jam, if you have it?"

Darcy nodded his acquiescence, moving to fill a plate as Elizabeth poured herself a cup of tea from the pot that was already on the table. Eventually they were both settled with their food, and the pair ate in silence for a time before Darcy cleared his voice.

"Have you any plans for the day?" he asked, and Elizabeth offered a slight nod, setting down her teacup.

"I have arranged to meet with Mrs. Reynolds after breakfast. I know she has been overseeing things admirably for many years, but I had hoped to familiarize myself with the running of the household and to offer what assistance I may. If it meets with your approval, that is."

"Of course," Darcy answered. "I am certain she would welcome your input." He paused before saying, "I have some business to attend to this morning myself, but I thought we might take our walk in the early afternoon, if that would be agreeable?"

Elizabeth's lips lifted in a genuine smile. "Yes, perfectly so. I am looking forward to it."

"Good. We will not venture too far, but dress warmly. The sun is out, however the temperature is dropping."

A meeting time was agreed upon, and although conversation remained stilted for the remainder of the meal, the prospect of a walk out of doors lifted Elizabeth's spirits to the degree that she scarcely minded.

When they had both finished their breakfast, Darcy adjourned to his study, while Elizabeth returned to the upstairs sitting room. She was eager to begin acclimating herself to the management of the household, if for no other reason than to give her some means of employment, although she did worry that the housekeeper might balk at the interference, after having operated independently for so many years. However, to her relief, Mrs. Reynolds, when she arrived, seemed to view Elizabeth's interest with admiration rather than resentment. The two soon agreed upon a weekly meeting to commence on the morrow with a tour of the kitchens and servants' quarters, and a formal meeting with Mrs. Webb, the cook.

They had just concluded their business and the housekeeper had stood to go, when, seeming to intuit something, she paused, saying, "Was there anything else, madam?" and Elizabeth could not help but smile at the woman's perceptiveness.

"Actually, there was something, yes. I was wondering... have you a list of the household servants?"

"A list, madam?" the older woman queried, furrowing her brow.

"Yes. Of their names, and occupations. The household is so large, I confess I am feeling a little overwhelmed. I should like to be able to address the servants by name, and I thought a list might be a good place to start."

The housekeeper beamed, instantly nodding her approval. "I understand. I suppose it can feel somewhat daunting in the beginning. I would be happy to compile a roster, if you wish it."

Elizabeth murmured her thanks, hoping that at least learning the names of the dozens of household servants would make her feel more like the mistress of the manor, and less like an outcast, set adrift in a sea of strangers.

The remainder of the morning passed quickly, and before Elizabeth knew it, she was meeting Mr. Darcy in the entrance hall for their planned tour of the park. The pair set off, and as soon as they reached the drive, Elizabeth breathed deeply of the cold, crisp air, as happy as a child on Christmas morning. After several days in a carriage, and the past two inside the house—enormous as it was—she relished the chance to stretch her legs and feel the wind on her cheeks.

Turning to face her husband, she was surprised to see that his lips were curved up into a shallow smile—the first truly amiable expression she had seen on his countenance since they had stepped into the carriage following their wedding breakfast—and Elizabeth could not help but smile back in return.

"I thought we would explore the area closest to the house," he offered as they turned onto a gravel path at the end of the circular drive. "The park is sizeable, and while there are some very pretty views down near the lake, we would need a horse or carriage to get there. I presumed today you would prefer to travel on foot."

Elizabeth nodded happily, a spring in her step. "Indeed, I would. I have missed walking, and am happy to go as far as you would like. I do not mind long walks."

"Yes. I remember you walking at least three miles to see your sister at Netherfield, but it was not quite so cold then as it is now."

Making their way down a narrow path, the pair strolled along until they reached a tree-lined avenue that terminated at a small enclosure.

"This is the rose garden," Darcy said as they traversed the uneven ground. "Of course, it is not much to look at now, but in the springtime, it is quite impressive. We grow over a dozen varieties of roses; some of them have been bred right here on the estate."

Reaching the opposite end of the garden, they climbed a set of shallow steps, passing under a lengthy trellis that emptied out into an elaborately landscaped garden, complete with polished marbles and a vast stone fountain at its center.

Elizabeth's jaw hung open in amazement, not only at the exquisiteness of the landscaping, but at the sheer magnitude of the space.

"These are the formal gardens. Besides the rose garden, they are the only ones accessible to guests touring the house. We do not get a great many visitors to the gardens, but if you seek solitude, it is best to avoid coming here, especially when the flowers are in bloom."

"It is magnificent," she breathed, her voice soft with wonder, and Darcy offered her another slow smile.

"It is much more impressive in the summertime. I am sorry you are not seeing it at its best."

Elizabeth tipped up her chin to meet his gaze. "Then I shall have even more of a reason to look forward to summer, but I think it lovely just the way it is."

Darcy stared back at her, and something about the expression in his eyes caused her heart to do a little flip inside her chest.

But just as quickly as it came, the moment slipped away, and Darcy took her arm, steering her in the opposite direction.

"Come, there is a great deal more to see."

Elizabeth walked side by side with her husband through the manicured space and out onto a wide expanse of lawn that stretched almost as far as the eye could see, making her gasp with delight.

"Oh, how wonderful to have so much open space!" Elizabeth cried, and Darcy nodded his agreement.

"It was put to good use when I was a boy. We would play pall-mall or nine pins when my Fitzwilliam cousins came to visit, and my parents hosted an annual picnic here each summer."

"It is certainly the perfect spot for gatherings," Elizabeth agreed. "There is so much room to run! And I can see how the even surface would lend itself well to sport. Perhaps we might engage in shuttlecock or archery when your sister comes this summer."

At Elizabeth's words, her husband stumbled slightly, and Elizabeth turned to see that his expression was even more grim than usual.

"My sister does not participate in those types of activities," he answered curtly, "and I have not played at such games since I was a child."

"Oh. Well, that is a shame. We had an archery target at Longbourn, though we did not have nearly so large a space to enjoy the pursuit."

Once again, Elizabeth turned to look up at her husband, laughing at his expression.

"Yes, Mr. Darcy, you heard correctly. I hope I do not shock you."

"No. Of course, I know many young ladies enjoy the sport... I am only surprised that you... that is, did all your sisters participate?"

Elizabeth grinned, then nodded. "Well, admittedly, Jane and Mary were never as fond of the activity as the rest of us, but even they would join in on occasion. Have I scandalized you, sir?"

"No. Though I will admit, I find it hard to picture you with a bow and arrow."

Elizabeth huffed in mock indignation. "I will have you know, I am quite capable when it comes to sport, Mr. Darcy, though I am not as accomplished at archery as my sister, Lydia. Her aim is second to none. She could even best my father."

"Well, thank you for the warning. I will be sure to stay on her good side," Darcy answered with a quirk of his lips.

Elizabeth turned to study his countenance, relieved to see that he did not look quite so somber as he had some moments before.

They continued on to the far side of the field where an enormous oak stood sentry, its thick branches stretching upwards towards the sky. To the left of the tree, a narrow lane meandered around a bend, and Elizabeth could see a ridge of wooded hills and a winding river in the distance.

"Shall we continue to walk," Darcy asked, "or would you like to return to the house?"

"Oh, no! I would prefer to continue, if you do not mind?"

Nodding his agreement, Darcy indicated they should take the lane, and they ambled along in silence for several minutes. They had just reached the bend in the road when the clatter of horse's hooves signaled the approach of a rider, who soon came into view. The gentleman approached at speed, but slowed his mount upon seeing them. Beside her, Elizabeth could feel her husband stiffen, and a quick glance in his direction indicated that any lightening of his spirits had instantly vanished.

The horse skidded to a stop before them, the rider lifting his hat in greeting.

"Mr. Darcy. Good afternoon."

"Mr. Boyle," Darcy replied curtly. Turning to Elizabeth he added, "I do not think you have had the pleasure of meeting my wife. Elizabeth, this is Mr. Boyle, Pemberley's steward."

Surprised at the obvious animosity between the two men, Elizabeth suddenly realized it was the steward's voice she had heard earlier in her husband's study.

Hastily, she dropped a shallow curtsy, which the steward acknowledged with a slight twist of his lips that appeared to be more of a grimace than a smile.

"Madam."

The threesome faced each other awkwardly as Mr. Boyle's horse shifted, pawing at the frost-covered path.

"Well, I will not keep you from your walk," said Boyle, and though his smile remained in place, his eyes were as cold as her husband's. "Sir. Madam." And with another quick lift of his hat, he cantered off in the opposite direction.

Darcy instantly resumed walking, and Elizabeth quickened her pace, hurrying to keep up with his long strides.

"I take it you and your steward are not on the best of terms?" she offered when she finally caught up with him.

"No."

"Has he been with you long?"

"Only since the autumn. But long enough to make a mess of things, it would seem." They continued on for a time before Darcy sighed heavily. "I suppose I am to blame. I never should have gone to Netherfield with Bingley so soon after Boyle's arrival. I hired him at the recommendation of someone I trusted, but it has proven to be a mistake. I am afraid he is the reason I did not wish to tarry any longer than necessary in Hertfordshire."

"Would you care to speak of it?" Elizabeth asked softly, and Darcy shrugged.

"There is not much to say. I hired Boyle in September, when my previous steward was pensioned out. Mr.

Beacham had been at Pemberley for many years before my father's death, and he was a tremendous help to me when I took over the running of the estate. When Beacham realized he could no longer keep up, I began searching for a replacement, and, as I said, Boyle came highly recommended. He had many years of experience managing properties larger than Pemberley, so he seemed the ideal choice. Unfortunately, we do not see eye to eye. During the time I spent at Netherfield, numerous letters were forwarded to me by Mr. Lawson. Letters from tenants of long standing whom Boyle had treated badly."

"Will you let him go?"

"At this time, I am uncertain. I had hoped being here to oversee things would help, but he shows no respect for my authority. I would like to give it a while longer, but in the end, the welfare of my tenants must come first."

An icy wind tugged at Elizabeth's bonnet and she glanced up at the dark clouds that now eclipsed the sun.

Shaking his head as if to dispel the matter, Darcy followed her gaze. "Come, the weather is beginning to turn. We should make our way back to the house." Tentatively, he extended his arm, and Elizabeth reached out, slipping her gloved fingers in the crook of his elbow as the pair retreated to the warmth of Pemberley.

Chapter 7

T he following morning, Elizabeth exited her chambers with a renewed lightness of spirit. The previous day had seen an improvement in Mr. Darcy's humor, the sun was shining brightly, and she was eager to commence her meeting with Mrs. Reynolds and Mrs. Webb. She knew that as the new mistress, her attitude and behavior would be thoroughly assessed, and she wished to do everything in her power to make the best possible impression.

Reaching the door Mr. Darcy had taken her through on her first evening, she lifted her skirts, holding onto the banister with her free hand and carefully descending the steep steps. She had just reached the first turning when the loud thumping of approaching footsteps from below made her move to the side, pressing her body against the wall lest she be run down. A moment later, the noise abruptly ceased as a young boy rounded the corner, coming to a sudden halt in front of her. His eyes grew round as he stared up at her, a pair of black Hessian boots clutched tightly to his chest.

"Begging your pardon, ma'am!" the boy gasped, the color all but leaching from his fair skin.

"There is no cause for alarm," Elizabeth replied with a

grin. "We were able to avoid a collision at least. Forgive me for startling you."

"Oh, no ma'am! 'Twas my fault. I shouldn't've been running."

Elizabeth's smile deepened. "Well, I am certain you must have had a good reason for running. Perhaps someone is even now waiting for those boots?"

"They're the master's, ma'am. Mr. Harris asked me if I could give 'em a quick shine. I wanted to get them done right quick, in case the master was wanting to wear 'em."

"Ah. In that case, I will detain you no longer. I have no doubt Mr. Darcy will appreciate your diligence."

Stepping away from the wall, Elizabeth descended a few steps before turning back to look up at the child.

"I am Mrs. Darcy, by the way. I hope you will forgive me for asking your name, but I am afraid I have yet to meet a good portion of the household."

The boy colored, but his chin went up a notch as he answered, "I'm the hall boy, ma'am. Simon's my name."

"Well, it is very nice to meet you, Simon. And now I had best let you be on your way, as I should be on mine. I have an appointment with Mrs. Reynolds, and I should not wish to receive a scolding for being late."

Simon's eyes widened even further as Elizabeth dipped her head, laughing softly as she continued down the staircase.

~

The servants' hall was everything Elizabeth remembered from her previous trip below stairs with Mr. Darcy. The space was vast, but immaculately clean. Everyone she encountered was impeccably turned out in neat uniforms, and the sheer number of servants meant nobody seemed harried or overworked. One young girl—a scullery maid who introduced herself as Amelia when Elizabeth asked—was especially friendly and spoke in glowing terms of her time in service there. Likewise, her meeting with Mrs. Webb was a delight. The cook shared further observations about Mr. Darcy and his sister—their dining habits and tastes in food—and Elizabeth made note of some dishes that were particular favorites with the intention of having those served over the Christmas holiday, when Miss Darcy was in residence.

Returning above stairs, she briefly toured the principal rooms, searching for her husband, but he was not in the library, the morning room, or his study, so she was left to conclude that he had business elsewhere on the estate. She was just about to return to the library to select a book when she encountered Mr. Lawson, the butler, who came bearing four letters addressed to her. Overjoyed at her first communication from home, Elizabeth thanked him with a smile, quickly retreating to her apartment and settling into a comfortable seat by the window.

Sifting through the stack, she saw there was a letter from Jane, one from Charlotte, one from her mother, and perhaps most surprisingly, something from her sister Kitty. As she was intrigued by what Kitty might have to say, she opened that letter first, her eyes growing round as they hurriedly scanned the page.

"Good heavens!" Elizabeth cried aloud. "It cannot be true!"

Setting Kitty's missive aside, she hastily broke the seal on Charlotte's letter, only to find a repetition of the same news: Mr. Collins had made Charlotte an offer of marriage, and he had been accepted! Elizabeth read the letter three times over, but despite Charlotte's assurances that she was content with her choice, Elizabeth could feel nothing but remorse for her friend.

She next picked up her mother's letter which was short and to the point. Mrs. Bennet only took the time to ask after Pemberley's furnishings and Elizabeth's trousseau, before reminding her daughter of her duty to produce an heir for her husband with all due haste. Elizabeth frowned in annoyance until her gaze settled on a handful of sentences that made her pulse pound faster inside her chest.

And Lizzy, see that you do not put Mr. Darcy off. I know how headstrong you can be in situations such as these, but you must make your willingness to do your duty understood. Men like Mr. Darcy are accustomed to having their way. Do not forget that your husband has ample means to acquire else-where that which is not freely given at home.

Re-reading the letter, Elizabeth could feel the heat building in her cheeks. There could certainly be no mistaking her mother's meaning. Elizabeth was to welcome Mr. Darcy to her bed as frequently as he pleased, lest he grow frustrated and find himself a paramour. A startled laugh burst from her throat. The idea of the ever-scrupulous Mr. Darcy seeking out companionship of that nature was positively comical.

Unless he already had a mistress. Was that the reason he

did not come to her? Had he only married her for practical purposes—as a helpmate to assist in the running of his household and a friend for his sister—without any intention of sharing her bed? Was the kindness he had shown her during the short days of their betrothal merely an act to ensure that she went through with the marriage?

A chill raised the hairs on the back of her neck but she quickly shook her head. That could not be it, as he had made a point of telling her he wanted a family...

But wanting children did not necessarily mean he wanted *her*.

No, she was being ridiculous—allowing her mother to put nonsensical ideas inside her head. Mr. Darcy most certainly did *not* have a mistress.

She would not give the idea another moment's thought.

Reaching for Jane's letter, she broke the seal, noting it was by far the longest—four pages written quite through in her sister's elegant hand. But despite the detailed accounting of all that had transpired at Longbourn since Elizabeth had gone away, she could not help but notice the underlying trace of melancholy in Jane's words.

Folding the letter, Elizabeth tucked it away with all the rest. Although her sister had not mentioned Mr. Bingley, she knew his desertion was at the heart of Jane's low spirits, and she resolved anew to speak to her husband about his friend. There had to be some way to convince Mr. Bingley to return to Netherfield, and once he did, Elizabeth had no doubt that he would be as taken with Jane as he ever was.

Yes, if there was a way to make it happen, she would see to it. After all, her entire marriage would be for naught if she could not help her dearest sister find happiness with the man she loved.

~

Dinner that night was filled with good food and polite conversation. Elizabeth made a point to be on her best behavior, steering their discussion to neutral topics and, to her relief, Mr. Darcy seemed to be in a good humor, easily answering her questions about Pemberley.

When the meal was concluded, the pair retired to the library, Darcy settling in with a book, and Elizabeth retrieving the embroidery she had left by the fire. They passed the time at their separate pursuits for a quarter of an hour as Elizabeth ruminated on the best way to approach the topic of Jane and Mr. Bingley; however, before she could formulate the proper course, it was Darcy who spoke.

"I did not realize you enjoyed needlework," he said. "I have not seen you employed in that manner before."

Elizabeth lifted her gaze, drawn from her private thoughts by her husband's voice. She smiled slightly as she answered, "I would not say I particularly enjoy it, nor am I especially accomplished, but it passes the time when I am not in the mood for reading."

Setting aside his book, Darcy sat forward in his chair, studying the embroidery frame in her lap.

"That is very pretty. 'Tis Longbourn, is it not?"

Elizabeth nodded, lifting the fabric so he could better see the pattern she was only beginning to fill in with colored threads.

"Yes. I asked my sister if she would sketch it for me

before I left. I thought it would be pleasant to have something to remind me of home."

Darcy's brows lifted in obvious surprise, though Elizabeth was not immediately certain if he was more amazed at her wishing to be reminded of her home, or that one of her sisters might be talented enough to produce such a likeness. As it happened, her question was answered when Mr. Darcy spoke next.

"I did not know any of your sisters boasted drawing or painting as one of their accomplishments. Was it Miss Bennet who made the sketch?"

Elizabeth's smile broadened. "No. Lydia." At the look on Mr. Darcy's face, a laugh burst from Elizabeth's throat. "I cannot say I blame you for what you must be thinking, but I assure you it is the truth. Lydia is the most creative of all my sisters, and the only one with any artistic ability. Of course, she has had no formal training, and her interest in drawing tends towards copying fashion plates and sketching gowns and bonnets, but the skill is there. I suspect she has the capacity to do much more with it if she would only exert herself."

Darcy seemed to ponder this information before saying, "It is a shame. If that sketch is any indication of her aptitude, she might be quite proficient if she had the right instruction."

Elizabeth was silent, returning her attention to her embroidery, but after a few minutes, she steeled her courage, saying casually, "Speaking of Longbourn, I had some letters from Hertfordshire today."

Her husband looked up. "All is well, I hope?" he inquired in a neutral tone of voice.

"Yes. Although, there was some surprising news. It

seems that Charlotte Lucas is engaged to be married. To Mr. Collins."

At this intelligence, Darcy frowned, an unreadable expression briefly moving across his features.

"That is unexpected."

"Indeed, I was quite shocked to learn of it. I cannot see my cousin making her happy, but she seems to be content with her choice. I suppose it is a prudent match for her, and Charlotte has never been the sentimental sort."

"Well then, the two of you have something in common," Darcy answered stiffly. "You have both made prudent matches."

Elizabeth stared back at him, but Darcy was already reaching for his book.

Quickly, before she lost his attention, Elizabeth said, "Have you heard from Mr. Bingley of late?"

Slowly, Darcy shifted his gaze in her direction. "Bingley? No. Not since just after we arrived at Pemberley. I believe he is with relations in the north."

"Oh. Yes, I understood he would be traveling for the festive season, I had only hoped... Do you think he will return to Netherfield in the new year?"

"I do not think it likely," he replied crisply. "His sisters wish to remain in Town."

At her husband's words, Elizabeth's stomach sank, but she did her best to school her features. "I see. Perhaps in the spring, then?"

"Perhaps," Darcy answered, turning his attention back to his book.

Elizabeth nodded dejectedly as Harpocrates, who was curled up in a ball beside her chair let out a soft snore. Reaching down, she stroked the hound's soft fur. Although she was unsure of the reasons, she could sense that her husband's happy mood was beginning to unravel, and thought it best not to continue to press him on the topic of Mr. Bingley at the present time.

The two sat in silence as Elizabeth searched her mind for another topic on which to converse, finally saying, "I made a trip below stairs today—at Mrs. Reynolds's invitation, of course," she added, carefully watching her husband's expression for any sign of displeasure. When none appeared, she continued, "I was able to speak further with Mrs. Webb, and to become better acquainted with some of the other servants. I... I hope to continue be of use to Mrs. Reynolds where I may."

Barely lifting his gaze from the pages of his book, Darcy answered. "You are free to apply yourself as you see fit, though it is not required of you. Pray, do as much or as little as you like."

For reasons Elizabeth could not readily identify, she felt her irritation building at the lack of interest in Mr. Darcy's tone. Did he truly have so little regard for her that he could not be bothered to care anything about her role as mistress of his home?

She knew she should leave well enough alone, but angry people are rarely wise, and so, against her better judgement, she said, "On my way to the servants' hall, I happened upon a young boy on the stairs. Dark hair, brown eyes, rather a lot of energy."

Slowly, Darcy's eyes lifted. "Yes, that would be Simon Edwards; he is employed as a hall boy. Why do you mention him? Did he give you some sort of trouble?"

"No, not at all. I was merely surprised to run into a

child on the premises. I dare say he cannot be more than ten years old."

Darcy fixed her with a quelling stare. "I believe he is eleven, or thereabouts."

"Is that not rather young to be in service?"

"I beg your pardon?"

"He is scarcely old enough to take care of himself, let alone anyone else. Should he not be in school?"

Closing his book with a snap, Darcy's gaze hardened.

"Not all children have the luxury of spending their time in a schoolroom. Do you mean to tell me there is no one like Simon in service at Longbourn? No stable boys or grooms?"

"Certainly not! Jack who works in the stables is nearly sixteen; Simon is scarcely out of leading strings."

Darcy glared back at her. "If you are implying the boy is being ill-used, you are mistaken. Simon is given simple tasks to perform in a safe environment. If he were not to work here, he would likely be someplace far worse."

Elizabeth pressed her lips together, willing herself not to say something that she would later regret, but in the end, she was unable to remain silent for long.

"I see. And are there others like Simon here?"

"Others?" Darcy repeated, his eyes narrowed. "Other children, do you mean?"

Elizabeth nodded.

"No."

Elizabeth looked away and Darcy released a frustrated sigh.

"I know the situation is not ideal, and it may not be what you are accustomed to, but it is a fact of life. Children of the lower classes are often forced to take work to help support their families. It is far worse for them in Town, where they are taken advantage of more often than not. At Pemberley, Simon is given clean clothes to wear, three square meals a day, and a safe setting in which to work—which is more than many children in his circumstances can boast. There is nothing egregious about his tasks, but if you have further questions, I would urge you to take them up with Mrs. Reynolds."

Chastened, Elizabeth bit the inside of her cheek. "Forgive me. I have no reason to think Simon is being poorly treated. I am angry at the unfairness of the situation, that is all."

Darcy regarded her with a steady stare, and when he spoke, his tone was gruff.

"Life is often unfair, Elizabeth. There are few of us who get what we hope for. Those who set out with lofty ideals are bound to be disappointed."

Surprised by the resentment in his voice, Elizabeth lifted her brow. What disappointments could someone like Mr. Darcy have faced? True, he had lost both his parents at a relatively tender age, but he certainly had never had to worry for his security. His situation could hardly compare to the plight of the truly less fortunate.

"Well, at least gentlemen in your circumstances have choices in life," she replied primly. "The same cannot be said for those who were not born with a silver spoon in their mouths."

"I beg your pardon?" Mr. Darcy bit out. "Of whom exactly do you speak?"

Once again, Elizabeth clamped her jaws together. She should not have allowed her agitation to get the best of her. Had she not sworn to cease provoking Mr. Darcy?

"Forgive me, I have said too much," she eventually replied.

"No," Darcy commanded, "if you have something to reproach me for, I should like to hear it."

Elizabeth remained silent for as long as she was able, but soon found herself powerless to contain the torrent of emotions begging for release.

"If you must know, I speak of the lower classes, especially the children, but not only of them. I refer also to all women in our society, even those fortunate enough to have been born into the higher social circles. Have you any idea what it feels like to be completely at the mercy of another person? To spend your life as the property of first a father, and then a husband? To know that when you marry, anything you may be fortunate enough to possess automatically becomes his?"

Darcy blinked back at her, his brow furrowed. "And all of this is somehow my doing?"

"No, of course not," Elizabeth answered bitterly. "You did not make the rules by which we live, though I dare say, like all gentlemen, you seem happy enough to abide by them."

"I see. And because I 'abide by them' as you put it, it must also follow that I agree with them?"

"Why should you not? You have all the benefits of the arrangement on your side. By entering into marriage, a woman automatically relinquishes everything to her husband, a man she may not be well-acquainted with nor even particularly like. A married woman cannot even deny her husband the rights to her own body."

Realizing too late exactly what she had implied, Elizabeth flushed, and her husband went utterly still. Fixing her with a piercing gaze, Darcy replied darkly, "I hope you do not speak of your own circumstances?"

Elizabeth felt the heat building in her cheeks and quickly looked away, saying softly, "No, of course not. I am merely endeavoring to point out that a woman gives up a great deal when she ties her lot to a man."

"Which is why there are marriage settlements! While it is true that women do not hold the same legal rights as men, a married woman is not entirely unprotected. A well laid out marriage contract can safeguard a woman's property, and often includes a generous income, not to mention a jointure to be used after her husband's death. Many women find themselves far better off after marriage than they were before."

"If you refer solely to money and property, then perhaps this is true—for some. But do not forget that the terms of the settlement are decided upon by a woman's father and her future husband, and then overseen by a male relation on her behalf."

Darcy reached up to rub the back of his neck as Elizabeth continued, "Someone in your position cannot possibly imagine what it is like to know uncertainty, or to fear for your future."

"Someone in my position?" Darcy repeated stiffly.

"Yes. A first-born son, heir to a great estate. From the time you were old enough to understand, you knew that all you surveyed would one day be yours. That you would always live a life of ease, and that nothing you wanted would ever be outside your grasp. The world is not like that for most."

Anger ignited in Darcy's gaze. "And of course, it is impossible to imagine that anyone with all of *this*," he said, as his eyes swept their luxurious surroundings, "might in fact want something vastly different?" Elizabeth blinked back at him as Darcy added, "Shackles made of gold are shackles still, Elizabeth."

An unexpected chill rippled down Elizabeth's spine as the two regarded one another. Elizabeth could see her husband fighting his emotions, and when he finally spoke again, his tone had gentled.

"Forgive me. I do not deny that there is some truth to what you say. It is a sad state of affairs that a woman should be seen as having less worth than a man, solely because of her sex."

Surprised by this shift in the conversation, Elizabeth lifted her brow. "Are you saying that you would support a woman having the same rights and privileges as a man?"

"Certainly. In fact, I believe wholeheartedly that the day will come when she shall have them. But change does not happen overnight. The best any of us can do is to speak out against injustice where we see it and support those causes that will foster such transformation."

Elizabeth could only stare back at her husband, who frowned before shaking his head in obvious disappointment.

"This surprises you," he said sadly, running his fingers through his hair. "Do you really think so little of me?"

Elizabeth lowered her lashes, shifting uncomfortably in her seat. "It is not that I think poorly of you in particular…"

"Ah, I see. So, it is men in general for whom you have such a low opinion."

Elizabeth did not answer, and after a moment, Darcy slid forward in his chair, staring at her with dark intensity.

"I am not the enemy, Elizabeth."

Slowly, Elizabeth nodded and once again their gazes locked until Darcy abruptly rose.

"Forgive me, it is getting late. I believe I will retire."

Startled, Elizabeth nodded, also coming to her feet. "Yes, perhaps we could—"

But before she had finished her sentence, Darcy offered her the briefest of bows before turning on his heel and exiting the room.

Three quarters of an hour later, Elizabeth paced the perimeter of her chambers, her agitation growing with each and every step. How dare he walk out on her in such an infamous manner! To rise and leave the room while she was in the middle of speaking! Of all the ill-bred, ungentle-manly behavior!

Throwing herself into a nearby chair, Elizabeth continued to rage at Mr. Darcy inside her head, but after a while, her agitation quieted as she reflected back on the entirety of their conversation.

While it was true that her husband often seemed to be going out of his way to provoke her, she had to admit that she had been pleasantly surprised by some of his opinions. Could the proud and arrogant Mr. Darcy truly wish to see a world where men and women were considered equals under the law? Where a woman could have her independence, beholden to no one but herself?

Elizabeth shook her head at such a revelation. Even her father, who was one of the most forward-thinking gentlemen she knew, was unlikely to make a statement as bold as that.

Sinking into the cushions, Elizabeth released an exasperated sigh. She had been married to Mr. Darcy for nearly a se'nnight, and still she was no closer to understanding him than she had been the day of their betrothal. One minute he was kind and attentive, telling her of his sister and sharing his concerns about his steward, and the next he was speaking in riddles and staring at her with nothing but coldness in his eyes.

It seemed as though she and her husband were like oil and water, each one destined to misunderstand the intentions of the other at every turn.

Lifting her gaze, Elizabeth stared in the direction of her husband's apartment, and her thoughts returned to her mother's letter. A child. She was to give Mr. Darcy a child... but how was she to do that when her husband showed absolutely no inclination towards visiting her in her chambers?

Elizabeth huffed. Not that she was in any hurry to undertake that particular wifely duty. It was bound to be an awkward business. And Elizabeth refused to heed her mother's ramblings about Mr. Darcy taking a mistress. The more she thought about such a thing, the more farcical it seemed.

Still, Elizabeth had never liked uncertainty, and the waiting and wondering about Mr. Darcy's intentions was proving to be far more difficult than she imagined. If they were ever going to consummate their marriage, she would just as soon get it over with.

Once again, her gaze drifted to the door to their shared sitting room. Could it be that he was waiting for some sign from her? She had tried to make her readiness apparent, but perhaps it was time to speak even more plainly on the matter…

Slowly, Elizabeth stood. How would Mr. Darcy react if she simply marched into his bedchamber right this minute?

A rush of heat crept up the column of her neck, and she briefly looked away. No, certainly she could not do anything so brazen as to parade into his bedchamber in the middle of the night.

Could she?

Elizabeth hesitated, and then, before she could change her mind, she quickly crossed the carpet, slipping into the shared sitting room.

Making her way to the door at the opposite side of the parlor, she lifted her hand, hesitating only a second before rapping firmly on the polished wood. Inside, she thought she could hear the soft murmuring of voices and the rustle of fabric, but the door in front of her remained tightly shut.

Elizabeth stepped back, folding her arms across her body. He could not have missed her knock, nor could he have any doubt as to who would be on the other side of the door, as it came from the room that connected their two apartments.

The clock on the mantle ticked out the seconds as Elizabeth's apprehension turned to annoyance. Was it possible he simply would not answer?

Tamping down her mounting vexation, she was just about to knock again when the latch clicked, and the door swung inward.

Mr. Darcy stood before her, tying the belt of a deep green dressing gown. His eyes briefly swept her form before fixing on her face, and Elizabeth could feel a flush rising to her cheeks. But if her husband felt any embarrassment, it was not evident from his expression.

"Elizabeth. Is anything the matter?"

"Yes. That is, no." Cursing her awkwardness, she defiantly tipped up her chin. "That is, I have something I wished to say."

Darcy's eyebrows lifted and she watched as he turned to speak over his shoulder.

"Harris, you may go down. I will ring for you if I require anything further."

Elizabeth heard a murmured reply and drew her dressing gown more tightly around her body. Blast! She had not taken the trouble to consider that his valet might still be within. She heard the door to the outer corridor close, but Darcy did not step back to allow her to enter his chambers. Instead, he swept out his hand, gesturing for her to step back into the sitting room. Elizabeth frowned, but after a brief pause, she did as he bid, and Darcy followed, closing the door to his bedroom behind him.

"Yes?" he finally asked, leaning one shoulder negligently against the wooden panel.

Discomfited by her husband's stare, Elizabeth turned away, pacing to the window before rounding on him with renewed purpose. He may be able to bar her from his bedroom, but she would not leave without an explanation.

With forced composure she said, "I was merely wondering whether I might anticipate the pleasure of your company in my bedchamber this evening. I had expected that once we reached Pemberley you would wish to..." Once again, Elizabeth could feel her cheeks heating, but forced herself to soldier on, "...join me in my chambers, however, as you have not yet seen fit to come to me, I decided it would be best to inquire as to your intentions, rather than to be taken unawares."

To Elizabeth's satisfaction, Darcy's countenance colored, but when he spoke, his voice was even.

"I beg your pardon. I had no intention of causing you undue distress. But since you ask, no."

Elizabeth blinked back at him. "No?"

Looking vaguely unsettled, Darcy stepped away from the door. "Forgive me, I had thought this to be your preference. Not all marriages involve…"

His voice trailed off as Elizabeth stared back at him.

At length he continued, "That is to say, you may rest easy. I have no intention of making any demands upon your person."

"Demands? I beg your pardon, but if I have given you the impression that I would not welcome… what I mean to say is that I have no particular objection. You were very clear about your desire for a family—for children—before we married."

Darcy frowned, a pained expression momentarily passing over his features.

"Yes, well… Desires change."

Darcy shifted his weight, and Elizabeth regarded him incredulously.

"What are you… Are you saying you have no intention of consummating our marriage?"

Darcy's eyes veered away and Elizabeth's own eyes grew round.

"*Is* that what you are saying?"

Across from her, Darcy sighed. "I am saying that nothing will happen tonight. Go to bed, Elizabeth." He turned, moving in the direction of his chambers, but when he reached the door, he looked back at her with something akin to pity.

"It has been a trying few days, with much to become accustomed to—for both of us. There is no need to make things even more taxing than they already are."

And without a backwards glance, he entered his apartment, closing the door firmly behind him.

Chapter 8

That night, Darcy did not sleep. By the time he left Elizabeth, it was too late to order another frigid bath—although he needed one, desperately—so instead he hastily dressed and descended the darkened staircase, letting himself out into the moonlit gardens.

The evening air was bracingly cold against his heated skin, which was a welcome relief after the events of the past half hour.

What had happened in that sitting room had been pure torture. And even though Darcy knew he had no one but himself to blame, it had been nearly impossible to stand there, listening to his wife all but ask him if he intended to share her bed.

Raking his fingers through his hair, Darcy cursed beneath his breath. It was his fault that things had gone this far. He should have addressed the situation days ago, as he had initially intended. Then she would not have come to him for an explanation, and he would not be forced to live with the image of her standing there in nothing but a thin dressing gown seared upon his consciousness for all eternity.

Turning onto the narrow lane that led to the stables, Darcy's thoughts shifted back to the moment he had opened the door to find Elizabeth on the opposite side. One look at her, and the breath had frozen inside his lungs, and it had taken every ounce of willpower he possessed to keep from gathering her in his arms.

Luckily, reason had prevailed, and he had been able to state his position calmly and unemotionally, and now there could be no mistaking his intentions.

At first, Elizabeth had appeared startled by his words, but that was only to be expected. Of course she would assume they would consummate their union, nor had he ever doubted she would submit to his will if he pressed the issue. But in the end, Darcy also knew she could feel nothing short of relief at his rebuff. In truth, it had surprised him greatly that she should have raised the matter in the first place. Knowing how she felt about him, he had assumed she would be comforted by his lack of demands upon her person. Especially after those comments she had made earlier that evening about a woman's rights to her body...

Just thinking about Elizabeth's body caused Darcy's own blood to heat and he sucked in another breath of the icy air. He should have known better than to think he could anticipate his wife's behavior. No matter how well he believed he understood the woman he had married, Elizabeth continued to confound him at every turn.

Having finally reached the stables, he opened the door and slipped inside, briefly acknowledging the startled groom who quickly absented himself at Darcy's curt nod.

Making his way to the corner stall where his chestnut Arabian stood in a shaft of moonlight, Darcy stretched out his hand, gently patting the animal's neck. The gelding snorted in appreciation, and it occurred to Darcy that if he were younger or more reckless, he might have saddled the beast then and there and taken off at a gallop, despite the fact that it was the middle of the night... But on this occasion, he simply allowed himself to stand by the majestic creature's side, breathing in the familiar scent of hay and horses and wishing that people were as easily understood as their four-legged companions.

Allowing his thoughts to drift back to their earlier conversation, Darcy sighed. He should not have quarreled with her. Had he not vowed only the previous day to treat her with civility, no matter the cost?

Yet when she had made those remarks about him never knowing deprivation, rage had clouded his judgement and he had lashed out. How dare she assume he did not know what it meant to give up your dreams. To find yourself shackled to a life that was not of your choosing. If only she knew how much he had sacrificed...

Darcy shook his head, locking those memories away.

In truth, he enjoyed sparring with Elizabeth, for it gave him a chance to see her lively mind at work. He liked hearing her opinions, even when he did not fully agree with them, for it allowed him to know her better. He relished the invested exchange of ideas that forced him to reexamine his beliefs, oft times refining his position. Before he had met Elizabeth, few people would have dared to express an opinion contrary to his own, and fewer still who could voice those opinions with such eloquence and fervor.

Stepping back out into the moonlit night, Darcy sighed. Elizabeth's passionate nature was one of the things he admired most about her, but he needed to remember that his aim was to keep their relationship civil. It was best not to provoke her. If they were to live the tranquil existence he had envisioned, he would do well not to engage her in further repartee. Theirs was no more than a marriage of convenience, and he needed to remember that and act accordingly.

~

The following morning, Elizabeth awoke to another note from Mr. Darcy. Reaching for the thick parchment with some trepidation, she read:

Elizabeth,

I will not be able to join you for breakfast as I have business to attend to elsewhere on the estate. I expect that I will be gone most of the day, but I look forward to seeing you at dinner.

FD

After reading the brief letter, Elizabeth re-folded the parchment, moving to the nearby window. She supposed she should be relieved. At least she would not have to face him over the breakfast table after last night's humiliation, and perhaps by the time dinner rolled around, she would have gained some measure of control over her jumbled emotions.

Upon returning to her bedchamber the previous evening, she had scarcely slept. Although her husband's reaction to her awkward query had not been a total surprise given his recent behavior, it was no less mortifying to be so soundly rejected. The gentleman who stood before her last night was not the same one who had spoken to her so tenderly of his desire for a family of his own, and she was no closer to understanding what had changed between them.

Turning away from the glass, Elizabeth released a ragged breath. She would not find the answers in the gardens below. Nor was she likely to get anywhere by continuing to force a confession out of the taciturn gentleman she had married.

In any case. Mr. Darcy's feelings for her were of no significance. After all, theirs had never been a love match, and she would do well to remember that. She need only content herself with being a good mistress to his home, and above all, to find a way to encourage him to support Mr. Bingley's pursuit of her sister. Anything else was immaterial by comparison.

Deciding to take breakfast in her apartment, Elizabeth rang for a tray, and when the dishes had been cleared, she made her way out into the corridor. In thinking about what she might accomplish as mistress of the house, it had occurred to her that perhaps some of the bedchambers were in need of refurbishing, and she made up her mind to go through all the rooms that were currently in use on the upper floors. Armed with a pencil and a sheet of parchment, she started with the family wing, before continuing on to the guest chambers on the opposite corridor... but as she had briefly noted on her first tour through the house, every space was impeccably turned out, and she could see little to improve upon in even the most infrequently used rooms.

With a heavy sigh, Elizabeth set aside her pencil and paper, descending the stairs and nodding to the lone footman on duty near the front door. Making her way to the library, she stopped briefly to pat Harpocrates, who was in her usual place in front of the fire before pulling a book at random from the stacks. Taking it to a comfortable chair by the window, she curled into it, but her mind was too restless to focus on the page.

A soft tapping at the open door brought a welcome distraction, and Elizabeth quickly rose as the housekeeper entered.

"Ah! Mrs. Darcy, I am glad to have found you. Might I have a word; if you have a minute to spare?"

"Yes, of course, Mrs. Reynolds. How may I be of assistance?"

Mrs. Reynolds's smile faltered as she reached into the pocket of her apron. "Forgive me, madam, I only wished to give you the list of the household servants you requested."

Elizabeth flushed, thanking the older woman and accepting the proffered note. Her eyes briefly skimmed the page before lifting to regard the housekeeper.

"Where is Amelia?"

Mrs. Reynolds blinked back at her, tilting her head in obvious confusion.

"I beg your pardon, madam?"

"Amelia. She is one of the scullery maids. And Simon. He is not here either."

"The hall boy?"

"Yes. He is still in our employ, is he not? I saw him only the other day."

The housekeeper frowned slightly. "Forgive me Mrs. Darcy, but is anything amiss? Has young master Edwards done something he ought not?"

"No! Of course not. He seems to be a very industrious boy."

"Another one of the servants, then? This Amelia you mentioned? I hope you will tell me if anyone has been—"

Quickly, Elizabeth shook her head. "No, no. You mistake me, Mrs. Reynolds. There is no problem with any of the servants. I simply wish to know them. To know their names and their histories… how long they have been with the family, that sort of thing."

Still looking somewhat taken aback, the housekeeper offered her a slow nod. "Certainly. Pray, forgive me, Mrs. Darcy. I am afraid I misunderstood your request. I assumed you would wish only for the names of those who work above stairs. But of course, I can compile a more comprehensive list. I shall have it for you by the end of the day."

Elizabeth smiled self-consciously, handing the folded parchment back to the housekeeper and thanking her for her time before settling back into her chair, but she was no longer in the mood for reading. Placing the book on a nearby table, she headed back out into the front hall, approaching the footman—she believed his name was Thomas—and asking for her pelisse and bonnet. Despite the cold, the sun was out, and a stroll in the gardens was certain to improve her spirits.

Upon returning to the house some thirty minutes later, Elizabeth retreated to the upstairs sitting room and completed her most recent letter to Jane. But when she finished, the clock on the mantle showed that there were still at least three hours before it would be time to change for dinner.

Releasing a breath, Elizabeth stood. Perhaps she should go to the music room and practice at the pianoforte… but to own the truth, given her current mood, music held little appeal. What was the matter with her? She should be happy to have a day of leisure with no demands on her time... But somehow, the stillness of the house was becoming almost oppressive. She missed the chaos and clamor of Longbourn —Lydia's raucous laughter, her mother's constant lamentation, Jane's quiet counsel. Even Mary's incessant pounding on the fortepiano. She could not continue to rattle around in this enormous house, all on her own. She needed to find some means of employment, or she would run mad!

Making up her mind, she squared her shoulders and turned towards the door. It was time she had a conversation with her husband.

Darcy was in the library returning a small stack of books to the shelves when Elizabeth entered the room, stopping short as soon as she crossed the threshold. She wore a white gown with pale blue flowers and a square neckline—the same gown, he recalled, that she had worn on the day she walked to Netherfield to see her sister—and her cheeks were flushed a soft pink. In his estimation, she had never looked lovelier, and it took all his willpower to greet her with detached civility. She smiled and her flush deepened as she stepped farther into the room.

"You are back from your business I see," she said, coming to sit tentatively on one of the sofas near the fireplace as Darcy nodded his affirmation.

"Yes, I have only just returned."

Setting aside his books, he went to join her, selecting an armchair nearby. Sinking into the cushions, he crossed and uncrossed his legs as Elizabeth looked up at him expectantly through her lashes.

"You have spent an enjoyable day, I hope?" he inquired at length, and Elizabeth offered him a shallow smile.

"Yes. I had a walk in the gardens and then I wrote a letter to my sister."

"Ah. Yes, the sun is out, making the air a little warmer than it was yesterday."

Elizabeth murmured her agreement as Darcy inwardly cringed, cursing his awkwardness. Was this what their marriage was to be? Clumsy conversations about the weather or the state of the roads?

"You have actually arrived in the nick of time," he began again. "I was just about to call for tea; if you would care to join me?"

Elizabeth answered in the affirmative, and Darcy went to ring the bell. A maid soon appeared bearing a porcelain tea service and Elizabeth stood to pour. Despite his best intentions, he could not help watching as her delicate hands lifted the pot, noticing how graceful her movements were as she slowly stirred in the sugar with a silver spoon...

Schooling his expression, he accepted the cup she offered him with a murmur of thanks. He briefly looked away, but his attention was drawn back as Elizabeth spoke.

"As we have a moment," she began hesitantly, "there is something I wished to discuss with you, if you do not mind."

Warily, Darcy turned back in her direction. "Of course," he answered neutrally, inwardly praying she was not planning to once again raise the subject of intimacy. He had barely been able to resist her once, and he was not certain he would be able to continue to do so if she pressed the topic.

"Well, it is just that I have been wondering," Elizabeth began, "what you would have me do. With my time, that is."

Darcy blinked back at her, surprised by the question, which was so different from what he had been expecting.

"Forgive me, I do not understand. If you speak of the running of the household, I thought I had made it clear that you are under no obligation in that regard; Mrs. Reynolds has everything well in hand. Your time is your own. You may spend it however you please."

Setting her teacup aside with a rattle, Elizabeth released a frustrated breath.

"But that is just it! I cannot simply spend my days in idle pursuits. I must have something useful to do!"

Darcy stared at her, taken aback by the sudden outburst, but soon composed himself enough to ask carefully, "Well, what did you do in Hertfordshire? I am certain you may occupy your time here in the same manner."

Across from him, Elizabeth's brows pulled together in a frown. "In Hertfordshire, I had my sisters to keep me company. I had relations nearby and acquaintances I had known all my life. My sisters and I would walk into Meryton to visit my aunt, or to frequent the shops. We called on our neighbors and attended local assemblies. I visited the bookshop and took long walks in the country-side. My father and I played chess together and discussed books. Mary and I practiced on the fortepiano and Jane and I sewed for local charities and visited my father's tenants. But here, I do not know anyone. I have not my sisters to keep me entertained, and this county and its people are unfamiliar to me. It is not yet warm enough for me to take long walks, and in any case, I do not know my way around, and fear I would be hopelessly lost if ever I left the gardens. I know there is the pianoforte, and the library is exquisite, but I must have something more to occupy my mind."

Darcy returned her gaze, equal parts irritated and ashamed. On the one hand, she was a grown woman, and certainly should not need him to create amusements for her. What did any woman do with her time? He thought back to his mother. How had she spent her days? In truth, he had no idea. He had been a boy of eleven when she died. When she was alive, he had been too busy living his own life— attending to his studies, playing out of doors—to have any comprehension of how she kept herself busy. He felt guilty for not knowing, and discomfited at the sudden realization that his impulsive offer of marriage had changed the trajectory of Elizabeth's life, uprooting her from all that was familiar. He had taken her away from her friends, her family... everything and everyone she held dear, and he had thrust her into a new life with very little forethought or regard for her feelings.

Worse still, in the week they had been at Pemberley, he knew he had done nothing to make the transition easier.

Why? Because he was angry. No, not angry. Hurt. But he had vowed to do better...

He realized belatedly that Elizabeth was staring at him expectantly, waiting for his answer. His mind raced back, trying to remember what she had said about her previous activities. Something that would occupy her days, that did not involve her sisters...

"Visiting tenants," he blurted. "That is something you

could do. If you wished to, that is. I would not want you to think it is required of you, but I am certain they would be eager to meet the new mistress of the house."

Elizabeth's expression lit, and Darcy breathed a sigh of relief at the thought that he had managed to come up with a solution to the problem.

"I would like that," Elizabeth began slowly, "but I suspect they are far removed from the house. At Longbourn, my sister and I would walk, but I expect I would not be able to do so here."

"No, you are correct. Even the closest farms are some distance away. But they are an easy enough ride." Darcy paused, rubbing his jaw as he realized he had not even thought to secure a horse for her. "Forgive me, I should have inquired before now but... had you a horse? At Longbourn, I mean? We might still have the animal transported if you wish."

Once again, Elizabeth picked up her teacup, her lips quirking up at the corners. "No, Mr. Darcy, I did not have a horse. Longbourn boasted only two such animals, and they were used for work on the farm and for drawing the carriage, which left little time for riding, so I never took the trouble to learn properly."

"Oh. I see. Well, there are several horses on the estate who are exceedingly docile. Perhaps the stable master could teach you, if you have the interest."

"I appreciate the offer, but I am no horsewoman," Elizabeth said with a laugh. "The few times I attempted it did not end particularly well."

Darcy nodded, mulling over the situation in his mind. "I suppose you could drive," he mused, and Elizabeth's brows lifted.

"Yes, but it seems like a lot of bother to take the carriage. I should hate to trouble your coachman or grooms, though it would be better than going on horseback, and more sensible than walking."

"No, no. Not the carriage. That is, of course you are welcome to take the carriage, if you would prefer it. But I meant that you could drive yourself. In the phaeton, or the curricle. They are rarely used, and therefore almost always available. It may be a bit cold in the winter months, but you would not be going far."

"You mean for me to... drive, on my own?"

"Yes, of course. Have you never done so?"

Elizabeth shook her head.

"Ah, I see. Well, I could instruct you, if you wish to learn. It is not difficult. I taught my cousin Anne, despite my aunt's protestations, and she took to the activity with great enthusiasm. Judging by your lively disposition and the pleasure you take in being outdoors, I think you might find that you enjoy it. And then you would be free to go anywhere on the estate you wish."

Elizabeth nodded before offering him a genuine smile. "Yes. I think I should like that, Mr. Darcy. Thank you."

Darcy briefly looked away, embarrassed at the warmth that flooded through him at the look of unaffected delight she bestowed upon him. Clearing his throat, he continued, "In the meantime, you will have my sister's visit and the festive season to keep you occupied. Georgiana arrives in less than a se'nnight, so you shall have another lady in the house. I hope you will enjoy each other's company."

Elizabeth's smile broadened. "Oh, I am certain we shall. I am looking forward to meeting her, and to spending my first Christmas at Pemberley. As a matter of fact, now that we are speaking of it, there was something else I have been meaning to ask…"

Darcy lifted his brows in anticipation as Elizabeth continued, "I was discussing the holiday with Mrs. Reynolds, and she indicated that it is your custom to give the majority of the servants the day off at Christmas, in addition to an extra week's wages."

Darcy nodded. "Yes. That was always my father's practice. I have not made any changes since I took over the management of the estate. Have you a problem with the arrangements? If you are concerned for your comforts on Christmas day…"

"Oh, no! That is not it at all. I have no objection to the servants being given the day. It was only that I was wondering… well, I was thinking that it might be nice to do something more personal than just adding a few shillings to their pay packets."

Darcy frowned. Whatever her suggestion, he knew the servants counted on those "few shillings" as she called them, and he had no intention of taking that away from them.

"Such as?" he answered cautiously.

"Well, at Longbourn, my sisters and I used to put up baskets for the household. You know, freshly baked bread, jam and honey, some sweetmeats, perhaps a small ham. And oft times we might embroider a handkerchief or put up some homemade toilet water…" Elizabeth's voice trailed off as she regarded his expression. "What is it? Why are you looking at me like that?"

"Forgive me, Elizabeth, but have you any idea exactly how many servants make up this household?"

"No," she answered, toying with the napkin she had

draped across her lap, "not precisely. I did ask Mrs. Reynolds for a list..."

"Well, I shall save you the trouble. Twenty-seven. And that is just inside the house. If we add in the gardeners, the grooms, the coachmen, the steward, the gamekeepers, and the stable hands, that number doubles. Then there is the house in London, which retains its own staff. Would you give baskets to the servants here and not to those working in Town? I assure you the households talk, and some of the servants, such as the coachmen and grooms, go back and forth between the two establishments. Christmas is in less than a fortnight, and you do not have your sisters to help you. The labor to put up these baskets would be far more than one person could handle, even if the goods you speak of could be procured in time."

Across from him, Elizabeth lowered her lashes and a soft flush colored her cheeks.

"Of course... I had not thought..." she murmured. "That is, I knew the household here was larger than at Longbourn... I simply did not anticipate..." Meeting his gaze she shook her head reproachfully. "Forgive me, it was a foolish idea."

Immediately, Darcy cursed his churlishness. "No, it was a fine idea. And I know they would have appreciated the gesture a great deal. Perhaps next year, if we were to begin earlier..."

Elizabeth nodded, but she left the room shortly afterward, leaving Darcy feeling that his first attempt at marital accord had been an abysmal failure.

Chapter 9

Dear Jane,

My new sister arrives today, and will stay through the new year. I would be lying if I said I was not apprehensive about making her acquaintance, but I will be happy for the company.

Pray, give my mother and father and all my sisters my fondest wishes for the festive season. I miss you more than I can say.

Your sister,
Elizabeth

Georgiana and Colonel Fitzwilliam reached Pemberley as anticipated on the afternoon of the twenty-first of December. Colonel Fitzwilliam turned out to be an exceedingly pleasant gentleman, who, while close to her husband in age, displayed none of Mr. Darcy's reticence or rigidity of manner. Though not as classically handsome as his slightly younger cousin, he displayed all the ease and affability of a well-bred man, and Elizabeth liked him at once.

Miss Darcy greeted Elizabeth with eager interest tempered with bashful reserve, but where her brother often appeared proud and self-important, Elizabeth could easily see that his sister was merely uncomfortable in the presence of someone unknown to her.

Upon entering the house, both the colonel and Miss Darcy congratulated Elizabeth on her marriage, saying all that was gracious and instantly putting Elizabeth at ease. The foursome conversed for some moments before Colonel Fitzwilliam expressed a wish to go for a ride, citing the need for fresh air after his long journey in the carriage. Though Darcy was obviously reluctant to leave his sister, Elizabeth could tell her husband wished to accompany his cousin, and she spontaneously suggested that the two ladies take tea together while the gentlemen went for their ride.

So it was that no more than a half an hour after their arrival, Elizabeth found herself in the sun-filled parlor on the first floor, seated across from her husband's sister. As Elizabeth served the tea, she furtively studied her new relation. Miss Darcy was a little taller than herself, and though only sixteen, her figure was already formed, and her appearance womanly and graceful. Though not the great beauty Miss Bingley had made her out to be, her features were pleasing to the eye. She was clearly timid, but she smiled readily, and Elizabeth could already see that her manner was unassuming and gentle.

Once tea had been poured, Elizabeth settled back in her chair before saying, "I believe I must thank you for this exquisitely designed sitting-room, Miss Darcy. Mrs. Reynolds mentioned that you were instrumental in its redecoration and that the room is a favorite of yours when you are at home. I hope you do not mind my claiming it while you were away."

Georgiana beamed back at her, and then flushed. "Oh, no! Of course, you must use it whenever you wish. Pemberley is *your* home now…" She lowered her lashes before adding, "But I am pleased you like it."

Elizabeth opened her mouth to offer some words of reassurance—she wanted to make certain Georgiana knew that Pemberley was still her home, every bit as much as it was Elizabeth's—but before she could form the words, the door eased open on its hinges and a sleek bundle of brown fur slipped into the room, briskly trotting in their direction, her tail furiously waving.

"Harp!" Georgiana let out a cry of delight, setting her teacup down on the table and reaching out to ruffle the hound's silky fur.

Harpocrates whined low in her throat, leaning heavily against Georgiana's legs and placing her head in the young girl's lap, causing Elizabeth to laugh.

"Well, I can see where her loyalty lies. I have never known her to come in here before now."

Georgiana continued to stroke the dog's head while glancing nervously at Elizabeth. "Do you mind very much? I can bring her back down if you wish."

"Nonsense! I do not mind in the least! I am only surprised. I have simply never seen her anywhere but the library."

Georgiana looked around guiltily before saying softly, "I am afraid her being here is my fault. Whenever I am home, I allow her to sleep in my chambers. She must have followed my scent. Pray, do not tell my brother. I am certain he would be angry if he knew."

Elizabeth smiled conspiratorially. "Your secret is safe with me. But I dare say your brother might surprise you. From what I have observed, he is excessively fond of that dog."

Georgiana offered Harp one last pat, and the hound happily curled up by the fire. Elizabeth regarded the young girl as she retrieved her teacup. From what she had witnessed so far, her new sister bore little resemblance to the character traits attributed to her by either Caroline Bingley or George Wickham. In fact, her behavior towards the dog had been the first sign of genuine enthusiasm Elizabeth had seen since the girl's arrival.

In an attempt to draw her out, Elizabeth steered the conversation towards Pemberley and then Lambton, the nearest village, which Elizabeth had not yet visited. And although Georgiana's answers were hesitant at first, she soon appeared to grow more comfortable, and before long was describing the local sites with genuine animation.

"You mentioned a dress shop," Elizabeth said, when she at last had a chance to speak. "Is the seamstress there sufficiently skilled? I am afraid my marriage transpired so quickly, I had not time to gather a trousseau, and I now find that I am in desperate need of some new gowns."

"Oh, yes! Mrs. McBryde is wonderful! She purchases all of her fabrics from the best warehouses in London, and she is always aware of the most current styles. She made the gown I am wearing now," Georgiana added timidly.

Elizabeth took in the blue muslin, which was simple in style, but Elizabeth could see that the fabric was very fine and the fit was flawless.

"It is lovely, though I will admit to being surprised you

would frequent a shop in Lambton when you spend so much of your time in Town."

At Elizabeth's question, Georgiana shifted uncomfortably in her seat. "I go to the modiste in Town but rarely, generally only when I accompany one of my aunts or cousins. I much prefer the shops in Lambton."

"Well, as you speak so highly of Mrs. McBryde, I will send a note around tomorrow. Perhaps she will agree to see me this week. As it is, I do not have much choice in the matter, as I certainly cannot wait until we are next in Town." After a moment, a thought occurred to her and she added, "Perhaps we might even go together, if you would like to accompany me."

"Oh, I should love that. But you need not go to Lambton. Mrs. McBryde will come here, to Pemberley, whenever you wish."

Elizabeth's expression must have given away her thoughts because Georgiana quickly added, "Or, we might visit her shop. Perhaps you would like that better, so that you can see some of the village. In any case, the shops here are not nearly so busy as the ones in Town, and Mrs. McBryde would always accommodate a member of the family, no matter when you came."

Elizabeth suppressed a laugh. How silly she must sound! She would have to get used to the fact that she was now the wife of the most prominent gentleman in the area. Naturally, every merchant in Lambton would be overjoyed to serve her, even if she should bang on their door in the middle of the night.

"And you must not worry about the workmanship or the quality of her fabrics," Georgiana continued. "I promise you will not be disappointed. Even my aunt, the Countess of Matlock, has frequented Mrs. McBryde's shop and has been very pleased. She says there is not another dressmaker so skilled in the entire county."

"It is settled then. Perhaps we might even go tomorrow if you think that is not too soon?"

Georgiana readily agreed and the two continued in amiable conversation until the clock struck the hour and Elizabeth startled.

"Goodness, it is later than I thought!" Rising, she continued, "I am certain you will wish for some time to rest and refresh yourself before dinner."

Georgiana also stood, and the movement seemed to alert Harpocrates, who yawned, clamoring to her feet and giving herself a brisk shake.

"I will take her downstairs," Georgiana said. "I dare not bring her to my rooms so early, or Fitzwilliam will notice she is missing."

Elizabeth nodded. "I can walk with you. I need to speak with Mrs. Reynolds about dinner. Shall I have warm water sent to your chambers so you may bathe?"

"Yes, that would be lovely. Thank you," Georgiana answered, as the pair exited the sitting-room.

Pausing, Elizabeth turned to her new sister. "Georgiana... Forgive me, do you mind if I call you by your Christian name? I feel rather silly addressing you as 'Miss Darcy' when we are now sisters."

"No, I would like that very much."

"Good. And you must call me Elizabeth. Or Lizzy, if you prefer."

Georgiana murmured her acquiescence before saying, "You are very kind. I confess that I did not know what to expect before we met. There are many who would have seen a younger sister as a burden. But you have made me feel very welcome here."

Impulsively, Elizabeth reached out, squeezing the girl's hand. "Georgiana, it is not for me to make you feel welcome! This is your home, and was such long before it became mine. I should never wish for you to feel displaced simply because I have married your brother."

Georgiana flushed and nodded, but Elizabeth could see that she was pleased.

"Come then, let us go down." She turned in the direction of the main staircase, but Georgiana stopped her with a press of her fingers.

"We can cut through the gallery. I will take Harp down the servants' stairs so no one sees."

Elizabeth nodded, and the pair changed direction. Glancing down at the hound who was trotting along beside them, she wondered how they would prevent the dog from running off on her own, but Harpocrates remained pasted to Georgiana's side.

Elizabeth smiled. "She is quite attached to you," she commented as they reached the end of the passageway.

"Oh, she is exceedingly loyal! She is like that with me and my brother. And I am certain she will be so with you before long."

They entered the gallery then, but before they had walked a great many paces, Georgiana stopped, staring up at the empty place on the wall.

"Oh! He took it down!"

Elizabeth, who had moved on ahead, returned to the spot where the young girl stood. "Yes. Your brother said he was hoping to hang my portrait there, though I do not know why he was so quick to remove the other painting. Surely it will be months before my likeness is completed, as the work has yet to begin."

Georgiana briefly looked away. "I am not surprised by his decision, only that it has taken him this long to do so. He does not come in here much. I think it makes him sad to be reminded of those he has lost."

Elizabeth nodded, thoughtfully. Of course. It made sense that it would be difficult to have such a tangible reminder of his parents together in happier times. "Yes, I can see where that would be difficult," she said quietly.

Georgiana turned to face her, offering her a shaky smile. "But I know having your portrait there will bring him much pleasure."

Elizabeth flushed. She did not know why her husband had insisted on having her portrait painted, but surely it was not so that he might preserve her image for his own gratification. Most likely it was only because he felt it the proper thing to do. But she did not wish to disabuse her new sister of the fact that theirs was not a love match. Instead, she answered honestly, "I am a little uneasy about it, to own the truth. I have never had my likeness taken. It is rather disconcerting to imagine some unknown gentleman staring at you for hours on end, noting every imperfection and committing it to canvas for posterity!"

Georgiana giggled. "I dare say you have nothing to worry about; you are so pretty." She colored slightly before continuing, "Although I do understand how you feel. It was very strange when I had mine done last year. But the artist Fitzwilliam hired was exceedingly kind, and my brother sat with me through the entire process." Her gaze softened. "He talked to me and told me stories to make me smile. So, I will always remember that time with fondness."

The portrait of Georgiana had just come into view and Elizabeth gazed up at it, noticing the half grin and the warm sparkle in the young girl's eyes. How sweet and unexpected to think of the aloof Mr. Darcy sitting with his sister throughout the procedure to make her feel more at ease.

"Well, I can see the results in the work. You look lovely, and very happy."

The two women reached the end of the long gallery and Georgiana bent to scoop Harpocrates into her arms.

"I shall go this way," she said, gesturing towards a door at the end of the corridor and Elizabeth nodded.

"Very well, I shall go down the front staircase so I might distract anyone who may be in the hall. I will see you at dinner."

Georgiana happily agreed, and Elizabeth turned in the opposite direction, quite delighted with her new sister.

Dinner that evening was a jovial affair. Elizabeth had made a point of inquiring about Georgiana's favorite dishes prior to her arrival and had seen to it that several of them—including the lobster terrine—were served. Colonel Fitzwilliam availed himself of several glasses of wine, and was fine company, keeping them all well entertained with stories from his recent stay in Newcastle, and by the time the second course was served, even her husband seemed to have relaxed and appeared to be enjoying himself.

When the meal was concluded, the entire party made their way to the withdrawing room. Elizabeth rang for tea for herself and Georgiana, while her husband and his cousin helped themselves to glasses of brandy. Elizabeth suspected that the colonel was already somewhat in his cups, but he remained genial and well-mannered and before long the conversation turned to his fondness for Pemberley and the time he had spent at the estate as a young boy. As the colonel continued to reminisce, Elizabeth noticed that her husband's good mood seemed to be quickly evaporating, his features soon settling into a mask of obvious displeasure. Glancing in his direction, she quirked a brow, but his only response was to stand abruptly, stalking to the decanter in the corner of the room to pour himself another drink.

Attempting to make up for her husband's barely concealed animosity, she turned to the colonel with a forced smile.

"I understand your parents' estate is but two hours from Pemberley, sir. I imagine my husband must have spent a good deal of time there when you were children."

"Aye," Colonel Fitzwilliam acknowledged, setting his empty glass on a nearby table. "Darcy and I were as close as brothers growing up, and our families were always visiting back and forth between the two estates. Is not that so, Cousin?"

Darcy, who had just returned with his drink, made a noise in the back of his throat that Elizabeth took to be a "yes".

Frowning in his direction, she once again turned to face his cousin, inquiring if she could refresh his drink. He looked on the point of accepting but to Elizabeth's further mortification, it was her husband who answered.

"I think my cousin has had enough," he said gruffly.

Across from him, Georgiana looked uncomfortably from one gentleman to the other, but to Elizabeth's relief,

Colonel Fitzwilliam seemed to take the rebuff with his usual good grace.

"Your husband is likely correct," he answered affably. "Any more and I may find myself under the table." Grinning at his own humor, he continued, addressing Elizabeth. "But you must call me Richard. We are family now, after all."

Beside her, Darcy let out a bitter laugh, taking another swallow of his drink. "I am afraid you are wasting your time, Cousin. My wife prefers to observe the proprieties when it comes to names."

A flash of anger sparked in Elizabeth's gaze at her husband's admonishment, but the colonel merely chuckled, turning towards her with an easy smile. "Well, in that case, you may address me in whatever manner you are most comfortable. I am sure I have been called worse than Colonel Fitzwilliam."

The colonel barked out a laugh as Elizabeth exchanged a heated look with her husband before endeavoring once again to change the subject.

"Did you spend Christmas here at Pemberley when you were a boy, then?" she asked.

"No, the Darcys always came to Briarwood for Christmas. But the Fitzwilliams would gather at Pemberley every summer. My sisters and our cousin Anne would hold tea parties on the lawn, while we boys would entertain ourselves with fishing in the stream, riding horses, climbing trees, and getting into all sorts of mischief."

Elizabeth smiled. "It sounds like an idyllic childhood."

"I assure you it was. Oh, the things we got up to! I remember one time, the four of us had just tied up our horses at the smithy in Lambton when Stratford—"

To Elizabeth's surprise, Darcy sharply cleared his throat, staring menacingly in his cousin's direction.

Elizabeth frowned up at him before turning to fix Colonel Fitzwilliam with a polite smile. "I beg your pardon, did you say there were four of you on this adventure? Have you brothers, sir?"

"Ah, yes. Just the one. Andrew—Viscount Stratford—is the eldest of my three siblings. On that particular day, it was Stratford and myself, along with Darcy and—"

With a yelp, Colonel Fitzwilliam leapt to his feet as Darcy's knee collided with the table that held the refreshments, sending the entire tea service crashing to the floor.

Georgiana cried out, hurrying to the bell pull to ring for a maid, while the colonel withdrew his handkerchief to blot at his sodden trousers.

"Forgive me," said Darcy stiffly. "I should have been more careful. I trust you have not been injured, Cousin?"

Colonel Fitzwilliam fixed Darcy with a sullen glare before saying, "No harm done."

A moment later, two maids entered, quickly clearing up the mess, but a pall seemed to hang in the air after their departure.

"Well, it is getting late," Colonel Fitzwilliam eventually stated, climbing to his feet. "I believe I will retire."

Elizabeth and Georgiana both stood as well, and he came forward to kiss his young cousin on the cheek before bowing to Elizabeth.

"Georgiana. Mrs. Darcy."

"Elizabeth, please."

Colonel Fitzwilliam nodded. "Very well. Elizabeth." Turning to his cousin he muttered, "Darcy," before heading for the door.

After the colonel retired, Georgiana and Mr. Darcy remained for another quarter of an hour, and the three spoke of inconsequential things, but Elizabeth could not help but feel that there had been more spilled that evening than just the tea.

Chapter 10

At breakfast the following morning, it was decided that Elizabeth and Georgiana would make a trip to Lambton to visit the local modiste, while Darcy and his cousin attended to some business with Mr. Boyle, the steward.

To Elizabeth's delight, the dress shop was all that Georgiana had claimed and more: the proprietress knowledgeable and welcoming, the space airy and bright, and the fabrics as fine as any Elizabeth had ever seen. Although she felt ill at ease over the prospect of purchasing such a large quantity of items at once, in the end, she had settled on three morning gowns and four dinner dresses, plus a ball gown, which Elizabeth had only purchased at Georgiana's insistence.

When they had finished with the modiste, Georgiana suggested a walk along the High Street so Elizabeth might become acquainted with some of the other shopkeepers, and they with her. In each shop they visited, Georgiana shyly performed the introductions, and although Elizabeth had expected a certain degree of deference, she was taken aback by the universal praise everyone they met heaped upon her husband—making a point to tell her of his kindness and generosity. In the booksellers, Elizabeth purchased a text on philosophy for her father and a volume of poetry for herself, and Georgiana acquired a new novel and some sheet music she had been looking for.

Upon exiting the confectionery next door, the ladies were greeted by a lightly falling snow, which produced shrieks of glee—especially from Elizabeth, who rarely saw snow in Hertfordshire—as they dashed for the waiting carriage.

Luckily, the roads were still clear and dry, and they were quickly returned to Pemberley, where they entered the front hall on a wave of laughter.

After divesting themselves of coats and bonnets and learning that the gentlemen were still out on the estate, Elizabeth suggested they change into dry clothing before meeting for chocolate in the upstairs parlor.

Georgiana readily agreed to the plan, and so it was that shortly thereafter, the new sisters found themselves curled up by a cozy fire, enjoying refreshments and one another's company.

Leaning back in her seat, Elizabeth released a sigh of contentment before turning to her new sister with a smile.

"Oh, Georgiana, thank you for a wonderful day! I cannot remember when I have had such a delightful time."

Georgiana flushed, before saying softly, "Nor I. I have always dreamt of having a sister to go shopping with, and now I know it is just as agreeable as I had imagined it would be. May we go again tomorrow?"

Across from her, Elizabeth laughed good naturedly. "Well, if this snow keeps up, I do not think we shall be going anywhere for some time. Besides," she added with an arch grin, "I expect I should wait at least a se'nnight before spending any more of your brother's money. I am already feeling uncomfortable about ordering so many dresses at once."

"Oh, Fitzwilliam would never mind about that! He is the most generous person in the world, especially when it comes to the people he loves. I know he would wish for you to have anything that would make you happy."

At this unexpected turn in the conversation, Elizabeth could feel the heat rising to her cheeks, and she quickly looked away. She knew Mr. Darcy was a far cry from loving her, but she was in no position to disillusion his young sister, who clearly thought her brother hung the moon.

Forcing another smile, she replied lightly, "Let us hope you are correct. I still feel the ball gown was an unnecessary indulgence, as I cannot imagine when I shall have occasion to wear it, unless it is at your come out!"

Elizabeth had hoped her cheeky retort might earn another smile from her usually shy new sister, but to her dismay, Georgiana's expression sobered and she turned to stare out the window at the falling snow.

Setting down her cup, Elizabeth slid forward in her seat. "Georgiana?" she asked, gently.

Turning away from the glass, Georgiana offered her a slim smile, but Elizabeth could see that the expression did not reach her eyes. Cursing her lack of decorum, Elizabeth reached for the younger girl's hand.

"Pray, forgive me. I forget sometimes that I am not with my own sisters, who are used to my teasing. If I have offended you in some way, please know that was never my intention."

To Elizabeth's immense relief, Georgiana squeezed her fingers before quickly shaking her head. "Oh, no. You have said nothing to offend me. It is just… when you mentioned my come out, I thought perhaps… that perhaps Fitzwilliam had said something to you, about wishing for me to marry soon. H-has he?" she asked tremulously.

"Goodness, no! I assure you my meaning was quite the opposite—that I should have no need of that gown for ages! You are still so young; I am certain your brother has no thought of you marrying for some years, especially if you do not wish it."

Seeing Georgiana visibly relax, Elizabeth continued gently, "Am I correct in assuming that you are in no hurry to wed?"

"N-no. That is, there was a time… But now I cannot abide the thought of it. Not after…" Her voice trailed off, and she lowered her lashes, picking at a loose thread on the waistline of her gown.

"After?" Elizabeth prompted gently.

"What happened last summer," Georgiana whispered. Her gaze lifted, taking in Elizabeth's perplexed expression and she quickly looked away. "He has not told you. I thought as much when I first arrived, and you were so kind to me… but then, just now, when you made that comment, I wondered…"

She let out a shuddering breath and Elizabeth dipped her chin, trying to get the younger girl to meet her gaze.

"Georgiana, I do not know what is troubling you, but even in the short time we have known one another, it is clear that you are a thoughtful, sensible young woman with an affectionate heart. Your brother loves you very much, and so do I. You need not confide in me if you do not wish it, but I am happy to listen if there is ever anything you would like to share."

Georgiana sniffled, and Elizabeth pulled a handkerchief from the sleeve of her gown. Her sister accepted it gratefully, pressing the starched cloth to the corners of her eyes.

"I... I would like to tell you, but if I do, I know you shall no longer see me as you do now, and I do not know how I could bear losing your regard."

"Nonsense. We have all done things we wish we had not. You have already witnessed my own impertinent tongue, which has got me into trouble on more than one occasion. Besides, I am afraid my regard for you is quite irrevocably fixed. Nothing you could tell me would alter my perception in the least."

Georgiana lifted her chin, a flash of daring in her clear blue eyes, before saying, "Not even if I told you that last summer, I very nearly eloped?"

Despite her best intentions, Elizabeth's eyes grew round as Georgiana continued, "And what is worse, it was with a man who showered me with empty flattery, when all along his chief object was my fortune of thirty thousand pounds, combined with the hope of revenging himself on my brother. Surely you have never done anything as foolish as that!"

Quickly schooling her features, Elizabeth took hold of the younger girl's hands, gently prodding her with quiet inquiries until the whole of it came pouring out. When Georgiana finished her tale, Elizabeth could only stare back at her in complete astonishment, but she worked hard to maintain a neutral expression. She would not have her sweet young sister believe that her shock was due to Georgiana's behavior. No, all the revulsion and dismay she felt were directed squarely upon herself, for her deplorable lack of discernment in believing that snake George Wickham.

Oh, how could she have been taken in by such a man! Even after Mr. Darcy had related the particulars regarding the living Wickham claimed he had been cheated out of, she had never believed him to be as bad as this!

I am as gullible as Jane, she thought miserably. *Willing to believe a relative stranger simply because he was charming and handsome, and he flattered my vanity.*

And the fact that she had thrown Wickham's virtues up to her husband during his offer of marriage! Yet, even then, Darcy had not defended himself as was his right. No, he would rather she continue to think badly of him than to put his beloved sister's reputation in jeopardy.

She realized belatedly that Georgiana had lowered her gaze, and that her entire body trembled with fear and apprehension.

Immediately, Elizabeth wrapped her arms around the other girl's shoulders, murmuring to her in soothing tones.

"Oh, Georgiana, forgive me for my silence! You must believe it was not a condemnation of you, or anything you have said. You have nothing to feel ashamed of, because *you* did not do anything wrong."

"How can you say so?" Georgiana wailed. "I very nearly threw everything away for a man who was only using me to get back at my brother. I am as good as ruined, and Fitzwilliam will never see me the same way. He can scarcely abide my company!"

"You cannot believe that!" Elizabeth cried in response. "Your brother adores you. He would never blame you for Mr. Wickham's machinations."

"He-he says he does not. But things have been different between us since it happened. Fitzwilliam cannot look at me without seeing my mistake, and what it nearly cost him.

That is why I assumed he would wish for me to marry… before the rest of the *ton* finds out what I did, and no gentleman will have me."

Elizabeth continued to hold the young girl, rocking her back and forth as Georgiana cried softly on her shoulder.

"Shh… Your brother would never force you to marry against your will, of that I am certain. His only wish is for your happiness."

Georgiana hiccupped softly. "I am a burden to him. And an embarrassment. That is why he does not want me here at Pemberley."

Elizabeth pulled back, her eyebrows lifting. "Not want you here at Pemberley? But that is not—"

"Yes, it is! He does not wish to be seen with me. He did not even want me at your wedding!"

Elizabeth stared back at Georgiana in confusion, but slowly, comprehension dawned, and she felt her face go pale with mortification.

"No, that is not true."

Georgiana's gaze slid away, but Elizabeth continued to speak quietly but firmly.

"What if I told you that you are not the only person in this room who has been taken in by Mr. George Wickham?"

"You?" Georgiana gasped, turning to face her with wide blue eyes. "Do you know Mr. Wickham?"

Elizabeth nodded, her lips tight. "Unfortunately, yes. He was a member of the militia quartered in the town of Meryton, very near my father's estate. We met by chance, and he wasted no time in attempting to weasel his way into my good graces, blackening your brother's name in the process. And I was naïve enough to believe every word he said."

"But... I do not understand. If that is the case, how did you come to hold my brother in such a tender regard?"

Elizabeth shifted uncomfortably, finally saying, "That is a rather long story, best saved for another day. The material point is that it was Mr. Wickham's presence in Meryton that caused your brother to keep you from our nuptials. It was not because he was embarrassed to have you there, but because he was trying to protect you."

"D-did he tell you that?"

"No. As I said before, I knew nothing of your history with Mr. Wickham until today. I will admit that I did wonder when your brother said you would not be able to attend the wedding, but now that you have told me your story, it is very clear to me that this is why he kept you away. Georgiana, your brother would do anything for you. I am certain his only thought was to keep you safe."

Georgiana sniffled quietly as Elizabeth continued, "And as for not wanting you at Pemberley, I am certain he merely thinks Town is better for you, at present." She paused before gently asking, "Are you not happy there?"

Georgiana sighed, lifting her shoulders before letting them drop dolefully. "I am not *unhappy*. Mrs. Annesley, my companion, is very kind, and there are many amusements... And I know my brother has gone to a great deal of trouble to find me the best possible masters; I suppose I am just lonely, sometimes."

Once again, Elizabeth gathered her sister into a quick embrace. If only she knew that Elizabeth was as lonely here at Pemberley as Georgiana was in Town.

"That is only to be expected when you are far from the

ones you love. But you must know that you are welcome to visit Pemberley as often as you like. And perhaps in the spring, your brother and I will be able to come to London for a visit. Would you like that?"

Georgiana nodded, once again dabbing at her eyes with Elizabeth's handkerchief. "Thank you," she murmured. "For listening to me, and for always being so kind. When Fitzwilliam wrote to tell me he had married, I confess I was worried you might be someone like Miss Bingley, or one of the other ladies who follow him around Town..." Georgiana's voice trailed off, a look of mortification igniting in her light eyes. "Oh, forgive me! You are not a friend of Miss Bingley's, are you?"

Elizabeth could not help but laugh at the poor girl's obvious distress. "No, I can assure you I am not. It is difficult to believe she and Mr. Bingley share the same parents. He is all affability and charm, while his sisters... well, the less said about them, the better."

Georgiana giggled, wiping the last of the tears from her cheeks as Elizabeth rose from her seat.

"Now, why do you not return to your chambers and splash some cool water on your face. The gentlemen are sure to be home at any moment, and we cannot have them thinking we are wallowing in misery without them here to entertain us."

The next four-and-twenty hours passed in a convivial manner. Darcy was gratified to see that Georgiana had taken to Elizabeth just as he had hoped, and the two spent all their time together, while he and Richard rode the estate with Darcy's steward. Their evening meals were pleasant, and after dinner the four of them would gather in the withdrawing room for coffee and conversation before retiring to their chambers.

On Christmas Eve, which was also the night before his cousin's departure, the ladies offered to exhibit, and Darcy and Richard settled into chairs near the pianoforte where Georgiana played carols and Elizabeth sang. When the performance was over, both men clapped heartily and Richard stood, moving to his young cousin and escorting her to a nearby settee.

"That was marvelous! Georgie, your playing is even better than it was the last time I heard you, and it was wonderful then. Truly, I cannot remember when I have been so well entertained."

Darcy agreed as Elizabeth came to take a seat beside his sister and his cousin continued, "Mrs. Darcy—forgive me, *Elizabeth*—I must thank you again for your gracious hospitality these last few days. It has been a real treat to be away from the barracks for a while, and to spend time with family."

"The pleasure was all ours, sir. We have enjoyed having you."

The party continued to converse for a while longer, before Georgiana expressed fatigue and she and Elizabeth said their goodnights, retiring from the room. Darcy likewise stood, but Richard held his attention with a steady gaze.

"A drink, Cousin?" he asked nonchalantly, making his way to the sideboard and selecting a bottle of port.

Darcy sighed. He might have known his cousin did not intend to leave Pemberley without subjecting him to a thorough grilling. He supposed he should count himself lucky to have avoided it for as long as he had.

"Very well," he said, slowly resuming his seat. "As you wish."

Removing the stopper from a crystal decanter, Richard filled two glasses, handing one to his cousin before settling into the opposite chair.

"You have been avoiding me."

"I beg your pardon?" Darcy replied, taking a swallow of his drink. "Have we not spent the past two days in one another's company?"

"Yes, but not alone. You have gone out of your way to see to that. Do you think I have not noticed?"

"If you are insinuating that was by design, you are mistaken."

Richard shrugged lightly before continuing, "I am not a fool, Darcy. And you are forgetting that I know you better than you know yourself. It has not escaped my attention that you barely speak to your wife, and every time I have mentioned Elizabeth when we have been in one another's company, you shut up tighter than the family vault. Not exactly the expected behavior for a man who is newly wed."

Darcy made no reply, and Richard let out an amused snort. "Ah, so I am correct. Trouble in paradise already, eh? She is not holding out on you, is she? Refusing to do her conjugal duty?"

"Don't be crass. That is my wife you are speaking of."

"Indeed; your wife. Your beautiful, young, charming wife..." Leaning forward in his chair he whispered slyly, "Does she truly never call you anything but Mr. Darcy? Even when you are—"

"Enough," Darcy snarled, "we are not having this conversation."

His cousin grinned, casually raising one booted ankle and resting it upon his knee. "Very well. I will desist. But you have not yet shared with me the details of how you came to be married so quickly, and to some unknown country miss, at that. You must know it came as quite a shock to the family."

"I have already told you. I met her in Hertfordshire, when I was visiting Bingley. Her father owns the neighboring estate."

"Yes, that much I gathered from the note you sent, concise as it was. But who is she? Who are her people? And why the need to marry with such haste? Unless...?"

Darcy sat straighter in his chair, bristling at his cousin's inuendo. "Do not be absurd."

His cousin shrugged. "It is not so far-fetched an idea. You met her in the autumn, and I know how you get around that time of year. I had thought perhaps you sought some female companionship to take your mind off your troubles, and—"

"Certainly not!"

"So, there was no compromise? You married her willingly?"

After a brief pause, Darcy offered him a single nod.

"Yet, it is not a love match."

"No."

"And Elizabeth?"

"What about her?"

Richard rolled his eyes. "Well, if she was not compromised, and this is not a marriage of affection..."

Darcy's jaw tightened but he did not answer.

Richard looked back at him skeptically and Darcy sighed.

"She was about to make an imprudent match. One that would have destroyed her. I could not stand by and let that happen."

He had not intended to tell Richard anything about the circumstances leading up to his betrothal, but now he felt a certain compulsion to get the entire business off his chest—all but the conversation he had overheard between Elizabeth and her sister on his wedding day. *That* humiliation he would take to his grave.

When Darcy was finished speaking, Richard rubbed his jaw in contemplation. "So, you were the lesser of two evils. Well, I suppose that explains Elizabeth's motives. That Collins fellow sounds truly deplorable. As for you, I cannot say I am surprised. I might have guessed this is how you would have come to be leg-shackled."

"I beg your pardon?"

Once again, Richard shrugged, taking another swallow of his drink. "You have always had a bit of an obsession with rescuing people." Darcy looked back at him incredulously, causing his cousin to chortle. "Oh, come now. You know it is the truth. First Wickham—how many times did you try to reform that blackguard?—and then there was the situation with Georgiana…"

Darcy instantly stiffened, a flash of anger igniting in his belly. "How dare you berate me for my care of Georgiana! If I had not gone to Ramsgate when I did—"

"Yes, yes, of course. We all thank Providence that you followed after her. But that was not the first time you have behaved in such a way; you have always been overly-protective where she was concerned."

"I am her guardian, not to mention the only immediate family she has left! You could scarcely expect me to behave differently. And as for Wickham, you know that relationship is complicated."

"Very well. I will give you those two. But it is not only them. You are forever running off like some knight in shining armor when anyone you care about is in trouble. Did you not recently write to me about saving your friend Bingley from the inconveniences of an imprudent marriage?"

The mention of Bingley made Darcy's stomach twist in an uncomfortable manner, and his gaze briefly veered away, but his cousin was still not finished.

"Even that flea-bitten creature," Richard continued, jerking his chin towards Harpocrates who was curled up on the hearth rug lightly snoring.

Darcy glared back at him and Richard sighed.

"I am merely saying there is a pattern. You cannot stand the thought of harm coming to someone you love—"

"That would be true for anyone!"

"Yes, but most people do not make it their life's mission to be their loved ones' sole protector." His voice gentled. "You know I understand why you do it, but you cannot wrap the world in cotton batting. Bad things happen. You cannot save everyone."

Darcy looked away, draining his glass and pacing over to the sideboard as his cousin's voice called out behind him.

"You have not told her, have you?"

Darcy froze, his hand on the decanter.

"Oh, come now Darcy. There is no point in dissembling nor in trying to deny it. If I had any doubt, the truth became painfully evident when you upended the tea service that first night."

"You were drunk. And that story was inappropriate."

"We both know it was not the story you objected to."

Lifting the crystal stopper, Darcy refilled his glass before returning to his place by the fire. For several minutes, the two sat in silence until Richard spoke.

"I know you do not wish to hear it, but you are making a mistake. She is your wife. Do you not think she deserves to know the truth?"

"What good would it do?" Darcy retorted. "There is no advantage to her knowing."

"Darcy. Think. She will find out eventually. Either a servant will let something slip, or a shopkeeper will make mention of it. Think how much worse it will be if she hears it from someone other than yourself."

"You are making too much of this. If she hears of it and comes to me, then of course I will tell her the truth. I simply do not see the point of digging things up that are better left dead and buried."

Richard studied him before saying softly, "Are you afraid she would think less of you, if she knew?"

Darcy turned away, a bitter laugh rumbling in his throat. "No. I assure you, *that* would be impossible." Standing abruptly, he placed his glass on a nearby table with a bang. "I have heard enough. I am going to bed."

He had almost made it to the door when he turned, staring back at his cousin with an inscrutable expression.

"You know you are always welcome here, Richard, and I hope you will visit often, but when it comes to my marriage, I must ask you to keep your opinions to yourself."

Chapter 11

On Christmas morning, Elizabeth awoke early. As the servants had the day off, she rose and donned a modest dress, twisting her hair up into a simple knot. Cassidy had been kind enough to offer to attend her as usual, but Elizabeth would not hear of it, and she certainly would not wish to awaken the girl at such an hour, even if she had been willing to accept her assistance. Walking to the window, Elizabeth stared out the frosted glass, noting with some relief that the ground below was clear of snow. Colonel Fitzwilliam would be leaving that morning to join his family at their country estate, and though Elizabeth was glad she would still have Georgiana's company, she missed her sisters. She imagined the scene at Longbourn—Mary laboriously pounding out Christmas carols on the fortepiano, Kitty and Lydia racing raucously through the house, pretending to kiss each other beneath the mistletoe that always hung in the entrance to the front parlor, while her mother encouraged them and Jane attempted to keep order. Her father would be hiding in his book room, no doubt with a glass of port and a large tome of history or philosophy.

Elizabeth sighed. Christmas at Pemberley would be very different from what she was accustomed to. Still, that did not mean it could not be pleasant. Yesterday, Georgiana had helped her decorate the entrance hall, weaving boughs of holly and ivy through the banisters of the grand staircase, and the Yule log had been wrapped in hazel twigs and placed in the library hearth. The effect had been understated yet festive, and the air smelled deliciously of evergreen and spice. Although they had enjoyed their Christmas dinner last night so that Mrs. Webb could have the day out, the cook had prepared a number of dishes in advance so they might still have a pleasant meal. Yes, it would be a lovely day.

Slipping out of her chambers, she softly padded down the steps. There were, of course, still a handful of servants on duty—who would be given their day out on the morrow—but the corridors were eerily quiet. Entering the small dining parlor, she was happy to see the sideboard had already been laid with dishes of soft-boiled eggs and rashers of bacon, as well as an assortment of pastries which sat beside crocks of jam and freshly churned butter. Helping herself to a plate of food and a cup of tea, she made her way to the table. She had almost finished her meal when the sound of footsteps in the outer corridor alerted her to someone's approach, and a moment later, Colonel Fitzwilliam appeared in the doorway. He seemed both surprised and pleased to see her, offering a slight bow as he entered the room.

"Elizabeth, good morning. Happy Christmas."

"Happy Christmas, Colonel. Will you join me for breakfast?"

"Just coffee, thank you. But I would be glad to keep you company while you finish your meal."

He took the seat beside her, pouring his coffee, and the

two exchanged pleasantries while Elizabeth ate what was left of her breakfast.

"You must be eager to depart so that you may spend the day with your family," she eventually offered, and Colonel Fitzwilliam nodded.

"Yes, though I am equally grateful for the time I was able to spend here at Pemberley. I always look forward to visiting with my cousins, and it was a pleasure to get to meet you at last."

Elizabeth flushed at the compliment as the clock on the mantle chimed the hour. Turning to peer out into the empty corridor, Elizabeth said, "I am surprised my husband is not yet down. He is normally an early riser, and I know we are to attend services at Kympton. I am certain he would wish to see you before you go."

Colonel Fitzwilliam pushed back his chair, tilting his head and studying her appraisingly before saying, "Actually, his absence is fortuitous, as I was hoping you and I might have a moment to speak before I left. Perhaps you would indulge me in a walk through the gallery?" he asked, coming to his feet.

Elizabeth's eyebrows lifted, wondering what her husband's cousin wished to speak with her about that could not be said right here in the breakfast room, but she smiled evenly.

"Of course."

Colonel Fitzwilliam helped her rise and the pair made their way through the empty hall and up the stairs. When they reached their destination, Elizabeth glanced inquiringly at her companion, who offered her a steady smile.

"I suppose you must know why I wished to speak with

you," he said as they began to walk, causing Elizabeth to gaze up at him in surprise.

"I confess I do not, sir. That is to say, not entirely, although I would guess it has something to do with my husband, as you suggested coming to the gallery. I assume you know he never ventures into this part of the house."

Colonel Fitzwilliam turned to look at her before barking out a laugh. "You are very astute, Mrs. Darcy."

"Elizabeth; please."

The colonel nodded. "Forgive me; *Elizabeth*." After a small hesitation, he continued, "The family was rather stunned to learn of my cousin's marriage."

He paused, staring down at her expectantly, and Elizabeth shrugged lightly.

"I supposed that was to be expected. We had not known each other long, and the decision was made rather precipitously. Still, your cousin is a man of seven-and-twenty. It cannot be so astonishing that he should take a wife."

To Elizabeth's surprise, Colonel Fitzwilliam chuckled. "Ah, but that just goes to show how little you know my cousin. In the years since Darcy reached his majority, I have never seen him take a serious interest in any young lady. In fact, up until this past autumn, he has spent most of his time doing everything in his power to fend them off. So, to hear he had married in haste to a woman whom he had not known above three months... well, I am certain you can see how it might come as quite a shock."

Elizabeth nodded, saying matter-of-factly, "You took me for a fortune hunter, I imagine. I cannot say I blame you. It is a logical assumption."

"But not an accurate one."

"No."

The colonel nodded, and Elizabeth's eyebrows lifted. "You believe me?"

"I do. Darcy said as much to me last night, but even if he had not, the time I have spent with you these last few days would have convinced me of it."

Elizabeth smiled. "Thank you for that. But if it is not my motives you question, I am at a loss to understand what you might wish to discuss."

"Ah, but I did not say I was not interested in your reasons for marrying, only that I believe you were not induced by material gain."

Elizabeth narrowed her gaze, and Colonel Fitzwilliam grinned back at her. "Do not worry, you have no cause for alarm. While I will admit to some curiosity on the matter, it is not for me to question your intentions." Elizabeth relaxed slightly as he continued, "I had wished more so to speak to you about my cousin."

The two walked on in silence before the colonel indicated a bench set back against the far wall. Elizabeth sat, Colonel Fitzwilliam taking the place beside her.

Elizabeth waited as her husband's cousin stared off into the distance, drumming his fingers absentmindedly against the wooden seat.

"You may have gathered this already," he finally began, "but Darcy is a difficult man to know."

The colonel paused, staring at her expectantly and Elizabeth struggled to keep her expression neutral, wondering exactly how she was to respond to such a statement.

"He is reserved, yes," she finally answered, "that I have noticed."

"Yes, he is naturally restrained, but in Darcy's case, it goes deeper than that. I am afraid my cousin has suffered many hardships in his life, and those experiences have caused him to build a shield of sorts around his heart. Those who do not know him well may interpret his behavior as hauteur or conceit, though I can tell you it is neither. He loves deeply, but his affection is not easily given."

Elizabeth's brow lifted slightly as she said, "I do not discount your superior knowledge, sir, but why are you telling me all of this?"

"I suppose I simply do not wish to see him hurt. He has already known a great deal of sorrow. He does not deserve any more."

"I have no intention of hurting him," Elizabeth answered softly.

Richard regarded her seriously. "Perhaps not. But he is entitled to a good deal more than the absence of malice. He deserves to be loved." He paused before adding, "It may not always be easy to see, but he is a good man, Elizabeth. A very, very good man. And for those lucky enough to earn his admiration, I can assure you that there is no truer friend."

Elizabeth flushed, nodding slowly. She wished she could give her husband's cousin the assurances he wanted, but to profess to loving Mr. Darcy—or even to intimate that she aspired to such a sentiment—would be disingenuous, and, to her detriment, she found she could not lie.

"I understand. And I can see that you are a good friend to him," she finally answered.

The colonel looked back at her solemnly. "He is like a brother to me. There is nothing I would not do to see him happy."

The two sat in silence, and, at length, the colonel stood.

"Well, I will not detain you any longer. The hour grows late, and I have said my piece."

He bowed, turning to go, but to Elizabeth's surprise, she found herself reaching out to lightly grasp his sleeve.

"Colonel? Thank you. I know I may not have given you the reassurances you hoped for, but your words have not fallen on deaf ears. I have heard you, and promise that I shall think on all you have said."

Colonel Fitzwilliam's lips curved up into a smile, and he offered her a single nod. "Then that is all I can ask. Oh, and Elizabeth? For what it is worth, I think my cousin chose well."

~

The remainder of the day passed pleasantly for all concerned. The small party of three attended services at Kympton village before returning to Pemberley where they adjourned to the library. Darcy and Elizabeth took turns reading aloud, and later Georgiana and Elizabeth played duets on the pianoforte, which pleased Darcy a great deal.

It was Elizabeth's idea to have an indoor picnic in the library. When she first proposed the scheme, Georgiana had looked up at her brother with wide eyes, as if she expected him to forbid it, but quickly overcame her scruples when he readily agreed. Together, they pushed the furniture aside, spreading a large counterpane before the fire. They feasted on mince pies and a cold collation of meats and cheeses, accompanied by an excellent French claret. For dessert, there were ratafia cakes, gingerbread, ice cream, and fresh oranges sent down from the orangery at Briarwood. When they had eaten their fill, they played vingt-et-un and spillikins until they all grew sleepy and retired to their separate chambers. It was only later that night, when Darcy had finally snuffed out his candle and lay in the darkness of his bedchamber, listening to the crackle and pop of the fire, that it occurred to him that he had not spent such an enjoyable Christmas for as long as he could remember.

~

"I fear I have neglected you this visit."

It was the day before Georgiana's departure, and Darcy had just happened upon her, alone in the library, which surprised him. She and Elizabeth had been inseparable since her arrival, and Darcy had been happy to hang back to allow the ladies to forge a friendship in their own right.

Looking up at him now, Georgiana set down the novel she had been reading, sitting up and untucking her legs to allow him room to sit beside her on the overstuffed leather sofa.

"Oh, no!" Georgiana replied. "You have no reason to reproach yourself; I know you have many matters that require your attention. Besides, I have had Elizabeth to keep me company." She smiled warmly before adding, "She is wonderful, Fitzwilliam. I am so happy you married her."

Darcy's color heightened at his sister's words and he gruffly cleared his voice.

"Yes, well, I am glad the two of you have become close. As a matter of fact, I assumed you would be with her now. I hope nothing is amiss?"

"Oh, no... that is, there is no trouble between the two of us."

Darcy furrowed his brow, instantly anxious.

"Is it Elizabeth? She is not unwell, or—"

But Georgiana was already shaking her head. "Oh, no, nothing like that. It is only that she received some melancholy news from home. I knew she would wish to write to her sister without delay, so I left her to her correspondence. I am certain she will join us when she is finished."

"Oh?" Darcy asked. "I hope it is nothing too serious. Do you know which sister it was that wrote?"

"Her eldest sister, Jane. And no, it is nothing so very terrible; no one is in ill health. It is… an ailment of the heart."

At his sister's words, Darcy could not help but shift uneasily in his seat before saying, "Ah. I see."

Darcy knew he should let the topic drop, but despite his best intentions, he heard himself ask, "Did Elizabeth mention the nature of the trouble?"

Georgiana looked up at him curiously, but nodded. "It seems her sister had formed an attachment to a gentleman whom she thought returned her affections, but he has left the neighborhood, and Jane, that is Miss Bennet, does not think he will be coming back. It is dreadfully sad, is it not?"

Darcy looked away. Clearly, his sister referred to Bingley. Had Jane Bennet truly been pining for his friend all this time? Elizabeth had said nothing about it. He felt a momentary pang of guilt for his part in Bingley's defection, but quickly put the thought from his mind. Miss Bennet was likely only suffering from a case of wounded pride. She would get over Bingley as soon as the next eligible bachelor rolled into town.

Turning his attention back to his sister's mournful countenance, he attempted to alter his expression with a reassuring smile. "Well, I am certain all will come right in the end. Miss Bennet is a very handsome young lady. I have no doubt she will soon secure the affections of some other eligible gentleman."

At his words, Georgiana stared back at him, a horrified expression in her wide blue eyes. "Fitzwilliam, how can you say such a thing? Miss Bennet was deeply in love! Her heart is broken, and Elizabeth does not think she will ever recover. One of her other sisters writes to say that Miss Bennet is not eating as she should, and that she rarely leaves the house. Some relations in Town have offered to host her for the Season, but she refuses to go. Elizabeth is very worried."

Darcy's smile faltered as a wave of contrition washed over him. Could all this be true? Was Miss Bennet's attachment to his friend actually one of genuine affection, and not the calculating scheme to entrap Bingley into marriage he had previously believed?

"Forgive me, I had not realized…" he murmured. "Still, Miss Bennet is young, and there are other amiable gentlemen in the world. I am certain she will get over this in time."

"Would you have got over Elizabeth?"

"I beg your pardon?"

"If Elizabeth had gone away, would you simply have forgotten about her and found some other girl to marry?"

"That is not… I hardly think…" Darcy sputtered, feeling heat once again building in his cheeks.

"People are not interchangeable, Fitzwilliam. Once the heart knows love—deep, abiding love—it does not mend as easily as a scraped knee."

Darcy looked back at his sister, unsettled by her words, but also deeply moved by the depth of her emotions.

"When did you get so wise?" he gently asked, and Georgiana flushed.

"I do not think I am so very wise. But I have grown up a good deal since last summer. I see things so differently now... I suppose that is why I feel for Miss Bennet. Even if she does find love again with someone else, that does not negate the pain she suffers now."

Chastened, Darcy averted his gaze. "You are correct, of course." Lifting his eyes to his sister's he added, "I trust... that is, I hope you do not still carry such pain. It would bring me immense sadness to think—"

Before he could finish, Georgiana stopped him with a vehement shaking of her head. "Oh, no. I do not speak of myself. I did not feel such emotions for Mr. Wickham. I suppose I was fond of him... but mostly I was just lonely, and flattered by the attention. I never carried him in my heart. I did not love him the way Miss Bennet loves her gentleman, or the way you love Elizabeth."

Darcy's mouth went dry as he struggled to form a reply, but before he could open his lips to speak, Georgiana continued, "Fitzwilliam... I hope you will not be angry, but I... I told Elizabeth. About Mr. Wickham."

"What? That is, you did? When?"

"A day or two after I arrived. I... I had not intended to tell her, but we got to talking and..."

"How did she react?" Darcy inquired. "She was not unkind to you, I hope?"

"Not at all! She was wonderful! She told me that I was not to blame. That *he* was the one who had behaved badly. She also told me she was acquainted with Mr. Wickham, that he had been quartered near her home in Hertfordshire..." She paused before asking softly, "Fitzwilliam, was Mr. Wickham the reason you did not wish for me to attend your wedding?"

Sheepishly, Darcy nodded. "Forgive me, I should have said something... I... I simply could not bear to have you come in contact with him again."

"Because you did not trust me?"

"No! Because I did not trust *him*. In truth, I still do not. But it was wrong of me not to be open with you, and it was unfair of me to keep you from our wedding. I did not think on it overmuch at the time, but looking back, I can see how you would have been hurt by the exclusion."

To Darcy's surprise, Georgiana leaned forward, enfolding him in a tight embrace. "You are forgiven," she said earnestly. Pulling back she continued, "As much as I would have wished to be there, all that matters is that you have married the woman you love. And nothing in the world could make me happier than that."

Chapter 12

The day after Georgiana's departure, Elizabeth woke early and made her way to the breakfast parlor. She smiled at Thomas, the footman on duty, before inquiring after her husband, and was informed that Mr. Darcy had already eaten, causing Elizabeth to smother a sigh. Now that Georgiana was gone, she was forced once again to face the grim reality that her life at Pemberley was to be one of isolation and idleness, whether she liked it or not.

Elizabeth ate her meal in silence. When she had finished, she made her way to the library, passing by Mr. Darcy's study as she went, but the room was empty.

After selecting a book, she retraced her steps, planning to go to the morning room to read. But when she once again walked past the study, she saw that her husband now sat behind his desk, penning a letter with bold, decisive strokes. Elizabeth watched him work for a moment before something must have alerted him to her presence, for his head came up and he startled, quickly coming to his feet and beckoning her forward.

"Ah, Elizabeth. Pray, come in."

"Forgive me, I did not mean to disturb you," Elizabeth

murmured, smoothing her skirts and tentatively crossing the threshold.

"You are not disturbing me. As a matter of fact, I was planning to seek you out in a few minutes anyway, so your arrival is well-timed." Returning his pen to the inkwell he came around the desk to pull out a chair so she might sit before returning to his place and slipping the letter he had been writing into a drawer.

"I wished to inform you that I have some business in the north that can no longer be delayed. I will leave at the end of the week."

"Oh, I see," Elizabeth answered, a sinking feeling settling in the pit of her stomach. While it was true that her husband did not provide her with much in the way of companionship, at least she had someone to converse with over dinner. If she was lonely now, she could not imagine how she would bear it with only herself and the servants in the house. "How long will you be gone?" she eventually asked.

"A fortnight. Possibly less. However, that was not the only reason I wished to speak with you. I have made some inquiries, and I believe I have found someone to paint your portrait."

"Oh! So soon?"

"I saw no point in delaying. And now that I have plans to travel, the timing seems auspicious as the artist has agreed to come to Pemberley as soon as may be. This way, at least you will have some company while I am gone."

Elizabeth blinked back at her husband, unsure if she had heard him correctly. "You would have the artist come here... to stay... while you are away?"

"Unless you have some objection. She has indicated that she is willing."

"She...?" Elizabeth asked, all confusion. "Are you saying you have commissioned a female artist?"

He eyed her warily before slowly nodding his head. "She is a young widow, recently arrived from France, to live with her brother in Town. Her husband was killed in the war, and she has been struggling. Of course, I would not have commissioned her solely on that basis, but I know the gentleman who referred her has extremely exacting standards. He hired Madame Gérard to paint a portrait of his daughter, and spoke very highly of her work."

"She sounds ideal; I was merely surprised, that is all. I confess, I had not even considered the possibility that the artist might be a woman."

Darcy regarded her with a quirked brow, before saying, "I will admit I had not thought of it myself at first, but after you railed at me about the predicament of women in our society, it seemed to be the least that I could do."

Realizing she was being teased—by Mr. Darcy of all people!—Elizabeth's mouth dropped open, but before she could come up with a witty retort, her husband sobered, continuing, "I know it might not have seemed like it at the time, but I do agree with you, Elizabeth. Women are not always given the same opportunities as their male counterparts, nor compensated fairly for their expertise. But it is not enough to hope—or even to believe—that someday things will improve. If we want the world to change, those of us in positions of power must begin to exhibit behavior that allows that to happen."

Elizabeth could only stare back at him, stunned that he

should have taken her words so much to heart. Flushing, she softly murmured her approbation and Darcy nodded decisively.

"It is settled, then. I shall write and tell Madame Gérard to come. In the meantime, there is another task that I have neglected, which I should like to remedy before I go."

Elizabeth looked back at him expectantly as Darcy continued, "I promised to teach you to drive. If you are still agreeable, I thought we might start your lessons this very afternoon. If the weather holds, we should be able to manage a few outings before I leave. I know of your fondness for being out of doors, and this way you will have use of the phaeton to tour the park at your leisure while I am away."

Elizabeth's mood immediately brightened, and she was quick to voice her agreement. "Thank you. I would like that a great deal. I am very much looking forward to learning."

"Good." Climbing to his feet, Darcy continued, "Come. I have several maps of the park I can give you to help you to get your bearings, and I will show you the prettiest drives. I can also point out some of the closer tenant farms, in case you wish to begin making calls, although you may prefer to wait until I return for that."

Darcy walked to a bookshelf along the far wall, and Elizabeth stood, following behind him. He reached up his hand, but instead of withdrawing a book or folio as she expected, he touched the edge of the one of the shelves, and a latch clicked.

Elizabeth gasped as the wall swung inwards, revealing the entryway to another room.

"Oh! A secret door!" she cried, and Darcy chuckled.

"Well, it is hardly a secret, as the entire household knows where it is located," he answered, regarding her with a look of amusement. "But yes, the entry is concealed. I suppose I thought it rather clever when I had it put in a few years ago."

Sweeping out his hand, he gestured for her to precede him, and Elizabeth slipped into the adjoining chamber, looking around her with interest. The space was large—at least twice the size of the study—with a bay window on one end and a marble fireplace on the other. Bookshelves filled with ledgers lined the walls and a long drafting table sat in the center of the floor. Near the fireplace, a comfort-able-looking sofa and two wingback chairs were grouped around a low table.

Where the study they had just left was formal and richly appointed, the room in which they now stood was warm and relaxed, the furniture upholstered in simple fabrics, and Elizabeth immediately felt at home.

"So," she said, turning towards him with a mischievous expression, "this is where you hide."

His forehead wrinkled before he answered seriously, "This is where I work. The room was once a parlor, but after my father's passing, I had it converted for my own personal use. It was the right size and in a convenient loca-tion as it adjoins the study."

"Why do you not simply use the study for your busi-ness?" Elizabeth asked curiously, as Darcy came around to lean one hip against the opened door.

"I do, for some things. Mostly correspondence and meetings with the household staff, or the occasional tenant. But the desk is too small to get any real work done." He turned, indicating the drafting table in front of them. "When I attend to the books, it is helpful to have a larger surface to spread things out. At least I find it so. Or perhaps my powers of organization simply need improvement."

Elizabeth's lips curved up at this small attempt at humor. Looking around the exceptionally tidy room, she was inclined to think Mr. Darcy was not at all lacking in the area of organization.

"So, you keep your ledgers here? In the house? My father has always left his estate books with our steward. When he has matters of business, or wishes to check the books—which admittedly is only once a quarter—he goes to the estate agent's office."

Darcy nodded slowly. "Yes, my father was the same. But when I took over the running of the estate, I found I wished to refer to the ledgers more often—sometimes daily —and it was an inconvenience to always be leaving the house. My steward comes here once a fortnight—more often if a situation necessitates it, which has certainly been the case with Mr. Boyle." Darcy's lips pressed together before he continued, "The only ledger I do not retain is the one pertaining to the household accounts. Mrs. Reynolds keeps that in her office. But she has been managing those records for years and does so flawlessly. I meet with her once each quarter, but I have never found so much as a shilling out of place."

Stepping over to the drafting table, Darcy retrieved a large portfolio, opening the cover and beginning to sift through its contents. "I have drawn up several maps of the grounds over the years; I will give you the ones I think will be the most helpful. You are welcome to keep them..."

As he continued to search, Elizabeth came to stand

beside him, picking up the discarded sheets of parchment he had set aside. Upon each one was an architectural drawing of some sort, and Elizabeth's eyes widened as she took in the illustrations.

"Are these yours?" she asked incredulously, lifting her gaze from a beautiful rendering of a cathedral, complete with spires, gargoyles, and incredibly detailed stained-glass windows.

Briefly lifting his gaze, Darcy nodded his confirmation as Elizabeth gasped in delight.

"You are an artist! I had no idea!"

At her words, Darcy's cheeks colored, and he shifted his weight, turning back to resume his search for the maps. "They are only sketches," he answered.

"Only...? But they are extraordinary! Perhaps it is you who should be painting my portrait."

Darcy's flush deepened and his attention once again turned in her direction.

"No, I have no talent for the human form. As you can see, I only draw structures: buildings, bridges, equipment, that sort of thing. Never people. And I know nothing of paints. I only sketch in pencil or charcoal."

"Still... these are..." She paused, slowly shaking her head before turning to look up at him. "You are exceptionally talented. Have you always been able to draw like this?"

Next to her, Darcy gave a small shrug. "I have always been fascinated with buildings, and any type of machinery. I used to construct elaborate edifices with my wooden blocks when I was a boy. When I got a little older, I started to sketch out the ideas in my head. I used to think that someday... Well, it is of no importance. Now I simply sketch to help clear my mind."

Elizabeth turned her attention back to the drawings, slowly flipping the pages until she came to a sketch of some type of machinery she did not recognize. She glanced up at her husband who stood at her right shoulder.

"What is this one meant to be? I do not think I have ever seen anything like it before."

Darcy offered her a lopsided smile, and he took the drawing from her, holding it up to the light. "That is a locomotive. It is powered by steam, so it can move without the aid of horses. It is designed to run on a track, similar to a wagonway."

Elizabeth stared back at him, her eyes round. "And you invented this?"

Darcy laughed lightly. "No. This particular engine was designed by Richard Trevithick, a mining engineer from Cornwall." He handed the drawing back to Elizabeth and moved a few feet away, digging through a stack of papers at the other end of the table. "Here. This is a more recent design for an engine that is being built in Leeds. I had the opportunity to view it recently when I was in the area on business."

Elizabeth studied the drawing for a moment before asking, "How exactly does it work?"

"Well, an engine like this one produces its pulling power by burning fuel, such as coal or wood, to create steam. The steam moves the reciprocating pistons, here, which are mechanically connected to the locomotive's wheels. Locomotives powered by steam result in a faster and more reliable means of transportation. For now, they are being built to haul minerals. But eventually, they could be used to transport people, as well as freight."

Elizabeth's nose wrinkled. "So, they burn the coal on board? That sounds dangerous."

"Not if it is done properly. Which is to say, it is no more dangerous than riding in a carriage, or sailing on a ship. Carriages overturn. Ships sink. People die. Does that mean we should all stay inside our houses?"

Sensing an inexplicable shift in her husband's mood, Elizabeth turned back to the drafting table, extracting another drawing and holding it up for his inspection. "I like this one. It looks like something out of a fairy story."

Seeming to relax, Darcy nodded, smiling back at her. "That is a glasshouse. And unlike the locomotive, this one I did design. See, it has a curved glass dome which uses wrought-iron for the sash bar, and there are perforated pipes under the stone floor to create steam to warm the air inside. It also utilizes ridge-and-furrow glazing, with the ridge running north and south and panes facing east and west."

Elizabeth laughed. "Goodness! I am not certain I understand any of that, but it is lovely, just the same. Will you build it? Here at Pemberley?" But she had hardly finished speaking before Darcy shook his head.

"No. With the tax on glass, it would cost a fortune. Besides, I have no need of a glasshouse, just as I have no need of a locomotive, or a cathedral. As I said, I only sketch for my own amusement. Sometimes, when I am trying to work out a particularly thorny problem, I find it helps."

"And do you ever do anything with the drawings, once you have completed them?" she asked.

"Such as?"

Elizabeth shrugged. "I do not know. It is only that it

seems a shame to hide them away. Would you mind... that is, could I keep this one?" she asked, holding up the sketch of the glasshouse.

Darcy blinked back at her. "If you wish. But what will *you* do with it?"

"Perhaps I will frame it and hang it in my sitting room," she answered playfully, and Darcy laughed, causing Elizabeth's pulse to quicken. She very much enjoyed making him laugh. He really ought to do so more often!

"If that pleases you," he answered.

Gathering the drawings into a neat stack, he placed them back in the portfolio before saying, "Now, let me get back to looking for those maps, and then we can begin our lesson."

A short while later, Elizabeth fairly skipped along the gravel path as she walked beside Mr. Darcy towards the carriage house. Her husband had apparently sent word of their planned outing, for when they reached the stables, two perfectly matched bays were already being led into the drive. At the approach of the horses, Elizabeth came to an abrupt halt, her earlier eagerness instantly dissipating.

Darcy slowed his pace, turning in her direction. "Is something the matter?"

"No, no. It is only that... I did not expect them to be quite so... large."

"Well, they need to be strong to pull a conveyance at a steady clip," he said, offering her a slow smile, "but I assure you, they are quite gentle." Taking her elbow, he steered her towards the animals. "Are you afraid of horses?

I know you said you did not ride… were you in an accident of some sort?"

"No. I simply have never had much experience with horses. Jane is the horsewoman in our family."

By this time, they had made their way to the spot where the bays stood, and Darcy reached up to pat the one closest to him affectionally on the side of the neck. "You have nothing to fear from Triumph and Victory. I have never seen a more docile pair of carriage horses. I purchased them two years ago at Tattersall's, and they have never given me a moment's trouble. I would not let my sister handle them, otherwise."

"Does your sister drive?" Elizabeth asked with interest. "You had not said so before."

Darcy nodded. "She generally prefers to ride, but I taught her to drive the phaeton last summer, and I think she quite enjoyed it." Turning back to the horses, he added, "Come, allow them to pick up your scent."

Cautiously, Elizabeth stepped forward, lightly running her fingers along the other mare's velvety nose. The horse snorted softly, pushing her muzzle into the palm of Elizabeth's hand.

"There, you see? She is as gentle as a kitten."

Elizabeth flushed, giving the animal one last pat as Darcy guided her past the stables and into the carriage house. Elizabeth blinked, allowing her eyes to become accustomed to the relative darkness, but found herself halting to take in a row of at least half a dozen vehicles of various shapes and sizes.

Once again, the tangible evidence of exactly how wealthy a man she had married momentarily took her breath away. Turning, she struggled to compose her features, but as luck would have it, Mr. Darcy had already begun walking towards a shiny black phaeton in the corner. Elizabeth followed, staring with interest at the low-slung vehicle.

"Well, what do you think?" he asked.

"Like your horses, it is bigger than I had imagined."

Darcy laughed. "Yes, there are smaller models, but I assure you it is easy to handle."

Just then, two grooms entered the space, leading the horses, and Darcy and Elizabeth stepped aside as the bays were harnessed, and the phaeton brought outside. Placing his hand at the small of Elizabeth's back, Darcy escorted her out into the frosty air, assisting her up before taking the place beside her. The horses pawed the dirt restively, and Elizabeth's grip tightened on the arm of her seat.

Sneaking a sideways glance at Mr. Darcy, she watched as he took up the ribbons, giving them a gentle flick, and the horses trotted forward. The cold, crisp breeze filled Elizabeth's lungs, stinging her cheeks and ruffling the curls peeking out from underneath her bonnet.

They drove in silence, until they eventually reached a small copse. Darcy pulled back on the ribbons and the horses slowed to a gentle stop. Elizabeth shifted nervously in her seat as he released the reins, allowing them to drop.

"Is that wise?" she inquired. "Will they not bolt?"

"No. They are extremely well trained. However, you are correct, it is not a good habit to get into. I should advise you to always hold tight to the ribbons, or tie them up properly if you stop."

Elizabeth nodded, saying nervously, "Did... did you wish for me to try now?"

"No, not quite yet," Darcy answered as he leaned down

to rummage beneath the seat. A moment later, he extracted a small wooden box, placing it on the bench between them. Elizabeth watched as he lifted the lid, and a gasp slipped from her throat as he withdrew a small pistol.

"I hope that is not loaded!"

"No; it is not. Though normally it would be. I asked the grooms to refrain from loading it so that I might show you how to do it properly."

"Forgive me, I do not understand. I was under the impression that you would be teaching me to drive, not to shoot."

Darcy looked back at her, a serious expression settling upon his features. "We shall get to the driving soon enough. However, it is imperative that anyone who takes out one of the Darcy carriages is trained on how to handle a weapon. All of the conveyances have a box like this one under the seat. The grooms are responsible for keeping the pistols in good order, and they are always loaded before the vehicle is taken out, and unloaded and cleaned when the carriage is returned."

"Is such a thing truly necessary?" she asked, wrinkling her nose.

"Which part? Having the pistols consistently cared for, or keeping a weapon in the carriage?"

"Both, I should imagine."

"Then, yes, in both instances. The proper care and maintenance of any type of weapon is of paramount importance. It is something that I am adamant about, and every one of my groomsmen is well aware of my feelings. Lack of attention to detail in this matter would result in an immediate dismissal. As for carrying a weapon, I do not know anyone of sense who would venture out without such protection. While you will only be driving within the park and it is unlikely that you will ever be set upon by high-waymen, the estate is vast, and any number of things could occur."

Elizabeth felt her eyes grow round and her expression must certainly have mirrored her alarm, because Mr. Darcy suddenly stopped, relaxing his tone.

"Forgive me. It is not my intention to frighten you. In the whole of my lifetime, I can only remember one instance when there was need of a pistol while on the estate, and that involved a fox we believe to have been rabid. However, it has always been my belief—and my father's, before me—that an ounce of prevention is worth a pound of cure." After a brief pause, he added, "However, if you are truly uncomfortable with the idea of learning to fire a weapon, I can have a footman accompany you when you go out. I had simply thought you would prefer your inde-pendence."

"No... that is, yes. I would prefer to be able to go on my own. I... I was only surprised, I suppose. But what you say makes sense, and I am willing to learn."

"Good. Knowing how to properly load and fire a pistol is a valuable skill to have, in any case. The results of doing so incorrectly can be catastrophic."

A flash of some emotion Elizabeth could not quite place flickered across Mr. Darcy's countenance, but was gone so quickly, Elizabeth thought she had imagined it.

"So, you taught your sister how to do this?" Elizabeth asked. "You said you had instructed her on driving."

Darcy nodded. "Yes. She was also a little hesitant at first, but she did very well, in the end. I have her keep a pistol in her saddlebag when she rides out alone, for the same reasons."

Over the next quarter hour, Darcy demonstrated how to load and unload the pistol. Afterwards, he helped Elizabeth to the ground, and they walked a little way into the copse. Once he had shown her the correct way to hold the weapon, Darcy aimed at a large oak before deftly pulling the trigger. An ear-piercing crack shattered the silence, and Elizabeth could not help but flinch in alarm. She had never been fond of guns or hunting, and had rarely accompanied her father or any of their neighbors on their shooting expeditions. She truly did not know if she could ever bring herself to use the weapon, even if the situation warranted it, although she did understand Mr. Darcy's reasoning.

Staring through the clearing smoke, she could just make out the neat bullet hole in the rough bark of the old tree.

"I hope you are not expecting me to be able to duplicate your marksmanship," Elizabeth said uneasily.

Darcy lowered his arm, carefully cleaning the pistol. "No. It is not necessary for you to hit the tree. I simply want you to know what it feels like to fire. As I said, it is extremely unlikely that you will ever need to do so, but it is best to be prepared."

After Darcy had reloaded, he placed the pistol in Elizabeth's hands, moving to stand behind her and guiding her into the correct stance. They had removed their gloves, and Elizabeth shivered as his warm palms pressed against her bare skin.

"Keep your arms straight. Hold the pistol in your right hand, and use your left to support your wrist. Good. Now place your index finger just above the trigger..."

Elizabeth could feel her insides trembling slightly, but her hands were surprisingly steady.

"Good. Very good. Now, whenever you feel ready, press the trigger."

Elizabeth did as she was told and the gun discharged with a loud bang, causing her to jolt at the recoil, which was more significant than she expected.

Slowly, she lowered her arms as Darcy's hands came up to rest upon her shoulders.

Elizabeth frowned into the smoke-filled air. "I did not hit it. I shall have to work on my aim."

"It does not matter; I would not have expected you to hit it on your first go. How do you feel?"

"It was different than I expected. Can I try again?"

Darcy smiled, taking the pistol and reloading it for her. This time the recoil did not unsettle her as much, and there was a satisfying crack after she pulled the trigger.

"I think I hit it!"

Darcy nodded. "You did. There, on the right side. Well done." Taking the weapon, he carefully cleaned the chamber, loading it once more before returning it to the wooden box.

"I think that is enough shooting for one day, but you did well." Suddenly, his expression grew serious. "However, I must ask you to give me your word that you will never touch this pistol if I am not with you, unless it is absolutely necessary. Do you understand?"

"Yes, of course. And you have no need for concern. I have not the smallest intention of firing that thing again, unless thoroughly provoked."

Darcy stared back at her before nodding somberly.

"Good. Now come, it is growing cold, and we should return to the house."

"Return! I thought you were going to show me how to drive?"

Darcy grinned, reaching out to take her arm. "And I have every intention of doing so. Who do you think will be driving us back?"

~

Over the next few days, Mr. Darcy took her driving on two more occasions. By the end of the week, Elizabeth had grown so comfortable with handling the horses, that her husband had little to do but to relax in the seat beside her, which pleased Elizabeth a great deal.

When they returned to the house after their third outing, she expected he would retreat to his study, as was his custom, but was surprised when he suggested adjourning to the library for refreshment, a proposition which Elizabeth readily accepted.

Darcy rang for tea, and the two settled into chairs by the fire.

"You have made great progress in a short period of time," Darcy began, relaxing in his seat. "Even Georgiana, who has been riding all her life, did not take to driving in the way you have done."

Elizabeth could not help but flush at her husband's praise. In truth, she had not expected to relish the activity to such a degree, but as Mr. Darcy had predicted, the horses were calm and steady, and the feeling of being out of doors and moving at a measured clip was exhilarating.

The two sipped their tea in silence for a while before

Elizabeth said, "Speaking of Georgiana, I had a letter from her today."

Setting down his cup, Darcy lifted his brow. "Oh? I have not heard from her save the one brief note she sent, letting us know she was safely returned to Town. How does she fare?"

"She is well, although…" Elizabeth paused and Darcy stared back at her, a deep furrow appearing between his brows.

"Is there something amiss? If she is unhappy, I hope you would tell me."

Elizabeth sighed. She did not wish to break Georgiana's confidence, nor to cause strife between brother and sister, but she could not help but think that her husband would benefit from knowing the truth.

"I would not say she is unhappy, precisely," she began carefully. "But I do think she is rather lonely. She misses Pemberley, and your company. I get the impression that she does not have many friends in London."

At Elizabeth's words, Darcy nodded slowly. "Yes. I am certain she is missing your society as well. I must confess if I were to gratify my own preferences, I would keep her here at Pemberley, always, but it is not what is best for her. She will come out soon, and should begin to accustom herself to mixing in larger circles. Being in London also gives her access to the best tutors. When I took her from school two years ago, it was under the provision that she would remain in Town so she could keep up with her studies. There is nothing for her at Pemberley."

"How can you say so?" Elizabeth answered heatedly. "There is you! And now me. Do you not think that being amongst those she loves is as beneficial to her development as being alone in a vast city, no matter how many masters that city may provide?"

Darcy sighed, leaning back in his chair and rubbing his temples.

"It is not that simple..."

Elizabeth bit her lip, finally saying, "Is this about Mr. Wickham?"

Darcy's eyes widened slightly at her words, but she could not say he looked entirely surprised by her question. Taking a breath, she continued, "Georgiana confided in me when she was here. About Mr. Wickham... and what happened at Ramsgate."

"Yes, she mentioned to me that she had. I am glad she felt comfortable enough to unburden herself to you. I had hoped she might wish to one day, although I confess, I am surprised it happened so quickly."

"I am glad as well. I think it helped for her to speak of it, especially once I told her Mr. Wickham was known to me already." She lowered her gaze briefly. "While we are speaking of it, I... I feel I owe you an apology... for my defense of that scoundrel. I was shocked when Georgiana told me her story, and I could not help but reflect on my own poor judgement. I should have known something was amiss when Mr. Wickham was so eager to relate such personal details to me upon so brief an acquaintance. But I saw only that which supported my prejudice."

Darcy stiffened at her words, but when he spoke, his voice was unaffected.

"It is not your fault. As I mentioned once before, Wickham is blessed with such happy manners, he has no trouble charming new acquaintances. It is only later that those he befriends realize their mistake." After a short pause, he continued, "As we are discussing the matter, there is something I would wish for you to know. Simon Edwards, the hall boy whose plight you were so taken with...? He is Wickham's natural child."

Elizabeth's teacup rattled against her saucer as she moved to set it on a nearby table. "Good heavens! But how can that be? Simon is eleven years old! Mr. Wickham would have to have been—"

"Full young, yes. And already conducting himself in a despicable manner. I was well aware of his dissolute tendencies at the time—it was one of the things that began to erode our friendship—although, in truth, we had not been close for some years before we reached our teens."

"I... I hardly know what to say! Even after everything I had learned, I still did not believe him to have behaved so infamously as this!"

Darcy grimaced, briefly lowering his gaze. "I do not wish to shock you, but I am afraid Simon is not Wickham's only offspring. He likely has upwards of half a dozen bastards running around the country. I have had the dubious honor of cleaning up after him on more than one occasion, however I knew nothing of Simon until about three years ago. His mother turned up at Pemberley seeking Wickham's direction. When I told her I did not have it, she broke down in near hysteria. She finally confided in me about the child. Her family had thrown her out when they initially learned of her predicament, and she had been residing with an elderly aunt, who had recently died. She had a good position as a seamstress in a dress shop in Sheffield, but without her aunt, there was no one to look after the boy. What she was hoping Wickham would do for her, I cannot imagine. I knew well enough he would never acknowledge the child, let alone offer any type of monetary assistance. But without some sort of intervention, she confided that her only recourse would be to place Simon in a workhouse."

Elizabeth's eyes widened as Darcy continued, "When I heard Miss Edwards's story, I agreed to meet the boy, and if he seemed suitable, to offer him a place at Pemberley. She brought Simon the very next day, and I was immediately taken with his obvious intelligence and willingness to learn. I took him on as hall boy, and he has been here ever since. He is well liked and valued by the rest of the household, and he seems happy."

"Does he know...?"

"That Wickham is his father? No. Nor does anyone in the house besides Mrs. Reynolds and myself. Richard is also aware of the situation, and now you, but the fewer people who possess this intelligence, the better. It is for Simon's own protection. Wickham is a master manipulator. If he knew the boy was here and under my protection, he would not hesitate to use that knowledge to his advantage."

Elizabeth nodded slowly. After all she had learned of Mr. Wickham in the past few weeks, she could well imagine that Mr. Darcy was correct.

"And what of Simon's mother?" she inquired softly.

"She seems to be doing well. She visits with Simon once a month and hopes to one day have enough saved for the two of them to be reunited somewhere nearer to Pemberley."

Elizabeth shook her head, struggling to tamp down the revulsion that twisted her stomach. "I am so ashamed! Not only for trusting Mr. Wickham so implicitly, but for the way I condemned you for Simon's treatment. What you have done for him, and for his mother... it is a very decent thing."

Darcy colored, shifting in his seat. "I did not tell you all this to earn your approbation. I simply felt that given the circumstances, it would be good for you to know."

Elizabeth nodded and Darcy soon changed the subject, the two of them moving on to discuss more neutral topics for the remainder of the hour.

Chapter 13

The day before her husband was to depart for the north, Madame Gérard arrived. Elizabeth was surprised to note that the artist was younger than she expected, perhaps only five or six years older than herself. She was a petite woman with auburn curls, expressive grey eyes, and a calm disposition. Her quiet serenity reminded Elizabeth a little of Jane, and she eagerly looked forward to having another young lady in the house with whom she might converse.

Alas, as it turned out, Madame Gérard had very little English, and Elizabeth—who had stubbornly insisted on learning Italian and Latin instead of a more useful language —was not much help, so the two were forced to communicate in Elizabeth's minimal and far-from-perfect French. Additionally, Madame Gérard had brought a French maid with her, and informed Elizabeth on the first evening that the two of them would take their meals within her apartment. Elizabeth had only nodded, and forced a smile, but she could not help but be disappointed that she would remain more or less alone for the duration of her husband's absence.

To add to her concerns, Elizabeth was growing more and more anxious about Jane, as the weeks progressed. Her letters had become less frequent, and although Jane tried to fill them with amusing anecdotes, Elizabeth knew her sister well enough to be able to read between the lines.

Caroline Bingley had written again to inform her sister that they remained in Scarborough, and would not likely return to Town until the spring. She also hinted heavily at her brother's interest in the sister of one of his close friends, and made it known that he was likely to give up the lease on Netherfield entirely by next summer. When Elizabeth had read the news, she could not help but grumble in frustration at Miss Bingley's impertinence. Despite Jane's protestations to the contrary, she continued to believe that Charles Bingley possessed tender feelings for her sister, and that it was only at Miss Bingley's insistence that he stayed away.

Setting aside Jane's most recent letter, Elizabeth vowed to speak with her husband again. She knew Mr. Bingley relied on his friend's good opinion, and if anything could be done to persuade him of Jane's affection, Elizabeth would see that it was accomplished.

The following days settled into an ordinary pattern. In the mornings, Elizabeth sat for Madame Gérard and then met with Mrs. Reynolds to discuss menus and household tasks. In the afternoons, she walked in the dormant gardens if the weather was fair, attended to her correspondence, or practiced on the pianoforte. Once or twice a week she visited Darcy's tenants in her phaeton, or simply drove around the park. To Elizabeth's surprise, she had come to appreciate driving a great deal, and she found enormous contentment in getting to know the families who worked Pemberley's land.

As promised, Mr. Darcy returned within a fortnight, and about a week after his arrival, Madame Gérard departed with the assurance that she had all she needed to complete the portrait at her studio in Town. And although Elizabeth knew she would miss her companionship, if she were being honest, she was glad to have her husband once again at Pemberley. In the two short months since their marriage, she had grown accustomed to his calm and steady presence —his confident stride echoing off the marble floors, the low rumble of his voice in the corridors, and the intensity of his gaze when he regarded her across the dinner table— which left her feeling both buoyant and bemused.

One day, shortly after Mr. Darcy's return, two letters of great significance arrived at Pemberley.

It was early afternoon, and Elizabeth was seated with Mrs. Reynolds in the upstairs sitting room when a knock sounded at the open door and Cassidy entered, offering a hasty curtsy.

"Forgive me for interrupting, ma'am, but the post just arrived and there is a letter for you. I thought I may as well bring it as I was on my way to fetch your dinner gown for pressing."

Rising, Elizabeth thanked the maid, and her heart rate escalated as she took the letter, seeing that it was from Jane and was a good deal thicker than any of her more recent communications.

Clearly noting the eagerness in her expression, the housekeeper also stood, smiling good naturedly.

"I believe we have finished here, Mrs. Darcy, so I will leave you to your letter."

Nodding her appreciation, Elizabeth prised up the seal, unfolding the thick sheaf of parchment and settling into a comfortable chair by the window to read, but she did not remain seated for long. News of a most shocking nature caused her to dart from her seat, her eyes scanning the page before she raced from the room.

She arrived breathless in her husband's study some minutes later, the tears she had been attempting to hold at bay already escaping from the corners of her lashes.

Mr. Darcy looked up at her entrance, surging to his feet upon beholding her flushed countenance and tear-stained cheeks.

"Elizabeth! What is the matter?" he demanded. "Are you ill?"

Struggling for composure, Elizabeth merely stood there, and Darcy quickly came around the corner of his desk, gently taking her arm and steering her to a nearby chair.

"You are unwell. Let me ring for your maid to attend you," he began, but Elizabeth was already shaking her head, as a wave of almost hysterical laughter threatened to burst from her throat.

"No, I am quite well. Forgive me for frightening you. It is happy tidings; the very best. Jane is engaged to be married! To Mr. Bingley!"

Elizabeth watched as Mr. Darcy's entire body seemed to slump in relief before he appeared to gather his equanimity, returning to the seat behind his desk and offering her a shallow smile.

"Well, those are glad tidings," he replied carefully. "They are well suited, I think. I hope they will be very happy together."

"You do not seem surprised," Elizabeth noted, studying

his expression. "Has Mr. Bingley already written to inform you of his intent to propose?"

Darcy shifted in his seat, and Elizabeth thought she saw him color slightly.

"Bingley is an indifferent correspondent. I have not had a letter from him in some time, though I am certain he will notify me eventually—likely at some point between now and when his firstborn enters university."

Elizabeth's smile broadened, and she could not help but laugh at her husband's attempt at humor.

Suddenly feeling awkward, she stared down at her lap, saying softly, "I beg your pardon for rushing in here and interrupting your work. I know you must think me silly, but this is all I have ever wanted—to see my sister this happy..." She choked back a sob before continuing, "There is no one who could deserve it more, and there is nothing I would not have sacrificed to make it happen."

"I know," Darcy answered soberly.

Lifting her gaze, Elizabeth studied his expression, and without forethought said, "You are not disappointed, I hope?"

"Disappointed? In Bingley marrying your sister? Why would I be?"

Across from him, Elizabeth lifted her shoulders in an indifferent shrug. "I had wondered if you disapproved of the match. Whenever I mentioned the possibility of Mr. Bingley returning to Netherfield, you did not seem to wish to discuss it. I thought perhaps you would discourage your friend from maintaining the acquaintances he made in the neighborhood."

Now, Darcy did look distinctly uncomfortable, but he continued to show his support, saying, "Bingley is a good friend. Like you with your sister, I have only ever wanted his happiness."

A shadow crossed his features, making his expression suddenly grave, and Elizabeth felt moved to change the subject, however it was Mr. Darcy who continued, "Will they marry as soon as the banns can be read? I am certain you will wish to be there, but travel may be unpredictable in winter."

Elizabeth once again took up her letter—as she had not got much past the news of her sister's unexpected betrothal —her eyes skimming the page.

"It appears they do not intend to marry until the spring. Mamma wishes to take Jane to Town to shop for a full trousseau, and insists on sufficient time to plan the wedding breakfast." Looking up at her husband, she added with a laugh, "No doubt the real reason is her desire to parade Jane through the neighborhood to receive all our friends' admiration and well-wishes. It is a good thing Jane and Mr. Bingley are so obliging."

Still looking somber, Darcy nodded, and Elizabeth climbed uncomfortably to her feet. "Well, I should leave you to your work..." Her voice trailed off as her gaze settled on a letter resting at the edge of her husband's desk. Although it was not facing in her direction, she could see the engraving on the outer envelope listed both their names.

"What is this?" Elizabeth asked, reaching idly for the heavy vellum.

Behind the desk, Darcy lifted his gaze, pausing before clearing his voice.

"It is nothing of consequence. Merely another invitation to a ball. I have not yet had time to pen my reply."

Elizabeth's eyebrows rose as she turned the letter over

in her hands, noting that the seal had not yet been broken. "As it is addressed to both of us, perhaps I might be allowed to determine its consequence for myself," she answered primly. "May I?"

Darcy appeared reluctant, but eventually nodded, watching as she unsealed the envelope and withdrew a heavy sheet of parchment.

"But this is a Saint Valentine's Day ball at Briarwood! And it is being held in less than a fortnight." Lifting her eyes, she continued, "You have not left us much time to prepare. Luckily, I purchased a gown I think should suffice, though I will need to order slippers…"

Across from her, Darcy's gaze hardened. "Do not bother; we are not going."

"I beg your pardon?"

"I was just about to send my regrets."

"Our regrets."

Darcy frowned, and Elizabeth folded her arms tightly across her body. "As the invitation is addressed to both of us, you were about to send *our* regrets." After a slight hesitation, she added, "Had you any intention of showing this to me? Or of asking if I would like to attend?"

Darcy colored, briefly looking away. "Forgive me. I am not yet accustomed to having to answer to another person when it comes to such decisions. I shall endeavor to consult you in future."

"Thank you." Elizabeth extended the invitation and Darcy took it, bending once more over his correspondence.

"And you may change your reply to an acceptance," she said sweetly as Darcy's hand jerked, splattering ink across the fine linen writing paper.

Slowly, he lifted his gaze. "You wish to go?"

"I do. It will be a nice change to be in company again, and there are still many of your relations I have not yet had the opportunity to meet. I assume some of them will be in attendance."

Darcy paled. "Very well, perhaps next year, we might—"

"Next year! I see no reason to postpone. As I said, I already have a suitable gown, and I am certain your aunt and uncle—"

"No. It is too late to accept. The ball is in ten days' time, and my aunt will not be expecting us. My reply is merely a formality. I never attend. I have not been to Briarwood since I was a boy."

"Then I am certain they will be overjoyed to see that you have made an exception this year," Elizabeth replied pleasantly.

Clearly struggling to regain his equanimity, Darcy released a shallow breath, fixing her with a fraught expression.

"Elizabeth, I doubt very much that they will have room for us to stay, and it is too far to travel there and back in one day."

"Then we shall find another place to spend the night. There must be an inn nearby."

Darcy blinked back at her.

"An inn?" he echoed incredulously.

Standing abruptly, he paced to the window, running his fingers through his hair. "No, it cannot be done. It would be the height of rudeness to accept with so little notice. Perhaps this summer we can invite my aunt and uncle for a visit..."

He turned back to face Elizabeth, whose heart sank inside her chest.

"Very well," she answered. "As they are your relations, I suppose the decision must also be yours." She turned, moving stiffly towards the door. "I should see about dinner…"

But she had not gone more than a handful of steps when Darcy called her name.

"Do you truly wish to go?" he asked.

She nodded back at him, and Darcy sighed before twisting his lips into something between a smile and a grimace before saying, "Well then, I suppose I should not delay any longer in sending our reply. And you had best see about ordering those slippers."

The morning of the ball, Darcy and Elizabeth departed for Briarwood directly after breakfast. Although the distance between Pemberley and the Matlock estate was an easy sixteen miles, icy roads meant the journey would take longer than usual. Elizabeth had suggested traveling a few days early, but Darcy had steadfastly refused. He claimed he could not possibly get away from the business of the estate for longer than two days, but Elizabeth could not help wondering if there was a different reason for his reluctance.

Looking across the carriage now, she could see that his jaw was tightly clenched and his spine rigid. And although an open book rested in his lap, he had not turned a page in at least a quarter of an hour. Elizabeth sighed. Perhaps this trip had been an ill-advised idea. When Darcy had first mentioned the ball, she had spoken instinctively—thinking only of the prospect of dancing and the chance to be in company again. Elizabeth was not formed for solitude, and the quiet days and nights at Pemberley, with no one but her husband for companionship, were starting to wear on her. What she had not considered was that she was likely leaping from the frying pan straight into the fire. It was clear her husband had not wished to attend. Indeed, he had made a point of telling her he had not been to Briarwood for years, since he was a young boy. Until now, it had not even occurred to her to ask why. Suddenly, an image of Lady Catherine sprang to mind, and Elizabeth stifled a groan. Was it not likely that this aunt and uncle were just as bad? These were more of her husband's Fitzwilliam relations, after all—Lord Matlock was Lady Catherine's brother. Would he be as hateful and cruel as his sister had been? And was his wife cut from the same cloth?

Stupid, stupid, Lizzy! Why do you never think before you act?

Despite her trepidation, a smile twitched at the corners of her lips. If she was only less impetuous, she would not be married to Mr. Darcy in the first place!

Turning to look out of the snow-flecked window, Elizabeth sighed. *Well, there is nothing to be done for it now. We are on our way, and I shall just have to make the best of it.*

Clearing her throat, she shifted to face her husband.

"Mr. Darcy, perhaps you might tell me something about your family. Whom do you expect to be at the ball?"

Darcy visibly started at the sound of her voice, as if he had forgotten she was in the carriage. Closing his book with a weary expression, he set it on the seat beside him, leaning back against the squabs.

"I do not believe it will be a large gathering, as the winter weather is not conducive to traveling. Mostly it will be family and a few local peers. I know Richard was not able to get away from his unit, but his elder brother, the viscount, will likely be in attendance, as well as Lord and Lady Matlock's two daughters and their husbands. I am certain Lady Matlock's mother, the Dowager Marchioness of Wheaton will also be there. She generally resides at Briarwood for the winter." After a slight pause, he added, "Lady Wheaton is also my godmother."

Elizabeth's eyebrows rose at this piece of intelligence. Apart from Georgiana and Richard—and Lady Catherine—she had met none of her husband's relations, and he rarely spoke of them. Of course, she had known his uncle was an earl, but until this moment, she had not truly apprehended the heights of society she had married into. An earl for an uncle and a marchioness for a godmother. One cousin who was a viscount, and who knew what else! However small this ball may be, she would be rubbing elbows with members of the first circles, a level of society she heretofore had almost no contact with. She glanced down at her simple burgundy pelisse and frowned. Perhaps she should have taken more care with her wardrobe. Although the ball gown she had purchased in Lambton was finer than any she had ever owned, and she thought it exceedingly pretty, it was likely to be inferior to anything the other ladies would be wearing.

Before she could think on it any further, the carriage began to slow, making a turn onto a narrow lane flanked on either side with majestic oaks. Across from her, her husband seemed to grow even more tense, the fingers of his left hand briefly tightening into a fist.

Elizabeth turned once again to peer out the carriage window, and her breath caught in her throat. She had expected Briarwood to be impressive, but nothing could have prepared her for the enormous edifice that stood before them. Where Pemberley was grand, Briarwood was nothing short of imposing. With architecture in the gothic style, it looked more like an ancient fortress than a home, and Elizabeth felt her apprehension begin to grow.

When they reached the end of the long avenue, the carriage swung into the circular drive where a line of liveried servants were already waiting. A footman opened the door, and Darcy stepped out before reaching back to hand her down. Taking her husband's arm, she allowed him to escort her up the long flight of stone steps to an enormous wooden door, which opened as soon as they reached the landing.

"Darcy! I can scarcely believe it! You are truly here."

An elegantly dressed woman rushed in their direction as they stepped into the cavernous entrance hall. Elizabeth looked from the woman to Mr. Darcy, who smiled for the first time that day.

"Aunt. It is good to see you, as well, although I hardly expect my presence to be such a surprise. I did write to inform you that we were coming."

The woman waved away his remarks. "One can say anything in a letter. I told Henry I would not believe it until I saw you on my doorstep. And here you are!" Turning to Elizabeth, she smiled, but there was uncertainty in her gaze. "And this must be your lovely bride."

Darcy nodded before saying, "Aunt, may I present my wife, Mrs. Elizabeth Darcy? Elizabeth, this is my aunt, Lady Cecilia Fitzwilliam, the Countess of Matlock."

"Your ladyship," Elizabeth murmured, and Lady Matlock's smile broadened.

"I am very pleased to meet you, my dear, although I hope you will call me 'Aunt'."

Elizabeth nodded, offering her thanks before saying, "I am very happy to meet some more of my husband's relations. You are very gracious to allow us to stay the night, especially on such short notice."

"Nonsense. Darcy knows he is always welcome here. But come, it is drafty here in the hall, and you must be tired from your journey. Let us go into the withdrawing room for a moment, and then I will show you to your chambers."

Beside her, Elizabeth could see her husband's shoulders tense, and the smile seemed to slip from his face, but he nodded to his aunt, gently taking her elbow and leading her down a brightly lit corridor. As they walked, Elizabeth took in her surroundings. Although the exterior of the manor had seemed dark and almost forbidding, the interior décor, while opulent, was tasteful, and the rooms they passed looked pleasant. They finally arrived at the door to a large, elegantly furnished drawing room where a silver tea service was laid out on a low mahogany table. The room's occupants all stood as their party entered, and Elizabeth dropped a polite curtsy as she was introduced.

"Darcy, you know everyone, of course. Elizabeth, these are my daughters, Alice and Eleanor, and their husbands, Mr. John Campbell and Lord Mathew Armstrong, the Earl of Halston."

Greetings were exchanged before Lady Matlock turned to an older woman seated imperiously in a throne-like chair at the opposite side of the room.

"And this is my mother, Lady Melanie Rice, the Dowager Marchioness of Wheaton."

Elizabeth lowered her gaze, dipping into a deep curtsy. "Your ladyship." Rising to her feet, she looked down at the older woman, whose piercing blue eyes seemed to see straight through to the very essence of Elizabeth's character. But a moment later her lips curved into a warm smile as her gaze shifted to her godson, who bent to place a soft kiss to her cheek.

"Lady Wheaton. You look lovely, as always."

"Humph! I am surprised you recognized me, given the length of time since we were last in company together. And what is this 'Lady Wheaton'? You know I prefer 'Melanie'."

Although her words were harsh, her tone was gentle, and Darcy chuckled softly. "Very well; Melanie. And you know it has not been so long as all that. I had the pleasure of seeing you in Town only last spring."

Just then, Lady Matlock came forward, encouraging them to sit, and Darcy escorted Elizabeth to a chair near his female cousins.

Elizabeth found Lady Matlock's daughters reserved, yet polite, and the ladies were soon engaged in conversation. Her husband had moved to take a seat closer to his godmother, and Elizabeth could not help but study them out of the corner of her vision, noticing that the dowager marchioness's gaze was often on her, causing Elizabeth's cheeks to heat self-consciously.

After about a quarter of an hour, Lady Matlock rose, nodding to Darcy and then Elizabeth. "I believe we have detained you long enough. You must be fatigued, and you will wish for some time to rest before tonight. Come, I will show you to your chambers."

Standing and making their farewells, Elizabeth and Darcy followed Lady Matlock from the room. The countess walked at a brisk pace, turning occasionally to speak to them over her shoulder.

"I have taken the liberty of placing you in the east wing. It has been recently refurbished and I thought you might... prefer it to the family wing."

They walked up a sweeping staircase and then down several long corridors before finally arriving at a heavy wooden door. Pressing the latch, the countess shepherded them into the large space, moving to the windows and drawing back the heavy brocade draperies.

"I hope you do not mind sharing these chambers," she called out as she worked, "the north wing is still being reno-vated, and it will be quite the crush with so many of our guests wishing to stay the night." Turning back to them, she offered a knowing smile, adding, "As newlyweds, I thought you would be the least likely to complain about having to double up."

Elizabeth could feel the heat rising to her cheeks, and quickly glanced at her husband. Although his expression remained impassive, she could see him tense.

"Of course," he answered evenly. "We are grateful for your hospitality."

"Good. I have already had your things brought up." Turning to Elizabeth, she added, "Darcy wrote that you would not be bringing your maid or valet. And while I am certain my nephew can manage on his own, you will want someone to help you dress and to do your hair. I will send one of my own maids to assist you."

"Thank you, your ladyship. That is very kind."

"Nonsense. There is no need to thank me. Indeed, I feel that I should be thanking you. I have no doubt you are the reason my nephew is here, and for that, you have my gratitude."

And with one last cryptic smile, she swept from the room.

⁓

When the door closed behind his aunt, Darcy turned to face Elizabeth. She looked somewhat discomposed, but whether that was due to his aunt's words, or the fact that they found themselves alone in a bedchamber, was difficult to know.

"Forgive me," he began, "I had not anticipated... I should have written to my aunt requesting separate chambers."

Elizabeth shrugged lightly. "It is not entirely unexpected that she would assume..." she blushed a soft pink before lowering her gaze.

"Well, in any case, you need not concern yourself," he replied. "The house is vast, with a large number of parlors. I will have no trouble finding a place to spend the night. I shall simply use this room to dress, otherwise, the bedchamber is yours."

"That is not—"

"It is."

Elizabeth flinched at his gruff tone, and Darcy gentled his voice. "Pray, do not concern yourself. It is no trouble. Now, I will leave you to rest and prepare for the ball. I shall return in two hours' time, if you think that will be sufficient?"

Elizabeth nodded, and before he could change his mind, Darcy turned on his heel and headed for the door.

After leaving Elizabeth, Darcy returned to the floor below, eventually locating his uncle and the viscount in the billiards room. The three men passed an amiable hour before separating to prepare for the evening's festivities. There would be an early supper for those already in residence, which included the immediate family and some other acquaintances who had traveled from farther afield. Afterwards the rest of the guests would begin arriving, many of whom would remain until tomorrow, so as not to risk traveling on the icy roads in the dead of night. Darcy sighed. He was likely one of the few guests who would have preferred risking life and limb to avoid staying even one night at Briarwood. He had almost suggested it, but Elizabeth would have thought him mad. Besides, he did not wish to hurt his aunt and uncle.

Exiting the billiards room, Darcy checked his watch. It had only been an hour and a half since he had left Elizabeth. He would have to wait at least a little while longer before returning to their chambers. Walking along the corridor, he hesitated before a set of tall French doors, finally easing them open. Inside the library, a fire crackled merrily in the hearth, but the room was miraculously empty.

Crossing to the sideboard, Darcy helped himself to a large tumbler of his uncle's brandy before settling into one of the brushed-velvet chairs. He was still dreading the remainder of the evening, but was glad to have some time alone to mentally prepare himself for what was to follow.

He was also thankful that his aunt had placed them in the east wing. It was an area of the house he had rarely, if ever, visited as a child, so it was mercifully devoid of memories. But even here in the library, he found that he was not as uneasy as he had anticipated. Perhaps it was because the room had been redecorated since the last time he had been here—the deep green flocked wallpaper and heavy leather furnishings he remembered replaced with a lighter, brighter color palette—or perhaps it was simply that the details of the house were muted in his memory after all this time.

Either way, he was grateful.

Settling back into the comfortable chair, Darcy suddenly realized that, for the first time since the day of his wedding, he was content. His journey to Scarborough had gone better than he had any right to expect, and seeing Elizabeth's reaction to Jane's news had been all the reward he could have wanted. And now that Elizabeth no longer had Jane Bennet's welfare to worry about, he was certain the two of them could settle into the uncomplicated, cordial existence he had envisioned before he went away.

Yes, all he needed to do was to make it through the next four and twenty hours, and life could go back to normal for both of them.

Somewhere nearby, a clock struck the hour, and Darcy swallowed the last of his drink before setting the glass on a low table. Elizabeth should be finished dressing by now. At least he fervently hoped she was. It was difficult enough to be alone in a bedroom with her. Walking in on his wife in a state of dishabille would surely push him over the edge.

Returning to the chamber in the east wing, Darcy tentatively knocked on the door, breathing a sigh of relief when

Elizabeth's cheerful voice called out for him to enter. Pushing open the door, he crossed the threshold, and froze. Elizabeth stood before the looking glass, wearing a gown of the finest muslin. The fabric was a soft white, embroidered with golden threads that seemed to shimmer in the candlelight. It hugged her body to perfection, and was somehow simple yet stately all at the same time. Around her neck hung the small topaz cross she had worn on the day of their wedding.

Stepping farther into the room, Darcy suddenly wished he had thought to present her with some of his mother's jewels. There was one necklace in particular that he could remember his mother wearing to grand events. It was a mix of diamonds and pearls, and Darcy thought it would suit Elizabeth's gown particularly well. He could just imagine how the jewels would sparkle against her alabaster skin...

Elizabeth cleared her throat, and Darcy realized he was still staring at her with his mouth agape. Snapping his jaws shut, he advanced in her direction, offering a rigid bow.

"Good evening," he murmured.

Elizabeth smiled, stealing his breath. "Good evening."

"You look lovely."

"Thank you."

For the first time, Darcy noticed that a maid stood behind Elizabeth, putting the finishing touches to her dark hair, and felt an unexpected pang of remorse. He should not have insisted they leave their own servants behind. At the time, he had feared that the presence of Cassidy and Harris might have encouraged Elizabeth to suggest extending their stay. But it occurred to him now that she was likely nervous, and would have been more comfortable were she attended by her own abigail.

Shifting his weight, he watched as his aunt's maid inserted one last jeweled hairpin into Elizabeth's curls before stepping back to admire her work.

In front of the mirror, Elizabeth twisted her neck this way and that before clapping her hands together. "Oh, it is perfect! Thank you, Betsey. You have been a godsend. And you must thank Lady Matlock on my behalf for the hairpins."

The maid flushed, dropping a brief curtsy before darting a glance in Darcy's direction and hurrying from the room. When she had gone, Darcy came forward, peering more closely at the diamonds that sparkled in Elizabeth's dark tresses.

"My aunt sent you hairpins?" he asked, momentarily distracted.

Elizabeth nodded. "It was very kind of her."

"Did you mention wishing to borrow them?"

Elizabeth turned away from the glass, a small wrinkle between her brows. "Of course not." After a slight hesitation she added, "I have no idea why she sent them. Perhaps the maid who unpacked for me reported that my gown was only muslin and not silk and she felt it necessary to ensure that I was at least appropriately coiffed for the occasion."

Darcy frowned. "I am certain that is not the case. My aunt has obviously taken a liking to you. I am just surprised, that is all."

"Surprised that anyone in your family should take a liking to me?"

"No, of course not," he answered, reaching up to rub the back of his neck. "That was not what I... I only meant that it seems rather sudden. You had scarcely been introduced, that is all."

Elizabeth shrugged. "Well, whatever the reason, I am suitably grateful."

Darcy lowered his gaze. "Elizabeth... I am sorry for suggesting that Harris and Cassidy remain behind. I realize now that it was an imposition to ask you to come without your own maid to attend you."

Across from him, Elizabeth's brows rose in obvious surprise. "Do not be silly; it was no bother. Your aunt was very kind to send Betsey to me, but I could have managed most everything on my own. You forget that having a lady's maid is not what I have been accustomed to. When you share a maid with four sisters, you learn to make do if you ever want to arrive anywhere on time!"

Darcy gazed back at her, struck anew with admiration for Elizabeth's practical nature and her unwavering independence. He knew there were few ladies in his social circle who would not have seen the idea of traveling without their own personal attendant intolerable. He could only imagine how someone like Caroline Bingley would have reacted had anyone so much as broached the possibility.

With an easy smile, Elizabeth walked to the vanity, retrieving a pair of white silk mousquetaires and pulling them on.

"I suppose you will wish to dress," she began, reaching for a silk wrap and settling it around her shoulders. "I shall return to the withdrawing room. Hopefully I can locate it again without getting too hopelessly lost."

With a light laugh, she turned in the direction of the door, but Darcy halted her with his voice.

"If you would prefer, there is a small parlor at the end

of the corridor. You might wait for me there, and we can go down together. I will not be long."

A look of relief brightened Elizabeth's countenance and she quickly agreed, dropping a slight curtsy before slipping from the room, leaving Darcy to his thoughts.

Elizabeth made her way along the corridor until she reached the parlor Darcy had described. The door was open, and she quickly crossed the threshold, coming to a halt when she realized the room was already occupied.

"Oh! Forgive me, your ladyship. I had not realized anyone would be in here. I hope I am not intruding?"

The dowager marchioness set down her book, gazing at Elizabeth attentively.

"You are not. Had I wished for solitude, I would have remained in my apartment."

Elizabeth smiled, and Lady Wheaton beckoned her forward. "Come in, come in. There is a draft in the corridor, and you will catch a chill."

Stepping farther into the room, Elizabeth took a seat on a settee by the fire as Lady Wheaton continued, "As a matter of fact, I am very glad you should have found your way here. I had hoped to have a few minutes alone with you this evening."

"Your ladyship?"

Apparently choosing not to elaborate, Lady Wheaton's gaze swept Elizabeth's person, beginning at the hem of her gown and slowly rising to the top of her head.

"You look very well; your gown is stunning. I approve."

"Thank you. It was actually Miss Darcy who encouraged me to purchase the fabric. I was not certain about it… it is so… different."

The dowager marchioness narrowed her gaze, her lips forming a small smile. "Indian, I dare say. And you are correct, it is unconventional, to be sure. But then, that is what makes it special." She continued to study Elizabeth before leaning forward in her chair, her gaze fixed on the loose chignon at the base of Elizabeth's neck. "Are those my daughter's hairpins?"

Despite her best intentions, Elizabeth could feel her cheeks heat. "Yes, ma'am. Lady Matlock sent them to my room, along with a maid to fix my hair. I was quite surprised, but it seemed wrong to refuse to wear them."

Lady Wheaton nodded sagely before saying, "She approves of you."

Elizabeth could not help but smile, Lady Wheaton's assessment being so similar to her husband's.

"I am not certain she knows me well enough to approve or disapprove," she hedged.

"She does not need to know you. You have succeeded in getting Darcy to return to Briarwood. That in and of itself would be enough to earn you her regard. And mine." After a slight hesitation she added, "I imagine you noticed I was observing you in the parlor earlier."

"No, ma'am, not at all," Elizabeth murmured, briefly lowering her gaze as the dowager marchioness let out an amused chuckle.

"Do not take up gambling, my dear; you are a terrible liar. Your eyes are far too expressive."

Elizabeth flushed but deftly changed the subject. "What

makes you think I am responsible for my husband's attendance tonight?" she asked.

"Oh, there can be no doubt of that. There are two
things Darcy hates above all others: balls and Briarwood.
He has not stepped foot on the estate since Robert's
death; and yet, two months after marrying you, here
he is."

Elizabeth's blush deepened as Lady Wheaton continued, "Seeing the sway you obviously have over your
husband has only served to make us all the more curious
about you."

Not quite knowing how to respond, Elizabeth found
herself at a loss for words, but she need not have worried,
as Lady Wheaton seemed perfectly content to carry the
conversation.

"I must say it came as quite a shock to the family—
indeed to all of society—when we learned Darcy had
married."

"Yes, so I understand," Elizabeth said quietly. At Lady
Wheaton's raised brows, she added, "Colonel Fitzwilliam
said something similar when he was with us at Christmas."

"Ah. Yes, Richard spoke well of you, which was
enough to persuade us that you were not a fortune hunter."

Once again, Elizabeth felt her cheeks heat, but Lady
Wheaton waved away her embarrassment.

"Forgive me. As you can see, I am known for my
candor. I used to be more restrained, but there are some
advantages to being my age." Leaning back in her chair she
continued to eye Elizabeth speculatively. "You were right
to think I was studying you earlier. From what Richard told
me at Christmas, I believe we have a good deal in
common."

She paused, and Elizabeth, whose curiosity was piqued by such a statement, waited anxiously for her to continue.

"I did not come to my title in the usual way, although, like you, my late husband's family was above my own in social standing. His father was a marquess, but Frederick was also a second son, intended for the church. When we married, I had envisioned a comfortable, if somewhat humdrum life as a parson's wife. I never dreamt I would one day call myself a marchioness."

"What happened?"

"His brother was killed—in a duel, no less—three years after we were married. Like you, I was unprepared for the life I was thrust into, and while most young ladies would have been euphoric about such a change in circumstances, I was unhappy at having so much responsibility heaped upon my shoulders. It took a good year, possibly longer, for me to come to terms with my new life, and for those members of the first circles to accept me as one of their own. In truth, there are some who never have, but that suited me well enough. I had my husband, and later my children, and I have been happy." After a moment, she added, "Besides all that, I have had Darcy and Georgiana, who are as dear to me as if they were my own. They have seen more than their share of heartache, and it has been a source of pride to have been able to be of service to them over the years."

"Yes, I could see downstairs in the drawing room that you and my husband are close."

"Indeed, we are. His mother, Lady Anne, was like another daughter to me. She and Cecilia were at school together, and it was Anne who introduced my daughter to Henry, that is, Lord Matlock. Such a tragedy, all that she suffered…"

A soft rapping upon the open door drew both ladies' attention as Darcy entered, an unreadable expression in his dark eyes.

"Melanie, I did not expect to find you here. I hope I am not interrupting?"

The dowager marchioness rose, shaking out her skirts, and Elizabeth did likewise.

"No, not at all," Lady Wheaton answered. "Elizabeth and I were just getting better acquainted. But now that you are here, let us go down. It is nearly time for supper, and if we are not quick about it, Stratford will help himself to all the choicest dishes."

Chapter 14

M r. Darcy escorted Elizabeth and Lady Wheaton to the dining parlor where a light repast had been set out for the family and close friends who had arrived early for the ball. Elizabeth's eyes widened as she took in the long table laden with more delicacies than she could ever remember seeing at one meal.

Darcy briefly excused himself to seat his godmother, as Elizabeth lingered near the door, surveying the silver platters heaped with haunches of venison and other cold game, imported cheeses and freshly baked bread, colorful salads, baskets overflowing with fresh fruits, and a variety of cakes and other sweet confections.

"Quite a spread, is it not?" a deep masculine voice said at her shoulder. "But still nothing to the real supper that will be served later tonight. Mother always outdoes herself at these events."

Elizabeth started, turning to face the gentleman who had come up beside her. Although they had not yet been introduced, his resemblance to Colonel Fitzwilliam left little doubt about his identity. However, before she could formulate a reply, Darcy returned, performing the introductions.

"Stratford. Allow me to present my wife. Elizabeth, this is my cousin Andrew, Lord Stratford."

Elizabeth dropped a polite curtsy, but to her surprise, the viscount merely grinned, taking her gloved hand and lifting it to his lips.

"Charmed. I will own, you could have knocked me over with a feather when I heard Darcy had tied the knot. And now you have succeeded in dragging him to Briarwood. No wonder you have Mamma eating out of your hand."

Elizabeth was saved from having to respond by Lady Matlock herself, who entered the room on the arm of a distinguished gentleman of middle years.

"Andrew, whatever are you on about?" she said, moving to stand beside their party.

"Oh, nothing of consequence. Mrs. Darcy and I were just discussing the fine table you have laid out here. I was telling her this is nothing to the meal we shall have later. Pray tell, what is on the menu this evening? Turtle soup? Oysters on the half shell? Sautéed asparagus?" Turning to Elizabeth he added, "Mother always makes a point of serving a supper filled with aphrodisiacs at her Saint Valentine's Day ball."

"And why should I not?" countered Darcy's aunt. "It is an evening intended to celebrate love, after all." Shifting her attention to Elizabeth, she indicated the silver-haired gentleman by her side. "Elizabeth, allow me to present my husband, Henry, Lord Matlock."

Elizabeth smiled amiably, and she and the earl exchanged polite greetings. Although his expression was not unkind, she noted that he did not project the same warmth or geniality as his wife or his two sons, and Elizabeth could not help but think that perhaps this was where her husband came by his standoffishness.

The party made their way to the table where Darcy pulled out her chair. As this was an intimate gathering of mostly family, the seating arrangements were informal, and Elizabeth found herself near the head of the table, with her husband on one side of her and the viscount on the other. Across from them, Lord Matlock sat beside the dowager marchioness.

"Now, Darcy," said Lady Matlock, once they had all filled their plates, "I intend to have you dance this evening. None of this skulking about on the periphery of the room as you are usually wont to do."

Elizabeth lifted her napkin to smother a smile, while furtively glancing at her husband. A slight frown wrinkled his brow, but he nodded courteously.

"Of course. I am looking forward to it, Aunt."

"Good." Turning to regard Elizabeth, she continued, "When it comes to dancing, there are only two rules for my Valentine's Day ball: First, all married gentlemen *must* dance both the supper set and the last set of the evening with their wives. And second," she paused here, turning to regard her nephew—who appeared more than a little relieved—before continuing, "they must choose a partner *other than their wives* to open the ball."

Elizabeth looked at Darcy openly now to see how he took the news, but to her surprise, he merely nodded before turning to address his godmother.

"In that case, Melanie, may I have the pleasure of the first set? That is, if you are not already engaged?"

Across from them, the dowager marchioness chuckled.

"My dance card remains open. The first set is yours, if you think you can keep up with me."

Stratford barked out a laugh, as Lady Matlock cleared her throat, looking pointedly at her husband who immediately turned to Elizabeth.

"Mrs. Darcy, might I solicit your hand for the first set?"

"It would be an honor, sir."

The viscount then hurried to ask his mother for the dance, and was accepted, before the conversation turned to other topics.

When the clock struck the hour, Lord and Lady Matlock rose. They would now prepare to receive their guests in the front hall, while the remainder of the party made their way to the ballroom.

Darcy assisted Elizabeth to her feet, and they moved to follow the flow of guests from the dining parlor. When they reached the corridor, the party in front of them—the dowager marchioness, who was deep in conversation with one of her granddaughters—turned right, but the viscount, who was standing at Darcy's other side, motioned to the left.

"Come, we can cut through the music room. Avoid the crush."

Darcy nodded, following his cousin down another passageway and shepherding Elizabeth through an open door into an elegant chamber. Elizabeth glanced around. The room was spacious and well-appointed, but the décor was more ornate than she was accustomed to. While the instruments within were every bit as fine as the ones at Pemberley, the space itself did not feel nearly as cozy or inviting, and Elizabeth once again had cause to be pleased with her own home by comparison.

She was so caught up in her thoughts, she had hardly noticed that they had crossed into an arched antechamber which connected the music room with the ballroom next door. The viscount moved aside to let them pass, but as soon as they stepped into the vestibule, his voice rang out in the small space.

"Stop right there."

Darcy drew to a halt, turning to the viscount who tipped up his chin, his eyes focused on the ceiling. Elizabeth and Darcy followed his gaze as Lord Stratford offered them an arch smile.

"You did not think my mother would host a Saint Valentine's Day ball without a kissing bough, did you? Always puts it in the same spot, too. This way the couples who wish to steer clear may easily avoid it, and the ones who are eager to steal a kiss know exactly where to go." He grinned wickedly. "Dear Mamma. She is nothing if not predictable."

Elizabeth turned to her husband, noticing that his frown had changed to a scowl.

Beside them, the viscount chuckled. "Oh, come now, Darcy. Do not be such a stick-in-the-mud. I know how you abhor public displays, but certainly you cannot object to kissing your own wife."

Her husband's eyes found hers, and Elizabeth felt herself flush under the intensity of his gaze. For a moment he remained still, as if considering the situation. Then, slowly, his hands came up to rest firmly but gently on the bare skin just above her gloves. Elizabeth's breath hitched as he lowered his head until his mouth was only inches from hers. Her eyes fluttered closed, and seconds later she felt the soft press of his lips against her own.

A current rippled up Elizabeth's spine, but before she could fully make sense of the sensation, her husband straightened, and Elizabeth's eyes opened to find him staring back at her impassively.

Beside them, the viscount offered a dramatic sigh. "Ever the gentleman."

Darcy ignored him, saying to Elizabeth, "We should go in."

Feeling a bit light-headed, she allowed her husband to lead her through to the ballroom, which was already beginning to fill.

Glancing around, Elizabeth's pulse quickened with excitement as she took in the elaborate decorations that included potted plants, hothouse flowers, and enough candles to make the entire space shimmer like spun gold. On a dais near the windows, a large orchestra was playing a lively tune, as liveried servants threaded their way through the crowd with silver trays of iced punch and champagne.

Moving through the growing throng on her husband's arm, Elizabeth's head swiveled this way and that, taking in the spectacle and making mental notes which she hoped would allow her to relate the entire experience to Jane in her next letter. As they progressed, Elizabeth could feel the eyes of people in the crowd tracking their progress, but Darcy seemed more at ease than she would have expected, stopping periodically to introduce her to those he was acquainted with.

Before long, the dancing commenced, and Darcy escorted his godmother to the floor as Elizabeth and Lord Matlock took up the place beside them.

True to his word, Darcy stood up with each of his female cousins, as well as his aunt, before retiring to converse with the viscount in a corner of the room. Elizabeth, however, danced every set. And although she enjoyed polite conversation with each of her partners, her eyes were routinely drawn to Mr. Darcy's tall form. She could not help but notice how well he looked in his formal attire, nor how gracefully he moved down the line during the sets in which he danced. In truth, she thought him the most handsome and elegant gentleman in the room, and for the first time since their marriage, she felt a strange sense of pride at being able to claim him as her husband.

Sometime later, after a spirited Scotch reel that left her breathless, Elizabeth allowed her partner to escort her to the edge of the room, where her husband was still in conversation with his cousin.

Darcy greeted her with cordial civility, but it was Lord Stratford's euphoric expression that caused her husband to turn on him suspiciously.

"Why do you look so gleeful, all of a sudden?" he asked, causing the viscount to respond with a roar of laughter.

"Am I that obvious? Well, if you must know, the supper set will be commencing shortly, and I have been waiting all evening to see you and your lovely bride take to the floor."

"How so?" Darcy asked, studying his cousin in obvious confusion. "If you have been eager to mock my dancing skills, you have had ample opportunity, as I have danced four sets already."

"Yes. But this is the *supper set*."

Darcy frowned back at him. "And?"

"Oh! I keep forgetting; you never pay attention to idle gossip," he answered, a mischievous twinkle in his eye. "Mother has decided to shock society this year by playing a waltz for the supper set. The room has been buzzing about it all evening. And I dare say, watching you two taking part shall be the highlight of my night."

And with that, he offered a brief tilt of his head before sauntering off in the direction of the refreshments.

Shifting his gaze, Darcy turned to look at Elizabeth, his brow wrinkled in consternation.

"Forgive me, I did not realize... Have you ever danced a waltz before?"

Elizabeth stared at him, before slowly shaking her head. "I have never even been present at a ball where one was played. We are not so fashionable in Hertfordshire. Amongst our *unvarying society*, such a dance is still thought to be highly indecent."

Behind them, Elizabeth could already hear the musicians warming up on the dais.

"I see. So then, I assume you do not know the steps," Darcy mused, and Elizabeth hesitated, chewing the inside of her cheek.

"No, not exactly," she answered.

"Then you do know them?" he asked, his brow lifted in surprise.

Looking left and then right, she stepped closer to her husband, saying softly, "My Aunt Gardiner was at a ball last spring where a waltz was played. She taught my sisters and me the figures, and we used to practice together at Longbourn, but I have never attempted the dance in public, and certainly not with a gentleman."

To Elizabeth's surprise, Darcy looked vaguely amused. Leaning down, he replied in a conspiratorial tone, "Perhaps it has slipped your mind, but the gentleman in question happens to be your husband. Certainly, you cannot think people will disapprove?"

Elizabeth frowned as other couples moved past them, taking to the floor. Perhaps Mr. Darcy was correct. She was a married woman now, after all, not a young maiden. There could be nothing scandalous about dancing in such a manner with the gentleman one was married to, though now she had a better understanding of Lady Matlock's stricture about husbands dancing the supper set only with their wives.

She looked up, suddenly realizing that Darcy was still staring at her expectantly.

"You seem quite eager," she stalled, still unable to make up her mind. "I thought you did not even like to dance."

Darcy's lips tipped up at the corners as the first strains of Beethoven filled the air. "Perhaps I am changing my opinion."

The music began to swell, slow and hypnotic, and before she could think better of it, Elizabeth smiled back at him, tucking her hand into the crook of his arm.

"Well, if we are to dance, we had best take our places."

Elizabeth allowed her husband to lead her to the floor where the waltz was already underway. Gazing at the swirl of couples moving in perfect harmony, she was temporarily transfixed by the beauty of the dance. A moment later, Darcy's arm wrapped around her waist, and she felt the warm press of his palm against the small of her back as they joined the circle of dancers. Turning in his direction, she allowed her left hand to settle lightly on his right shoulder. They were still at least six inches apart, but the pose felt unspeakably intimate, and Elizabeth could feel a rush of heat creeping up her neck at the novel sensation of being held in such a familiar embrace.

However, before she could dwell on it further, Darcy stepped forward, and all thoughts flew from her mind as Elizabeth fixed her attention on following the movements of the dance. She worried briefly that she would embarrass herself, as she had only practiced the steps a handful of times, and never in a ballroom filled with other couples, but it soon became apparent that whatever skill she lacked, her husband more than made up for.

Mr. Darcy led as he did most things, with a quiet authority that put Elizabeth immediately at ease. He changed positions in a way that was natural and fluid, signaling in which direction he meant for them to go with a subtle tilt of his head, or the gentle pressure of his hand against her back. Before long, Elizabeth realized it was almost as though they had become one being, moving together in perfect unison. The room spun as the thrill of the dance took over, and a small laugh bubbled up her throat.

Darcy looked down at her, an answering smile brightening his features. "Enjoying yourself?" he asked.

"Oh, yes!" Elizabeth breathed. "It feels like flying!"

No sooner were the words out of her mouth than the couple dancing next to them careened in their direction, causing Darcy to tighten his hold, anchoring Elizabeth against his body as he swiftly pulled her out of the way. Elizabeth stumbled slightly at the abrupt shift in position, but Darcy effortlessly matched his steps to hers, continuing through the movements of the dance as if nothing out of the ordinary had occurred.

"Are you well?" he murmured against her ear when they were clear of the other couple, and Elizabeth nodded shakily. With their bodies now pressed together, she could feel the hard muscles of his chest as the vibration of his deep baritone reverberated through her body. Taking an uneven breath, she inhaled the subtle scent of shaving soap and starch, and her heart rate escalated. It briefly occurred to her that one of them should step back, as they were now dancing in what must be viewed as an indecently tight embrace, but for some reason neither of them altered their position, and they stayed as they were until the dance ended some minutes later.

The music ceased, and Darcy immediately stepped back, releasing his wife. Elizabeth stared up at him. Her cheeks were flushed a soft pink, and her eyes sparkled with laughter. God she was beautiful! For a moment he just stood there, transfixed by the picture she made, his body still reeling from the sensation of holding her in his arms. Other dancers drifted past them, making their way to the edges of the floor for a short respite before the musicians began the second dance in the set.

Pulling himself together, Darcy gently cupped Elizabeth's elbow, leading her to a corner of the room where the dowager marchioness sat with another matron.

"You two made quite a handsome couple out there," Lady Wheaton said, as soon as they arrived. "I trust you found the dance agreeable?"

"Oh, it was wonderful!" Elizabeth answered, laughter in her voice. "I have never danced a waltz before!"

Lady Wheaton's gaze shifted from Elizabeth to Darcy and back again, a slim smile playing at the corners of her lips.

Darcy cleared his throat, turning to his wife. "May I get you some refreshment? We should have a few more minutes before the next dance begins."

"Thank you, but no. I think I need only rest my feet. I have not sat out a dance yet."

Darcy nodded, saying to his godmother, "Melanie? How about you? Some punch?"

"Yes, thank you, Fitzwilliam. I could do with some refreshment; however, I believe I will accompany you. I have been sitting too long in one attitude, and shall relinquish my seat to your wife."

Lady Wheaton stood, and Darcy offered her his arm as Elizabeth slipped into the seat she had vacated.

Making their way through the crowd, Darcy was pulled from his thoughts of Elizabeth when his godmother spoke beside him.

"She has been watching you, you know."

"I beg your pardon?"

"Your wife. Elizabeth. Her eyes follow you, even when she is dancing with another. There is interest there, whether you believe it or not."

At Melanie's words, Darcy's heart pounded as he attempted to school his features. "I am afraid I do not have the pleasure of understanding you," he said stiffly.

"Oh, but I think you do."

They had reached the refreshment table and Darcy stepped forward, accepting a cup from one of the footmen.

After handing the libation to Lady Wheaton, the two moved to a quiet corner where they could converse with some degree of privacy.

"You are in love with her," the dowager marchioness said simply, taking a sip of her drink. "And you are grieved because you do not believe she returns your feelings."

Darcy started, struggling to compose his features. His godmother had always been known for her perception, but he was not prepared to have anyone speak to him so candidly, nor did he have any intention of discussing his marriage.

"People wed for many different reasons," he answered carefully.

"Yes, yes. *People* do all sorts of irrational things, especially when it comes to marriage. They wed for money, for connections, for social standing. But we are speaking about you. And you did not marry Elizabeth for any of those reasons."

Darcy looked away, his jaw tight. "No."

When he said no more, his godmother regarded him with interest, before taking another swallow from her cup. "It can be difficult to find oneself in a marriage of unequal affection. Believe me, I know."

Instantly, Darcy's eyebrows rose. "You?" he asked incredulously. "I always thought yours was a love match."

"Oh, it was. But it did not start out that way."

"Ah. The marquess did not... that is..." Darcy felt his cheeks color and his godmother laughed at his discomfort.

"No, my dear. Frederick was not the problem. I was." At Darcy's look of surprise, she continued, "I fancied myself in love with another, but he was not of our station, and my father refused to consider the match. Frederick Rice was the second son of a marquess. His family was titled and ours was not. He was kind, but dull, or so I thought at the time."

"But you agreed to marry him anyway?"

"I suppose you could say so. That is, I did not lock myself in my chambers or steal away in the night. Barring that, there was very little I could have said or done to prevent it. My father agreed, and so it was settled.

"What changed? Did you come to feel more for him once he inherited the title?"

Lady Wheaton shook her head, staring back at him with a lively expression. "Goodness, you do think well of me. No. I fell in love with him long before that. As it turns out, I was completely mistaken about Frederick's character. What I had taken for tedium and monotony, in fact, turned out to be steadiness and stability, and a passionate nature he showed to no one but me. As I came to know him better, my feelings began to alter. But most importantly, he loved me, and he never missed an opportunity to tell me so.

"Still, it took time. Time for me to learn to be a good wife, and for Frederick to learn to be a good husband." Handing her empty glass to a passing servant, she paused, studying Darcy with an inscrutable expression. "You are very like him, you know. And you are proud; all the Fitzwilliams are. But heed my advice. Do not let your pride keep you from expressing your true feelings. All living things need nourishment to grow. A flower will not bloom in the darkness."

Across the room, the musicians had returned to the dais and the air soon filled with the sound of the violinists tuning their instruments.

Next to him, his godmother smiled. "But enough of that

for now. It is time for your next dance, and we should not keep your lovely Elizabeth waiting any longer."

The following quarter of an hour passed in a blur. The second dance was also a waltz, and Elizabeth found that she enjoyed this one even more than the first. Embracing her husband did not feel quite so awkward as it had before, and she soon became more confident in her execution of the steps. Darcy seemed pensive, and was quieter than usual, but Elizabeth did not mind as she was swept up in the music and the beauty of her surroundings. When the dance ended, Darcy once again took her elbow as the company adjourned to the supper-tables. To Elizabeth's surprise, there were no less than four dining parlors in use, but Darcy escorted her to the largest of the lot, where the immediate family would take their meal.

Inside the room, the tables were covered with the finest French linens and lavishly decorated with silver candelabras, flowers, ornate tremblents, and raised frames topped with fresh pineapples. The effect was grand in the extreme, and Elizabeth could not prevent the small gasp that escaped her throat as they entered the room.

Darcy looked down at her with a sardonic smile. "My aunt does not do things by half measures," he murmured, and Elizabeth laughed.

"No, I should say not!"

They proceeded to a pair of vacant seats at the far side of a long table, and Darcy pulled out Elizabeth's chair. Although her experience with private balls was limited, the few she had attended usually featured a buffet supper of white soup, lobster patties, and cold meats and cheeses, but she was surprised to see that Lady Matlock had planned an extravagant hot supper smartly served by dozens of footmen in navy-blue livery.

The meal was laid out *à la française*, and Elizabeth's eyes grew round as she stared down the table. Roast fowls, sliced ham, lobster, ragout of veal, crayfish in jelly, tartlets, and raised game pies were all elegantly displayed on gleaming platters. In addition to the savory dishes, there were savoy cakes, blancmange, meringues, orange custard, as well as an abundance of fresh fruits and other assorted confectionaries.

As soon as Elizabeth was seated, a footman filled her glass with wine, and she took a small swallow. She would have to be careful not to overeat, nor to indulge in too much drink, lest it go to her head.

The meal began with sturgeon smothered in black truffles and was followed with a negus ice that was so delicious, it took all of Elizabeth's willpower not to lick the last droplets from the dish.

The next remove consisted of a turtle soup unlike any Elizabeth had ever tasted. As Darcy was engaged in conversation with his cousin Eleanor, who was seated at his other side, Elizabeth turned to the woman on her right, a Mrs. Keating, who had been introduced to her as one of Lady Matlock's oldest friends.

"This soup is superb," Elizabeth began. "Our cook makes a version that is also very fine, but I have never tasted a turtle soup quite like this one."

Mrs. Keating nodded in agreement. "Oh, yes. Cecilia's chef is a wonder. French, you know. The man puts sherry in everything. No doubt that is what makes it all taste so good."

Taking another spoonful of the rich broth, Elizabeth smiled. "I shall have to remember to give Lady Matlock my compliments. Goodness, if all the dishes are as good as what we have had already, I do not know how I shall have the energy for dancing the remainder of the sets!"

Lifting her glass, Elizabeth took another sip of wine, surprised to realize she suddenly felt somewhat light-headed. *How strange! I certainly cannot have drunk so much as to be inebriated,* she thought, staring at her half-full goblet.

Returning to her soup, she attempted to listen to what Mrs. Keating was saying to her—something about a trip she had taken to Paris—but in truth, it was becoming increasingly difficult to concentrate.

Elizabeth finished her soup, carefully setting her spoon on the edge of her plate. There was an odd tingling in the back of her throat, and the palms of her hands were beginning to prickle. Staring down at her empty bowl, her heart began to beat a faster rhythm as realization slowly dawned. Moving her hands to her lap, she surreptitiously ran the tips of her fingers over the opposite palm. As she suspected, she could feel a scattering of tiny raised bumps at the base of her wrist.

As if sensing her disquiet, Darcy leaned towards her in his chair.

"Is anything the matter?" he murmured, before lifting his wine glass and smiling at his cousin Alice, who was seated across the table.

"My palms are beginning to itch," Elizabeth whispered

back, already tugging on the mousquetaires that had been resting beneath her napkin.

"Is it the gloves? Have you worn them before?"

Elizabeth shook her head. "'Tis not the gloves. I think it is the soup."

Darcy's brow furrowed. "I do not understand."

Elizabeth opened her mouth to speak, but a wave of nausea washed over her, and she could feel beads of perspiration gathering along her hairline. Fighting to retain her composure, she turned her head, saying softly, "There must have been some sort of shellfish in the soup. I need to leave the table. I am going to be ill."

The thought of causing a commotion in front of Darcy's closest relations made Elizabeth shudder, but it was nothing compared to the notion of casting up her accounts all over Lady Matlock's imported linen tablecloth. She made to stand, but before she could so much as push back her chair, Darcy was on his feet. All eyes swiveled in his direction as conversations around the room slowly ground to a halt.

"Pray, forgive me, Aunt, but I feel the beginnings of one of my megrims. I believe I must seek my chambers."

Lady Matlock paled. "Oh, dear! Yes, of course. I shall send a footman to fetch some powders."

"No, that will not be necessary. I simply need to lie down. Elizabeth, might I ask you to accompany me?"

Elizabeth managed to nod, pressing her lips together as her stomach churned. Before she knew what was happening, Darcy had her on her feet, her arm secured tightly in his. A footman moved to open the door as they swiftly made their way across the room. Behind them, conversation resumed, and Elizabeth could hear Lady Matlock speaking to one of the guests in a subdued tone.

"He suffers terrible headaches. Has ever since that autumn. It is not surprising that being back here—"

The door closed, and Elizabeth heard no more. Turning her attention to tamping down her nausea, she allowed Darcy to propel her along a wide passageway.

"Can you make it to our chambers?" he asked quietly. "Or shall I bring you to the ladies retiring room instead? It is just through those doors."

Gathering her strength, Elizabeth shook her head. There would be a maid stationed in the retiring room, and possibly other guests as well. As if reading her thoughts, Darcy nodded. Wrapping his arm securely around her waist, he steered her in the opposite direction, opening a heavy oak door that led to a narrow set of steps.

"The servants' stairs," he said, and Elizabeth breathed a sigh of relief. If they did not reach their room before the inevitable occurred, at least she would not have to worry about making a public display on the grand staircase.

Leaning heavily on her husband, she turned her thoughts inward, focusing on taking short, shallow breaths. *You can do this, Lizzy. You will not make a spectacle of yourself in front of Mr. Darcy.* When they reached the first landing, Darcy stopped to look at her, and Elizabeth closed her eyes, borrowing support from the wall beside her.

"Are you able to keep going?" she heard him ask.

Elizabeth did not answer, but she opened her eyes and attempted to climb the subsequent set of stairs. She must have stumbled, because the next thing she knew, her husband had slipped one arm beneath her knees, gently scooping her up. Elizabeth moaned, burying her head in the soft folds of his coat. She was certain the jostling motion of being carried would make things worse, but Darcy kept her anchored against his body, ascending the remainder of the steps with long, easy strides. Finally, she heard the creak of a door being pushed open and the ground evened out as they stepped into the upstairs passageway, but she kept her eyes closed until they came to a halt and her husband released his hold, gently setting her on her feet before the door to their apartment.

For a moment, the world tilted, and she was barely aware of Mr. Darcy lifting the latch and shepherding her across the threshold. She expected he would leave her then, but instead, he closed the door behind them, turning to look down at her with obvious concern.

"Shall I call for a physician?"

Keeping her jaws clamped tightly shut, Elizabeth shook her head. There was no need for a doctor. She knew from past experience that once her stomach was emptied, the worst would be over.

Taking a breath, she attempted to gather her thoughts. She knew she should thank Mr. Darcy for his kindness, but she was afraid to so much as open her lips. Once again, she closed her eyes, concentrating on calming her churning stomach. If she could just get herself under control so that she could say a civil word to her husband and walk with some degree of dignity to the adjoining dressing room where there was a chamber pot and a wash basin... but it was not to be. They had scarcely entered their chambers when Elizabeth realized she was losing her battle, and, without a backwards glance, she turned away from Mr. Darcy and bolted from the room.

～

Much later, Elizabeth found herself lying in a heap on the cold marble floor. She could not say how long she had been hunched over the chamber pot in the compact bathing room, but it felt like hours. Slowly drawing her knees up to her chest, she curled against a nearby wall, pressing her shoulder to the hard surface as her body trembled. Reaching for the edge of the large copper tub, she used it to pull herself unsteadily to her feet, before taking in her appearance in the looking glass that stood in the corner of the room.

To her dismay, her once-beautiful muslin gown was now damp with sweat and wrinkled beyond repair, and most of her hair had escaped its pins, leaving long spirals cascading over her shoulders and down her back. Drawing in an uneven breath, she made her way to the wash basin, splashing cool water on her face and neck before rinsing her mouth.

Thank heavens Mr. Darcy had left immediately after doing his duty and escorting her to their apartment. She had heard the click of the latch as soon as she had gained the solitude of the bathing room. Even in her misery, she had felt an enormous sense of relief at having been spared the indignity of her husband witnessing such a humiliating display. At least there was that one small mercy to be thankful for.

Staring down at the polished floor beneath her feet, she wondered if it might be safe to return to the bedchamber. Though she suspected she would need a chamber pot close at hand for the remainder of the night, her body was exhausted, and she longed for the comfort of her bed—not to mention someone to assist her with removing her gown and stays, which were making her stomach feel worse.

She was just contemplating the wisdom of ringing for a maid, when the creaking of a floorboard on the opposite side of the door caused her entire body to go rigid with alarm. Had someone entered her chambers in the time she had been holed up in the small room?

Slowly moving towards the door, she pressed her ear to the thick panel and listened, but the noise had ceased.

Perhaps it is one of the maids, come to lay the fire, she thought. For all she knew, the ball might be over by now.

But surely she would have heard a maid knock before entering... and laying the fire would have entailed a great deal more noise. Elizabeth held her breath until she finally heard another soft creak, as if someone stood just outside the door, shifting their weight.

Closing her eyes, she pressed her palms to the smooth wood, and when at last she spoke, her voice was a low croak.

"Mr. Darcy?"

"Yes?"

The reply was immediate, and far too close for comfort.

Elizabeth's shoulders sank as mortification seeped into every fiber of her being. Reaching for the latch, she cracked the door open.

There, on the other side, stood her husband, still impeccably dressed, a small furrow between his dark brows.

"I thought you left," she whispered.

"I did. But only to make a brief trip to the kitchens. How are you feeling?"

Her misery and mortification momentarily forgotten; Elizabeth gaped back at him in confusion. "You went to the kitchens?"

Darcy nodded. "I did not know what would be best, but

I brought some plain biscuits and a pot of ginger-root tea. Mrs. Reynolds always makes it for my sister when her stomach is unsettled."

Elizabeth blinked back at him, as he continued, "Does it surprise you that I know where the kitchens are located? I should. I spent enough time nicking food from them when I was a boy. Or are you to reprimand me for not following my own strictures about entering the servant's domain without invitation or warning? If the latter, I can assure you I sent a footman to speak to the cook in advance of my going down."

Elizabeth shook her head, leaning heavily against the door jamb as her knees suddenly threatened to give out. "I assure you, sir, that was not my intention. I am in no condition to reprimand anyone at present."

Immediately, Darcy came forward, wrapping his arm around her shoulders and guiding her farther into the room. "Forgive me," he said, "I should not have kept you here talking when you are still so unwell."

Leading her to an upholstered bench at the foot of the bed, he helped her to sit before saying, "You should change into your nightclothes. Shall I fetch a maid?" he asked uncertainly. "The one who assisted you earlier, perhaps? I do not recall her name…"

"Betsey. But, no. If the ball is still going on, I am certain she must be needed elsewhere. I think I can manage if you would only undo the buttons at the back of my gown and untie my stays?"

Darcy's cheeks colored, and Elizabeth knew she should feel some degree of embarrassment at suggesting such a thing, but she was exhausted beyond caring, and he was her husband, after all. Besides, she did desperately wish to change out of her gown. The tightness of her stays was not helping her queasiness.

Although he would not meet her eye, Mr. Darcy offered her a single nod, and Elizabeth turned her back. She felt the dip of the cushion as he took a seat behind her. Drawing a shallow breath, she waited for what seemed like an eternity before she felt his fingers, warm and gentle as they brushed against her skin.

A chill shot up her spine, and Elizabeth suspected it had little to do with the temperature of the room.

She felt the fabric of her gown loosening, and seconds later the pressure around her middle eased as Darcy began unfastening her stays. Relief coursed through her as she inhaled again, feeling instantly better.

Behind her, Darcy cleared his throat. "Where is your nightdress?"

With one hand gripping the bodice of her gown, Elizabeth tilted her chin in the direction of the rosewood chest on the far side of the room. "The top drawer. On the left-hand side."

Darcy rose, returning in a matter of minutes with the neatly folded gown. His eyes veered away, and he shifted on his feet.

"Shall I…?"

"No. I will only be a moment."

Clutching the garment to her chest, Elizabeth stood, making her way back to the small bathing room. When she returned to the bedchamber, Darcy was facing the fireplace, clearly intent on giving her what little privacy he could. Gratefully, Elizabeth scurried to the large four-poster bed, peeling back the counterpane and slipping between the cool, crisp sheets. At the rustling of the bedclothes, Darcy turned to face in her direction.

"Are you feeling any better?" he finally asked.

Elizabeth risked a brief nod. "Yes, a little."

"Good. I am glad." After a pause, he added, "Are you absolutely certain I should not fetch a doctor?"

"Yes, I believe the worst is over. Now, I only need rest." She was quiet before continuing, "Mr. Darcy, I—"

"Forgive me, but—"

They both spoke at once, then stopped.

Again, Darcy cleared his throat. "Pray, continue."

"Oh. I… I only wished to apologize. I never presumed you would return to our chambers after…" Elizabeth's cheeks burned as she continued, "well, knowing that I was about to be… ill."

Across from her, Darcy's brow furrowed. "You are apologizing for being ill? Elizabeth, do you think I have never seen anyone throw up their dinner?"

"Well, n-no," she stammered in embarrassment. "Still it is… unpleasant. You should not have had to…" She lowered her gaze as Darcy came to stand closer to the bed.

"Elizabeth, life is filled with things that are truly unpleasant; this is not one of them. As far as I am concerned, any person who would turn their back on someone in need of care, simply because their delicate sensibilities might be offended, is a poor excuse for a human being."

"Thank you," Elizabeth murmured. "Not only for taking such good care of me, but for drawing everyone's attention to yourself when we left the dining room." After a moment, she added, "Do you really get megrims?"

Darcy nodded. "Sometimes."

A sudden chill made Elizabeth's body tremble, and Darcy instantly sobered.

"We need not speak any further now. You must rest and try to regain your strength."

Elizabeth nodded, moving to slide beneath the covers when a frisson of alarm caused her once again to sit bolt upright in the bed.

"The hairpins!" Her fingers flew to her hair, searching through the thick curls. "Are they still there? Oh, what will your aunt say if I have lost any of them? They must cost a fortune!"

"Shh… Elizabeth, pray, do not upset yourself," Darcy soothed, coming to sit at the edge of the bed. "They are only hairpins."

"Diamond hairpins! If any of them are missing—"

"Then I will replace them. Here, let me see."

Obediently, Elizabeth turned her head, and after a short hesitation she felt her husband's strong, sure fingers gently probing what was left of her elaborate coiffure.

"Do you see them?" she asked breathlessly. "There are six altogether."

"Yes, they all seem to be in place." A light tug and then another followed as Mr. Darcy gently pulled each of the precious jewels from her tangled locks.

"There, last one," he said at length. "All present and accounted for."

Darcy stood, and Elizabeth shifted to face him, her entire body going slack with relief.

"Thank goodness. There is a case for them, there, on the dressing table."

Darcy crossed the room, returning the jewels to their proper place before coming back to the bed.

"What about the rest of the pins?" he asked. "Would you be more comfortable if I removed those as well?"

Elizabeth stared back at him in surprise. In truth, she knew she could likely take the ordinary pins out herself, as she was not worried about dropping them or leaving any behind... but the feeling of her husband's hands in her hair had been inordinately pleasant, and so she found herself offering him a slow nod. "If it is not too much trouble...?"

Darcy returned to her side, once again taking a seat on the bed and setting to work. Slowly, Elizabeth's dark curls tumbled around her shoulders as the remainder of the pins were removed one by one.

"Better?" he asked quietly when he had finished.

"Yes, thank you."

Once again, Elizabeth slipped beneath the covers, watching as he set the simple wire pins on the dressing table beside the velvet box. When he came back to stand beside her, Elizabeth gazed up at him sleepily.

"Can I get you anything?" he asked quietly. "Some of the tea, perhaps?"

Elizabeth shook her head. Her stomach was feeling significantly better since she had emptied it, but she would prefer not to take any chances.

"Very well. I shall place it here by the bed in case you change your mind during the night."

He turned in the direction of the table where he had left the teapot, and Elizabeth allowed her eyelids to drift closed. She could hear him set down the cup and saucer, and then the soft creak of the floorboards as he moved away. She thought to open her eyes so she might bid him a good night and thank him again for his kindness, but the lure of sleep was too strong.

After that, she remembered nothing.

~

Slowly, Elizabeth opened her eyes, blinking against the soft gray light filtering into the room through the crack in the curtains. Pulling herself up against the pillows, she stared across the room, suddenly realizing she was not alone. There, curled into an armchair by the fireplace, Mr. Darcy slumbered, his head resting awkwardly against his shoulder.

Elizabeth sat up straighter in the bed. The rustling of the covers seemed to rouse Darcy to wakefulness, for he suddenly startled, opening his eyes and blinking back at her.

"You are still here," Elizabeth said softly.

Lifting one hand to massage his neck, Darcy offered her a slow nod. "Forgive me, I know I told you I would find another place, but I could not very well leave you alone when you were so ill. I had intended to ask if you would prefer that I fetch a maid, but you fell asleep before I had the chance."

"No, I would not have wanted you to inconvenience a maid… that is, I am glad you stayed."

Again, Darcy nodded, rising stiffly to his feet and coming closer to the bed. "How are you feeling this morning?"

"Much better."

"Good. I am relieved to hear it. I will go fetch a fresh pot of tea, and some breakfast if you think you are well enough to eat. I will also inform my aunt that we will need to trespass on her hospitality for a while longer."

"Oh, no! That will not be necessary. I know you wished to return to Pemberley, and as I said, I am feeling much improved. If I am correct and my indisposition was caused by something I ate, the worst is over."

"Ah, yes, forgive me. I did not have the opportunity to tell you last night, but you were correct in assuming it was the soup. I inquired when I went down to the kitchens. The cook used lobster to make the stock."

"Well, then, there is almost certainly no cause for alarm. Whenever I have had a similar reaction in the past, I have been restored to good health once the food has been purged from my stomach. I am only a bit tired now."

Darcy stared back at her dubiously, causing Elizabeth to force a shallow smile. "Truly, I only wish to go home. I will feel infinitely better once I am back at Pemberley, and I see no reason to distress your aunt and uncle."

"Well, if you are certain... Though I would still feel better if you were to see a physician before we left."

Swinging her legs over the side of the bed, Elizabeth replied, "I shall make a bargain with you. If we return to Pemberley and I am still feeling unwell, I will give you leave to send for a physician first thing tomorrow. Will that suit?"

Across from her, her husband sighed, but eventually agreed, leaving to tell the coachman to prepare the carriage, while Elizabeth went to ring for a maid, feeling better than she had in a very long time.

Chapter 15

Upon Darcy's orders, the carriage moved at a slow and steady pace towards home. Turning away from the fogged glass, he gazed across the compartment at Elizabeth's sleeping form. There was slightly more color in her cheeks, but she still looked drawn, and there were dark circles beneath her eyes. Nevertheless, it was a vast improvement over her appearance the previous evening. When she had opened the door to the bathing chamber and he had seen her before him, barely able to stand, her fair skin almost translucent in the candlelight, he had been truly frightened. More frightened than he could ever remember being in the entirety of his adult life.

Even now, the thought of what might have happened sent a shiver of terror down his spine. Although Elizabeth had been quick to assure him that she had suffered similar symptoms in the past, Darcy had learned at a young age that life could never be taken for granted. What if it had been more serious than she suspected? After all, what did any of them know about the poisonous effects of food on the body? If he had lost her...

Just thinking about it made his blood run cold. To imagine her bright light extinguished... No, it was impossible. He simply could not conceive of a world without Elizabeth in it.

Turning once again to stare out at the passing countryside, he thought back to that morning when she had asked to go home. Knowing that she had come to regard Pemberley as her home had filled him with an unexpected surge of joy, but that elation had been short-lived. Oh, certainly he was grateful that she had found some measure of contentment in her new life, but why should she not? Pemberley was a beautiful estate, and she had grown comfortable there. Being ill, in a strange place, it was only natural that she would wish to be somewhere familiar, somewhere safe. But that had nothing to do with him.

Sinking further into his seat, Darcy released a ragged breath. No, it had been irrational to think that Elizabeth could be truly happy at Pemberley—away from society and her friends and family and everything she loved best. Elizabeth was not made for isolation. She was too vibrant and spirited for such a confined way of life. She had been unhappy from the moment they arrived, and he had done nothing to make things easier for her.

In the years since his father's passing, he had become accustomed to a solitary existence, but it was different for Elizabeth. She came from a household bustling with activity. She was used to commotion and lively conversation. He had taken all that away from her, dragging her off to a large empty house with only himself for company. And it was destroying her.

No, Elizabeth needed excitement and intellectual stimulation to thrive. She was like a rare and beautiful creature he had removed from her natural habitat, only to find that by placing her in captivity, he had destroyed all the things that had made him love her in the first place.

As the thought echoed inside his head, a groan escaped his lips as he finally accepted what he had attempted to conceal from himself since the very beginning.

He loved her. Desperately. God, what a fool he had been, thinking he would be able to settle for a cordial, uncomplicated marriage with someone like Elizabeth.

Turning his thoughts back to his conversation with his godmother the previous evening, he shook his head. Ever perceptive, Melanie had guessed at his true feelings... indeed she had recognized them even before he was willing to admit them to himself.

But more than that, she seemed to believe Elizabeth might actually share those same sentiments...

"Her eyes follow you, even when she is dancing with another. There is interest there, whether you believe it or not."

But Melanie did not know the truth. She had not stepped onto that balcony at Netherfield to hear Jane Bennet enumerating in great detail exactly how much Elizabeth detested him.

No, Melanie had seen Elizabeth at her best—in company, laughing and effervescent and full of life. If Elizabeth had looked at him with anything resembling affection last night, it was merely gratitude for bringing her to Briarwood.

With a soft groan, Darcy allowed his head to fall back against the leather squabs. No, this time, Melanie was mistaken. Elizabeth did not love him. She would never care for him as he cared for her.

But to Darcy's surprise, he suddenly realized that it did

not matter. So long as she was alive and well and happy, he would be content.

And at least in that regard, there *was* something he could do. He could never give her back all he had taken from her, but he would find a way to make her happy— happier than she was now. He could not continue to keep her in a cage. He needed to give her her freedom, whatever the cost.

The following morning, Elizabeth made her way to the breakfast parlor at an accelerated pace. She had awoken in good spirits to find another missive from Mr. Darcy propped up upon her bedside table, the contents of which read:

> *Elizabeth,*
>
> *I hope you had an easy night. If you are feeling well-enough recovered, I would be pleased to take breakfast with you in the small dining parlor at your convenience.*
>
> *FD*

Immediately after reading Mr. Darcy's note, she had rung for Cassidy, dressing and pinning up her hair as quickly as possible. She had slept far later than was her custom, and she knew enough of her husband's habits to guess that he had already been awake for several hours. She hated that she had kept him from his morning meal, and worried her delayed appearance had likely caused him undue distress.

Crossing into the dining room, she was relieved to find him seated at the table, leaning back leisurely in his seat, a newspaper laid out before him. He rose at her entrance, stepping forward to pull out her chair.

"Elizabeth; good morning. You are looking well. I trust you are feeling better?"

"Yes, thank you," she answered, sliding into the seat he offered. "I believe I am as good as new, though ravenously hungry."

"Well, that I am certain we can remedy," Darcy responded with a smile. "Pray, help yourself to tea, or coffee, and I will fix you a plate."

He moved to the sideboard, selecting small portions of everything on offer, until the plate in his hand was laden with a variety of sweet and savory dishes. As he worked, Elizabeth reached for the teapot, saying, "I hope you will forgive my late arrival. I had not realized you would wish to dine together, or I would have had Cassidy wake me earlier."

Making his way back to the table, Darcy set down her meal before returning to fill a plate of his own.

"It is of no significance. You needed your rest, and I had business to attend to this morning, so it worked out well."

Coming to sit beside her, he waited for her to begin before turning to his own breakfast.

They ate in silence for several minutes before Darcy said, "You might be interested to know that I had two letters from Briarwood this morning. My aunt wrote to inquire after my headache. My godmother, however, asked to be remembered to you and said she hoped you were feeling better."

Elizabeth's fork froze in midair as Darcy offered her a slow smile. "I should hardly have been surprised. Melanie has always prided herself on her powers of observation."

"Oh, dear. I hope she does not suspect it was the dinner that made me unwell. I should hate to cause your aunt any offence. Do you think I might write to assure Lady Wheaton that it was merely a temporary complaint?"

"Of course. I am certain she would welcome a correspondence. She seemed quite taken with you, as was my aunt."

Elizabeth flushed, but turned her attention back to her breakfast. "Very well, then I shall write to both of them this very afternoon. I enjoyed their company and would like to know each of them better." After a moment, she added, "I confess, before we arrived, I worried your aunt and godmother might be cut from the same cloth as Lady Catherine, but I was pleasantly surprised. I especially appreciated Lady Wheaton's candor. I liked her a great deal."

Across from her, Darcy's face broke into a grin. "Melanie cannot abide Lady Catherine. She refers to her as 'The Dragon' amongst the rest of our relations."

Elizabeth laughed, as Darcy continued, "I also had a letter from Bingley. He wrote to share the happy news of his betrothal and mentioned that they had set the wedding for the end of June."

"Yes, Jane said the same in her most recent letter. I am surprised she would wish to wait, but no doubt she was thinking of our traveling so far on icy roads, in addition to wishing to appease my mother's inclinations. I know

Mamma was quite put out by our own nuptials being so rushed."

Elizabeth had said the last in jest, but looking over at Mr. Darcy, she could see that he had taken her words far more seriously than she had intended.

"I am sorry you did not have all that," he offered quietly. "The time to shop, and to plan. I should not have rushed you to the altar as I did."

"Oh, there is no need to apologize for that," Elizabeth replied, hoping to put him at ease. "In my case, it is just as well that we married quickly. I do not have Jane's patience for my mother's attentions, and I have never set much store on fripperies the way my youngest sisters do."

"Still, it would have given you more time to… to say your farewells and to become accustomed to the idea of being a bride. I was selfish not to have given that to you."

Once again, Elizabeth met her husband's eyes, surprised by the depth of emotion she saw reflected in his gaze.

"Well, it is over and done with, in any case," Elizabeth said easily. "Jane and I are different people, and I am only happy to know that she will have the wedding she has always dreamt of."

Darcy nodded, and the two spoke of more trivial things. However, when the meal was concluded, and Elizabeth turned away from the table, Darcy called out her name.

"If you are not feeling too fatigued, I wonder if you might do me the honor of accompanying me to my study?" he asked. "There is something I wished to discuss."

Although she could not imagine what her husband would wish to speak with her about that could not have been addressed over the breakfast table, Elizabeth readily agreed, following him from the room.

Entering the study some moments later, Elizabeth settled into one of the chairs facing his desk. She could not think there was any cause for alarm, given Mr. Darcy's genial manner over breakfast, but she felt the need to wipe her palms against the fabric of her skirts, just the same.

Darcy took his usual seat, restlessly drumming his fingers upon his blotter. There was no disguising his apprehension, and Elizabeth was left to wonder if she had been too hasty in assuming the meeting was not a portent of bad news.

Finally, he spoke.

"I realize I have been remiss in not speaking of it sooner, but I wished to discuss the monetary compensation that was promised to you in your settlement. I have no excuse for the delay, other than the fact that it is not something I have had to deal with before. However, I should like to remedy that oversight now."

"I-I beg your pardon," Elizabeth stammered. "I do not understand. Has something changed since you signed the marriage contract with my father? Your terms were extremely munificent, so I certainly have no cause for complaint."

"No, there has been no change. But though it was all laid out on paper, I realized that I have never spoken of it with you… and I would like you to know how to access the funds that have been set aside for your use."

Sliding out one of the drawers of his desk, Darcy withdrew a small purse, as well as several sheets of paper, laying them out on the polished surface. Ignoring the purse, he reached for the documents, picking them up and handing them to Elizabeth as he spoke.

"The twenty-five thousand pounds I settled upon you at the time of our marriage has been placed in a London bank in your name. The funds are yours alone, to do with as you wish. Those letters are copies of my correspondence with Mr. Adkins, the bank manager, and Mr. Harrington, my man of business in Town. You will see that their direction is included on each of the letters. To withdraw funds, you need only write to either of them, and they will assist you in obtaining whatever you require."

Having briefly skimmed the letters, Elizabeth could only fix a wide-eyed gaze upon her husband as her heart hammered within her chest. Twenty-five thousand pounds! It was a fortune! And although she had seen the number in the marriage settlement her father had shown her, she had never conceived of having that money placed in a separate account, solely in her name, to do with as she pleased...

Belatedly, she realized her husband was still speaking, and once again returned her attention to the sound of his voice.

"Of course, those funds should not be used for anything having to do with the household, or for your own particular needs. Mrs. Reynolds will help you to obtain anything you wish for the house, and there are accounts of credit at all the local shops in Lambton, and at many in Town. Any articles of clothing, or other personal notions you may wish to acquire, will of course be covered by me."

Still somewhat stunned, Elizabeth could only murmur, "That is exceedingly generous."

"It is no more than what you were promised when we wed." Reaching for the purse, he continued, "I also wished to discuss your pin money. While you should have little need of ready cash, I will see that you receive your monthly allowance in coin, so you will have more portable funds, should the necessity ever arise."

Taking the purse he offered, Elizabeth was surprised by its weight.

As if in answer to her unasked question, Darcy said, "That is your allowance for the two months we have been wed, and next month's besides. Again, I apologize for neglecting to see that you had it before now."

Closing her fingers around the leather pouch, Elizabeth stared back at her husband. "I... I hardly know what to say. While I certainly appreciate the gesture, I cannot imagine that I should have any use for pin money when all my needs have already been met."

"Still, it is what was promised to you," Darcy repeated. "Besides, life is uncertain. There may come a time when you will be glad to have it."

Elizabeth lifted her brow at her husband's cryptic message, but before she could dwell on it any further, he continued with forced indifference, "Which reminds me, I had a thought... I know you will want to travel to Long-bourn for your sister's wedding in the early summer... what say you to spending the Season in Town? You could travel as soon as March or April, if the weather is fair, and stay as long as you like. See your family... I believe you mentioned you have relations in London, and I know Georgiana would be delighted to have you there."

At her husband's words, Elizabeth's pulse instantly quickened. Oh, to see her beloved aunt and uncle! And Jane! And to be once again out in society, free to go to the theater and museums...

"That sounds wonderful!" she gasped. "I should love to be able to spend time with Jane before her wedding, and it will be marvelous to see Georgiana again, but... can you get away from the estate for all that time?"

Across from her, Darcy shifted awkwardly in his chair. "I would not be going. As you surmised, I cannot leave Pemberley for the foreseeable future. Not with the issues I am having with Boyle. But there is nothing tying you here. Darcy House is well situated, close to all the shops, and you will have your own carriage, so you may travel to Longbourn as often as you wish..."

Elizabeth stared back at him. "You... you mean for me to go on my own?"

Darcy looked slightly uneasy, but nodded his agreement. "It occurred to me that you must be lonely here. And just because I am forced to stay, does not mean you should be also."

Elizabeth looked away, the exhilaration that had filled her only moments before evaporating in an instant. Go to London on her own? Leave Pemberley, and live apart from her husband, as if she was a kept woman, or worse yet, the wife of a man who wanted nothing whatsoever to do with her? Was this the life he envisioned for them?

"I thank you for your consideration," she answered slowly, "but I would not wish to go on my own. If you cannot leave Pemberley, then I shall stay also. I would like to attend Jane's wedding, of course, but there is no reason for me to be gone for more than a fortnight, at the most."

Darcy frowned at her, as if perplexed by her reaction.

"Are you quite certain? I thought you would enjoy spending the Season in London."

"No, upon reflection, I would be happier at Pemberley.

I look forward to exploring the gardens and the remainder of the park when the weather improves, and I have always preferred the countryside to Town."

Slowly, Darcy nodded. "Very well, as you wish. In any case, April is still weeks away, so there is no need to come to a decision now. Perhaps you will change your mind."

"Perhaps," Elizabeth answered, but she knew she would not. As much as she wished for the comfort of her loved ones, she would not live as a society wife, cast off by her husband.

The two spoke of ordinary things for a time before Elizabeth rose, Darcy following her lead.

"Well, I should leave you to your work. I will see you at dinner, then?"

"Yes, of course. I look forward to it." And without further conversation, Elizabeth quit the room, reflecting yet again on how little she understood the man she had married.

One day, about a week after their return from Briarwood, Elizabeth was on her way to the library when the sounds of raised voices drew her attention to Mr. Darcy's study. Ducking into a small alcove on the opposite side of the corridor, she strained to hear what was being said, instantly recognizing her husband's deep baritone, and the clipped tones of another gentleman. Though she could not make out the words, the distinct northern accent led her to believe it was Mr. Boyle, the steward. The voices were muffled at first, but grew suddenly clear as the door to the room was opened.

"I tell you again, you are making a mistake," said Boyle, in an agitated manner. "If you do not hold her accountable, there will be others, you mark my words."

"I have heard your opinion, and my decision is final. Nothing will be accomplished by such means; it was not my father's way, and it will not be mine. You shall have a month's pay, but I will ask you to vacate the premises by the end of the week."

Realizing they were about to exit the room and she would soon be discovered, Elizabeth hastened from her hiding spot, but she had not gone more than a handful of steps when Boyle stalked down the corridor, jamming his hat on his head as he went. Brushing past Elizabeth without a word, he took the stairs at a brisk pace, barely stopping to allow the startled footman in the front hall to open the door.

Changing direction, Elizabeth cautiously made her way to her husband's study where she found Darcy standing stiffly by the window, staring vacantly out at the frozen gardens.

The latch engaged with a soft click as Elizabeth closed the door, and Darcy turned to face her with a weary expression.

"You heard that, I suppose."

Elizabeth nodded. "I gather you let him go?"

"Yes. In truth, I should have done so long before now. I kept hoping things would improve, but it was evident from the beginning that he was not the right man for the post. While the estate prospered, his treatment of my tenants was something I could no longer condone."

He paused then, and Elizabeth asked gently, "Could you not have helped him to see things from your perspective?"

"No. Believe me, I have tried, but it was becoming an

untenable situation. My father always prioritized people over profits, and since taking over the management of the estate, I have strived to follow his example. I am relieved to have now found someone who will support me in that endeavor, rather than contradicting my wishes at every turn as Boyle has done."

Surprised, Elizabeth's eyebrows lifted. "You have already hired his replacement?"

Darcy's expression lightened as he nodded his head, moving to the desk and lifting a letter from his stack of correspondence. "A Mr. Ellis. I stopped to see him last month on my return from Scarborough and offered him the position, but I only received his reply today. He is to start within the fortnight."

"You seem pleased."

"I am pleased. I think Ellis is exactly what Pemberley needs. My only regret is not engaging him sooner." Motioning for Elizabeth to sit, Darcy lowered himself into the chair behind his desk. "I met with him last summer, when the post initially became vacant. He was raised not far from here, and I was impressed with his knowledge of the land and his ideas for modernization. But above all that, I liked him. He has a calm, steady demeanor and a sharp intelligence. I believe he is the right man for the job."

"He sounds ideal. If you do not mind my asking, why did you not offer him the position last summer?"

Leaning back in his chair, Darcy released a breath, idly fingering the chain of his pocket watch. "He is young, only six and twenty, and he has never had the management of any estate, let alone one as large as Pemberley. Mr. Boyle came highly recommended and has been working as a steward for above fifteen years. I worried that being relatively new to running Pemberley myself, I would be making a mistake in hiring someone with so little practical experience. I see now that I was wrong. Ellis may be young, but he is ambitious, and more importantly, he shares my values and my vision for the future. I think we will do well together."

"Then I am very happy you were able to secure him," Elizabeth answered.

"As am I." Darcy offered her a shallow smile, but Elizabeth could see his eyes were still troubled.

"Is there something else worrying you?" she asked hesitantly, and once again, Darcy sighed.

"Indeed, there is something. It was one of the things Boyle and I were at loggerheads over, and I have been puzzling it out for some time with no good resolution."

"Well, I cannot promise I will do any better in coming up with an answer, but I would be happy to listen if you think it would help."

"Thank you, yes," Darcy eventually replied. "I would value your opinion. It involves one of my tenants, a Mrs. Kirk."

Upon hearing the name, Elizabeth furrowed her brow. Though she had been visiting Darcy's tenants for some weeks now, this particular individual was unfamiliar to her. "I do not recognize the name," she answered. "She is not amongst the tenants upon whom I have paid calls."

"No, I am not surprised. Her farm is one of the farthest from the house. She is a widow, and, unfortunately, since her husband's passing, she has been unable to keep up with the demands of running a profitable enterprise. Her income has been greatly reduced, and she is no longer able to pay her rent. Though she has two grown sons, both have left the estate in the last year: one joined the navy and the other married and moved south to be nearer to his new wife's family. Since their departure, it was my understanding that Mrs. Kirk had been using hired hands to help her bring in her crops, but I believe the low yields in recent years have made it impossible for her to keep them on. She is now in arrears on her rent by several months, and the house itself has fallen into a state of disrepair. It was Boyle's opinion that we should begin the process of an eviction."

"And you disagreed."

Darcy responded with a curt nod. "I simply cannot see putting someone in her circumstances out on the street. She has lived on this land all her adult life. As a matter of fact, before her marriage, she worked as a maid in Pemberley's kitchens."

Elizabeth sat back in her chair, worrying the topaz cross she wore around her neck. Her heart went out to this woman she did not know, as it took very little to imagine how easy it would be for any woman—even one from a much higher social circle than Mrs. Kirk—to slip into a state of genteel poverty. Indeed, were it not for her marriage to Mr. Darcy, and Jane's impending nuptials to Bingley, her own mother's prospects would not look so very different when her father died.

"I see," she finally answered. "Yes, that is a dilemma. But I must agree with you. Putting her out would not be the charitable thing to do."

"No. Still, Boyle has a point. She cannot stay on indefinitely if she cannot farm the land nor pay her rent."

"No, I suppose not." After a slight hesitation she added, "Perhaps one of her children might take her in? The son who married and moved away?"

"Yes, I think that may be the only option. But she is proud. She would likely be loath to ask, and I do not know if her son has the means to keep her. However, beyond the broader issue, there is the more pressing concern of her current well-being. If things are as bad as I fear, she may not even have sufficient food on the table, or coal to heat her home. I have attempted to call there twice, but was not admitted on either occasion."

Slowly, Elizabeth nodded. "Yes, I would imagine not."

At Darcy's raised brow, she continued, "If things are as you suspect, she would not wish for you to see her in those circumstances. She may have even worried that you had come to demand the rent, or to tender an eviction."

Darcy's jaws clenched together, but he nodded his agreement. "I would like to say you are wrong, but I am afraid I cannot."

Elizabeth chewed her lip, her thoughts churning. "Perhaps..." she mused aloud.

"Pray, continue. I am at a loss and would welcome any suggestions you might have."

"Well, I do not have any recommendations for the larger problem, but do you think it would help if I were to call on her? At the very least, I could bring a basket of food. I do not know if she will grant me entry, but I am a stranger to her, and she may be more welcoming to another woman than to the master of the estate."

Slowly, Darcy nodded. "It cannot hurt for you to try. And if she accepts your assistance, at least it would be a start."

Elizabeth smiled. "Very well. If the weather is fair, I shall go tomorrow, and then perhaps we will have a better idea of how to proceed."

~

The instructions Darcy gave her for finding Mrs. Kirk's farm were easy to follow, and within half an hour Elizabeth was pulling up before a small stone cottage. Securing the horses, she carefully stepped to the ground, circling around to the back of the phaeton, and retrieving the wicker hamper she had asked Mrs. Webb to fill.

From what she could see, the dwelling was neatly-kept, although the paint on the shutters was chipped and faded, and the thatched roof looked like it could use some repair. Squinting up at the leaded windows, she noticed that, despite the late hour, the curtains were drawn.

Elizabeth frowned. Perhaps she should return at another time... For a moment she stood on the dirt path, debating the merits of paying some additional calls first, before deciding to carry on as planned.

Moving to the front door, she shifted the basket in her arms before rapping her knuckles upon the rough wood. A faint scuffling sound came from within the cottage, but the door in front of her remained firmly shut.

Stepping back, Elizabeth tilted her head, peering once again at the front window. She thought she saw one of the curtains flutter, as if someone had quickly dropped it back into place.

Returning to the door, she knocked again, but was greeted with the same silence.

She had just made up her mind to leave the basket and return another day when the handle twisted and the door was cracked open just enough for Elizabeth to see the sliver of a dark-haired woman in an apron and cap.

Too young to be Mrs. Kirk, Elizabeth thought. Perhaps

things were not as dire as they had feared if Mrs. Kirk was able to keep a maid.

The woman stared at her warily as Elizabeth offered up a winning smile.

"Good morning. Is Mrs. Kirk at home, by chance? I am Mrs. Darcy."

The girl's eyes widened at the name, and she glanced nervously over her shoulder.

"The mistress is feeling poorly today. She ain't receiving no callers."

Elizabeth did not miss the fact that the girl's eyes had darted to the basket more than once.

"Oh, that is a shame. I have been out since early this morning, and it is rather colder than I had anticipated. I had hoped to break my trip here before returning to the house."

Once again, the maid looked over her shoulder, but this time the door opened a bit wider as an older woman came into view.

The maid stepped back and Elizabeth's smile broadened. "Mrs. Kirk, I presume?"

At the woman's slight nod, she quickly continued, "I am pleased to make your acquaintance. I am Mrs. Darcy. I hope you will forgive me for not visiting before now. I have been paying calls on all of my husband's tenants since my arrival, but there are so many of them, it has taken me longer than I had anticipated!"

Mrs. Kirk nodded, peering up at her. "Aye, I had heard the master married."

Her gaze shifted to the basket Elizabeth held, and Elizabeth extended it in her direction.

"I hope you will accept this small token as an apology of sorts, for not calling sooner."

Reluctantly, the older woman reached out her hands, regarding the basket with a mix of discomfiture and desire.

Taking this as her opening, Elizabeth continued, "I hate to impose, but I was wondering if I might come in for a moment. I have been driving around the park for some time, and was hoping for a short respite before returning to the house."

The woman hesitated, and Elizabeth thought it more likely than not that she would refuse. But finally, she seemed to make up her mind, taking a step backwards and swinging the door wider so Elizabeth could enter.

Crossing the threshold, Elizabeth paused, allowing her eyes to become accustomed to the dim light. A fire burned low in the grate, doing little to warm the air, and a single tallow candle guttered on a scarred wooden table in the corner of the room.

Mrs. Kirk ushered her to a worn armchair by the hearth, and Elizabeth sat.

Across from her, the older woman shifted uncomfortably before saying, "I'm afraid I am out of tea, but I can offer you some barley water if you'd like."

"Oh, no, pray do not trouble yourself," Elizabeth was quick to reply. "I am just happy to sit by the fire for a few minutes." Glancing around, she noticed that the small front room was sparsely appointed, but while the furnishings were slightly tattered, the space was clean, and she could see that what was there had once been of good quality.

Taking a seat across from her, Mrs. Kirk followed her gaze. "You'll have to excuse the state of things," she said stiffly. "I wasn't expecting company."

"Oh, please, do not concern yourself," Elizabeth

answered with a smile. "You are doing me a great service to allow me to stay and rest awhile."

The two lapsed into silence, and Elizabeth searched her mind for some neutral topic upon which they might converse, finally recalling something Mr. Darcy had told her the previous day.

"It is lovely to meet someone who has such a long history on the estate," she began. "My husband tells me you used to work up at the house, before your marriage."

For the first time since Elizabeth had entered the cottage, Mrs. Kirk's cheeks lifted into a faint smile, and she nodded agreeably.

"Aye, so I did. Worked in the kitchens, under Mrs. Shaw, the cook, God rest her soul. Couldn't read nor write; kept all her receipts in her head. But her food was fit for a king. Not fancy, mind. But some of the best victuals I've ever tasted, before or since. I learned everything I know about cooking from her."

"My, she certainly does sound like a treasure!" Elizabeth answered. "I wish I had had the opportunity to make her acquaintance."

Mrs. Kirk nodded sagely. "Had a big heart, too. Used to take the table scraps and cook pies for the tenants and villagers who were having trouble getting by. Never made a fuss about it, neither. Just left 'em at their doors. But everyone knew where they come from. Aye, she was a kind soul."

Mrs. Kirk's expression clouded, and Elizabeth shifted in her chair, uncomfortable about the fact that the exchange had veered dangerously close to Mrs. Kirk's own precarious circumstances. She was about to attempt to turn the conversation, when her hostess continued, "After seeing

Mrs. Shaw's example, I've always made it my business to do my bit as well. I ain't never had much, but I've always shared what I could. No matter how bad you think you have it, there's always someone that has it worse."

"That is very good of you," Elizabeth murmured. "I am certain Mrs. Shaw would be proud to know her charitable nature had had such a profound effect."

Mrs. Kirk nodded, and the two women chatted on amiably for a brief interval before Elizabeth stood.

"Well, I should be going, but I cannot thank you enough for your hospitality. I do hope our paths will cross again very soon."

And although Mrs. Kirk smiled her agreement, Elizabeth could not help but wonder if the older woman would be quite so willing to admit her on a second occasion.

Chapter 16

Dear Georgiana,

You were correct in assuming your brother had not mentioned his upcoming birthday, so I thank you for the intelligence. The books you suggested sound like a perfect gift, and I would be happy to procure them from the bookshop in Lambton on your behalf. Pray, write again and let me know if there is anything else I might do to make the day a special one.

Your sister,
Elizabeth

"You wished to speak with me, madam?"

Elizabeth looked up from her letter, setting down her quill as the housekeeper entered the room.

"Yes, Mrs. Reynolds. Thank you for coming so quickly. Is my husband still from home?"

"Aye. I believe he is at the estate office, preparing for the arrival of the new steward."

Elizabeth nodded. Although she was eager to speak with Mr. Darcy about her meeting with Mrs. Kirk earlier that day, she was glad to have him out of the way for the present.

Motioning for the housekeeper to come in, Elizabeth sat forward in her chair.

"I understand Mr. Darcy will be celebrating a birthday next month," she began, "and I had wished to ask... what is generally done? To commemorate the occasion, that is."

Mrs. Reynolds stepped farther into the room, but her brow furrowed as she said, "To be truthful, Mr. Darcy has never been one for celebrations, madam, and he is often in Town at this time of year. I do not remember anything in particular being done to mark the day since he was a boy."

"Oh. I see." Although she was not surprised her husband would shy away from anything that caused him to be the center of attention, she somehow found herself strangely disappointed. At Longbourn, birthdays were always celebrated with great fanfare, and she could not imagine letting the day pass without some sort of festivity.

"Still, I feel we must do something," she mused. "Perhaps a special dinner?" she asked hopefully, and to her relief the housekeeper's eyes brightened.

"Yes, I think that would do. I could have cook make some of his favorites, with a cake for dessert..."

Elizabeth was instantly cheered by the housekeeper's words. While she knew Mr. Darcy was not fond of sweets, certainly something out of the common way was expected on one's birthday.

Elizabeth instantly expressed her approval before saying, "Is there a particular dish you could recommend? Perhaps something that is not generally served? I would like it to be special."

Mrs. Reynolds pursed her lips, her gaze turned inward.

"Now that I recall, there *was* something our old cook, Mrs. Shaw, used to make when the master was a boy... Yes! I remember now, it was a sort of stew... Hotch-Potch was the name. Oh, goodness, I have not thought of that in years. It was a dish Mrs. Shaw learned from her Scottish gran, and I have never tasted its like before or since. Oh, Mr. Darcy used to love it! I believe it was served on his birthday more than once."

"That sounds perfect! In fact, I met with one of the tenants only this morning who remembered Mrs. Shaw from her time as a kitchen maid here at Pemberley, and spoke very highly of her cooking. Do you think Mrs. Webb would be able to duplicate the recipe?"

Mrs. Reynolds frowned. "Ah, now there is the problem. There is no recipe. I believe Mrs. Shaw used to make it from memory. And while I have no doubt that Mrs. Webb could cook something like it, I fear it would not be exactly the same."

Elizabeth's enthusiasm waned, but she did her best to keep her smile in place. "Oh. Well, I suppose that will have to do. Please speak to Mrs. Webb and see if she is up to the task. We have several weeks, so perhaps she will be able to perfect a close approximation in that amount of time."

The housekeeper agreed, and the two continued to discuss the menu for the rest of the meal until one of the footmen came to alert them that Mr. Darcy had returned to the house.

～

"But this is outrageous!" Darcy thundered a short while later. "If things are as bad as you estimate, something more must be done for her at once!"

Elizabeth watched her husband, anger mottling his cheeks and his jaw tight. She had known he would be distressed by Mrs. Kirk's situation, but was nevertheless taken aback by the depths of his anguish.

"I would have to agree that her circumstances are not the best, and she did look somewhat frail, but at least she still has a roof over her head, thanks to you."

Darcy began to pace, running his fingers through his hair. "That is not enough. I cannot stand idly by while one of my tenants lives in such mean conditions. Especially a woman of her advanced years, with no husband nor son to look after her. I will go again tomorrow and insist she see me. We must be allowed to assist her with food and coal for the fire at the very least, until a more permanent solution can be resolved upon." He turned to face Elizabeth, studying her expression. "You do not agree?"

"No," she answered slowly. "I will allow that some action should be undertaken, it is only your methods I question."

Darcy hesitated, blowing out a frustrated breath before saying, "Very well. What would you suggest?"

"I do not know… It is just that if she was reluctant to let you see her when you called before, she will be more so now. Even I had to use subterfuge to gain entry, and although she accepted the provisions I brought, there is no telling whether she will actually keep any of them. From some of what she said, I believe she is as likely to give the food to some other unfortunate soul whose circumstances she deems more dire than her own."

"Then what can be done? If she will not accept our assistance, I am at a loss."

Elizabeth gazed into the near distance, thinking back to what her husband had told her about the elderly widow. "You were correct when you said that she is proud; she will not want charity. If only there was some way to help her without making her feel that what we are offering is merely a handout due to her reduced circumstances…" Suddenly, an idea struck her and she instantly brightened.

"What is it?" Darcy asked. "Have you thought of something that may help?"

Elizabeth nodded. "Indeed, I think I have."

Darcy stared back at her, but Elizabeth only shook her head and smiled enigmatically.

"I am afraid it must remain a secret for now. But if you put your mind to a more permanent solution to the problem of the rent, I shall take care of the rest."

The evening of Darcy's birthday, Elizabeth found herself at the top of the principal staircase, pacing along the empty corridor as she waited for her husband to emerge from his rooms. As luck would have it, he had spent the entire day out on the estate with Mr. Ellis, the new steward, so Elizabeth had had no opportunity to speak with him until now. And the closer they came to the dinner hour, the more apprehensive she grew. Would her husband be pleased with her surprise? Would he even take note of the meal Mrs. Webb had spent an entire day preparing?

Mrs. Reynolds had clearly relayed his dislike of any

type of special attention... Would he grow taciturn and remote at her attempt to celebrate the occasion?

Finally, when she thought she could not stand it any longer, she heard a door opening farther down the passageway, and then the steady rhythm of approaching footsteps. A moment later, Darcy rounded the corner and stopped short, clearly startled to find her lying in wait at the top of the stairs.

"Good evening," Elizabeth said, forcing a cheerful smile. "I supposed you would be along soon. I thought I would wait so that we might go down to dinner together."

Recovering himself, Darcy nodded, offering his arm, which Elizabeth took.

"Of course."

"I trust you have had a pleasant day?" she continued as they began to walk.

"I have," Darcy answered, slowing his pace as they descended the steps. "Ellis and I rode out to survey the north side of the estate. He has some interesting ideas for rotating a few of our crops, as well as a plan to dam up a portion of the river where there has been flooding. I continue to be impressed with his knowledge and enthusiasm."

Elizabeth listened as her husband continued, "And you? I hope you have also spent your day in an agreeable manner?"

They reached the bottom of the steps and turned to the right, crossing the entrance hall.

"Indeed," Elizabeth answered with a small smile. "Like yours, it has been... productive."

They had just reached the dining parlor. Crossing into the room, Elizabeth released her husband's arm, watching as he paused, taking in the sparkling silver candelabras and the vases of fresh flowers that adorned the table, which was laid with Pemberley's best china.

"Happy birthday," she said, her voice bright.

Darcy blinked. His body had gone utterly still, and there was an unreadable expression in his dark eyes.

Elizabeth's smile slipped. *He does not like it.* Oh, why was she forever making the worst choices where he was concerned?

Licking her lips, she said cautiously, "Georgiana wrote to inform me of the date some weeks ago, and Mrs. Reynolds and I thought to have a celebratory dinner. I hope you are not cross."

Slowly, Darcy shook his head. "No, I am not cross. To own the truth, I had not even recollected the date until now. Thank you. This was very thoughtful." He hesitated before leaning in to place a light kiss upon her cheek. Elizabeth's stomach did a strange little flip as his hand settled at the small of her back, and she allowed him to lead her to her place at the table.

Darcy took the seat beside her as Lawson approached, proffering a bottle of wine for his master's inspection.

Darcy's brow lifted as he looked at the label. "French champagne? We are celebrating, I see."

"If you would prefer something different, sir, I have brought up a claret and a bottle of Madeira as well."

"No, no," Darcy replied, waving his hand. "Pour the champagne. I will only turn eight and twenty once, so we may as well enjoy ourselves."

Lawson did as he was directed, just as the first footman entered with a tureen of soup. Elizabeth served as Darcy looked on.

"White soup? Now this does feel like a special occasion."

"I hope you are not displeased? Mrs. Reynolds said you enjoyed it."

"No, not at all. It is one of my favorites."

They ate in relative silence for some time, Elizabeth's heart rate quickening with each minute that brought them closer to the next remove. Finally, the footmen entered with trays of jugged steak with potatoes and sole with wine and mushrooms, before setting down an elegant porcelain écuelle before Mr. Darcy and lifting the lid.

Elizabeth watched as her husband stared at the colorful stew. His brow momentarily furrowed before he turned to her with a slow smile. "This looks delicious. Thank you."

Elizabeth's heart sank slightly as she watched him carefully serve for both of them, taking a bit from all of the offerings on the table. Elizabeth shifted in her seat, scarcely able to attend to her own plate as she watched her husband take his first bite of the traditional Scottish dish.

Her breath caught, as she anticipated his reaction. She did not have long to wait. Darcy's eyes grew round, and he fairly stopped chewing, before going in for another forkful.

With forced calm, Elizabeth turned in his direction. "Is anything the matter?"

"No... It is only that this stew tastes remarkably like... But, no, it is impossible. I have not had anything like this since I was a boy."

Elizabeth nodded, smothering her smile. "It is a Scottish dish called Hotch-Potch."

"Yes! That is it! I had forgotten... The cook we had when I was growing up—"

"Mrs. Shaw," Elizabeth supplied, and Darcy set down his fork.

"Elizabeth. How is this possible? I might think you had lured the poor woman out of her much-deserved retirement if I did not know for a fact that she passed from this earth some three years ago. And she was the only person I ever knew who cooked anything that tasted like this."

"You are enjoying it, then? You did not say."

"It is wonderful! The dish was a favorite of mine when I was a boy. But how could you know that? And how could you have directed Mrs. Webb in its preparation, if indeed Mrs. Webb cooked the dish? The meat, the vegetables, the seasonings, everything is exact!"

At last, Elizabeth released a joyful laugh. "Yes, Mrs. Webb prepared it, though not without some help. If the dish tastes as you remember, you owe your thanks to Mrs. Kirk."

Darcy stared back at her, his thick brows drawn together. "Mrs. Kirk? Forgive me, I am not following."

"Well, it was Mrs. Reynolds who first suggested the stew. She remembered that you were fond of it as a boy, but she also told me that Mrs. Shaw had made it from memory, and that the recipe was one that had been handed down within her own family in Scotland. At first, I thought to have Mrs. Webb prepare something similar from whatever receipt she could uncover... but then I remembered that Mrs. Kirk used to work in Pemberley's kitchens before she married, so I thought to ask her if she could help."

"You are very clever! And she remembered the recipe?"

"Alas, no. Mrs. Shaw never shared it and Mrs. Kirk was not a cook at the time, only a kitchen maid. But she did remember the taste of the dish, in very great detail as it turns out." At Darcy's furrowed brow, Elizabeth continued, "Mrs. Webb started with a basic recipe, and I took the dish to Mrs. Kirk. She pronounced it quite good, but she was certain the spices were wrong, and she distinctly remembered that Mrs. Shaw used a mix of lamb, venison, and beef, and that she used leeks instead of turnips. Mrs. Webb, bless her soul, made three more attempts, and on the fourth try, Mrs. Kirk declared that the Hotch-Potch was exactly as she remembered. Still, I did not know if her memory could be trusted. It has been a great many years, after all."

Darcy's eyes suddenly lit with understanding as he said slowly, "And unless I miss my guess, you left each of those dishes with Mrs. Kirk. You were able to get her to accept the food as she believed herself to be doing you a service, rather than seeing the food as merely an act of charity."

Elizabeth flushed. "Just so. She was a bit reluctant at first, but I was able to convince her that I was absolutely relying on her assistance. If she questioned why I brought such large portions, she did not share those thoughts with me."

Darcy released a low chuckle. "Tell me, did it truly take four attempts for Mrs. Webb to perfect the recipe?"

Elizabeth grinned. "Perhaps she might have done it in three. But I will say that Mrs. Kirk was looking much heartier the last time I saw her—though she may be a bit tired of eating Hotch-Potch!"

Darcy laughed again, and the pair continued to enjoy their meal, conversing on other topics before finally circling back to the elderly widow.

"Speaking of Mrs. Kirk, you will be happy to know that I believe Ellis and I may have come up with a more permanent solution to the problem of the rent," Darcy said. "In truth, I had thought to use a similar tactic to your own."

"Oh? I would be interested to hear it. I agree that something must be done, and the sooner the better."

Darcy nodded. "It had occurred to me that the best course of action would be for me to take over a portion of her land. She would retain the house, of course, and the immediate acreage surrounding it—enough to maintain the kitchen garden, and to keep some small livestock if she wishes—and the estate would farm the rest. In exchange, I would be able to substantially reduce her rent, and perhaps even pay her something for her trouble."

Elizabeth frowned. "She would know it was charity. Clearly you would have no need of her acreage when I assume a large portion of land belongs to the estate already."

"Yes, I had thought of that. I would need to come up with a story... some reason why that particular parcel of land was of value to me."

Elizabeth set down her fork as the footmen began to clear the table. "The idea has merit. If you are able to come up with a plausible motive."

Darcy sighed. "I am afraid I do not have one at the moment. I was hoping I could start by relaying the scheme. If she agrees, I will speak to Ellis about what we might do with that land. I am certain if we put our heads together, we can come up with something."

Just then, the servants' door opened and Peter, the first footman, entered bearing a silver tray laden with oranges, grapes, and pineapple—all sent down from Briarwood—as well as a sizeable fruit cake, studded with currants and soaked in brandy.

Elizabeth glanced apologetically at her husband. "You will have to forgive me. I know you do not prefer elaborate desserts, but it seemed intolerable to have a birthday dinner without a cake. When I asked Mrs. Reynolds what you might prefer, she said she remembered you favoring fruit-cake when you were a boy."

She stopped speaking, realizing that Mr. Darcy was staring at the dessert with a strange expression. But after a brief hesitation, his eyes found hers.

"Pray, forgive me, I was lost in my memories. I haven't had a cake like this since before... that is, since I was a child. But as usual, Mrs. Reynolds's memory has served her well. Currant cake used to be a particular favorite, and one my mother had prepared for many a birthday dinner."

Relieved, Elizabeth offered him an expressive smile. "Then you will have some?"

"Yes," Darcy answered quietly. "I shall have some; I shall eat it with relish."

When the meal was over, Darcy accompanied Elizabeth to the withdrawing room where a parcel wrapped in plain brown paper awaited them. Spying the package, Darcy looked over at her in confusion.

"Your birthday gifts," Elizabeth said with a grin. "Go ahead, open it."

Slowly, Darcy took a seat, and Elizabeth settled in beside him, tapping her foot in nervous anticipation as he untied the strings to reveal a small stack of books.

"I hope you like them; they are from your sister. Georgiana sent me the titles, and I purchased them in Lambton on her behalf. If you have already read them, I beg you do not enlighten her. I know she would be crushed."

Darcy nodded, sifting through the pile. "I have only read one, this book of poetry, but it was several years ago, and this is a much finer copy than the one I initially purchased." He continued to stare down at the books, picking up each one and turning it over in his hands... almost as though he were trying to make sense of the fact that they had all been specifically selected with him in mind.

Strangely, Elizabeth felt the beginnings of a lump forming at the back of her throat, but before she could grow too maudlin, she reached down to a basket at her feet, extracting a sealed letter and another slim parcel.

Handing him the letter, she said, "This is also from your sister. She enclosed it in the correspondence she sent to me last week and asked that I give it to you today."

Darcy offered her a half-smile, taking the note and slipping it inside the pocket of his coat. He opened his mouth to speak, but before he could say anything Elizabeth quickly passed him the remaining package.

"And this is from me."

Darcy's eyebrows lifted, but he took the item from her hands, peeling back the stiff paper until the gilded lettering stared up at him: *A Book of Architecture, Containing Designs of Buildings and Ornaments. By James Gibbs.*

"I know it was published some time ago," Elizabeth said in a rushed breath, "and you have likely already read it. But Mr. Dowling at the bookshop said he could not remember ever selling you a copy, and he recommended it quite highly when I asked for something in the field."

Slowly, Darcy shook his head. "No, I have never read

anything by Mr. Gibbs." Lifting the volume from the paper, he ran his hands reverently over the leather cover.

"But you know of him?" Elizabeth asked.

"Yes, of course. He was one of Britain's most influential architects. His works include many of the country's preeminent buildings, including the Radcliffe Camera at Oxford University." After a moment, he added, "What made you think to purchase this for me?"

"I... I do not know. It just seemed, from your sketches, that you had an interest in such things. Of course, if you do not like it, I am certain—"

"No; forgive me. That did not come out as I intended. I do like it. I like it very much." He turned away, but not before Elizabeth caught the slight sheen at the corners of his eyes.

Reaching out to collect the wrappings, Elizabeth began neatly folding them and returning them to the basket.

"So, what shall we do now?" she asked cheerfully. "Shall I play for you? Or we might retire to the library..."

Turning back to look at her, Darcy cleared his throat. "No. I thank you, but I find I am more tired than I realized. I think I will take my new books and turn in early, if you do not mind?"

"No, of course not," Elizabeth answered, though she could not help but feel a little disappointed.

Elizabeth climbed to her feet, and her husband did likewise.

"I will bid you a good night then," Darcy said with a bow. He moved towards the door but then stopped, turning once more in her direction.

"Thank you, Elizabeth. For the wonderful dinner, and the gifts. Truly. It is a day I will not soon forget."

～

The door to Darcy's apartment closed behind him with a hollow click. As usual, Harris was waiting, but Darcy barely spoke to his valet, sending him away with a wave of his hand.

Pouring several fingers of brandy, he settled down in an armchair by the fireplace, the book Elizabeth had given him resting in his lap.

His birthday. How could he have forgotten?

Staring into the empty hearth, Darcy shook his head. In truth, it was not unusual for him to overlook the date. Indeed, he had not celebrated his birthday in any meaningful way since his father died. Usually, it was Harris who reminded him of the occasion by wishing him well when he greeted him on his birthday morning, and likely would have done so today had it not been his morning out.

Of course, Georgiana always remembered the day, but for the last few years, his sister had been away at school. And while she had always commemorated the occasion and written him happy tidings, there had been no gifts. No celebratory meals.

Until today.

Swallowing down the knot that had once again settled at the back of his throat, Darcy cracked open the volume in his lap, reverently flipping through the pages. How could she have known exactly the type of book that would suit his tastes? Even his sister and Richard, who was his closest friend and confidant, would never have thought to purchase him something like this…

Closing the leather cover, Darcy allowed his head to fall back against the cushions, one hand coming up to massage his brow. The entire evening had been a sort of heavenly torture. Seeing the deliberate care and consideration Elizabeth had put into making the dinner a special one had filled him with admiration. It had instantly taken him back to his boyhood—which had been both a blessing and a curse—and had made him feel nurtured and cherished in a way he had not experienced since before his mother's passing. But more than that, it had made him fall even more deeply in love with his wife.

Taking another swallow of his drink, Darcy stifled a groan. He was slipping. Ever since the ball, when he had finally acknowledged his feelings for her, Elizabeth had been gaining a stronger grip on his heart with each and every day that passed. And he was powerless to stop it.

Devil take it! What in blazes was wrong with him? He was supposed to be distancing himself from Elizabeth, not allowing her an even firmer foothold on his heart. Well, there was no point in denying it any longer, he was at his most vulnerable where she was concerned.

Which was one of the reasons he had suggested they separate. Why had she turned down his offer to decamp to Town? He was certain she would have jumped at the chance to be closer to her family and away from him...

Taking another swallow of his drink, Darcy sighed. There was still a chance that she might change her mind. And if not, perhaps he would be the one to go. Ellis was already proving to be a trustworthy and reliable custodian for the estate, so Darcy's presence at Pemberley was not as vital as it had been before.

In any case, it was becoming clearer every day that something would have to change. Being with Elizabeth was dangerous. Despite his best intentions, she was beginning to matter to him in a way that could only end in heartbreak. The feelings she provoked in him were too raw, too unsettling. He could not continue to battle the riot of emotions she incited within him simply by being who she was.

No, he could not allow himself to want her. He would sooner feel nothing at all.

In the weeks following her husband's birthday, Elizabeth's days settled into an easy routine. The weather was slowly improving, and in addition to her visits to the tenants in her phaeton, she was finally able to spend prolonged periods of time walking through the gardens, which were beginning to come to life after the long winter.

Mr. Darcy remained busy with his new steward, whom both he and Elizabeth liked very much. Several days after their dinner conversation, her husband had gone to see Mrs. Kirk, and to everyone's delight, the older woman had agreed to allow Mr. Darcy to take back the majority of her land, in exchange for a substantial reduction to her rent. Elizabeth had visited her several times since then, and was relieved to see that her circumstances already appeared somewhat improved, and the lines of worry around her eyes had all but disappeared.

One day in early April, Elizabeth was curled up in an armchair in her chambers when a soft scratching drew her attention to the corridor outside.

With a wry smile, Elizabeth set down her novel, picking up her skirts and hurrying to admit her canine visitor lest she damage the polished mahogany beyond repair.

As soon as the door was opened, Harpocrates scampered into the room, streaking across the carpet and bounding onto the seat Elizabeth had just vacated, curling into the cushions.

Shaking her head, Elizabeth shut the door, coming to perch on the arm of the chair and scratching the hound behind her ears in a way that made her sigh with pleasure.

"You are getting far too spoiled," Elizabeth said, a smile in her voice. "What would Mr. Darcy say if he knew you spent your afternoons sleeping in my bedchamber?"

In answer to her question, Harpocrates let out a soft snort, and Elizabeth laughed outright.

"One would almost think you could hear and understand every word I say, you little minx."

To Elizabeth's surprise, in the three months since Georgiana's departure, the hound had transferred her affections to herself, spending more and more time in Elizabeth's company within the house. And as the weather began to improve, Elizabeth had even taken to allowing the dog to join her when she walked in the gardens.

Coming to her feet, she looked down at the animal now in mock severity.

"Well, if you insist on stealing my chair, I shall have to move a second one in here so we might both be comfortable," she said with a rueful smile.

Which suddenly reminded Elizabeth that she had meant to speak with Mrs. Reynolds about that very subject. Although the chair she was currently using was serviceable, she had seen a small chaise in one of the guest chambers that she thought would fit perfectly in her little nook beside the bookcase the housekeeper had procured for her. It would be far more comfortable for reading, and would even be big enough for her furry companion.

Giving the dog one last pat, she turned on her heel, determined to seek Mrs. Reynolds out to ask her about it then and there.

~

Upon reaching the entrance hall, Elizabeth paused to question a passing footman as to the housekeeper's whereabouts, and was informed that she could be found in one of the parlors towards the rear of the house. The room in question was not one Elizabeth visited frequently, though she did vaguely recall Mr. Darcy showing it to her when she first arrived. It was in an out of the way location, and the heavy, masculine décor was not to her taste. And as Pemberley boasted more parlors, sitting rooms, and saloons than one could possibly need, she tended to make use of the ones more suited to her personal preferences.

Entering the walnut paneled room several minutes later, Elizabeth stopped just inside the door, not wishing to disturb Mrs. Reynolds, who was giving instructions to one of the young parlor maids on the far side of the room. However, it did not take long for the housekeeper to notice her presence.

"Oh, Mrs. Darcy! Forgive me, I did not hear you come in. Was there something you required?"

"No, no, that is, it is nothing of great import. Pray, finish what you were doing. I am happy to wait."

Nodding her acquiescence, Mrs. Reynolds returned her attention to the maid, while Elizabeth wandered aimlessly towards the tall windows, running her fingers lightly along the back of a green velvet sofa. Upon reaching the fireplace, she paused, her interest captured by a pair of miniatures that hung above the mantlepiece. Coming closer, she studied the portraits, which showed two young men of a similar age to herself. The first drawing was clearly her husband, his features arranged in the same serious expression she had seen him adopt on numerous occasions... but it was the second likeness that held her attention.

"That is all for now, Nellie. You may go."

Having dismissed the maid, the housekeeper came forward, stopping when she reached Elizabeth's side.

"Very like him, is it not?" she asked, indicating the miniature of Mr. Darcy. "It was done about eight years ago, when the master was at university."

Slowly, Elizabeth nodded. "Yes, very." Darting a glance in the housekeeper's direction she indicated the second portrait saying cautiously, "Is that not Mr. George Wickham?"

Instantly, there was a change in the older woman's expression, her lips turning down at the corners.

"Aye. The master has told you of him no doubt. He was the son of my late master's steward, raised here on the estate and brought up at Mr. George Darcy's own expense. He is now gone into the army," she added, "but I am afraid he has turned out very wild."

"Yes, so I hear," Elizabeth answered, unwilling to admit to knowing the gentleman herself. "I suppose I was just surprised to see his portrait on display beside my husband's. It is my understanding that they do not get along."

"Aye," the housekeeper repeated. "This parlor was my late master's favorite room, and these miniatures are just as they used to be then. He was very fond of them. The present Mr. Darcy never comes in here."

Ah. Well, that would explain the situation, Elizabeth thought. She wondered if her husband even knew the miniature of Mr. Wickham remained on display. He must not, or she was certain he would have had it removed.

Suddenly, Elizabeth was struck by something, and she turned once again to face the housekeeper.

"Forgive me, Mrs. Reynolds, but did you say a moment ago that the late Mr. Darcy was called George? I had been under the impression that his name was Robert, but perhaps I am misremembering..."

To Elizabeth's surprise, the housekeeper looked as though she had been struck, but she quickly averted her gaze, composing her expression.

"His given name was Robert, madam, but his second name was George, just like his father's before him. It is a family name, passed down for some generations. As old Mr. Darcy's father bore the same moniker, my late master always went by George to avoid confusion."

"Oh, I see." Something was niggling at the back of Elizabeth's mind, but she set it aside, turning away from the miniatures and changing the topic of conversation to her reason for seeking the housekeeper out in the first place.

"Certainly, Mrs. Darcy," Mrs. Reynolds eagerly replied. "I shall have a footman move the piece this very afternoon."

The two spoke for some few minutes more before one of the maids arrived to report a problem in the kitchens, and Elizabeth waved the housekeeper off with a smile before taking a seat in one of the leather wingchairs facing the fireplace.

What was it about the late Mr. Darcy's name that was nagging at her? While the housekeeper's accounting made sense, Elizabeth could swear she had heard Mr. Darcy's father referred to as Robert, and not George. Had her husband ever mentioned his father by name? Elizabeth racked her brain, but she could not recall him doing so. No, it had to have been someone else. Colonel Fitzwilliam, perhaps?

Suddenly, Elizabeth straightened in her chair. No, it had not been the colonel. It was her husband's godmother who had used the name, she was almost certain of it.

Turning her thoughts back to the day of the ball, she once again heard the dowager marchioness's voice inside her head.

"There are two things Darcy hates above all others: balls and Briarwood. He has not stepped foot on the estate since Robert's death..."

How strange. Why would Melanie have referred to the late Mr. Darcy as Robert, when he had always gone by George?

All at once, Elizabeth's pulse quickened as realization sent a shiver down her spine.

No, Melanie had not referred to the former Mr. Darcy as Robert. Because when she had used the name, her husband's godmother had been speaking of someone else entirely.

Chapter 17

"Why did you never tell me you had a brother?"

At Elizabeth's words, Darcy visibly started, setting aside the sketch he had been working on and slowly coming to his feet, his expression grim.

"I beg your pardon?"

"Robert," Elizabeth elaborated, walking farther into the room off her husband's study. "He *was* your brother, was he not? Or do you deny it?"

Darcy flinched, but he answered evenly, "I have no wish to deny it. However, there is nothing to tell. He died long ago."

Elizabeth stared back at him, her mouth dropped open. "Surely there must be something to tell, as you have taken great pains to erase his existence."

Darcy's face was devoid of expression, but Elizabeth could see how his hands gripped the edge of the table in front of him. At length, he turned his back, pacing to the window and pulling his fingers through his hair.

"Who told you?" he eventually asked, staring out into the gardens.

"Mrs. Reynolds said something just now... but it was actually your godmother who first mentioned him. She told me you had not been to Briarwood since Robert's death. When she said it, I assumed she meant your father. I only realized today when Mrs. Reynolds referred to the late Mr. Darcy as 'George' that I was mistaken."

Coming to stand beside him, she said quietly, "There were other clues as well, though I was not clever enough to pick up on them. The story Colonel Fitzwilliam was attempting to tell about your boyhood, when you knocked over the tea service. And the empty space in the gallery. It was your brother's portrait that hung there, was it not?"

Darcy offered her a single nod, and Elizabeth could see by the pallor of his complexion and the rigid way he held his body that the conversation was exceedingly difficult for him. But despite his obvious discomfort, something told her that she would not be doing him any favors by leaving the truth locked away.

"Will you show it to me?" she asked gently.

Darcy turned to face her, a question in his dark eyes. "Show you…?"

"The portrait. Is it here, in the house?"

He paused, then nodded. "Yes. In the attics."

Elizabeth smiled encouragingly, reaching for his hand, and Darcy sighed in defeat.

"Very well. If you wish it."

Without another word, he tucked her hand into the crook of his arm, escorting her from the room. When they reached the uppermost story of the house, he led her down a long passageway before ascending another flight of stairs which opened into a vast attic. Sunlight filtered in through the dormer windows, illuminating the dust motes that floated in the stagnant air.

Releasing her arm, Darcy threaded his way through the

clusters of shrouded furniture and the neat stacks of castoff belongings, Elizabeth trailing after him. At length, they reached a corner of the room where a painting wrapped in moleskin leaned against the far wall.

Darcy hesitated before slowly reaching up and peeling back the heavy cloth.

Elizabeth's heartbeat quickened as the drape fell away, revealing the portrait of a young boy. Although he had her husband's strong jaw and straight nose, his coloring was fair, like Georgiana's, but it was the expression on his face that affected her the most. With his lips drawn up into a genuine smile, and his eyes sparkling with mirth, the image radiated an almost palpable joy.

"My brother, Robert," Darcy said, not removing his eyes from the portrait. "He was killed in an accident when he was twelve years old, and I was ten. This was painted just before his death. As a matter of fact, it was not even completed until... afterwards."

Turning her face towards his, Elizabeth reached out, gently squeezing his hand.

"It happened at Briarwood," he continued, "in the autumn of '94. We were there for a shooting party. A couple of us boys found a set of dueling pistols, and there was a wager... to see who could come closest to hitting an old archery target in the woods. The gun Robert was using misfired..." Darcy visibly swallowed, and Elizabeth laced her fingers with his, tightening her grip.

"How terrible," she whispered.

"Yes," he replied solemnly. "It was."

They stood in silence for several minutes, both staring into the eyes of the young Robert Darcy, who looked back at them impassively, fixed forever in time and place. Eventually, Darcy turned away, replacing the white drape that had covered the painting. When his gaze once again found hers, Elizabeth's heart shattered at the unmistakable anguish she saw reflected in his eyes.

Spotting the shrouded form of an old settee tucked away near one of the high windows, she drew her husband there, gently pulling him down to sit beside her on the narrow seat.

"Will you tell me about him?" she asked quietly.

Bracing his elbows on his knees, Darcy dropped his head into his hands. For a long moment, he was silent, and Elizabeth began to think he would not answer. Then, slowly, his posture straightened, and he began to speak in a hollow tone.

"Robert was, in virtually every respect, a model son, and the best brother anyone could ask for. He was friendly and clever, and a natural sportsman. He loved to make people laugh, but he was also exceedingly kind. He had a soft spot for animals, and he would champion anyone he felt was being treated unfairly.

"I know it sounds like I am idealizing him, but I assure you I am not. Anybody who knew him would say the same. He had a way of making everyone he spoke with feel as though they were the most important person in the room. When he was alive, Pemberley was a home filled with laughter, and liveliness, and joy. And when he went, he took all of our happiness with him."

Not knowing what to say, Elizabeth murmured, "It must have been very difficult... for your parents to lose a child, and for you to lose such a wonderful brother."

Darcy nodded, saying, "It was my mother who suffered worst of all. She was already increasing with Georgiana when the accident occurred, and her grief nearly destroyed her. She took to her bed, withdrawing from the world. Knowing she was carrying a child, she did her best to cope, but Georgiana was delivered too early, and there were... difficulties. Three days after my sister's birth, my mother was gone."

Elizabeth sucked in a breath as her husband continued, "We thought we would lose Georgiana, too, but despite all odds, she survived. My father tried to hold everything together—caring for his newborn daughter, and beginning to teach me the management of the estate; but he was never the same. Losing Robert and my mother changed him... it changed us, as a family, and it altered everything I thought my life would be."

He turned to face Elizabeth, but there was a blank sort of emptiness in his eyes.

"So, now you know the truth. Pemberley was never my birthright. Robert was the heir. And there is nothing I would not give to have him here instead of me."

Elizabeth opened her mouth to speak, but before she could so much as gather her thoughts, Darcy rose abruptly to his feet.

"Pray, forgive me... I cannot..."

And without a backwards glance, he fled from the room.

The following morning, Elizabeth awoke to another note from her husband.

Elizabeth,

Urgent business takes me to Leeds. I expect to be gone a fortnight. Should you have need of me before then, Ellis has my direction.

FD

Setting aside the brief missive, Elizabeth sighed. Mr. Darcy had been virtually silent at dinner the previous evening, and had retired shortly thereafter. He had made no mention of a trip, and Elizabeth could not help but wonder whether it was truly business that called him away, or whether he was merely running from his memories.

In truth, Mr. Darcy was not the only one who had been deeply affected by their conversation. Since their encounter in the attic, Elizabeth had spent a great deal of time thinking about the man she had married. She had been so certain she understood his character... but how much did any one person ever really know about another? And how easy was it for false perceptions and faulty first impressions to color one's opinions? After all, she thought, had she herself not been most unhappily deceived by her own lack of discernment when it came to Mr. Wickham?

Her thoughts drifted back to the argument she had had with Mr. Darcy shortly after her arrival at Pemberley, when she had brazenly accused him of being unacquainted with any type of privation.

"Someone in your position cannot possibly imagine what it is like to know uncertainty, or to fear for your future."

"Someone in my position?"

"Yes. A first-born son, heir to a great estate. From the time you were old enough to understand, you knew that all you surveyed would one day be yours. That you would always live a life of ease, and that nothing you wanted would ever be outside your grasp. The world is not like that for most."

Recalling her words now, Elizabeth cringed. That she had had the impudence to stand before her husband and castigate him for never knowing adversity... he who had suffered more loss in his young life than anyone should have to bear.

What would it be like to be a boy of ten and to see the older brother you idolized mortally wounded? And worse still, to know that the life you lived and all you possessed had been intended for another? How would such a circumstance shape the person you grew up to be?

Slowly, Elizabeth was beginning to understand that losing his brother—and then his mother not long afterwards—had affected her husband deeply. Not only had he been pitched headlong into grief and despair, but there had been responsibility, too, piled upon his shoulders. Obligations he had never prepared for, nor even desired, but had he run from them? Had he palmed off his estate on stewards and men of business as so many of his class did, so that they could live a life of leisure and indolence? No, he had risen to the occasion. He had become the best possible master of Pemberley. He had packed his own dreams away in order to care for his sister and his tenants; his servants and staff; his friends and his relations.

"And me," she whispered.

Yes, Mr. Darcy cared for everyone in his circle... but who was there to care for him?

∾

For several days after her husband's abrupt departure, Elizabeth nursed her melancholy, but as her character was not formed for ill-humor, on the fourth day, she made up her mind to pay a call on Mrs. Kirk. She had not been to visit the older woman recently, and Elizabeth was anxious to see how she was faring.

As luck would have it, the weather that day was especially fine, with the sun shining brightly in a clear blue sky, and the idea of a long drive through the park was a balm to Elizabeth's low spirits.

After sending word to have the phaeton readied, Elizabeth retrieved her bonnet and spencer before making her way out of the doors that led to the gardens. She had just reached the gravel drive when a sound behind her captured her attention, and she turned to see Harpocrates scampering up the path, her long tail waving in the breeze. Stopping in her tracks, Elizabeth folded her arms despite the laugh that was building in her chest.

"And where did you come from?" she asked, even though the animal was unable to hear her, and certainly would not answer if she could.

Nonetheless, Harp responded by whining low in her throat and wriggling the back end of her body.

Elizabeth laughed without reserve, shaking her head at the animal's antics.

"You should not be out here. You must learn that you cannot accompany me whenever I leave the house."

The hound cocked her head, staring at Elizabeth with wide, dark eyes, which caused any hope she might have had of standing her ground to completely give way.

"Oh, very well. Just this once. But you shall remain in the carriage!"

~

A short while later, Elizabeth was pulling the horses to a stop before Mrs. Kirk's compact cottage. Looking up at the stone dwelling, Elizabeth could see a marked improvement from her first visit—the shutters were now painted a bright white, the roof was newly thatched, and a large parcel of nearby land had been freshly turned.

Gathering her skirts, Elizabeth climbed down from her conveyance, reaching in to collect the basket of provisions she had brought with her and giving Harp a brief pat on the head.

"You stay here," she said, though, naturally, the hound did not so much as turn in her direction. Instead she stared off into the near distance, her tail thumping against the floorboards. Following the animal's gaze, Elizabeth was surprised to see a familiar figure rounding the corner of the house, whistling a lively tune.

"Simon!"

Stepping away from the carriage, Elizabeth approached the boy, who set down the shovel he had been carrying and immediately doffed his cap.

After he had offered her a formal bow and a polite greeting, Elizabeth looked around in some confusion before saying, "I am surprised to see you here. I did not realize you worked outside the house."

Nodding his acknowledgement, Simon replied, "I'm still up at the manor in the mornings; then here in the afternoons. The master arranged it for me. Been coming out for a few weeks now."

"I see," Elizabeth answered. *No wonder things seemed so much improved around here,* she thought. It was certainly a benefit to Mrs. Kirk to have Simon on hand to assist with the farm, but she could not help but worry that the boy was being taken advantage of.

"That is good of you," she continued, "to agree to be of service to Mrs. Kirk, in addition to your regular duties."

At Elizabeth's words, the boy's eyes grew round, and he quickly shook his head.

"No, ma'am! I'm the one who should be thanking Mr. Darcy for sending me. He knows how keen I am to work the land. I been asking him since I come if he could find a place for me with one of the tenants. I know I'm still too young to be of much use, but this is a right good start."

Relieved, Elizabeth nodded before a sudden thought occurred to her.

"Surely you do not walk here? It is very far from the house."

"No, Misses. Mr. Ellis brings me out in the gig. Comes to fetch me back at the end of the day, too."

"Well, that seems a sensible arrangement." After a moment, she added, "Tell me, Simon, are you fond of Mr. Ellis? That is, do you find him amiable?"

"Oh, yes, ma'am! I know some folks don't like him being so young and all, but he's real smart. Told me he's worked the land since he was no bigger than me, and he knows all sorts of things about different plants and how to get 'em to grow. Treats people right, too."

The two chatted for a while longer and then Elizabeth said her goodbyes and began to make her way towards the house, but she had not walked more than a few steps before she turned to once again face the young boy.

"Simon, might I ask a favor? Will you have Mr. Ellis come see me this afternoon when he drops you at the house? You may let him know there is a matter of some importance I would like to discuss."

~

On the twelfth day following the start of his self-imposed exile, Darcy's carriage trundled to a halt in Pemberley's circular drive. Looking out at his ancestral home, he suppressed a heavy sigh. He knew he had taken the coward's way out by leaving, but speaking of Robert had been more painful than he had anticipated, and he comprehended enough of Elizabeth's nature to be certain she would not rest until he divulged more than he was prepared to share.

Still, he had missed her.

Allowing his footman to unlatch the door, Darcy stepped to the ground, steeling his resolve. He needed to get a hold of himself. How was he supposed to distance himself from the woman he had married when he could scarcely last a fortnight without her?

Climbing the wide stone steps, Darcy entered the hall, removing his hat and coat and handing them off to a waiting footman as his butler hurried into view.

"Mr. Darcy, sir! We were not expecting you until the day after tomorrow. You have had a pleasant journey, I hope?"

"Yes, thank you, Lawson. I was able to conclude my business earlier than expected, and we made excellent time on the roads."

"Very good, sir. Shall I have hot water sent up?"

"No, I will bathe at the usual time," he replied, already heading towards the stairs. "There are some matters of business I should attend to before dinner. Has Mrs. Darcy gone out?" he called over his shoulder, silently berating himself for not even making it five minutes without the almost overwhelming desire to see her.

The butler hesitated for only a moment, but it was enough to make Darcy stop, turning to look sharply at the trusted servant.

"No, sir. Mrs. Darcy retired to her chambers directly following the midday meal. I believe she is… indisposed."

"What?" Darcy snapped, turning on his heel. "Why did you not say something as soon as I arrived?"

Not waiting for an answer, he stalked towards the curved staircase with ground-eating strides, taking the marble steps two at a time.

Striding down the corridor that led to the family wing, all sorts of terrible images assaulted his senses. Had she inadvertently eaten something at luncheon that had made her truly ill, as she had been at Briarwood? Why on earth had Lawson not thought to alert him as soon as he alighted from the carriage!

Fear gripped his stomach as he came to a halt outside her apartment, and he lifted his hand, rapping insistently on the polished wood. When no answer came, he knocked again, harder this time. He had just resolved to try the handle when the latch clicked, and the door opened.

Elizabeth's startled gaze met his through the narrow opening.

"Mr. Darcy! Forgive me, I did not expect... That is, I did not realize you had returned. Is... is anything the matter?"

"I have come to ask you that very question. Lawson said you were unwell."

He thought he saw her relax ever so slightly, but noticed that a light flush suffused her cheeks.

"No. That is, I am not..." She sighed, opening the door wider before looking up and down the passageway. "Pray, come in."

Shifting uneasily, Darcy hesitated before finally stepping across the threshold and allowing Elizabeth to close the door behind him.

Once inside her chambers, he instantly regretted his decision. He had expected to find her tucked up in bed, with a maid by her side. Instead, she was alone, standing before him in a soft pink dressing gown which she moved to wrap more securely around her body. She looked lovely, if a little pale, and Darcy found himself thinking of the last time he had seen her in that dressing gown, the night she had come to his bedchamber, shortly after their arrival at Pemberley.

Clasping his hands behind his back, he attempted to banish such thoughts, turning his mind to the matter at hand.

"Are you ill? Lawson said you went up right after luncheon. I thought perhaps..."

"Oh! No, it is nothing like that. I am only a bit..." she waved her hand vaguely before continuing, "Pray, do not concern yourself. I am certain I shall feel better tomorrow."

Darcy's gaze sharpened. "How can you know that? Should I not send for a doctor?"

To his surprise, Elizabeth arched her brow.

"No, that will not be necessary, unless you plan to send for him on a monthly basis."

It took a minute for her meaning to register, but when it did, he could feel an intense heat creeping up his neck, and he quickly looked away.

"Ah. I see. Yes, of course. I… well. I shall leave you to rest, then."

"Yes, thank you," Elizabeth answered. "I appreciate you coming to check on me."

Still unable to meet her gaze, Darcy bowed awkwardly, moving towards the door. But he had not gone more than a few steps before stopping to turn once again in her direction.

"Is there nothing I can bring you? Some tea? Or brandy, perhaps?"

Elizabeth offered him a shallow smile, but he could see now that there was a tightness around her mouth, and her eyes lacked their usual luster.

"That is kind, but there is no need. Very few things offer any relief. A hot bath sometimes helps, but I have had one already. I think I will simply rest, as you suggested."

Slowly, Darcy nodded. He knew he should leave, but for some unknown reason, his legs refused to cooperate. Instead, he found himself continuing to speak.

"What are the others?"

"I beg your pardon?"

"You said there were but a few things that offered you any relief—a hot bath being one of them. What are the others?"

"Oh." To his surprise, Elizabeth's color deepened. "Well, sometimes Jane would rub my back. I... I suppose I could ask Cassidy to attend me, but I would feel a little silly. A maid is not quite the same as a sister."

Darcy regarded her for a long moment.

"What about a husband?" he asked, scarcely recognizing his own voice.

Elizabeth blinked back at him. "A... a husband?"

"I could do it; rub your back, that is. If you think it would help."

Elizabeth stared up at him, her eyes round, and Darcy held his breath, although for the life of him he could not determine whether he was willing her to say yes, or no. After a moment that felt more like an hour, Elizabeth offered him a slow nod.

"Very well."

Turning away, she loosened the belt of her dressing gown, slipping it from her delicate frame and draping it neatly over the back of a chair. Beneath the robe, she wore a simple cotton night rail. As nightclothes went, it was of a modest design, with long sleeves, a high neck, and a hemline that touched the floor. In truth, it was about as far from indecorous as such an article of clothing could be... were it not for the golden rays slanting in through the window behind her, causing every curve of her figure to stand out in sharp relief.

Darcy swallowed, and their gazes locked before Elizabeth lowered her lashes. His eyes followed as she walked to the bed, climbing atop the quilted counterpane and relaxing onto her stomach with a soft sigh.

For several seconds he could only stare, his feet rooted to the carpet as his heart continued to hammer in his chest.

Inside his head, a small voice was screaming at him to get out while he still could... but then Elizabeth smiled, and in a matter of seconds, he was moving to her side.

Perching carefully upon the edge of the mattress, he focused his gaze on her upturned face.

"Where exactly...?"

"My lower back. At least, that is where the pain is most severe... if... if it is not too much trouble."

Darcy nodded, slowly shifting his attention to the spot where the dip in her spine met her perfectly rounded bottom as a slight sheen of sweat broke out across his brow.

Lifting his hands, he allowed his palms to settle against her form, his fingers automatically curling into the folds of her nightgown. The heat of her body seemed to scorch his skin through the light cotton as Darcy began to knead the taut muscles of her back.

Beside him, Elizabeth released a breathy moan, and Darcy did his best to ignore the stirring in his loins, focusing his attention on moving his thumbs in slow, steady circles along the column of her spine.

Gradually, Elizabeth's eyes fluttered closed and her breathing slowed to a steady rhythm. After a while, her measured breaths began to lull Darcy into a light stupor, and he could not say how long he sat beside her, gently caressing her through the thin fabric of her shift. It was not until the clock on the mantle chimed the hour that Darcy drew back, reluctantly removing his hands as Elizabeth opened her eyes.

"Better?" Darcy asked hoarsely, and Elizabeth offered him a contented nod.

Standing, Darcy turned away, reaching for the extra blanket at the foot of the bed and pulling it up to cover her.

With his body still angled mostly away, he forcibly cleared his voice.

"I shall leave you now. Pray, do not concern yourself over supper; I will have Mrs. Reynolds send a tray."

"Thank you," Elizabeth murmured, and without further conversation, Darcy turned and walked stiffly from the room.

∾

A quarter of an hour later, Darcy paced to the window of his chambers, staring out at the rain-soaked garden.

He never should have touched her. He had convinced himself that his intention had only been to relieve her suffering; he had never been able to bear seeing her in pain. But he should have called her maid to attend her, as she had suggested. Or perhaps his housekeeper. Good God, any of the female members of the household would have sufficed. Anyone but him!

Darcy groaned. The truth was… he had wanted to touch her. He had been desperate to feel the warmth of her body underneath his hands… hell, he had yearned for the feel of her ever since that first week at Pemberley when she had come to his bedchamber wearing nothing but her night-clothes, her chin tipped up at a defiant angle.

Turning away from the glass, he stalked to the sideboard, lifting the waiting decanter and pouring himself a drink.

No, even that was not the truth. In actuality, he had wanted to touch her long before that. Almost from the earliest moments of their acquaintance, when he had seen her striding across the lawn at Netherfield, her petticoats six inches deep in mud.

Taking a swallow of his brandy, he dropped into a nearby chair. There was no point in denying it any longer. He had loved her from the beginning. But had he told her that? Had he expressed his genuine admiration and regard when he had made his addresses to her? Had he spoken one word of love, or affection, or esteem? No, he had not. He had scarcely managed to keep a civil tongue in his head. Yet he had the temerity to feel slighted when he found out that his new bride was not madly in love with him! Why should he have expected that she would be? He had done nothing to earn her regard, and he had certainly made no attempt to assure her of his.

What had possessed him to insist on moving forward with his offer after she had made it clear that she had no intention of accepting her cousin? If anyone had asked him at the time, he would have said that he considered it a matter of honor, as he had already spoken with her father. But deep down, he knew that was a lie. It was not honor that had propelled him along his path to ruination, nor were his motives entirely altruistic. It was desire, plain and simple. He wanted Elizabeth—had wanted her since he first laid eyes on her at that assembly, if he was being honest with himself—and so he had contrived a way to have her. And he had done it in such a manner as to make it seem like an act of noble generosity, to boot. He had been so caught up in the fantasy he had created—this dream of a life with the most captivating woman he had ever known— that he did not make even the smallest effort to ascertain the desires of her own heart.

And her heart did not belong to him. At least not in the way his belonged to her.

"... you have not simply married without affection; you have married a man you vehemently dislike. You, who always said you would only marry for love."

Once again, Jane Bennet's words echoed in his ears, but for the first time, he realized that Elizabeth's sister had been wrong. Elizabeth *had* married for love. A love far deeper than any she could ever feel for him.

"This is all I have ever wanted—to see my sister this happy... There is no one who could deserve it more, and there is nothing I would not have sacrificed to make it happen."

She had not married him for his money or his standing in society. She had done it for Jane. She had traded her own happiness for that of her beloved sister—the one person in the world she loved better than any other.

But could he truly blame her for that? Would he not have done the same for Georgiana?

No, he could not find fault in her reasons for marrying him, nor in her behavior since the day they had become man and wife. She had lived up to her end of the bargain—she was an excellent friend to his sister, a capable mistress for his estate, and a valuable helpmate to him.

It was not her fault he wanted more.

If only it were possible to turn back the clock and do things differently... Perhaps if he told her of his true feelings, there was still a chance that she could grow to care for him.

If only he could find the courage to try.

~

The following morning, Darcy awoke with renewed determination. He had made up his mind. He would find Elizabeth and pour out his heart. He would tell her he loved her, and that he wanted to start again. He would find a way to be a better husband. A better man. The kind of man Elizabeth deserved.

Hurrying through his morning routine, Darcy exited his chambers at a brisk pace. According to Harris, Elizabeth had rung for her maid some time ago, and he hoped to catch her in the breakfast parlor. It was another beautiful day, and he had already determined that the rose garden would be the perfect setting for him to finally reveal his true feelings to the woman he loved.

Striding into the breakfast room, he drew to a halt at the sight of the empty table, disappointment already settling like a stone inside his stomach. Turning to the footman on duty, he attempted to keep his voice neutral.

"Good morning, James. Has Mrs. Darcy breakfasted already?"

"Yes, sir. She left about a quarter of an hour ago. I believe she is walking in the gardens."

Instantly, Darcy's mood lightened, and he thanked the servant before hastening from the room. The gardens were extensive, but he was hopeful that he could locate her quickly. Now that he had determined to speak his mind, he did not want to waste a moment.

A short while later, Darcy ducked under the trellis that led to the formal gardens, but before he could enter the enclosure, his feet ground to a halt.

Directly across from him, Elizabeth was seated on a stone bench, surrounded by a profusion of early spring blossoms. She looked exactly as he had dreamt she would... except for the fact that she was not alone. A gentleman Darcy had never seen before sat by her side, their shoulders so close they were practically touching. As he watched, Elizabeth handed him a folded sheet of paper, and the gentleman smiled, tucking it away in the inside pocket of his coat. The man could not have been much older than himself, and Darcy could see that his clothing was well-tailored and his bearing open and relaxed. But it was Elizabeth's expression that caused Darcy's stomach to twist in a way that almost made him cry out in pain. She looked... happy. No, not just happy, she looked effervescent. Her skin flushed a soft pink and her lips curved up into the kind of smile he had not seen since he had brought her to Derbyshire.

The man leaned in, saying something Darcy could not hear, and Elizabeth laughed in obvious delight, reaching out to touch his sleeve. Darcy stood transfixed, watching until he could bear it no longer before turning away. But it was no use. He knew that image would be seared upon his consciousness for as long as he lived.

And that was when he made up his mind. He would be gone from Pemberley the following morning; and this time, he had no intention of coming back.

Chapter 18

Elizabeth stood on a high rocky rise overlooking Pemberley's lands, her bonnet held loosely in one hand, Harpocrates crouched contentedly by her side.

Four letters. That was the extent of the communication she had received from her husband. One for each week he had been gone. Every letter, precisely the same. A single sheet of parchment telling her everything and nothing, all at the same time.

The weather was fair. Georgiana sent her regards. They had attended a musical performance or gone riding in Hyde Park. His business occupied much of his time. He could not yet say when he would return to Derbyshire.

And with every letter that arrived, Elizabeth had attempted to set pen to paper to compose her reply… only to end up relegating every effort to the fire.

For what was there to say? She could not bear the thought of sending a similarly insipid response, and yet she dared not expose her heart for his derision.

Staring out at the horizon, Elizabeth released a melancholy sigh. The truth was, she missed him. And she was sensible enough to realize it was not simply because she was lonesome. She missed *him*.

In the five months since she had come to Pemberley as a new bride, the clouds had lifted from her eyes, and everything she thought she knew about the proud and arrogant Mr. Darcy had fallen away, leaving a very different sort of man standing in his place. A man who was noble and generous, steadfast and kind.

How had it taken her so long to understand his true nature, despite all of those around him who had spoken up on his behalf? Richard, Georgiana, Lady Wheaton. Even the servants and tenants under his care. But beyond that, how could she so easily dismiss what she had witnessed with her own eyes?

Time and again, her husband had shown himself to be a good man—the very best of men—and yet she had dismissed each instance out of hand.

Of course, it was true that when they were newly married, they had not understood each other very well, but she could not blame everything on faults of understanding. No, when it came to Mr. Darcy, she had willfully misunderstood.

I am not the enemy, Elizabeth.

No, he was not the enemy. Yet she had never seen him as a friend, let alone a partner. Nor had she treated him as such. And it was only now, when it appeared it may be too late, that she was beginning to deeply regret her actions.

The sound of a throat being cleared pulled Elizabeth out of her reverie, and she quickly turned in the direction of the noise. Lawson, the butler, stood several paces away, looking as dignified as he could manage after walking half a mile from the house and then trekking up a steep incline.

"Excuse me for intruding, madam, but you have a caller."

For a moment, Elizabeth's heart stuttered in her chest, thinking that perhaps her husband had returned at last… but of course, Lawson would not have referred to his master in such a way. Nor was Fitzwilliam likely to seek her out upon his arrival, she reminded herself ruefully.

Taking a step in the butler's direction, she returned the bonnet she was holding to her head, swiftly tying the ribbons. The movement drew Harpocrates's attention, and the hound scrambled to her feet.

"A caller?" Elizabeth asked in some confusion. In the five months she had been in residence, no one had called upon her, nor had she been introduced to any of the local families in the neighborhood, so she could not imagine who should be coming to see her now.

"Yes, madam," Lawson answered, "the Dowager Marchioness of Wheaton. I have taken the liberty of escorting her to the yellow drawing room and ringing for tea."

"Oh!" Elizabeth could not prevent the exclamation that fell from her lips. *Melanie is here?* Elizabeth had had a letter from her husband's godmother only last week, and she had said nothing about a visit…

Attempting to compose her features, she thanked the butler for his kindness in coming all this way to fetch her before saying, "Pray, tell Lady Wheaton that I am happy to receive her. I will return to the house directly."

~

Entering the drawing room a short time later, Elizabeth hurried towards her husband's godmother, who stood at the back of the room, gazing out into the gardens. At the sound of approaching footsteps, she turned, allowing Elizabeth to take her hands and kiss her gently on the cheek.

"Lady Wheaton! It is wonderful to see you. Pray, forgive me for not being here to greet you when you arrived. I spend a great deal of time outdoors now that the weather has improved."

Allowing Elizabeth to escort her to a chair, the dowager marchioness sat, carelessly waving away Elizabeth's regrets.

"Nonsense. One can hardly blame you for not being at home when your guest has the audacity to appear unannounced. It is I who should be apologizing to you for the impromptu visit. And you must call me 'Melanie'. Only the people I don't like call me 'Lady Wheaton'."

Elizabeth flushed and nodded her agreement before saying with a small smile, "Well then, perhaps we can agree not to quarrel over the greater share of the blame. In any case, I am very happy to see you, although I am afraid Fitzwilliam is not at home…" Her voice trailed off as the dowager marchioness studied her appraisingly.

"Yes, I am well aware of my godson's whereabouts. I have had letters from both Georgiana and my grandson, Richard, though none from Darcy himself. He has been in Town for some time, it would seem."

Elizabeth felt a flush building in her cheeks, as though it were somehow her fault that her husband had deserted her with scarcely a word of explanation.

"Yes. Above a month."

"Humph. Exactly as I thought. But I suppose it is just as well, since it is you I have come to see."

"Well, I am delighted to receive you," Elizabeth replied, attempting to hide her surprise. "Shall I have Mrs. Reynolds prepare a room? I would be happy for the company."

"No, my dear. I cannot stay. I am on my way to Town myself, so my visit will be brief."

Elizabeth voiced her disappointment, but before she could say anything further, there was a cursory knock at the opened door, and two maids entered, bearing the tea service and a tray of small sandwiches. Once the maids had gone, Elizabeth stepped up to pour, before settling down beside the dowager marchioness.

"I hope you will forgive the scarcity of sweet confections," she added, nodding towards the plate of food. "As I am sure you are aware, Fitzwilliam is not fond of them, and our kitchen staff is accustomed to catering to his preferences."

Pausing with her teacup in midair, Lady Wheaton stared back at her in puzzlement before barking out a laugh. "Darcy, not fond of sweets? Good heavens! When he was a boy, he could not get enough of them. I once saw him devour an entire plum pudding, and I do not remember a time when he did not have sweetmeats hidden in his pockets."

Upon hearing this revelation, Elizabeth could only stare at her husband's godmother in surprise. Of course, she knew one's tastes often evolved over time, but how did a boy who carried candies in his pockets grow into a man who eschewed sweets of any kind?

"I had no idea," she mused aloud. "He did seem to enjoy the cake I had our cook prepare for his birthday, but besides that one instance, I have never seen him eat anything beyond fresh fruit and the occasional dollop of jam. It is very curious…"

Melanie regarded her with a forthright gaze. "Is it? As a matter of fact, I find it fits the pattern quite well." Deliberately setting aside her cup and saucer, her husband's godmother continued, "My dear, has it never occurred to you to wonder why your husband has hied off to London, and what has kept him there these many weeks? And pray, do not say it is business. I know you are far too intelligent to believe *that*."

Once again, Elizabeth could feel the heat building in her cheeks, but she met Lady Wheaton's piercing gaze with as much composure as she could muster.

"No. I do not believe it is business that sent him to Town, nor do I believe it is business that keeps him there. I… I am afraid it is me."

The dowager's eyebrows lifted. "You think Darcy has gone to Town because he is displeased with you?" she queried, and Elizabeth offered a tremulous nod.

"I am certain of it. Not long before he left, we… we spoke of his brother. I could tell I had upset him with my questions. I thought it might help for him to speak of it, but I can see now that I should have left well enough alone."

"Ah, I see. Well, in that case, there may be some truth to what you say. Robert's death was an unspeakable tragedy. In many ways, it destroyed this family, and it certainly altered the course of Fitzwilliam's life. I do not think he has ever got over it. So, yes, in a way, it is understandable that he would retreat to London to lick his wounds. But I do not believe he stays away because you make him unhappy. In fact, I dare say it is quite the opposite."

"Forgive me, I am afraid I do not understand."

"Oh, my dear child… Why do you think your husband avoids sweets when he loves them so much? Moreover, why does he rarely go out in society? And why, on the rare occasions that he is forced to attend a ball, does he refuse to dance?"

Lady Wheaton stared at her intently, but Elizabeth could only shake her head in bewilderment.

"I do not know. I always assumed it was because he found no pleasure in such amusements."

Beside her, Melanie offered up a sad smile before gently taking Elizabeth's hand. "No, my dear. It is because those things bring him joy. And he does not think he is deserving of that sort of happiness. He denies himself as a punishment of sorts—because he survived, and Robert did not."

"But that is preposterous! His brother's death was an accident!"

Melanie lifted her shoulders in a delicate shrug. "I did not say his response was rational. And in truth, he may not even realize what he is doing. I am certain he thinks he is merely shouldering the responsibilities he has inherited in the best way possible. But he is not living. Not really. He has locked a part of himself away for a very long time. Fortunately, I believe there is now someone close to him who holds the key."

"Me?" Elizabeth asked incredulously, staring back at her husband's godmother with wide eyes.

Lady Wheaton chuckled softly. "Yes, you, Elizabeth.

Unless I miss my guess, Darcy has not retreated to London because you do not make him happy, but rather because you do."

~

Following Lady Wheaton's departure, Elizabeth claimed a headache and retired to her chambers.

The more she learned about her husband, the more she felt as though she were finally seeing the man she had married clearly for the first time… as if all the pieces of a puzzle had suddenly snapped into place. And while she was still reeling from Melanie's revelations, she knew it was not her husband's heart she needed to examine, but her own.

Since the beginning, she had maintained to everyone who would listen that she held Mr. Darcy in contempt. She had even gone so far as to tell Jane that the gentleman was the last man in the world whom she could ever be prevailed on to marry. And yet she had married him, all the same.

Oh, she had been quick to hold Lady Catherine accountable at the time. But she knew she could not lay the blame for her marriage entirely at Lady Catherine's door. In point of fact, she was every bit as obstinate and headstrong as Fitzwilliam's aunt had accused her of being. If she truly had not wanted to marry him, nothing and no one could have prevailed upon her to do so. Which left her to ponder the implications of her actions. Had she secretly wished to marry Mr. Darcy? No, it was not possible! And yet she had agreed to the match, of her own free will. True, Lady Catherine had goaded her into accepting, but Elizabeth had not made even the smallest attempt to extricate herself from her promise.

So why had she done it?

It would be a stretch to say that she had been fond of Mr. Darcy before their marriage, but he had always intrigued her. Even when he was being haughty and supercilious, he had captivated her in a way no other gentleman had, before or since. He was educated and clever, with a quick wit that rivaled even her beloved papa's. He was a caring and affectionate brother to Georgiana and a concerned and considerate landlord to his tenants. As far as she could tell, he had no abominable habits. He did not drink to excess or gamble, nor did he behave disreputably.

And all at once, Elizabeth had a rather shocking revelation: She admired her husband, and she was well on her way to being truly happy in her marriage. Not because she had been able to bring Jane and Mr. Bingley together, and not because she lived in a beautiful home with every possible luxury at her disposal, but because Fitzwilliam Darcy was a man she could look up to and respect. In truth, he was one of the most honorable men she had ever known.

"All this time, I have been lying to myself," she whispered. *"I do not despise him at all!"*

But was that enough? For a marriage to truly work, Elizabeth knew there had to be affection on *both* sides, and Darcy did not love her. Oh, she knew he cared about her. She knew he found her clever, and that he admired her lively disposition. But admiration was not love.

Unbidden, the thought of her husband turning to another woman for affection swam to the forefront of her mind, but she quickly pushed it away.

Coming abruptly to her feet, she made her way to the writing desk in the corner of her chambers. Elizabeth sat, slowly picking up her pen. Her fingers trembled slightly as she contemplated the consequences of her actions. For once the words were committed to paper, there would be no going back. Yet, something had to give. She could no longer continue on with things the way they were.

Reaching for the inkwell, she removed the stopper, dipping her pen and tapping it gently against the rim before touching it to the parchment.

Dear Fitzwilliam...

The moon cast inky shadows along the lane as the Darcy carriage made the last turn onto the familiar gravel drive. Ahead of them, Pemberley House stood on rising ground, a pale stone edifice, majestic in the moonlight. Inside the plush compartment, Darcy was surprised at the sudden melancholy that overtook him at the sight. Pemberley had been both his home and his vocation for the better part of eighteen years, and yet he was only now beginning to realize how much the estate meant to him. He would miss it when he was gone.

The coach drew to a gradual stop, and Darcy allowed his footman to unlatch the carriage door. Ascending the wide stone steps, he had just reached the landing when the front door was opened from within. Lawson, his butler, waited on the other side, his posture straight, his clothing spotless, his countenance smooth. As if it were a perfectly natural occurrence for the master of the house to turn up in the middle of the night.

Stepping across the threshold, Darcy removed his hat, passing it into the butler's waiting hands.

"Lawson, forgive me for arriving at such an indecent hour. We were to have stopped in Sheffield for the night, but I thought to take advantage of the full moon and travel straight through. I am sorry if I pulled you from your bed."

"Not at all, sir; I was still awake. It is good to have you home."

Darcy offered the trusted servant a half-hearted smile. It was on the tip of his tongue to tell the butler that in fact he would be leaving again on the morrow, but there would be time enough for that. Better to wait until after he had spoken to Elizabeth. He would not wish for her to learn of his decision from her maid or one of the other servants.

"Thank you, it is good to be home. But pray, retire for the evening. The hour is late." He turned to go before adding, "Oh, and you might tell Harris there is no need to attend me when you go down. It has been a long day for him as well, and I can manage on my own for tonight."

Indeed, he would likely need to get used to managing on his own. He had already determined that it would be too much to expect his man to relocate with him. Harris had a mother and two sisters living in Shropshire. It was not likely that he would wish to abandon them to move hundreds of miles away.

With a last nod to his butler, he began moving towards the stairs, but was surprised by the sound of a throat being cleared behind him. Turning his head, Darcy regarded the longtime retainer.

"Yes, Lawson? Was there something you wished to say?"

To Darcy's surprise, the butler colored. "Yes, sir. That is, I simply wished to advise you that if you were looking for Mrs. Darcy, I believe she can be found in the annex, off your study."

Startled, Darcy instinctively glanced in that direction, his eyebrows raised. "At this hour?"

"Yes, sir. She has taken to spending a great deal of time in there, especially in the evenings..."

"I see. Thank you, Lawson."

Mounting the steps, Darcy crossed the landing, making his way down the long corridor that led to the back of the house.

The door to his study was open, and Darcy entered, padding quietly across the carpet and slipping through the hidden door adjacent to his desk.

Inside the adjoining chamber, a fire burned low in the grate, casting the room in shadow. Darcy blinked, slowly becoming accustomed to the low light. Drawing a breath, his lungs filled with the scent of orange blossoms, and his heart clenched painfully at the familiar fragrance that was solely Elizabeth's.

And then he saw her, tucked up on the long sofa, his hound curled contentedly at her feet. In the flickering candlelight, her skin glowed like polished marble, and for a long moment, Darcy simply stood there, drinking her in. He had almost forgotten how breathtakingly beautiful she was...

Reluctantly tearing his gaze away from Elizabeth's sleeping form, he pulled a chair from the center of the room, perching lightly on its edge. The movement seemed to rouse Harpocrates from her slumber, for the animal lifted her head, her nose twitching in recognition as she leapt to the floor. Leaning down, Darcy offered the hound an affectionate pat before turning his attention back to his wife.

Fighting an almost overwhelming desire to gather her in his arms, Darcy reached out, settling one hand upon the curve of her shoulder. The shadow of a smile pulled at the edges of her lips, but then her eyes opened and she instantly stirred, wrenching herself upright.

"Forgive me," Darcy murmured. "I did not mean to frighten you."

Elizabeth shook her head, as if trying to make sense of the situation before saying, "You have returned."

"Yes. Only just. Lawson said I might find you here."

Darcy thought he could see her color heighten, and she briefly looked away.

"Yes... I... I come here to read sometimes. I find it cozier than the library. I hope you do not mind?"

"No, of course not. I have told you before, this is your home, Elizabeth. You are welcome to use any room you wish."

Elizabeth's gaze fell to her lap, her delicate fingers toying with the folds of her gown. "You were gone some time. I was not certain when you would return."

"Yes, forgive me. My business took longer than I anticipated."

Elizabeth's eyes once again found his, and she stared at him expectantly. Darcy merely regarded her in silence before saying, "I trust everything here is well?"

"Yes. Perfectly well."

"Good. I am glad to hear it."

The longcase clock chimed the hour, and Darcy looked away before reluctantly climbing to his feet.

"Well, it is late. I expect we should retire."

Elizabeth's eyes seemed to widen slightly, but she made no move to stand.

"I thought… I wondered if there might be something you wished to say to me?" she asked quietly.

A log popped in the grate as a knot formed inside Darcy's chest. She could not possibly know of his plans, but perhaps she had guessed… Inwardly, Darcy sighed. He knew he should wait until morning. He was tired, and being here, alone with Elizabeth in the middle of the night was dangerous. He should not indulge himself. But damn it, he *wanted* to indulge himself. Especially as this would likely be his last opportunity for some time. Possibly forever.

"Actually, there was something. I had planned to speak to you in the morning but, as we are both here…"

Elizabeth instantly sat straighter in her seat, her eyes lit with an expression Darcy had never seen in them before.

Turning away to hide his own tumultuous feelings, Darcy stepped in the direction of the sideboard.

"If we are going to sit up a while, I think I will pour myself a drink. May I get something for you?" he asked, turning to face her again. "Some wine, perhaps? Or… shall I ring for tea?"

"No, I would not wish to disturb anyone at this hour. But I will have a little brandy, if you do not mind."

He paused, one hand resting lightly on the decanter. "Of course. Forgive me for not offering, I have simply never seen you indulge in spirits before."

Pouring a measure of the amber liquid into two tumblers he crossed back to where Elizabeth sat, handing her a glass.

"Thank you. I do not do so often, but my father used to let me sip from his brandy from time to time." She offered him a shaky smile before taking a small swallow. "Dutch courage."

At Elizabeth's words, Darcy's brow furrowed in confusion. What did she expect him to say that she should need brandy as fortification? Surely if she suspected what he had to tell her, she would be elated with the news.

Stepping around Harpocrates who was now splayed before the fire, Darcy settled back into his chair. They sat for several minutes in silence, sipping their drinks until Darcy finally cleared his voice.

"Elizabeth, while I was in Town, I ran into an old acquaintance who, it turns out, was looking to liquidate some of his holdings. After giving the matter some consideration, I have made the decision to purchase one of his estates. The land is fertile, and I believe it has the potential to do well. Unfortunately, the house is in a state of disrepair, and there has been some mismanagement in recent years... in any case, it will be necessary for me to... go there, to stay for a while... at least until I can hire laborers and make the required repairs, and find a decent steward..."

His voice trailed off, but Elizabeth remained silent, her face devoid of expression. Interpreting her silence as concern, Darcy quickly continued, "You will remain here, of course. Ellis will continue to run things, and he and I will be in constant communication. He has proven himself, and I feel no misgivings about leaving Pemberley in his capable hands."

After a moment, Elizabeth said almost inaudibly, "Might I ask, where this estate is located?" and Darcy hesitated briefly before answering.

"It is in Scotland."

Elizabeth's eyes slid closed and she sucked in a breath. When she spoke, her voice was strained.

"You are moving to Scotland?"

"No, not moving; not permanently. But I do expect to be there for some time. At least a year." Across from him, Elizabeth paled, and Darcy quickly continued, "But you must not worry for your security. I took the liberty of meeting with my solicitors while I was in Town, and as far as your income is concerned, nothing will change. You will always be well provided for."

"I see."

Sensing that perhaps she did not fully understand what he was telling her, Darcy leaned forward in his chair, his eyes latching onto hers. He knew it would take all the willpower he could summon to force the next words from his throat, but he needed to say them, just the same.

"As far as your... personal life is concerned, that will be solely your own. You may have any of your relations come to stay, for as long as you like—your parents, or any of your sisters. And if... if there is anyone else, an acquaintance, or...or a friend... I want you to know that you have my blessings, to do whatever you feel will add to your happiness. I... I would like to know that you are happy..."

To Darcy's surprise, Elizabeth came abruptly to her feet, causing him to nearly knock over his chair in his haste to do likewise.

"Thank you... I..." Elizabeth looked away, visibly swallowing before turning back in his direction. "Forgive me. I think the brandy has gone to my head. I am suddenly very tired."

"Yes, of course. I beg your pardon; it is late, and I should not have detained you. We can discuss the particulars in the morning."

Elizabeth nodded, allowing Darcy to take her glass and

set it on a nearby table before escorting her to her chambers and bidding her a quiet good night.

~

Entering his own apartment, Darcy was surprised to find his valet within, his nightshirt and dressing gown laid out neatly on the bed.

Closing the door, Darcy shook his head, reaching up to untie his cravat. "Harris, you need not have come. I told Lawson to let you know I would manage on my own."

"Yes, sir, he informed me, but I wanted to see to your belongings. And I thought you might wish for a bath after a long day on the road."

Tugging his neck cloth free of his collar, Darcy turned around so Harris could assist him in removing his coat.

"You could have left the trunks until morning, though now that you mention it, a warm bath does sound heavenly."

Harris showed the barest hint of a smile before moving to the wardrobe.

"It is already prepared, sir."

Nodding gratefully, Darcy made his way into the adjoining chamber where the large copper tub stood ready and waiting.

Shrugging into his dark-green dressing gown a quarter of an hour later, Darcy crossed back into his bedchamber, only to discover that his valet was still there.

"Harris, really! You could have unpacked my trunks twice over in the time you have been up here. Anything else that needs doing can wait until tomorrow."

"Yes, sir. I was just on my way out, but I wished to alert you to a letter that arrived while we were away."

Crossing to the desk, he bent to retrieve the missive as Darcy sighed. Sometimes his valet was almost too conscientious. Did the man really think he would have any interest in going through his post in the middle of the night?

"You needn't have bothered to bring anything up. I will look through everything in the morning."

"Yes, sir. I have placed the majority of your correspondence on the desk in your study, but there was one letter I thought you might wish to see now."

Rolling his eyes to the heavens, Darcy stifled a groan. What on earth could be so important that it would not wait until morning? Surely if an express or any other letter of an urgent nature had arrived while he had been gone, Lawson would have notified him of it as soon as he entered the house.

Harris handed him the letter, and Darcy glanced briefly at the direction, his eyes growing round before lifting to the valet's.

"It was sent from Pemberley to the house in London over a week ago," Harris supplied, "but evidently it arrived after our departure. Mr. Willis sent it back, and Mr. Lawson set it aside to give to me upon our return."

Once again, Darcy stared down at the letter. Though he had only seen her penmanship a handful of times, he would recognize the graceful, flowing hand anywhere. The writing was Elizabeth's.

"Thank you, Harris," he said distractedly. "You may go."

The valet offered him a shallow bow before exiting

through the dressing room, and Darcy slowly made his way across the carpet, lowering himself into an armchair by the hearth. He stared at the folded parchment for some time, turning it over in his hands. Elizabeth had written to him. Why? She had never done so before... Had she been ill while he was away? She had seemed a bit pale when he had walked her to her chambers... but surely Mrs. Reynolds would have sent word immediately if there had been any cause for alarm.

With a rueful smile, he shook his head. What was he doing, speculating on the contents of the letter when the answer was right there in his hands? All he need do was to break the seal and read it.

But still he sat, studying the outline of an orange blossom pressed into the deep red wax. He had never seen her seal before. Had never even thought to ask if she had one.

What was he waiting for? Why was he afraid to open the letter to see what she wrote?

Leaning back in his chair, Darcy closed his eyes. No, it was not fear that kept him from opening the letter. It was hope. A fleeting wish that there might yet be some words inside that would alter the course of their marriage for the better. He knew the chances were slim, but perhaps...

Finally, with unsteady fingers he broke the seal, unfolded the thick vellum, and began to read.

Dear Fitzwilliam,

Be not alarmed on receiving this letter. I write without any intention of paining you, nor of rehashing that topic that was so disturbing to you prior to your abrupt departure. I am truly sorry if my questions caused you distress, and sorrier still if you felt it necessary to flee your home to avoid further discourse on the matter. I do not always think before I act, and in many ways, I am certain I have not been the wife you anticipated.

I know that ours has never been a love match, and I can find no fault with you in that. You did not promise me a marriage of affection, and I did not ask for one.

But now, I suddenly find that I am no longer content to continue as we have begun. I want a true marriage, in every sense of the word. I want to share your bed and bear your children, and most importantly, I want to love you, the way you deserve to be loved.

Because I do. I love you, so very much. And I feel exceedingly foolish for taking so long to realize the truth, and even more so for divulging something so momentous in a letter. I suppose I am taking the coward's way out, but had I attempted to speak of such feelings, only to see indifference or pity in your gaze, I do not think I could carry on in this marriage with any degree of equanimity.

So now, my dear husband, I must ask you for a favor. If your wishes and desires match my own, pray, put me out of my misery and tell me so at once. Come home to Pemberley, and let us build a life together—one filled with joy and laughter and love.

However, if you do not return these sentiments—if your desire is merely for a marriage of convenience, devoid of any emotional entanglement, I must beg you to destroy this letter. Consign it to the fire, and banish its contents from your mind. Return to Pemberley without one word of acknowledgement, and I shall know how to act.

Rest assured, if this is your wish, I will remain silent on this subject forever.

Until we meet again, I will only add, God bless you.

Yours,
Elizabeth

Chapter 19

Elizabeth sat on the newly upholstered chaise lounge in her spacious apartment, her feet tucked up beneath her, staring into the empty grate. Her marriage was over, and she had no one but herself to blame.

How could she have been so stupid as to have poured out her heart in that letter?

Well, there was no point in dwelling on it now. She had made her choice, and her husband had made his. After what had transpired between them tonight, there could be no mistaking his wishes.

Drawing a shaky breath, her thoughts drifted back to the moment she had opened her eyes to find him sitting beside her. At first, she had believed it to be a dream, until she had breathed in his familiar fragrance and felt the warmth of his palm upon her shoulder, and she had hardly been able to contain the spark of joy that had ignited in her chest.

But then he had spoken, his voice devoid of emotion as he calmly informed her that he was leaving—this time for good.

After that, it was all she could do not to dissolve into a puddle at his feet. At least she had saved herself that embarrassment.

And in the end, perhaps it was best that he had decided to go. He had likely realized how difficult it would be for them to remain in the same house after she had admitted to feelings he could never return.

A tear slid down her cheek just as a sharp rap sounded at the door to her sitting room, the room that connected her chambers to her husband's. Hastily dashing the evidence of her distress from her face, Elizabeth rose as the door swung open on its hinges, and Darcy stalked into the room.

Drawing the neckline of her dressing gown more tightly around her body, Elizabeth struggled for composure as her husband advanced in her direction. When he was within several feet of where she stood, he stopped and stared at her, his expression fierce.

The way he was looking at her—his eyes almost wild with emotion—made Elizabeth's stomach clench, and it was all she could do to prevent her gaze from dropping to the floor.

"Did you mean what you wrote in this letter?" he demanded without preamble.

As if in a daze, Elizabeth blinked, slowly shifting her attention from her husband's face to the sheet of parchment he clutched between his fingers. She did not need to ask about the origins of the dispatch he held; even in the low light, Elizabeth recognized her own hand.

"What does it signify?" she eventually answered, not even bothering to keep the defeat from her voice. "You have made your feelings and intentions perfectly clear, so there can be no cause for me to repeat my own. I beg of you, let us part with at least some of our dignity still intact."

She turned away, but to her surprise, Darcy reached out,

seizing her hand and pulling her back to face in his direction.

"Elizabeth, look at me. Please. I need to know. Did you mean what you wrote? Are you... are you in love with me?"

Elizabeth could feel her chin begin to tremble, and cursed herself for the inability to conceal her feelings. Well, there was no point in denying it. He would never believe her if she lied to him now.

"Yes," she whispered.

She barely had time to register his sharp inhalation and the emotions that crossed his countenance in quick succession—shock, incredulity, and finally, elation—before he had closed the space between them, his lips capturing hers in a searing kiss.

Elizabeth leaned into him, her palms pressed to his chest and her heart pounding against her ribs. When he finally pulled away, she could only look up at him in confusion, her entire body trembling with a mix of disbelief and desire.

"Wha— I don't—"

Her thoughts were a jumble, but before she could form a coherent sentence, he was kissing her again, soft, passionate kisses trailing along her jaw and the curve of her neck.

Finally, he rested his forehead against hers, his breathing ragged as he choked out, "Dear God, Elizabeth. You are everything to me."

Startled, Elizabeth drew back, tipping her gaze up to meet his. "But... How can you... You said you were leaving!"

"That was before I read your letter."

"I do not understand. I sent that letter weeks ago!" Elizabeth cried, still trying to make sense of the situation.

"It missed me. I had some business in the north, and the letter arrived after I left Town. The butler at Darcy House forwarded it here, and Harris just gave it to me. God in heaven, do you think I would have planned to go to Scotland if I had known?"

"Then you do not... wish to get away from me?"

To Elizabeth's surprise, Darcy barked out a laugh. "Get away from you? I never want to let you out of my sight! I am hopelessly in love with you; I have been from the beginning."

Elizabeth stared up at him skeptically. "Now I know you are lying. You most certainly did not love me at that assembly in Meryton. As a matter of fact, I distinctly recall—"

She did not finish her sentence, as Darcy once again pressed his lips to hers, kissing her thoroughly until they both began to laugh.

Sobering ever so slightly, he tipped up her chin, his fingers lightly caressing her jaw.

"Very well, I confess that was not one of my better days. But I realized my error almost as soon as those words left my mouth. And I came to love you very soon afterwards, although I was too blind to admit it, even to myself."

"Then why...? How...? Oh, Fitzwilliam, I do not understand! There were times during our betrothal that I thought perhaps you held me in some tender regard, but once we were married, you were so distant! It was as though you could scarcely bear to look at me!"

Darcy blinked back at her, his eyes round. "What did you just say?"

"Surely you do not deny it?" Elizabeth exclaimed. "From the moment we arrived at Pemberley, you were withdrawn and aloof, and you never—"

"No, not that. My name. Just now, you called me Fitzwilliam. You wrote it, too. In the letter."

"Oh. Yes. I… I suppose I did."

"Say it again."

Elizabeth huffed. "You, sir, are evading the question."

"Please."

"Very well. Fitzwilliam. Now, you cannot expect me to believe that you—"

Once again, Darcy's lips were on hers, and despite her best intentions, her hands were in his hair, drawing him closer until they finally pulled apart, gasping for air.

"Forgive me," Darcy breathed. "I did not mean to kiss you like that."

Elizabeth lightly shook her head, still reeling from her husband's attentions. "It would seem, *Mr. Darcy*, that you have latched onto a very effective way to keep me from speaking my mind."

She had intended the words to be a reprimand, but she knew there was laughter in her voice.

To her surprise, Darcy colored, lifting her hand and placing a chaste kiss upon her knuckles.

"Pray, forgive me," he repeated. "It was not my intention to keep you from speaking, nor to evade the question. I simply did not realize how much it would mean to me to hear you refer to me by my given name. But you are correct. There is much to talk about. Let us sit, and I will try to explain."

❧

Taking Elizabeth's hand, Darcy led her to an alcove near the window, and the two took seats across from one another. At first, neither spoke as Darcy attempted to gather his thoughts while Elizabeth waited patiently.

"Before I begin, I would like to offer you an apology. I know I behaved abominably during the early days of our marriage. I have very little to say in my defense, except that I was angry, and hurt. I was so wrapped up in my own feelings, that I thought very little of yours. I could have—should have—done more to see that you were happy here. Despite what I knew about your feelings for me, you did not deserve my disdain, and for the way I treated you, I am truly sorry."

Elizabeth looked up at him, a small furrow wrinkling the space between her brows. "What you knew? I am sorry, I do not—"

"I heard you, Elizabeth," he said quietly. "At Netherfield; the day of our wedding. Speaking with your sister."

Darcy watched as she continued to stare at him in confusion until finally he could see the spark of realization in her eyes. Immediately, the color drained from her face, and those same eyes widened with alarm, but Darcy continued to speak, anxious to have it all out in the open.

"You had gone up to change, and I went to check on the carriage. When I returned to the house, you had not yet come down, so I decided to have one last look around my bedchamber, to make certain nothing had been left behind. After I inspected the room, I walked out onto the balcony for a breath of air, and I heard your voice. Yours and your sister's, coming from the next room. The windows were open and I—"

Elizabeth blanched, holding up her palm to halt his speech. "Pray, do not continue, I beg you. I know what you heard."

"I am not certain why it affected me the way it did... I knew it was likely you did not have strong feelings of affection towards me. Our marriage came about so quickly, and we had never discussed such sentiments. But to hear that you despised me..."

"Oh, God, Fitzwilliam. I am so sorry. I never would have wished for you to overhear such things, and on our wedding day! How you must have detested me."

Immediately, Darcy shook his head. "No. That is, I suppose I did, at first. But what began as anger towards you soon took its proper direction. Eventually I realized you were not to blame for my disappointed hopes. I never told you I loved you. Not even when I made my offer, though it was how I felt. And you never claimed to love me, nor did I stop to ask your opinion."

Across from him, Elizabeth was shaking her head, but Darcy reached out, capturing her hand.

"It is all right, Elizabeth. You do not need to dissemble to spare my feelings."

"But you are wrong! I did not hate you. Not then. Not in my heart. I would never have married you if I did."

"But your sister..."

Elizabeth sighed. "Yes, I know. And I *did* say those horrible things. But that was only because my pride was wounded by what I overheard you say at that assembly, the night we met."

At the memory of those unkind words, a knot formed in Darcy's throat. God, how could he ever have uttered such a callous remark, and within the lady's hearing, no less! He opened his mouth to speak, but to his surprise, Elizabeth's grip tightened around his fingers.

"No, pray, do not apologize for that. I have had some time to work things out, and I have long ago forgiven you for what happened that night. The point is that we were both wrong. Wrong to have said those things, and wrong to have made assumptions based on conversations we were never meant to hear."

Slowly, Darcy nodded. He knew he should steer their discussion into more tranquil waters, but there was still one thing weighing on his mind, and he had to know the truth.

"Elizabeth, there is something I must ask. Before I left for Town, I saw you... in the rose garden. With... a gentleman."

To Darcy's surprise—or possibly it was relief—Elizabeth's brow furrowed. "I do not recall... Was it Mr. Ellis? Or one of the gardeners, perhaps?"

"It was not a gardener, and it was not Ellis. I was too far away to see his face, but this man was taller, with a slimmer build. He was well dressed, and I saw... I saw you hand him something. It looked like a letter."

"I cannot imagine," she began, but suddenly he could see her expression change, and a light flush infused her cheeks. "Oh. Yes, if it was just before you went away... it must have been Mr. Anderson. He is... a business acquaintance, of sorts."

"A business acquaintance," Darcy repeated numbly, and Elizabeth's blush deepened.

"Yes. Forgive me, but I would prefer not to elaborate at

the moment. For now, all you need to know is that Mr. Anderson is a very happily married man who has been helping me with a project I have been working on. Nothing more."

When Darcy did not answer, Elizabeth reached out, her delicate palms cupping his face. "Fitzwilliam, please, I need you to trust me on this. *You* are the man I love. Only you."

Pressing his lips together, Darcy attempted to regulate his emotions. He wanted to believe what she was saying... No, he *did* believe her. And although he could not comprehend her reasons for failing to elaborate, Elizabeth was correct in one thing. They needed to trust one another.

Slowly, he offered her a single nod, and Elizabeth smiled, chasing away all of his misgivings. But before he could say anything further, she stood, settling herself in his lap, her hands coming up to rest lightly against his chest. He had barely got over the shock before she was kissing him in a way that made his insides tremble.

"No more talk," Elizabeth breathed, and with a herculean effort, Darcy nodded, drawing away from the warmth of her body.

"Yes, you are correct. It is late. There will be plenty of time to discuss everything in the days ahead."

He made to rise, but to his surprise, Elizabeth clung to him, staring into his eyes with mock indignation.

"Where are you going?"

"To my chambers. As I said, it is late and..." Darcy's voice trailed off as Elizabeth glared at him.

"After everything we have just shared, you would simply walk out that door?" she asked incredulously.

"I am hardly abandoning you! It is past midnight; I was merely suggesting we both get some sleep."

Elizabeth's eyes fixed on his, and held. "I am not sleepy."

Darcy swallowed. When he spoke, his voice was hoarse with emotion. "Elizabeth…"

Her lips brushed the underside of his jaw, sending a ripple of desire down the length of Darcy's spine.

"Make me your wife."

Despite the racing of his heart, a wry smile tugged at the corners of his mouth. "You are already my wife."

"Not truly. And I wish to be. Please, Fitzwilliam. Take me to bed."

Darcy's smile faded and he stared back at her seriously. "Now? Are you certain?"

Elizabeth nodded.

Attempting to rein in his emotions, Darcy answered slowly, "There is no rush. I do not wish for you to feel compelled to do anything solely to prove a point…"

To Darcy's surprise, Elizabeth laughed. "No rush! We have been married above five months!"

Slipping his arms around her waist, Darcy pulled her close, breathing softly in her ear, "I know. And I have wanted you every minute since the day we wed."

"Well, then," she replied with a smile, "what are we waiting for?"

A small gasp slipped from Elizabeth's throat as Darcy stood, cradling her in his arms as he approached the bed in long, fervent strides.

Gently, he lowered her to her feet, kissing her tenderly as his hands came up to caress her shoulders through the thin fabric of her gown.

"That day in your chambers," he murmured, "when I touched you, I never wanted to stop. I wanted to touch every inch of you."

"I wanted that, too. I still do."

With trembling fingers, Elizabeth reached for the tie at her waist, tugging until the knot came undone. Reaching up, she drew the garment away from her shoulders, allowing the silky fabric to drop to the floor.

Darcy's heart was galloping in so violent a manner, he wondered that it had not exploded from his chest. Slowly, he mimicked her actions, removing his own dressing gown before lifting her gently onto the bed. For a moment, they merely stared into one another's eyes before Darcy settled his palm on the curve of her hip.

Never in his life had he desired any woman the way he did her. He wanted her with a desperation that frightened him, but the thought of causing her pain in the process of loving her made him feel physically ill.

"I am terrified of hurting you," he whispered.

"You will not hurt me," Elizabeth answered, staring up at him with absolute trust in her eyes.

"It is just that… we have waited so long, and I want this to be perfect."

"Fitzwilliam. Do you love me?"

"More than you can possibly imagine."

Elizabeth smiled. "Then it is already perfect."

Elizabeth was right. It was perfect.

When it was over, Darcy rolled them onto their sides, gathering her against his chest. In the silence of the darkened chamber, he could hear the rhythmic cadence of her breathing, but otherwise, she was quiet. Too quiet.

Drawing himself up on one elbow, he stared down at her. "Elizabeth? Are you well? Have I hurt you?"

In the sliver of moonlight falling through a gap in the draperies, Darcy could just make out Elizabeth's nod, but after a brief hesitation, she drew a shuddering breath before turning to face the opposite wall. Instantly, Darcy's heart plummeted as he reached out his hand, gently caressing her cheek, which was wet to the touch.

"Oh, God, Elizabeth. I *have* hurt you. I should have taken more care, gone more slowly. I—"

Beside him, Elizabeth shook her head against the pillows. "No... it is not... You did not..." Her voice cracked and she choked out a small sob as Darcy gently turned her back to face him.

"Elizabeth, please. Tell me."

Reaching up to dash the tears from her cheeks, she forced a tremulous smile.

"Forgive me... I am being silly..."

"No, you are not. Whatever you are feeling... if it is causing you this type of distress, then it is certainly not silly."

"It... it is only that when we... that is when you..." Elizabeth flushed scarlet and Darcy nodded, showing her that he understood.

Taking a deep breath, she continued, "It is just that I did not expect to feel..."

Darcy searched her face, dread building inside his chest. Heaven help him. If she was to catalogue the precise nature of the physical pain he had caused her, he was not certain he could bear it. An apology already on the tip of his tongue, he whispered, "To feel...?"

"How much you loved me."

At Elizabeth's words, Darcy's heart fractured, and he took her in his arms as she wept softly against his shoulder.

"I told you it was silly. It is not as if I doubted you when you *said* you loved me, but when you held me, and... the way you touched me..." She sniffed softly before adding, "I am sorry for being such a ninny and frightening you."

"Hush," Darcy crooned, "There is nothing to be sorry for. Though I will admit, my mind conjured up a far less pleasant explanation, so thank you for telling me."

Elizabeth tipped up her chin, staring back at him with shining eyes.

"It is I who should be thanking you."

"What for?"

"For marrying me," she murmured sleepily. "And for loving me so well."

And with that, Elizabeth released a contented sigh, and drifted off to sleep.

Much later, Darcy lay awake in the half-light, Elizabeth's soft body curled against his side. He knew he should try to get some sleep, but it was no use. He could not pull his eyes away from her. Elizabeth. His wife, finally, in every sense of the word.

Once again, his thoughts drifted back to the moment he had placed her on the bed, and everything that had followed after.

In all the fantasies he had indulged in since their marriage—and if he were honest, there had been many—Elizabeth had always been a willing participant. But nothing could have prepared him for the way the flesh and blood Elizabeth had responded to him when they had come together for the first time.

She had not been nervous or shy. She had been eager and inquisitive and joyful and bold.

He could tell he had surprised her with some of his attentions, but after only the slightest hesitation, she had leaned into his touch, encouraging him with light caresses and soft breathy moans.

He had tried to go slowly, for her sake, but also for his. He knew now that there would be countless nights like this one, but this night—the night of their first coupling—would never come again, and he did not want to miss a moment of it. He wanted to remember everything. Every touch and taste and sound and scent: The curve of her bottom. The sweetness of her lips and the saltiness of her skin. The hitch of her breath. The hint of orange blossoms that clung to her hair. The gentle press of her hands against the muscles of his back. The way her nails bit into his shoulders when he entered her body.

He had stopped moving then. He had told himself that he would desist immediately at the first sign of pain. But before he could draw back, she had pulled his head down and kissed him. Tenderly at first, but then ardently. And then her lips were at his ear, whispering his name, and he had been lost, and found.

After that, there had only been sound and sensation and passion and joy. So much joy that he thought his entire body would combust from the power of it.

And then Elizabeth was lying in his arms with tears on her cheeks and tenderness in her gaze.

And that was when he knew. That she was his and he was hers and nothing short of death would ever tear them apart.

~

Elizabeth rolled onto her side, breathing in the heady scent of shaving soap that was uniquely her husband's. Her eyes fluttered open, blinking at the rays of sunshine streaming in through the partially opened curtains. Fitzwilliam was still beside her, propped up against a mound of pillows. A book lay open across his lap, but his gaze was fixed on her.

"Good morning," he said softly.

Stretching languidly, she smiled up at her husband.

"Good morning," she murmured sleepily. "What time is it?"

He did not answer right away, instead reaching out to tuck a wayward curl behind her ear. As if with great difficulty, his gaze shifted briefly to the bracket clock above the fireplace before returning to her face.

"It is a quarter past eight. You slept well, I trust?"

Elizabeth blinked back at him in confusion before her eyes widened in alarm.

"A quarter past eight! Why did you not wake me?" Bolting upright, she clutched the counterpane to her chest. "I must get dressed! That is, I must find my nightdress..."

Her gaze frantically scanned the room before she turned once again in his direction.

"Why are you still sitting there? Cassidy will arrive at any moment! Do you wish for her to walk in here and see us in this state?"

The smile Darcy had clearly been attempting to smother erupted into soft laughter, fueling Elizabeth's ire.

"Not particularly," he drawled, "though it might be rather entertaining, now that you mention it."

"Fitzwilliam, do not tease! You must return to your chambers at once!" She moved to leave the bed, but her husband's arm gently wrapped around her waist, drawing her back to his side.

"Shh... You may rest easy. No one is coming. I returned to my chambers over an hour ago and rang for Harris. He was instructed to notify Cassidy and the rest of the staff that you and I would be spending the day in our apartments, and that we were not to be disturbed, for any reason. So, unless the house catches on fire, I do not expect any of the servants to so much as enter this wing without being summoned."

Elizabeth stared back at him as a gasp fell from her lips.

"But that is very nearly worse! The entire household will suppose that we are... that is, they will know that we..." Elizabeth's cheeks grew hot, causing more laughter to rumble in Darcy's chest.

"That we are spending the day in bed together? Yes, likely they will, but it cannot be helped."

"Fitzwilliam Darcy! Pray, tell me you are not serious. You cannot mean to spend the entire day in this bed?"

"Hmm..." he murmured, kissing her lightly at the corner of her lips. "No, you are correct. That might be somewhat confining. Perhaps we will only spend the *morning* in your bed, and then we might spend the *afternoon* in mine."

Elizabeth's gasp turned into a laugh and then a sigh of pleasure as Darcy began peppering her neck with gentle kisses. It was not long before Elizabeth had ceased thinking about the servants altogether.

~

"Fitzwilliam?"

"Mmm…"

"May I ask you a somewhat… indelicate question?"

Several hours had elapsed since Elizabeth had first awoken, but she and her husband were still ensconced in their apartments, although they had finally left her bed. Darcy had rung for a light breakfast to be sent up, after which they had withdrawn to the sitting room between their two chambers to curl up on the sofa, content to simply talk and bask in one another's company after so long apart.

Darcy looked back at her now before reaching out to brush the backs of his fingers along her cheek. "You may ask me anything you wish, always." With a wry smile he continued, "I would think after what occurred last night—and again this morning—there can be no more secrets between us."

Elizabeth flushed, briefly looking away before steeling her courage and once again meeting his gaze. "Do you… do you have a mistress?"

Darcy's eyes widened but after a slight hesitation, he released a startled laugh. "A mistress? Whatever would make you ask me such a thing?"

Lifting her chin, Elizabeth answered, "I do not think it such an extraordinary question. Perhaps it is impertinent of me to ask it, but I am not naïve. I am aware that many men of your social standing keep mistresses. It is just that if you have one, I would prefer to know about her."

Darcy leaned back against the cushions, studying her seriously now. "Yes, it is true that many gentlemen do keep mistresses. But that does not explain why you should think that *I* would have one."

"You have not answered the question."

To Elizabeth's surprise, Darcy suddenly rose, pacing to the fireplace before turning back in her direction.

"Elizabeth, have you not listened to a single word I have uttered these past twelve hours? I have not thought of another woman since my eyes landed on you at the Meryton assembly. I am a man who is hopelessly, helplessly, and completely intoxicated by his wife. I thought I had made that abundantly clear last night."

Elizabeth's cheeks colored, as Darcy continued, "Now, would you mind telling me what would make you ask me such a question?"

"It is just that you were always leaving! And I know you were not coming to me for... for... Well, I knew we did not have a full marriage, so I assumed..."

"So you assumed I would fulfill my baser needs elsewhere? Good God, Elizabeth! Do you know me so little? Do you honestly believe that one warm body is the same as any other? *Yes*, I was always leaving. And *yes*, it was because I was overcome with desire... for you! I wanted you so badly I could hardly think straight at times. When we first came to Pemberley... that night you knocked at the door to my bedchamber... You have no idea what it cost me to walk away from you!"

"Then why did you?"

"Because I believed you indifferent! Because I could not bear to lie with you, knowing I was not your choice. I did not leave because I did not love you. I left because I *did*. It was simply too difficult. Being here, wanting you every minute of every day. Craving something I could never have."

"But you did have me!"

Darcy shook his head sadly before returning to the sofa and settling once again by her side. "No, Elizabeth. I did not simply want the pieces of you that you were obligated to give. I wanted all of you: Your heart, your mind, your body. Your love and your affection and your respect. If I could not have all of those things, then I wanted nothing at all. So, yes. I left. I would have gone mad if I had not. But it was *you* I desired. None but you."

Elizabeth was silent, merely staring back at him, her eyes luminous with unshed tears. Then, all at once, she launched herself into his arms, holding him tightly and murmuring apologies against his ear.

"Forgive me. I should never have asked you such a question, nor ever thought it of you."

Releasing a breath, Darcy said with more composure, "No, I am glad you asked if it was troubling you. I would never wish for you to have thought something of that magnitude and kept it to yourself."

It was on the tip of Darcy's tongue to once again raise the topic of the gentleman he had seen with Elizabeth in the rose garden, but he managed to restrain himself. If he was asking

Elizabeth to trust him, he needed to do likewise. He could not very well condemn her for thinking he would take a mistress and then turn around and tar her with the same brush.

She had promised to tell him when she was ready and Darcy was determined to be patient, even if it killed him.

Chapter 20

When Elizabeth finally rang for Cassidy, she scarcely knew how she would be able to face her maid. She was well aware that gossip in a great house like Pemberley spread like wildfire, and there was no doubt in her mind that the servants' hall was buzzing with the unexpected return of the master, as well as the news that he and Elizabeth had spent the entire day in their rooms.

But when the maid arrived, she merely offered Elizabeth a cheerful smile, before disappearing into the dressing room to prepare her mistress's bath, humming a merry tune as she went.

Dinner that night was a blissful affair, which for Elizabeth, had very little to do with the food—which was delicious, as always—and a great deal to do with the smoldering glances her husband continually sent her over his wine goblet, and the way his fingers repeatedly brushed hers every time he served her a slice of mutton or a portion of pickled salmon.

When the meal was over, the pair adjourned to the library, where Darcy pulled her into his arms as soon as the heavy wooden doors had closed behind them.

"I have wanted to hold you all evening," he murmured, and Elizabeth smiled up at him.

"Well, I am glad you restrained yourself. I am certain the staff is already scandalized by the way you were looking at me throughout dinner."

Darcy released a soft chuckle. "They are lucky that is all I did. I must admit that I am finding it very difficult to be in such close proximity without kissing you," he added in a hoarse whisper, before brushing his lips softly against hers.

Elizabeth flushed, but took his hand to lead him farther into the room. "Come, let us select a book to read," she proposed, but she had not gone more than a few steps when her attention was diverted by a large object draped in heavy fabric standing at the rear of the room.

"What is this?" she asked, stopping abruptly and turning to look at her husband.

"Ah," Darcy replied with a rueful expression, "I had almost forgotten; it is your portrait. I collected it from Madame Gérard before I left Town."

Elizabeth's brow lifted as she responded with a nervous laugh. "Goodness, I had almost forgotten about it myself! I hope the end result is not too terrible. If it is, you must promise that we will hang it in an upstairs sitting room, preferably one that gets very little use."

"I do not think that will be necessary," Darcy said with a grin. "I cannot imagine it will be anything less than lovely with you as the subject, but I will own that I have not yet seen it myself."

Taking her hand, they crossed the carpet together, and with one last press of his fingers, Darcy reached up to unveil the painting.

As soon as the cloth came away, a gasp slipped from Elizabeth's throat. The portrait was a remarkable likeness, and seeing her face captured in such a way was truly an uncanny experience, but it was not her countenance that caused her eyes to widen in surprise.

"But that is…"

Darcy nodded. "Longbourn, yes."

Elizabeth's gaze darted from her husband's face to Madame Gérard's handiwork. In the painting, she sat on a stone bench in a garden bursting with color, her former home rising up behind her.

"I hope you are not displeased," Darcy said cautiously. "Madame Gérard suggested a variety of different backgrounds, but I thought you might like to have something to remind you of home. It was actually your needlework that gave me the idea."

"But how…?"

Beside her, Darcy shrugged lightly. "I wrote to your father to ask if he was agreeable to the notion, and when he said that he was, I arranged for Madame Gérard to travel to Hertfordshire. I confess we did have to wait until the spring due to both the weather and Madame Gérard's schedule, which is why it has taken so long for the painting to be completed."

Turning back to study the portrait, Elizabeth shook her head in disbelief. "It is beautiful," she whispered.

Darcy came up behind her, wrapping his arms around her waist and pulling her gently to his chest. "No, *you* are beautiful."

Elizabeth turned in his embrace and Darcy took her face in his hands, pressing his lips to hers in a gentle kiss.

"I am glad you like it," he murmured.

Elizabeth slid her arms around his neck, a soft moan slipping from her throat as he continued to feather light kisses along her jaw.

"Elizabeth?" he asked softly, a moment later.

"Yes?"

"I am not really in the mood for reading."

Elizabeth laughed, her eyes sparkling as she moved to look up at him. "That is just as well. Neither am I."

"So, tell me, Mrs. Darcy, what would you like to do today?"

It was late the following morning and the pair had just finished breakfast in their private sitting room. Leaning back contentedly in her chair, Elizabeth regarded her husband with a playful smile.

"Ah, so it is 'Mrs. Darcy', now, is it?" she teased, as her husband came around to help her to her feet.

"It seems a fair trade, as you have finally begun calling me 'Fitzwilliam'," he quipped.

"Very well, I shall allow it," Elizabeth said with a laugh. "As for today, I thought we might take a drive, if you are agreeable to the idea. The weather is fine, and we have been in this apartment for the better part of two days. Besides," she added more seriously, "there is something I would like to show you."

Darcy readily agreed, ringing to have the phaeton prepared and brought around to the front of the house.

The carriage was readied in good time, and a short while later, Darcy was handing Elizabeth up before taking the seat beside her on the narrow bench. They set off at a brisk pace, and Darcy could not help but smile as he watched Elizabeth's skillful handling of the horses.

"You drive well," he offered. "No one would ever know you had not been doing this all your life."

Darting a glance in his direction, Elizabeth beamed back at him. "Well, I cannot take all of the credit. I did have an excellent instructor."

"You enjoy it, then? I had hoped you would."

"Oh, yes! Very much. I am glad you encouraged me to learn. I do still relish a nice long ramble, but I can travel so much farther this way. And it is gratifying not to have to rely on anyone else to ferry me about."

For a moment, Darcy simply studied her profile, suddenly struck with the overwhelming desire to take her in his arms. Stripping off his gloves, he reached out to caress her cheek and Elizabeth grinned before swatting him away.

"Now, now, none of that," she replied archly. "You mustn't distract the driver."

"I beg your pardon. Though in all fairness, I did tell you it was going to be difficult for me to keep myself from kissing you, especially when we are alone."

"But we are not alone," Elizabeth answered expressively. "Look, there is a whole flock of sheep in that meadow, and I am quite certain the big one is staring at us."

Darcy barked out a laugh before slipping his hands back into his gloves and settling once again into his seat. "Very well. I will attempt to keep my ardor under good regulation for the remainder of the drive. I would not wish to be responsible for shocking any of the livestock."

They continued along for the next quarter of an hour or so, making amiable conversation. The sun shone brightly in an azure blue sky, and a light breeze ruffled the curls that had escaped Elizabeth's bonnet. Darcy pointed out some areas of natural significance as they passed, but mostly he was content to gaze at his wife. He was just about to ask how much farther they were to travel when Elizabeth turned off the lane and Darcy peered back at her.

"Are we going to see Mrs. Kirk?" he asked, noting the route they were taking.

"No, not exactly," Elizabeth answered, but her lips were tipped up into a mischievous smile.

Darcy frowned. He knew every inch of the estate like the back of his hand, and there were no other farms or objects of interest on this side of the property.

Eventually, Elizabeth steered them onto a narrow track before pulling on the ribbons and bringing the horses to a stop as Darcy looked around in confusion.

"Have you lost your way?" he asked. "There is nothing down this path but some fallow pastures."

"No, I know where I am going. But we are getting close, so now I must ask you to close your eyes."

Shifting on the bench, he regarded her curiously. "Close my eyes?"

"Yes, otherwise it will ruin the surprise. Do not worry, I will not run us into a ditch."

Noting the sparkle in her eyes, Darcy's mouth tipped up at the corners. "I am not worried. Your driving is flawless. However, this track is not so well traveled as the main road. Are you certain you know where you are going?"

"Quite certain."

Darcy offered her an exaggerated sigh before closing his eyes as she had directed, and once again, the carriage lurched forward.

"You must not peek," Elizabeth warned from her place beside him. "Are you certain your eyes are closed?"

"On my word of honor, I cannot see a thing." Darcy clutched the armrest in mock distress as the phaeton bounced over the uneven ground.

Elizabeth laughed. "Very well. Not much farther now."

Darcy could feel the angle of the carriage shift as they began to climb a slight incline. After a few minutes, the terrain leveled out, and they soon drifted to a halt.

"We are here," Elizabeth said softly. "You may open your eyes."

Slowly, Darcy did as she instructed, and his breath caught inside his chest. Directly in front of them, the sun glinting off every surface, was an image he had only pictured in his imagination: A glasshouse, larger and more brilliant than any he had ever seen.

Elizabeth turned to look at her husband, who had gone completely still, staring at the structure in front of them.

"It is a glasshouse," Elizabeth explained reflexively. "The one from your drawing."

When Darcy remained silent, the first prickles of apprehension crept along the back of Elizabeth's neck, and she rushed on, speaking quickly to fill the silence. "As you can see, it is not yet finished. We are still awaiting panels for the roof, and there is some additional work to do on the inside. But Mr. Anderson assures me it will be completed within a fortnight, so long as the glass arrives on time."

Finally, Darcy turned to look at her. "Anderson?" he repeated.

Despite her trepidation, Elizabeth smiled consciously. "Yes. Mr. Anderson is the gentleman you saw me speaking with that day in the garden. He is the architect in charge of the project."

Slowly, Darcy shook his head, as if trying to make sense of a foreign tongue.

"I do not understand. What...? How...?"

Elizabeth licked her lips, running her palms over the fabric of her skirt. "Well, the land, as I am sure you are aware, was Mrs. Kirk's. I knew you had been trying to find a use for it, so when I had the idea to build the glasshouse, I consulted with Mr. Ellis to see if it might be suitable—"

"Ellis assisted with this?" Darcy interrupted, his brow raised, and Elizabeth nodded.

"He was the one who found Mr. Anderson, and Anderson hired the laborers. I would never have been able to accomplish any of this without Mr. Ellis's help."

Turning away from her, Darcy climbed down, slowly approaching the glasshouse, and Elizabeth scrambled after him.

"You mustn't be angry with Mr. Ellis," she called. "Building the glasshouse was my idea. He wanted to speak with you before we began any of the work, but I convinced him to keep it a surprise." Coming up beside him, she added, "And you did say he could take direction from me on anything concerning the estate before you left."

Darcy nodded absently, moving closer to the structure and beginning to make his way around its perimeter. Elizabeth followed at a rapid pace.

"When I showed Mr. Anderson your illustration, he was quite impressed. Of course, he did need to make a few alterations, as the sketch was not drawn to scale. But he built the roofline exactly as you specified. At least I believe he did. I explained everything as best I could. He said he had never heard of a glasshouse being built in the manner you described, but he thought it very clever."

Darcy glanced briefly in her direction, but Elizabeth could see that his attention was elsewhere.

"I was not certain about the location," she continued, "but both Mr. Anderson and Mr. Ellis felt it would suit due to the elevation and the fact that there is a water source close by."

When Darcy did not answer, Elizabeth went on, "I know it is a substantial expense, but if it is the money you are concerned about, I promise I did not drain the coffers. I paid for everything myself."

Finally, Darcy stopped, turning sharply in her direction. "What?"

Elizabeth's pulse quickened at his tone, but she lifted her chin defiantly. "I used my pin money, as well as a portion of the funds from my settlement. You said it was mine to use for anything I wished."

"Elizabeth, when I said that, I meant things for yourself! For gowns, or jewels, or for refurbishing your rooms!"

Elizabeth's color heightened, but she lifted her shoulders in an indifferent shrug. "My rooms were redecorated before I arrived, and I am very happy with them. I have never been one for jewels, and I have all the gowns I need." After a moment, she added quietly. "I wanted you to have your glasshouse."

Darcy turned away and Elizabeth's heart sank inside her chest. She had been so certain he would be pleased to see one of his drawings brought to life, but it suddenly occurred to her that she may have made a horrible mistake.

"I know you said you had no need of a glasshouse, and I do realize the expense is not insubstantial, but I thought…" Cautiously, she stepped up behind him. "Are you very angry?" she whispered.

Slowly, Darcy shook his head. When he moved to face her, Elizabeth could see tears shining at the corners of his eyes.

"Come here."

Elizabeth stepped into his embrace, relief flooding through her as she felt his arms tighten around her body.

"I am not angry. I am… stunned. This is the most generous thing anyone has ever done for me. I am speechless."

Elizabeth pulled back, searching his eyes. "Then you approve of it? Truly?"

Darcy lifted her hand, placing a tender kiss upon the knuckles. "I approve of it. It is magnificent."

"Oh, I am so relieved! And I do think it will prove useful. We could grow oranges, or lemons, or even those pineapples your aunt likes so much."

Darcy laughed. "We could. Although, there were some new species of plants I had been thinking about experimenting with…"

The knot in Elizabeth's stomach slowly began to loosen as she studied her husband's face. "And you are not cross about the expense?" she persisted.

Darcy shook his head. "Only about you using your own funds. And I intend to repay every penny. The glasshouse will be used for the betterment of the estate, and the estate shall pay for it."

Elizabeth attempted to demur, but Darcy remained adamant.

"I do not know why you are being so stubborn," she finally said. "You were exceedingly generous with my settlement, and you did make a point of telling me the money was at my disposal to spend as I saw fit."

At Elizabeth's words, Darcy sighed, running his fingers through his hair. "Elizabeth, when I told you that, this is not what I had in mind. I... I wanted you to know that you had options. That you would always be able to take care of yourself—to live a good life, dependent on no one, regardless of whether or not..."

His voice trailed off, and all at once, Elizabeth understood. That money was her means of escape. He had wanted her to understand that she need never stay with him merely for the sake of her financial well-being. That she would always be safe and secure, regardless of whether or not she remained with him as her husband. He had not attempted to send her away because he wanted to be rid of her... he had done it because he thought *she* wanted to be rid of *him*.

He had been in love with her all along, and yet he had still put her happiness before his own. Despite the hurt and humiliation she had caused him, he only wanted what was best for her. He had even been willing to give up his home —to exile himself to Scotland—for her sake.

Choking back the sob that was pushing its way up her throat, Elizabeth shook her head, reaching for his hand. Darcy looked down at her, concern wrinkling his brow.

"Elizabeth? Have I said something to upset you?"

Shaking off her melancholy, Elizabeth forced a laugh. "No, I was only thinking about how much I love you. Come. Let us go inside and I will show you around."

Together they walked towards the entryway, crossing

the threshold and then exploring every corner of the space. Darcy marveled at the size of the footprint, and Elizabeth explained that Mr. Anderson had made a point of running pipes beneath the floor to ensure that the entire area could be heated from below as well as above.

After they had spent some thirty minutes going over every nook and cranny, they agreed that Darcy would meet with the architect when Anderson returned to the estate, so that he might oversee the completion of the project.

"Come, it is getting late," Darcy finally said, placing a hand on Elizabeth's back and guiding her outside, "let us return to the house.

Elizabeth nodded her agreement as a sudden gust of wind tugged at her bonnet, causing a shiver to course down her spine. In the last half hour, a covering of clouds had rolled in, blocking out the sun, and the air had grown unexpectedly cool.

Squinting up at the sky, Darcy paused, shrugging out of his coat. "You are cold. Here," he offered, draping the soft wool over Elizabeth's shoulders. "Forgive me, I should have suggested you bring a wrap. It is still early in the season, and the weather can be changeable."

Elizabeth nodded, slipping her arms through the sleeves and breathing in the familiar scent that was solely her husband's.

"Yes, I am beginning to see that."

When they reached the phaeton, Darcy assisted Elizabeth up before moving to untie the horses. Settling onto the padded bench, Elizabeth rubbed her hands together and then slid them inside the pockets of her husband's coat. Her knuckles came into contact with something hard and flat, and Elizabeth instinctively wrapped her fingers around the foreign object. It was cool to the touch, but too large and thick to be any type of coin. She turned it over in her hand as her husband climbed up beside her.

Well, whatever it was, she should leave it be. It belonged to Fitzwilliam, and she certainly had no intention of being the type of wife who searched through her husband's pockets.

Next to her, Darcy gathered up the ribbons with one hand, reaching for her with the other. Elizabeth smiled, pulling her hand from the pocket of his coat and realizing too late that she still held the mysterious object in her palm. Opening her fingers, Elizabeth looked down, startled to see her own face looking back at her.

A small murmur of surprise slipped from her throat as she stared at the miniature in the round silver frame. The drawing was rendered in what appeared to be charcoal on vellum, and although it was not sketched in color, it was flawlessly executed, with subtle shadings that made it fairly leap from the page. Even after seeing her portrait, Elizabeth could not help but be struck anew by Madame Gérard's talent.

"Oh, how lovely," she cried, briefly glancing at her husband. "I had no idea you commissioned Madame Gérard to do a miniature as well!"

Continuing to study the portrait, she marveled at the attention to detail, fascinated that something so tiny could appear so incredibly lifelike!

Suddenly becoming aware of her husband's silence, she flushed in embarrassment, realizing he must be thinking her remarkably vain to be so taken with her own likeness.

Peeking up at him from beneath her lashes, she was already forming an apology when something in his expression caused her to draw in a breath, her senses reeling.

I only sketch in charcoal.

The words he had spoken the day she had first discovered his drawings suddenly reverberated inside her head as she continued to study the miniature.

"Madame Gérard did not draw this, did she?" she said softly, turning to look up at him.

Darcy shifted in his seat before answering with a single shake of his head.

"But you said you never drew people!"

"I do not. Or at least, I did not. You were my first."

"Your first…? But this is exquisite!"

Darcy colored. "It is passable, though not nearly as lovely as the original. What you hold in your hand is also not my first effort. I made at least a half a dozen attempts prior to this one, and it is still not quite right. The eyes lack a certain depth…"

Elizabeth blinked back at him. "I see nothing lacking, not in the eyes or anything else. Fitzwilliam, you have a gift! If this is what you can do with charcoal, imagine what you could create with oils or watercolor. Your work could hang in the finest galleries in London!"

Darcy laughed, seeming to relax a little. "I appreciate your enthusiasm, but I have never wished for any of that. *You* are the only subject I would ever have any desire to paint. You and our children, perhaps, if we are ever blessed with any."

Elizabeth shook her head, still marveling at the tiny portrait resting in the palm of her hand.

"Well, I am going to hold you to that promise. The next

time you wish to have my likeness taken, you shall be the one to paint it."

Darcy offered her an enigmatic smile before leaning in to whisper in her ear. "Elizabeth, I assure you that were I to paint your portrait, it would not be suitable for hanging in the public gallery."

Elizabeth felt her cheeks grow warm as her husband continued, "As a matter of fact, let us return to the house at once. I feel a sudden urge to retrieve my charcoals."

Later that night, Elizabeth lay in her husband's arms, a satisfied smile curving her lips as Darcy stroked her back in slow, lazy circles.

"Pray, what has you looking so amused, Mrs. Darcy?" he asked, and Elizabeth gazed up at him, her eyes sparkling.

"Oh, I was just thinking that now that I have a better under-standing of what you were sacrificing all those months, I am even more impressed by your restraint. Had I any knowledge of exactly what I was missing, I might not have been so chari-table about waiting five months to consummate our union."

Darcy choked on a laugh before saying dryly, "Well, as you so aptly stated, I *was* always leaving."

Elizabeth shifted to look up at him, her brow furrowed. "Would you have really gone to Scotland?" she asked, and Darcy sobered.

"Yes. Though whether I would have stayed there is the greater question. I am not certain I would have had the strength to give you up, even if I had wanted to."

"Well, luckily we shall never know," Elizabeth replied, "thanks to my impertinence in writing you that letter."

Drawing back just enough to look into her eyes, Darcy fixed her with a penetrating gaze.

"Elizabeth, that letter was one of the greatest gifts I have ever received. I will treasure it always, and I thank Providence you had the courage to send it. I shudder to think what our future might have looked like if you had not."

"I suppose we both would have lived a very lonely existence. At least I am certain I would have."

Darcy gathered her even more closely to his side, placing a gentle kiss upon her temple.

For several minutes they simply lay in one another's embrace, listening to the sound of their breathing, which mingled with the ticking of the clock.

"So, what will happen now?" Elizabeth eventually asked. "To the estate, in Scotland, I mean. Will you still purchase it?"

"No. I have already written to my friend to tell him I cannot take it on. As I said, it needs a great deal of work, and I am no longer in a position to oversee a project of that magnitude."

Inwardly, Elizabeth sighed in some relief. She had been afraid that despite their newfound intimacy, her husband might still wish to move forward with the purchase, and she could not bear the idea of being separated from him, even for a fortnight.

"Will he be able to find another purchaser?" she asked. "As happy as I am to hear that you will no longer have reason to leave Pemberley, I would hate to think that he will suffer because of your change of heart."

"Nor would I. But I am certain everything will work out in the end. He already had several other interested parties. It is an excellent piece of property that he is selling at a very reasonable cost." He paused before continuing, "In any case, with the glasshouse and the spring planting, I have more than enough to keep me occupied here without taking on any additional responsibilities."

Elizabeth glanced up at him, a small frown wrinkling her brow. "Fitzwilliam, I am curious about something. This afternoon, you said you thought the glasshouse would be a worthwhile investment for the estate… but if that is the case, why did you never have one built before? Especially as you had spent so much time on those designs."

Beside her, Darcy shrugged. "As I said, I knew it would be a costly proposition, and I suppose it simply never seemed to be all that important."

"But if it was a project that would have brought you joy…" Her voice trailed off as she remembered Melanie's assertion that her husband intentionally denied himself the things that made him happy, and a profound sadness settled like a stone inside her heart. Leaning back against the pillows, she regarded the man she had married. In many ways, he was the picture of strength and vigor: tall, handsome, powerful. But on the inside, she suspected there was still a scared little boy, weighed down with guilt and overloaded with responsibility.

"Tell me," Elizabeth said softly, "what do you think you would have done, had you not inherited Pemberley?"

Staring off into the distance, Darcy lifted his shoulders in a shrug. "There was never much time to dwell on such things. I knew I would be heir to the estate from the time I was ten years old."

"Still," Elizabeth persisted, "you must have given the matter *some* thought, even as a young boy."

Darcy was silent for a time before saying, "Lady Catherine always spoke of my marrying Anne and taking over Rosings. I do not know if there is any truth to the story that she and my mother planned the match when my cousin and I were in our cradles—I never asked—but I suppose it makes sense. As Robert was to have Pemberley, it would have been an advantageous arrangement for all concerned."

Turning to look at her, Darcy quickly added, "But you have no cause for alarm. That scheme would never have come to fruition. Not only because Pemberley went to me when Robert died, but more importantly, because neither Anne nor I desired the match. It was only my aunt who continued on in her delusions."

Elizabeth nodded before saying gently, "You have not really answered the question. You have told me what your family desired, but not what you would have chosen for yourself."

Darcy sighed, and his mouth opened and closed several times before he finally spoke. "I suppose... if I had the right to choose, I might have studied mechanical engineering, or perhaps architecture. I would have enjoyed building things."

A small smile lifted his lips, but just as quickly as it came, his expression shuttered, and he shook his head before saying succinctly, "In any case, it does not signify; such notions are nothing more than the fancies of a small boy. I have known for most of my life that Pemberley would be my destiny."

Darcy looked away, and Elizabeth reached out, gently forcing him to meet her gaze.

"You are wrong to say it does not signify; of course it does. Dreams are always important. *Your* dreams are important."

When Darcy did not answer, she continued, "Do you remember when you spoke of my settlement, and you said you wanted me to know that I had options?" Darcy nodded, and Elizabeth went on, "Well, I suppose when I built the glasshouse, I wanted you to know that too. You have choices, Fitzwilliam. Just because you are the master of Pemberley, that does not mean you must give up on all of your own aspirations."

Darcy's eyes searched hers, and after a long moment, he gathered her tightly in his arms, placing a kiss upon her cheek before murmuring a quiet "thank you" in her ear.

After that, her husband was quiet for a while. He continued to hold her, but Elizabeth could tell he was mulling something over in his mind. When he finally spoke, his voice was soft.

"I would like to take you somewhere; will you come with me? Tomorrow, if the weather is fair?"

Elizabeth gazed up at him, immediately giving her consent, but instinct told her not to press him on their destination.

Pulling her back into his embrace, Darcy placed one last kiss upon her lips before blowing out the candle, but it was some time before either of them slept.

The following morning, Darcy had a pre-arranged meeting with one of his tenants, but the pair set out directly after luncheon. Darcy confided only that they would be traveling some distance from the estate, but chose to use the phaeton rather than one of the larger carriages so they could forgo a driver and footman.

This time, her husband took up the ribbons, which meant Elizabeth was free to enjoy the beauty of the countryside as they drove.

The ride was uneventful. The roads were well-maintained, the weather clear, and Darcy and Elizabeth were content to be in each other's company—sometimes speaking, sometimes simply holding hands and watching the scenery go by. But in due course, they turned off the turnpike road and onto a smaller lane, and Elizabeth sat straighter in her seat, suddenly taking note of their surroundings.

"But this is Briarwood, is it not?" she asked, and Darcy, who had grown quiet some time ago, nodded.

Elizabeth refrained from saying anything more, wondering if her husband wished to show her something within the house. But her suspicions were contradicted when he steered them away from the drive that led to the manor and onto a narrow track that ran through the woods. They continued on for some distance before the path petered out, and Darcy reined in the horses. Tying up the ribbons, he turned to Elizabeth.

"I am afraid we will have to travel on foot from here, but the distance is not great."

Always happy to walk, Elizabeth easily gave her consent, and Darcy assisted her to the ground.

Uncertain of where they were going, but sensing her husband's disquiet, Elizabeth reached for his hand, lacing her fingers with his. Darcy offered her a faint smile and they began to stroll at a gentle pace, winding their way through the wood. Although the day was sunny and warm, the tall trees blocked out the light, and a carpet of dry leaves crunched beneath their feet. Finally, they reached a small clearing and Darcy drew to a halt.

Elizabeth looked up to see his face was drained of color and his breathing had grown shallow.

And all at once, she knew where they were.

"This is where it happened," she murmured. "Where your brother lost his life."

Although it had not been a question, Darcy offered her a brief nod. "Where he was wounded, yes. I have not been back here since that day. Indeed, I have scarcely set foot on the estate since the accident, as I am certain you have deduced."

Elizabeth looked away, her stomach twisting uncomfortably. "Yes. Pray, forgive me. I am so sorry I made you come. For the ball. I would never have suggested it if I had known."

"No," Darcy replied with a shake of his head, "it was good that we came. Richard was right. I have been running from my memories for too long. That is why I wanted to bring you here."

He paused, and Elizabeth studied his face. His complexion was still ashen, and she could see a mix of grief and anguish in his eyes.

"Elizabeth," he began slowly, "when I told you about Robert—about the accident—I was not entirely truthful with you. Or at least, I did not tell you the whole of it. But yesterday, when you showed me the glasshouse... and then last night, when you were so kind to me... I realized I needed you to know the truth. I should have told you before... before that night when we..." His gaze veered away, and Elizabeth could see him swallow. "It was not fair of me, but I wanted you so badly, and I knew if I told you…"

His eyes dropped to the forest floor as he whispered hoarsely, "After everything we have been through, I could not bear to lose you."

Her heart breaking, Elizabeth lifted his hand, pressing a kiss to his palm. "Shh… You will never lose me. But I think you are correct, you must be free of this, whatever it is. Come, let us sit."

Still holding his hand, Elizabeth led him to a fallen tree, perching on its edge and pulling her husband down to sit beside her. When he did not speak, she began herself.

"When you showed me the portrait, you said Robert's death was an accident. That there had been a wager, and the gun your brother was using misfired."

Drawing an uneven breath, Darcy nodded. "Yes, all of that is true, but I did not tell you the entire story. The boy Robert was competing against, the one who initiated the wager… it was Wickham."

Elizabeth gasped softly as Darcy continued, "But that is not even the worst of it. Elizabeth, Wickham did not challenge Robert. He challenged me. *I* was the one who was supposed to be holding that pistol. I was the one who should have been killed. Robert took my place because I was a coward. And he paid with his life."

Chapter 21

Darcy's voice broke, and Elizabeth wrapped her arms around his waist, holding him close. His breathing was ragged, and Elizabeth could feel his heart beating wildly against his chest.

"Tell me what happened," she said, shifting so she could look up at him.

Darcy nodded, but for a moment, he merely stared out into the distance, as if gathering his thoughts. Then, slowly, he began to speak.

"It was mid-October, and Lord and Lady Matlock were hosting a shooting party at Briarwood. On a whim, my father asked Old Mr. Wickham if George would like to accompany us. This was not entirely unusual, as George was my father's godson, and my father was fond of the boy. As he was of an age with both my brother and me, the three of us were close, often spending time together—exploring the park, fishing, climbing trees and doing all manner of things young boys get up to together. My father always tried to look out for George, but that autumn especially so, as he had lost his mother in childbirth the previous summer. In any event, his father agreed, and so, we all set out for Briarwood: My parents, Robert, George, and me. Stratford was away at school, but Richard was home, and the four of us were eager to spend a fortnight away from our studies.

"The first few days were tremendous fun. The weather was unseasonably warm, and I remember Lord Matlock had recently acquired a fine Arabian mare that we all took turns riding. But on the third day, it rained. Robert and Richard were engaged in a chess match and were happy to spend the afternoon at that. I would have been content to sit in the library with a book, but George was never one for reading. He wanted to explore 'the castle' as he called it. He was certain there must be hidden passageways or buried treasure or something of the sort. I assured him there were no such things, or I certainly would have heard about them on one of my many visits to the estate. Nevertheless, we set out. We started in the attics before moving on to the lower floors. After a while, we came to a small chamber where my uncle displayed some military curiosities he had collected: a suit of armor, swords, that type of thing. I had been in the room before, and had never thought much of it, but George was captivated. He became especially enamored of an old set of dueling pistols my uncle had on display. He took them down, pretending to fire at me. I knew the weapons were not loaded, still it made me nervous, and I told George the pistols were likely valuable, and we should go before someone came and caught us playing with them. Eventually, George agreed, returning the pistols to the wall, and we left.

"I thought that was the end of it until that night, after supper. George came up to me in the salon and said he had an idea. There was a clearing in the woods with an old archery target that we had come across the previous day. George proposed taking the pistols and engaging in a shooting match there. Initially, I refused. Not so much out of any fear of firing the weapons, but because I was afraid we would be caught and severely punished if my father or my uncle found out. But Wickham continued to pester me about it until finally I acquiesced.

"In truth, I think a part of me hoped he would have forgotten about it by the next day, but unfortunately he did not."

Here Darcy paused, staring down at the ground and prodding a stone with the toe of his boot.

Elizabeth reached out, running her fingers along the sleeve of his coat. "What happened?" she asked quietly. "The day of the accident."

Darcy turned to look at her, slowly drawing a fortifying breath. When he spoke again, his voice was flat.

"That morning, Wickham awoke early and went to retrieve the pistols. By the time we met, they were loaded, though I do not know where he got the gunpowder or the bullets. I did not ask, then or later.

"I had already made arrangements to go for a ride with Robert that morning, so Wickham and I agreed to meet at the clearing. During our ride, I think my brother could tell something was troubling me. We were extremely close, and he always had a way of recognizing when I was uneasy. When he asked me about it, I told him it was nothing of any importance, but it was evident he did not believe me.

"In any case, after our ride, we separated outside the stables. Robert was to resume his chess match with Richard, and I told him I was going to find George. I watched as he turned towards the house, and I made my way here.

"When I reached the clearing, Wickham was already

waiting—the target set up, the pistols ready. I had never fired any type of weapon before—never even held one that was loaded—and I was beginning to have serious misgivings. But I did not wish to be taunted for my lack of courage, so I took the pistol he handed me without a word.

"Wickham fired first. He hit the top edge of the target. It was nowhere near the center, but he whooped and shouted and predicted that I would fare far worse.

"I stepped up to the spot where he had stood. I remember that my knees were shaking and my palms were so slick with sweat, I could barely hold the gun. Then I looked over at Wickham. His lips were twisted into his usual smirk, and I knew if I did not fire, I would never be able to live the incident down.

"Turning back to the target, I lifted the pistol, prepared to pull the trigger, when suddenly, a voice called out for me to stop.

"Wickham and I both turned around, and there was Robert, leaning against a tree trunk, his arms folded across his chest."

Slowly, Darcy shook his head, his eyes lifting to meet hers.

"Elizabeth, I cannot tell you the relief I felt in that moment. Robert had followed me! And all at once, I knew everything would be well. My brother would scold us for taking the pistols, confiscate the weapons, and take us back to the house. I was certain he would find a way to return them to the place where they belonged, with nobody the wiser, and Wickham would not be able to call me a coward for not firing."

"I can understand very well how you must have felt,"

Elizabeth said, slipping her hand into his. "But that is not what happened, is it?"

"No. Instead, my brother laughed, chiding Wickham for not including him in the scheme. I could not understand what he was about, but then he stepped into the clearing, coming up to me and taking the pistol from my hands. His back was to Wickham, and he smiled at me in the easy manner he always had, before giving me a wink that was so quick, I almost thought I imagined it. Then he turned towards Wickham, and demanded to shoot in my place. He even offered George a half a shilling for the privilege. As usual, Wickham was taken in by the prospect of making money off the arrangement, and he instantly nodded his agreement.

"After that, everything happened so fast. Robert stepped up and aimed the weapon... and..."

Darcy's voice cracked, and Elizabeth's hold tightened around his fingers.

"You do not have to tell me any more," she whispered, struggling to force the words out around the lump in her throat. But Darcy shook his head.

"After Robert fired, I do not remember much. I recall seeing him lying on the ground... and there was so much smoke... and blood... and..." Darcy choked out a sob, and Elizabeth moved into his embrace, resting her head against his shoulder.

"Hush," she crooned. "It is over now. It was a long time ago."

"No... I have to tell you the rest." Drawing a sharp breath, Darcy continued, "After it happened, it seemed as if time stood still. But then, I could hear Wickham shouting. He was saying we needed to go for help. I remember him shaking me... but I... I just stood there, staring at my legs. Some blood had spattered on my trousers.... and my lungs were burning from the smoke... and all I kept thinking was how angry everyone was going to be... because we took the pistols, and because Robert was hurt, and my trousers were likely ruined..."

"Oh, Fitzwilliam."

Again, Darcy shook his head, as if he could shake away the memory, before turning to look at her with haunted eyes.

"But I have not told you the worst of it. When Wickham finally got through to me, when I looked up at him, and I saw the panic in his eyes... instead of going for assistance, or staying to comfort Robert... I... I ran. Dear God, Elizabeth! I left. I took off into the woods and I kept running until I could not go another step.

"Richard found me curled up in a small cavern some time later. I did not learn what had happened until that night, but Wickham had gone for help. He found my father and my uncle, and they rushed out to the clearing and carried Robert back to the house. He was still breathing. The doctor was summoned, but there was nothing to be done. He died early the next morning."

Despite already knowing the outcome, a chill snaked down Elizabeth's spine as the knot in her stomach tightened. "And you?" she whispered.

"Richard brought me home. It did not take much for him to deduce that I had been with my brother and Wickham when the accident occurred—there was blood on my clothing, and my face and hands were covered in soot. But when we got to the house, everything was still in chaos. Servants were rushing around, fetching water and bandages. My mother was in hysterics, and my aunt and the other ladies were trying to comfort her while the men tended to my brother alongside the physician.

"Nobody noticed us at all.

"Richard took me to my room. He washed me up and burned my clothing in the fireplace. To this day, he and Wickham are the only ones who know I was there. We did not… I do not think any of us intended to keep my presence there a secret. It is only that nobody asked. Everyone's focus was on Robert, and when he passed… well, after that, nobody spoke of the accident any more. We returned home to Pemberley, and my mother took to her rooms. I learned the following day that she was with child. It was still early days, and she and my father had not shared the news with anyone prior to our trip to Briarwood."

Finally, Darcy stopped speaking and Elizabeth cradled him in her arms as he whispered raggedly against her neck.

"So, now you know. Robert died because of me. I wanted to blame Wickham; I wanted what had happened to Robert to be his fault, but I could have stopped him. I could have refused to participate, and I did not. And Wickham was the one who went for help, while I…"

Elizabeth pulled back, forcing him to look at her.

"Fitzwilliam, you were a boy! A child! It was an accident. A tragic, senseless, horrible accident, but an accident nonetheless. You are no more to blame for what happened than I am."

Slowly, Darcy shook his head, continuing as if Elizabeth had never spoken.

"After it happened, I just kept wondering, 'why?' Why did my brother not try to stop us? Why did he not confiscate those weapons and march us straight back to the house? Why did I let Robert fire that pistol? Why had I agreed to Wickham's scheme in the first place? Why, why, why. But there were never any answers. Not then, and not now."

Elizabeth opened her mouth to speak, but Darcy was not finished. "You asked me yesterday why I had never built a glasshouse at Pemberley. This is the reason. Because I do not deserve it. I do not deserve to have my dreams come to fruition when my brother—"

"Stop! You stop that right now, Fitzwilliam Darcy. Your brother's death was a terrible loss, but punishing yourself will not bring him back! You have done an admirable job of running Pemberley; no one can doubt your devotion to the estate and all its inhabitants. But that does not mean you must let all your own ambitions fall by the wayside."

"It just feels... wrong. Pemberley was supposed to be Robert's. I do not deserve—"

"It is not wrong for you to be happy! If everything you have told me about Robert is true, he would want that for you."

When he did not answer, Elizabeth reached out her hands to cup his cheeks, her eyes fixed on his.

"You are not to blame, Fitzwilliam. You are a decent, honorable, wonderful man. Indeed, you are the very best man I have ever encountered."

To Elizabeth's surprise, Darcy released a rough, mirthless laugh. "You did not always think so."

"No," she replied quietly. "I did not. But I was young and foolish, and I did not understand you then as I do now. I wish I had taken the time to know you better, instead of letting my pride and vanity rule my emotions."

Darcy did not reply, and the two sat together in silence

for some time. Finally, Darcy stood, pulling Elizabeth with him and kissing her lightly on her forehead.

"Come, it is growing late. Let us go up to the house. I am certain my aunt will be happy to put us up for the night; we need not travel back to Pemberley until tomorrow."

Elizabeth studied his face. His color had returned to normal, but he still looked drained.

"Is that what you wish?" she inquired gently.

Darcy looked away before saying, "I am not opposed to the idea, if that is what you are asking." Elizabeth lifted her brow and Darcy forced a faint smile. "Truly."

"No," Elizabeth answered, "let us return to Pemberley. We can still make it back before nightfall, even with a stop to rest the horses. I will drive, if you wish."

"No, there is no need for that. But the trip home will take at least two hours. Are you certain?"

Elizabeth nodded. "It has been an emotional day. I think we would both rest easier in our own bed."

"*Our* bed?" he asked, with a quirk of his lips.

"Yes. Ours. I do not care whose chambers we choose, but one thing is certain—I have no intention of being separated from you again, not even for the night. If you must leave Pemberley, I mean to go with you. And I intend to sleep by your side tonight and every other night from this day forward. Have you any objections?"

Darcy smiled down at her. "None whatsoever."

"Good. Then let us go home."

Later that night, Darcy slipped into his wife's chambers, closing the door quietly behind him. The room was in shadow, with only one candle burning on the bedside table. Removing his dressing gown, he pulled back the covers, climbing into bed beside Elizabeth's curled up form. He thought she was already asleep, but when he blew out the candle, she rolled over, melting into his embrace.

"You are still awake," he murmured, stroking her hair. Feeling her nod beneath his hands, he said softly, "I know you must be tired. Let me just hold you for a moment."

"You may hold me all night if you wish."

Shifting slightly against the pillows, he stared into her face until he became accustomed to the darkness and he could see her bright eyes gazing back at him.

"Thank you, Elizabeth, for what you did today. For coming with me, and for everything you said."

Again, Elizabeth nodded in the dim light. "I am glad you were able to unburden yourself. Maybe now you will be able to heal. Not to forget," she added, "but to begin to move past it."

Darcy was silent, remembering what she had said that afternoon, about the night they first met. How she had not understood him properly because she had allowed her pride and vanity to rule her emotions. And there was something else, too. Something she had said to him before...

"Elizabeth, the night I returned from Town, when we spoke in your chambers, you said something about that assembly in Meryton, where we first met. When I tried to apologize for making that ill-mannered comment, you said you had had some time to work things out, and that you were no longer angry about it. What did you mean by that?"

Elizabeth pulled herself up against the pillows, her eyes

luminous. She stared at him seriously for a moment, as if trying to determine how much she ought to say.

"The day of that assembly," she finally said quietly, "it was the anniversary of your brother's death, I think."

Darcy startled, but after a slight pause, he nodded his confirmation. "It was. But how did you...?"

Beside him, Elizabeth shrugged. "When you first told me about Robert... about the accident, you said it had happened in the autumn. The assembly took place on October the 19th. I remembered the date because it was but two days after my sister Mary's birthday. I was not certain if I was correct, but it made sense to me that you would not have been disposed to dance on such an occasion, nor even to be out in company at all. But I did wonder why you chose to attend. I am certain Mr. Bingley would have understood if you—"

Darcy stopped her with a shake of his head. "He did not know. I have never told him about Robert, so he could not have been aware of the significance of the date. In truth, I accepted Bingley's invitation to Netherfield *because* the dates coincided with the anniversary of Robert's death. I have never liked to be in Derbyshire at that time of year, so I almost always spend the autumn in Town. A trip to Hertfordshire seemed just the thing, until I arrived and realized that we were expected at a dance on that particular day. I wanted to beg off, but I knew Bingley would be hurt. I decided I would go and simply do my duty to Bingley's sisters, then feign a headache and leave... but Bingley kept hounding me, nagging at me to dance, and finally I snapped. I just said the first foolish thing that popped into my head. I never meant to insult you, only to get Bingley to desist. When I realized what I said, and that you had over-heard me…"

"Shh," Elizabeth murmured, "all is well. I guessed it was something of that nature. And no, you should not have said what you did, but neither should I have presumed to understand your character based on one overheard remark."

Darcy gathered her to his chest. "As usual, you are far too generous, but thank you for saying so. I am glad to have everything out in the open now. Since leaving Briarwood, I feel as if a great weight has been lifted from my shoulders. I cannot claim it will be easy to let go of a lifetime of guilt and sadness, but I wanted you to know I heard you, and I am willing to try. As long as you are by my side, I feel as though anything is possible."

"I will always be by your side, reminding you that you are a remarkable man, and that you deserve every happi-ness this life has to offer."

"*You* are my happiness. You shine so brightly; you are like the sun, chasing away the darkness. You light up every room you walk into, and you spread warmth and joy wher-ever you go. I simply cannot imagine my life without you in it. If anything were to happen to you…"

"Nothing will happen to me," Elizabeth answered with a smile. "I am far too stubborn. So, I am afraid, Fitzwilliam Darcy, that you are quite stuck with me. At least for the next sixty or seventy years."

And with that, Darcy brushed his lips gently over hers, holding her in his arms and listening to the soft hum of their mingled breathing until they both drifted off to sleep.

~

In the days that followed their trip to Briarwood, Elizabeth began to notice a slow but steady improvement in Fitzwilliam's mood. It was not a complete transformation, but he smiled more often, and his general demeanor was lighter than she had ever known it to be.

One afternoon, about a week after their return from his aunt and uncle's estate, the pair took a drive to view the progress on the glasshouse, which was almost complete. When they returned home, Elizabeth rang for tea, and the two settled into comfortable chairs in the morning room with the day's post. Darcy had correspondence from both Richard and Georgiana, and Elizabeth was elated to find a letter from Jane. The Bennet women were all presently in Town, staying with the Gardiners and shopping for Jane's trousseau, and Elizabeth was anxious for news.

Prying up the seal, Elizabeth curled into her seat, unfolding the heavy parchment and beginning to read, but it did not take long for her to sit up in alarm, a sharp gasp falling from her lips.

Darcy immediately stood, coming to her side. "Good God, what is the matter? Is someone ill?"

Still in a state of astonishment, Elizabeth shook her head, once again scanning the letter before lifting her eyes to meet her husband's worried gaze.

"No, it is nothing like that, but... Jane and Mr. Bingley are married!"

Darcy stared back at her, his brow furrowed in confusion. "What? I do not understand. I thought the wedding was set for the end of June."

"As did I. But it seems they were married in Town last Friday." Once again, Elizabeth turned to her letter, reading on before looking up at her husband.

"Apparently, between my mother's histrionics and her obsession with visiting every warehouse in London, and Caroline Bingley's barbed remarks, even my sweet sister had reached her breaking point. Charles saw how unhappy she was, and acquired a common license. They married in a private ceremony, with only my Aunt and Uncle Gardiner as witnesses."

Releasing a soft chuckle, Darcy shook his head. "Well, good for him! I am glad he took matters into his own hands rather than see your sister unhappy." He paused before pulling over a nearby chair and perching on its edge. "Elizabeth, as we are speaking of Bingley and Jane... there is something I need to tell you."

Elizabeth looked at him quizzically as he haltingly continued, "I warned Bingley away from your sister. I wrote to him when we first returned to Derbyshire and advised him not to pursue the acquaintance."

Elizabeth was quiet for a moment, and Darcy quickly rushed on, "I promise you I regretted it soon afterwards, but at the time, I was suffering from a great bitterness of spirit. I have no excuse, except to say I was angry, and hurt. I knew you had married me against your inclination, and I told myself I was doing Bingley a service by keeping him from a loveless marriage. I know it is unforgiveable, and you have every right to be angry."

"I forgive you," Elizabeth answered simply.

"How can you? If I had my way, Bingley and your sister would never have married."

"Yes," Elizabeth said with a slow smile, "but that is only if you had not changed your mind and rectified your error. If not for that, Bingley might never have returned to Hertfordshire." At Darcy's perplexed expression, Elizabeth continued, "You sought Mr. Bingley out in Scarborough and gave him your blessing, did you not?"

Darcy's mouth dropped open as he asked, "How did you...?"

"It was something Jane mentioned in one of her letters; Miss Bingley had written to inform her that she and her brother were to remain in Scarborough where they had traveled for Christmas. I did not think anything of it at the time, but then you also referred to that town when you spoke of having secured Mr. Ellis. You said you stopped to see him on your return from Scarborough." Elizabeth grinned at him mischievously. "Although in truth I did not know for certain it was Mr. Bingley you went to see until just now."

Darcy shook his head, as Elizabeth reached out, taking his hand. "Thank you. I can never repay you for bringing them together again."

"You should not be thanking me. In fact, if you owe your thanks to anyone, it is to Georgiana. It was something she said when she was here at Christmas that made me realize your sister's feelings ran deeper than I had imagined. If I had not interfered, Bingley might have found his way back to Hertfordshire even sooner."

Elizabeth shrugged lightly. "Well, in the words of William Shakespeare, 'all's well that ends well'. They are happily married now, and that is all that matters."

"Still, you must be disappointed," Darcy pressed. "About missing the wedding."

Again, Elizabeth shrugged. "Of course I would have liked to be there, but in the end, all I have ever wanted is what is best for Jane. I would never wish for her to postpone her happiness on my account."

"That is very generous of you," Darcy answered before saying lightly, "In any case, if you do feel the burning need to attend a wedding, you may still get your chance. I have just learned there appears to be another romance playing out right here at Pemberley." When Elizabeth looked at him with raised brows, he continued, "Ellis and Miss Lucy Edwards."

"Simon's mother?" Elizabeth exclaimed. "I had no idea they were even acquainted!"

"Nor had I. Apparently, Simon introduced them when his mother visited last month. It seems she and Mr. Ellis have since struck up a correspondence."

"Well, I am certainly pleased for them, although I am not sure I would call one meeting and a handful of letters a serious attachment."

Darcy's eyes sparkled as he answered, "That is because you did not see the expression on Ellis's face when he spoke of her."

"Oh, my! And... you are not opposed to the match?"

"No, of course not. Why should I be?"

Elizabeth shrugged. "I thought perhaps you would view Simon's mother as... unsuitable, given her circumstances."

"Because she was young and naïve and allowed herself to be taken in by a reprobate like George Wickham? I would be quite the hypocrite if I thought that way, given the fact that my own sister came very close to finding herself in the same circumstances. In truth, Ellis and Lucy Edwards do not have such different backgrounds. And Ellis is exceptionally fond of Simon, and vice versa; he has been a wonderful influence on the boy. I would be very pleased if he and Miss Edwards found their happiness together."

Moving to retrieve his correspondence, Darcy settled

onto the settee by Elizabeth's side, as she turned to look up at him.

"What does your sister write?" Elizabeth inquired. "She must be looking forward to spending the summer here at Pemberley. When does she come?"

Darcy's face instantly sobered, and he shifted in his seat, his sister's letter held loosely in his hand.

"Actually, I had wished to speak to you of that. Stratford is traveling from Town to Briarwood in a fortnight, and he has offered to escort Georgiana to Pemberley then, if we are agreeable."

"Oh, so soon!" Elizabeth exclaimed. "The last she wrote me, she had not expected to be here until July."

"Yes, well, that is when she generally comes. But I wanted to speak to you before making any fixed arrangements. I know we have only recently reconciled, so it would be understandable if you did not wish to have relations underfoot," Darcy said consciously, and Elizabeth's eyes widened.

"Of course I want her here! Have I not been telling you so all along?"

"Yes, but that was… before. I thought perhaps you were only lonely when Georgiana was here in the winter. And now…"

"Well, yes. I was lonely. But that is not why I wished to have her here. Pemberley is her home, and we are her family. I will always want her here, for as long as she wishes to stay."

Pulling her into a light embrace, Darcy kissed her softly. "Thank you." Drawing back, he asked, "And you will not mind? You will not feel crowded?"

Elizabeth choked out a laugh. "Crowded! You cannot

be serious? Pemberley is enormous. You are forgetting that I came from a home with four sisters. And I shall love having the company."

Darcy beamed back at her. "Then I shall write Stratford this very afternoon."

He stopped speaking then, but Elizabeth could tell there was still something he was mulling over in his mind. When she asked him what it was, he flushed slightly before saying, "I was thinking that, if you are agreeable, perhaps we might have Georgiana stay for some time past the end of the summer. After all, she would be here again at Christmas anyway, and I do not like her traveling when the roads are so treacherous."

Instantly, Elizabeth threw her arms around his neck, showering him with kisses. "Oh, but that is wonderful! She will stay here permanently, then?"

"Well, not permanently, mayhap, but at least until the spring, if you truly do not mind."

"You know I do not! But, what has happened to change your mind? You were so adamant that she should be in Town for the benefit of the masters, and to become more comfortable in society."

Gently pulling away from Elizabeth's embrace, Darcy focused on the letter in his hands. "Yes, well, all of that was true, to an extent. I do think Georgiana could benefit from being in society more often, but when I thought further on the subject, I realized you were right—nothing is more important than spending time with her family. I want her to know she is loved and wanted. I do not think even the most accomplished masters can compete with that. In any case, she will not lack for instructors. There are plenty of men and women right here in Derbyshire who would fit the bill, and I do not doubt there are some who would come from London for the right inducement."

"Oh, she will be so happy," Elizabeth cried, her eyes sparkling with delight. After a moment, she added, "But what of Mrs. Annesley? Will you give her her notice? I suppose Georgiana will have little need of a companion while she is here with us."

Darcy's brow furrowed as he settled back in his chair. "Actually, I am of a mind to keep her on, if she wishes to stay. Georgiana will go back to London eventually, and she enjoys Mrs. Annesley's company. Besides, even while my sister is here at Pemberley, there will still be obligations that call the two of us away. I should not wish for her to be lonely. And with her come-out only a year or two away, it could only benefit her to have another woman of sense and decorum to guide her."

"Another woman?" Elizabeth teased. "And who might the first one be, if I am allowed to ask?"

"Why, you of course. I cannot think of any other lady in the entire kingdom I would rather have my sister emulate."

Chapter 22

Georgiana arrived on the eleventh of June. The reunion was a happy one for all concerned, and life soon settled into an easy rhythm.

While Darcy spent his days with Ellis out on the estate, or with Anderson, supervising the completion of the glasshouse, the ladies took walks in the garden, played for one another in the music room, conversed over their embroidery, or read books in the library. Mrs. Annesley was a pleasant addition to their household, and Elizabeth quickly came to regard her as another member of the family. Several times a week, the three of them frequented the shops in Lambton or drove out to visit tenants together.

It was on one such visit that Elizabeth introduced Georgiana and her companion to Mrs. Kirk, and to Elizabeth's delight, the two older women soon developed a close friendship. Before long, Mrs. Annesley and Georgiana were paying calls at the Kirk farm on a regular basis, which left Elizabeth with several hours a week in her husband's sole company, a circumstance which gave neither of them any cause to repine.

Thus, one balmy afternoon several weeks after Georgiana's arrival, Darcy and Elizabeth found themselves alone in an upstairs parlor—Darcy poring over a book on architecture he had recently acquired, as Elizabeth gazed out into the sunlit gardens.

They had been together in that attitude for some time before Elizabeth belatedly realized her husband had been speaking to her, whereupon she turned away from the glass, her cheeks warm with embarrassment at having been caught out.

"Forgive me, I was not attending," she admitted. "What were you saying?"

Darcy smiled back at her, relaxing further into his seat. "Nothing of great import. I was merely speaking of the plans Ellis and I were making for the glasshouse. Am I allowed to ask what has you so preoccupied, my love?"

Elizabeth lifted her shoulders in a light shrug before saying, "To own the truth, I was actually just recalling your proposal."

Immediately, Darcy's brows drew together as he set down his book with a grimace. "I cannot imagine that would be a memory worth revisiting. It pains me to think of how I offered for you. I said nothing of my love or admiration. I wish I could take every word of it back and start again."

Intrigued, Elizabeth asked, "And pray tell, what would you say, Mr. Darcy, if you were to offer for me now?"

Darcy stared back at her seriously. "I would tell you that you were the most remarkable woman I have ever known, and I would admit that I was desperately in love with you. Then I would get down on bended knee and beg you, most fervently, to put me out of my misery and agree to be my wife."

Elizabeth looked back at him, a mischievous grin pulling at her lips. "Yes, I daresay that *is* an improvement.

Still, there is one aspect of your original proposal I was quite fond of, and I would hate to think you would have omitted it."

Darcy inclined his head, the crease between his brows becoming even more pronounced. "I cannot imagine I said anything redeeming. From what I recall, the entire business was badly done. But pray, do enlighten me. What portion did you find to your liking?"

"Well, I was specifically thinking about the bit where you mentioned wanting children," she replied with an arch smile. "You have not changed your mind about that, I hope?"

"No," he replied slowly. "Elizabeth, is there something you wish to tell me?"

"Perhaps."

In an instant, Darcy was on his feet, gathering Elizabeth in his arms. His palms came up to caress her cheeks as his lips found hers in a fierce kiss. When he finally drew back, Elizabeth released a joyful laugh.

"Then you are pleased?" she asked.

"Pleased?" Darcy cried, "I am beyond ecstatic! But tell me, how are you feeling? Should we not send for a physician or a midwife?"

Once again, Elizabeth laughed. "No, I think it is a bit too early for that. And we shall not know anything for certain until the babe quickens."

Darcy stared back at her, a dubious expression on his face, and Elizabeth reached out to smooth the furrow between her husband's brows. "Pray, do not make yourself uneasy. Despite being somewhat more fatigued than usual, and having developed a severe aversion to the kippers Mrs. Webb has been serving at breakfast, I assure you I am in perfect health. If anything, I am far more concerned with Lydia's predicament. Tell me, have you written to my father?"

Helping Elizabeth back into her seat, Darcy nodded in the affirmative. "Yes, first thing this morning. Though I am not certain it will do any good. From what you have told me, he seems disinclined to stop her going, no matter what anyone says about it, but at least we will have made the attempt."

Elizabeth sighed. To her dismay, Lydia had received an invitation to travel to Brighton for the summer as the particular friend of Mrs. Forster, the wife of the colonel of the regiment lately stationed in Meryton. Elizabeth had already written to express her apprehension about such a scheme, but her father had only laughed off her concerns, saying there would be no peace at Longbourn if Lydia was not allowed to go.

Chewing her lip, Elizabeth attempted to quiet the uneasiness in her stomach as she regarded her husband.

"You do not think... Would Wickham really pose a danger to her, do you imagine?" she asked.

"No, I do not think it likely. He is far more apt to seek out another young heiress, someone who is alone and unprotected. But I have long ago ceased to put anything past George Wickham. I will feel much better if your father heeds my warning and keeps your sister at home where she belongs."

~

Despite Darcy's and Elizabeth's pleas, Mr. Bennet gave his blessing for Lydia to accompany Mrs. Forster to Brighton, but to everyone's relief, the youngest Bennet daughter seemed to be comporting herself in a respectable manner— or at least in as respectable a manner as Lydia Bennet was capable of. So, they could only hope their fears where Wickham was concerned would remain unfounded.

Elizabeth continued to be in good health and even better spirits, but she and her husband had both agreed to keep her condition to themselves for the time being. And if Georgiana or Mrs. Annesley questioned her sudden desire to take breakfast in her apartment, neither one voiced their suspicions.

So it was that on a sunny morning in mid-July, Darcy entered Elizabeth's chambers to inform her that his sister and Mrs. Annesley had recently departed for the bookshop in Lambton with the intention of visiting Mrs. Kirk afterwards.

"Which means," he continued, stepping farther into the room, "that you and I can spend the entire morning together. What say you to a drive 'round the Park?"

Elizabeth accepted the proposal with great enthusiasm, but she had no sooner spoken than a knock sounded at the door to their sitting room, and Darcy went to answer. She watched as he exchanged a few hushed words with one of the footmen, before taking a letter off the salver and unfolding it to read.

His eyes scanned the page for no more than a moment before his expression darkened, and he folded the parchment, slipping it into the pocket of his coat and murmuring a few hurried words to the waiting servant. Closing the sitting room door, he crossed back to the spot where Elizabeth sat, his expression sober.

"Forgive me, my love, but I am afraid we shall need to

postpone our excursion. An urgent matter has come up that requires my attention, and I must leave directly."

Elizabeth's brows pulled together as a knot formed in the pit of her stomach. Though her husband's outward appearance was calm, she had grown accomplished at reading his moods, and there was a look in his eyes that she could not be entirely comfortable with.

"It is nothing serious, I hope?" she asked, and Darcy frowned, but promptly shook his head.

"No, nothing for you to worry about. I shall be back before dinner."

He turned to go, but then stopped, slowly pivoting in her direction. "Oh, and Elizabeth? Pray, stay inside the house today. I am going to send a footman in search of my sister and Mrs. Annesley as well. I would feel better if you were all to remain indoors until I returned."

The tightening in Elizabeth's stomach intensified, and she hastily pushed back her chair, coming to her feet.

"Fitzwilliam, you are frightening me. Please, tell me you are not in any danger?"

With a small smile, he lifted her hand, placing a gentle kiss upon her knuckles.

"Not at all. It is only that I will be away from the estate, and I would be easier knowing you are indoors, where the servants can look after you. Will you promise me?"

"Of course, if you wish it," Elizabeth agreed, "but..."

However, before she could continue her thought, her husband placed one last kiss upon her cheek before turning on his heel and exiting the room.

～

After Fitzwilliam's sudden departure, Elizabeth made her way to the library, hoping to keep her mind occupied with a book while she waited for Georgiana and Mrs. Annesley to return from Lambton. But Darcy had not been gone a quarter of an hour when a knock sounded at the library door and Mr. Lawson entered.

"Forgive me for disturbing you Mrs. Darcy, but you have a caller," he intoned, as Elizabeth lifted her gaze, surprised to see the usually unflappable butler looking distinctly ill at ease.

"It is a young lady," he elaborated, "who claims to be your sister."

Setting her novel aside in alarm, Elizabeth stood, her pulse quickening as she made her way across the carpet.

"My sister?" she repeated, and the butler nodded.

"Yes, madam. She did not say any more than that, but I have taken the liberty of placing her in the front salon."

Elizabeth nodded, thanking the butler before hastening from the room. However, she did not have to go all the way to the salon to have her curiosity satisfied. Crossing into the entrance hall, she could see a woman wandering the vast space, however, upon her approach, the young lady turned, causing Elizabeth's breath to catch inside her throat.

"Lydia! What are you doing here?"

At Elizabeth's words, her youngest sister giggled, removing her bonnet and skipping merrily in Elizabeth's direction.

"Lizzy! Is this not a marvelous surprise! You were not expecting to see me today, I am certain! But then, I was not expecting to see you, either. In fact, I had no notion we were so close to Pemberley until this morning." Lifting her gaze, she stared up at the gilded ceiling hung with its crystal chandelier, turning in a slow circle.

"Lord, Lizzy! I knew Mr. Darcy's house would be grand, but I did not expect anything like this! He must be even richer than anyone imagined when you married him."

One of the footmen stationed near the front door coughed, and Elizabeth felt her face heat with mortification. Taking her sister firmly by the arm, she steered her towards the nearest withdrawing room.

"Come, Lydia. You must be fatigued from your journey. I will ring for tea, and you can tell me all about this unexpected visit."

Once they had settled into the parlor and the tea had been ordered. Elizabeth turned to face her sister, who was walking around the spacious chamber, lifting various ornaments and examining every aspect of the room's décor.

Tamping down her growing agitation, Elizabeth called, "Lydia, pray, come sit down. You must tell me how you came to be here all on your own. I am growing quite concerned."

Setting a Chinese vase back upon a nearby table, Lydia laughed, before coming to take the seat her sister indicated.

"You were shocked to see me, were you not?" she gayly inquired. "I could tell by your expression."

"Lydia," Elizabeth warned, and her youngest sister drew her lips into a pout.

"Well, I ought not to tell you, as it is meant to be a secret..."

Elizabeth glared back at her, and Lydia released another throaty giggle. "Oh, very well," she easily relented, sliding to the edge of her seat. "I am dying to tell someone. You may congratulate me, Lizzy, for I am to be married! We are even now on our way to Gretna Green, and by the end of the week, I shall be Mrs. George Wickham!"

Elizabeth gasped. "What? You cannot be serious!" she cried. "You have eloped? With Mr. Wickham?"

Lydia's grin broadened. "Is it not romantic? My darling Wickham surprised me less than a se'nnight ago, and we left Brighton directly. Mrs. Forster thinks I have returned to Longbourn, and George is supposed to be on an errand in Town. By the time anyone realizes we have run off, we shall already be man and wife. Is that not a fine joke?"

Elizabeth sank back against the cushions, her pulse racing. "A joke? Is that how you see this? Lydia, you will be ruined!" After a moment, an even more shocking thought occurred to her and she could not keep her eyes from widening in alarm.

"Lydia... you have not... that is, have you allowed Mr. Wickham to..." her voice trailed off, but Lydia merely regarded her with a baffled expression.

Drawing a steadying breath, Elizabeth continued, "Have you allowed Mr. Wickham to take liberties with you since you left Brighton?"

To Elizabeth's further dismay, Lydia did not even have the good sense to look embarrassed by her question, continuing to stare back at her in satisfied audacity.

"A lady does not kiss and tell," she answered coyly, but at Elizabeth's horrified expression, she continued, "Oh, Lizzy, do not be so dramatic! It was merely a few kisses. And I can hardly be ruined when I shall be a married woman before anyone even realizes I have gone."

Turning away from her sister, Elizabeth shook her head, her thoughts reeling. In some respects, she knew she should not be surprised. Was this not the very thing she had been afraid of when her father had agreed to allow her youngest sister to go to Brighton? Still, seeing her worst fears had actually come to fruition left her at a loss for words, and dearly wishing her husband was not from home.

Shifting her attention back to her sister, she opened her mouth to speak, but just then a maid arrived with the tea, and she was forced to bite her lip in frustration until the woman left the room.

Upon seeing the tea service, Lydia squealed with delight at the assortment of cakes and pastries, taking a plate and quickly filling it with the iced confections as Elizabeth poured the tea with shaking fingers.

"I shall take extra sugar, if you please," Lydia piped up around a mouthful of cake. "After all, I am company, and your Mr. Darcy certainly looks as though he can afford the cost. I am sure *he* never skimps on sugar or tea the way Mamma does. Once I am married—"

"Lydia," Elizabeth hissed, finally reaching her breaking point, "you cannot marry Mr. Wickham; I expressly forbid it!"

Setting down what remained of her teacake, Lydia stuck out her chin. "I most certainly shall marry him; and you have no right to forbid me to do anything. As soon as Wickham returns with the funds he is owed, we will be able to—"

Lydia did not have the chance to finish her explanation before Elizabeth broke in. "Lydia, what are you speaking of? What funds? Where is Mr. Wickham now, and why are you here on your own?"

Lydia set down her cup, looking uncertain for the first time since her arrival. "I am not supposed to say. In fact,

Wickham would be very cross if he even knew I had left the inn."

Attempting to rein in her exasperation, Elizabeth fixed her sister with a pointed stare. "Lydia, I cannot make heads nor tails of a word you have uttered since you arrived. I think you had better start at the beginning, and I beg you to speak sensibly, and leave absolutely nothing out."

~

"...and then last night we arrived at the Rose and Crown— do you not think that a fine name for an inn? The night before we stayed at a horrible place called the Spotted Pig, but Wickham said—"

"Lydia, pray, forgive me," Elizabeth cut in, rubbing her temples to quell the headache that was already forming. "When I said to leave nothing out, I did not mean that I required a detailed accounting of every minute of your journey. Perhaps you could skip to the part about the money?"

"Oh. Yes. Well, Wickham said we could not continue on to Scotland until he collected a debt that was owed him. This morning, he awoke early and spent an age writing a letter, and once he had sent it off, he told me he must go out and that I should stay in our room until he returned. And I had every intention of listening to him, Lizzy, truly I did. But then the maid who brought my tea told me we were not five miles from Pemberley, and really, I *was* getting rather bored in that tiny bedchamber all alone—"

"A debt?" Elizabeth interrupted. "What sort of debt?"

Flopping back against the cushions, Lydia shrugged. "Some rich toff cheated him out of thirty thousand pounds.

But Wickham said he was certain he had a way to get it back, and once he does, we shall be on our way to Gretna Green!"

Elizabeth felt the blood drain from her cheeks and a low humming filled her ears, but Lydia continued to talk, oblivious, as always, to her sister's mood.

"Oh, Lizzy, only think! Thirty thousand pounds! I shall be as rich as you are, I daresay, and I shall make Wickham buy me the finest gowns, and a carriage of my very own!"

Elizabeth could only stare at her sister as she attempted to suppress her growing dread. *Thirty thousand pounds.* The exact sum of Georgiana's dowry. It could not be a coincidence.

"Lydia, listen to me. This is extremely important. Did Mr. Wickham say where he was going, or from whom he was planning to collect this money?"

"No," Lydia replied, setting aside her teacup and reaching for another one of the tiny iced cakes. "He never mentioned any names, but he did say he had a long ride ahead of him, and would not return for many hours. That is why I knew I should have plenty of time to pay you a visit."

"Did he tell you anything else?" Elizabeth pressed. "Or say in which direction he was going?"

"I do not think so. Or if he did, I was not attending." Lydia paused to lick a drop of icing from the tip of her finger, before sitting a bit straighter in her chair. "Oh, wait, I do recall something. I believe he said they were to meet in a wood somewhere. Yes, now that I think of it, I am fairly certain about that part. But Lizzy, why should you care so very much? If you think to have Mr. Darcy follow Wickham and call him out, I shall not allow it."

"You will not allow it?" Elizabeth spat, her anger surging. "Might I remind you that you are but sixteen years old, and hardly in a position to make the rules? Now, think! You have five minutes to tell me everything you remember, or I can promise you will be exceedingly sorry."

Lydia stared back at her, her eyes wide. "I...I do not recall anything further. Truly. Only that the place he was going had 'wood' in the name. Rosewood, mayhap? Or, something like it..."

Elizabeth froze. "Briarwood? Lydia could that have been it?"

"Yes! At least I think so. Do you know of such a place?"

Elizabeth nodded numbly as her mind spun. It made perfect sense. Of course Wickham would lure her husband to the one place he felt especially vulnerable. Oh, why had Fitzwilliam not confided in her? She would never have let him face such a thing alone! Suddenly her eyes lit, and she immediately leapt to her feet.

"We must leave at once! There is not a moment to lose!"

Lydia remained seated, gaping at her in surprise. "Leave? But I have only just arrived. You have not even shown me about the house." Her lips formed a small moue of displeasure, but Elizabeth only grasped her sister's arm, tugging her to her feet.

"Never mind the house. We are going after Wickham. I have every reason to believe it is my husband he is meeting, and if I am correct, they are both in grave danger."

∾

Grateful that Georgiana and Mrs. Annesley had not yet returned, Elizabeth informed Mr. Lawson with forced cheer that she and her sister were going for a drive around the Park. She did not like to lie, but she knew the butler would never allow her to take the phaeton all the way to Briar-wood without several footmen accompanying them.

To her vast relief, Lawson merely nodded his agreement, and the phaeton was readied in very little time. In just over a quarter of an hour, she and Lydia were on their way. But they had scarcely made it down the gravel drive when Lydia tugged at Elizabeth's elbow, her gaze pinned over their shoulders.

"Lizzy, I believe we are being followed."

Elizabeth's stomach instantly sank and she drew in a sharp breath, tugging at the ribbons to bring the geldings to a halt. Steeling her courage, she twisted in her seat, certain she would see one of Pemberley's grooms galloping after them. Instead, the road was empty save the hound who was even now trotting up behind the phaeton.

"Oh, no! Harp!"

From beside her, Lydia let out a loud guffaw. "Lord, Lizzy! The sun must have addled your wits. Clearly that is a dog and not a harp." She continued to laugh at her own joke as Elizabeth handed her the ribbons before climbing to the ground.

Harpocrates raced to her side, tail waving.

"Harp is her name. It is short for Harpocrates. She must have slipped out somehow." Elizabeth groaned, knowing they were losing precious time. "We shall have to go back. We cannot leave her here."

"Goodness, she is only a hound. I am certain she will

grow tired of chasing the carriage in time and go home on her own. Besides, did you not say we were in a hurry?"

"Of course we are in a hurry," Elizabeth snapped. "But it is not safe for her to be out here on her own. She is deaf. And if anything happened to her, I would never forgive myself." Scooping the animal into her arms, Elizabeth lifted her into the back of the phaeton. She was worried Harp would simply leap back down, but instead the dog curled herself into a tight ball, tucking her nose between her paws and letting out a contented sigh.

Breathing a sigh of relief herself, Elizabeth climbed back up to her seat, taking the ribbons from her sister and preparing to turn the phaeton, but Lydia reached out, staying her movements.

"Why do we not simply bring her along? She looks happy enough now that she is inside the carriage."

Elizabeth frowned. "No. I cannot take any chances. Fitzwilliam is excessively fond of that dog. If she were harmed in any way..." She could feel a lump forming at the back of her throat just thinking of her husband, who even now might be in mortal danger. Would the time it took to go back to the house put him at even greater risk? Although she remained fairly certain Darcy had gone to Briarwood, she had no idea how long it would take her to locate the clearing he had shown her, or even if that spot was Wickham's intended meeting place.

Behind them, Harp let out a soft snort, and an idea suddenly sprang into Elizabeth's mind.

"Lydia, you are a genius!" Reaching out to give her sister a quick embrace, she snapped the reins and the horses lunged into motion.

Perhaps Harp's following after them had been just the stroke of luck they needed.

~

Elizabeth knew they were making good time on the road, but the racing of her pulse and the sick feeling in her stomach made the drive seem interminable. To distract herself—and also because she believed her sister had a right to know—she related the whole of what she had come to learn about Mr. Wickham, save his involvement in Robert's accident. When she had finally finished her tale, Lydia was quiet for a long time. But just when Elizabeth feared she would not speak at all, her sister turned to look at her, her face pale.

"So, he did not love me," she whispered. "He was only using me to get at Mr. Darcy's money."

"I am afraid so." Gathering the ribbons in one hand, she reached over to squeeze her sister's gloved fingers with the other. Despite Lydia's reckless decision to elope with a man of questionable character, she did not doubt that her sister's heart had been engaged. Learning the truth would likely hurt her a great deal.

More gently, she said, "I am so sorry, Lyddie. I know you truly cared for him."

Lydia looked away, the wide brim of her bonnet obscuring her expression. But when she turned back to face her sister, her jaw was set at a determined angle and her dark eyes held a steely edge.

"How dare he take me for a fool! Make haste, Lizzy! We cannot let him get away with this."

Elizabeth was already driving as fast as she was

comfortable, but seeing the fire in her sister's gaze spurred her on, and she coaxed the horses to an even brisker pace.

They had not gone much farther when she felt Lydia's slim fingers grasp her forearm, and her brows lifted as she turned to study her expression.

"Oh, Lizzy! I have just remembered. Wickham has a gun. I saw him loading it this morning before he left."

Elizabeth nodded, turning back to face the lane. The revelation did not shock her, but hearing it confirmed made her heart beat a tiny bit faster in her chest.

"I am not surprised; I am certain Fitzwilliam has one as well." Knowing her husband's feelings regarding the need for protection when traveling, as well as his past dealings with Wickham, she did not doubt he would have come prepared... but that did not help to keep the fear at bay.

She trusted her husband would exercise caution, but where there were pistols involved, accidents could always happen, as Fitzwilliam knew all too well. How would he react to being back in the place that had caused him so much heartache? And how would Wickham use those emotions to his advantage?

Elizabeth shuddered, pushing the horses even faster. She was not sure how much longer she could continue to keep her feelings in check, but several minutes later, she saw the tall stand of trees that marked the entrance to Briarwood's lands. Slowing the horses to a trot, she turned onto the smaller lane.

"Is this it?" Lydia asked.

Elizabeth nodded, steering the team away from the house and towards the place she remembered her husband taking her the last time they came.

"Do you think we will be able to find them?"

"I hope so. I remember where we parked the carriage when Fitzwilliam took me here before. If he is in the area, I believe Harp will be able to pick up his scent."

"Lizzy, I have not wanted to say anything… but what if Mr. Darcy is not here? Perhaps we have got it all wrong, or have arrived too late…"

Elizabeth shuddered, praying that was not the case, but when they finally reached their destination, she knew she had guessed correctly, as Fitzwilliam's mount stood before them, tethered to a nearby tree. She and Lydia exchanged a brief glance as she pulled the geldings to a stop, tying up the ribbons and reaching underneath the seat. When she straightened, Lydia gasped.

"Lizzy! You have a pistol? Do you know how to shoot?"

Elizabeth nodded, slipping the weapon into her reticule. "Fitzwilliam taught me. I am not sure I am very good at it, but hopefully I will not need to be."

A sharp whine arrested their attention, and Harp, who had awoken as soon as they stopped, pushed her muzzle against Elizabeth's shoulder.

Elizabeth frowned, her gaze shifting to her sister. "Lydia, take off your bonnet."

Lydia's eyes narrowed. "Why? What do you want with my bonnet?"

"Just take it off. Hurry, we are wasting time."

Lydia huffed, but did as she was asked, handing the bonnet to her sister. Reaching for the ribbons, Elizabeth wrapped them around her palm before giving them a sharp yank.

"Lizzy! What are you doing! You have ruined it!"

"Hush! I need something to tie to Harp's collar so she does not run off."

"Why did you not use your own ribbons?" Lydia grumbled.

"Because yours are longer."

Looping the scrap of silk through the dog's collar, Elizabeth climbed to the ground, Harp eagerly jumping down behind her.

Lydia followed, muttering under her breath. "Very well. But you will need to buy me a new bonnet when this is over. Something very fine, from one of the shops in Town."

Lydia continued to pout, but Elizabeth scarcely noticed. She had turned her attention to Harp, wondering how she would communicate to the animal that they were attempting to track her master. But no sooner had they stepped into the woods then Harpocrates put her nose to the ground, sniffing at the dry leaves before setting off at a brisk pace and dragging Elizabeth behind her. Lydia lifted the hem of her skirts, scurrying along at her sister's side.

"Does she know where she is going?" Lydia hissed, swatting aside a stray branch as they threaded their way through the trees.

Elizabeth nodded, although in truth she had no idea if Harp was leading them to Fitzwilliam. For all she knew, the hound had picked up the scent of a fox or a rabbit. *Oh, please let us find him. Please let him be safe.*

The words reverberated inside her head as they continued through the thick undergrowth. Finally, after about a quarter of an hour, the silence was broken by the sound of raised voices drifting towards them through the trees.

"You are talking in circles, Wickham, and wasting my

time. I have already told you, you will not get a penny from me. Now tell me where she is."

Turning to face her sister, Elizabeth pressed a finger to her lips, and Lydia nodded her understanding. Treading as softly as they could on the fallen leaves, the sisters crept closer to the voices as Wickham growled, "It is *you* who are wasting time. I shall reveal nothing until I receive the money that is owed me."

Finally reaching the edge of the clearing, Elizabeth pressed up against the trunk of a great oak, as Lydia came to stand beside her. Through the thick undergrowth, she could see her husband standing about twenty feet away, while Wickham lounged against a tree trunk opposite him.

"Well then, there is nothing more to discuss," Darcy replied calmly. "Since I have no intention of paying for the information, I shall find Miss Lydia on my own."

He turned to go, but the sound of a pistol being cocked arrested his steps.

From their hiding place, Elizabeth let out a soft cry, pressing her hand to her lips to muffle the sound.

Slowly, Darcy shifted his gaze to his opponent as Wickham continued, "You are not leaving here until I have my funds. And you would do well to give me what I require. I kept my mouth shut when it came to your sister, but I shall not do so again. Even if you were able to track down the trollop, it is too late to save her reputation. She has been well and truly ruined, and I will waste no time in making sure the entire population of Hertfordshire knows about it."

Beside her, Elizabeth could feel Lydia stiffen, but before she could so much as turn her head, she felt a sudden tug on her hand, and the ribbon she had tied to Harpocrates's collar slipped through her fingers.

Before Elizabeth could do anything to stop it, Harp broke free, bolting into the clearing. Elizabeth lunged forward, attempting to restrain her, but it was too late. The hound raced to the center of the space.

Harp's head snapped back and forth between Wickham and Darcy while a strangled sound emanated from the back of her throat.

Wickham startled, turning sharply in Elizabeth's direction, and her stomach dropped as she stared down the barrel of the gun. Through the sound of her pulse pounding in her ears, she could hear Darcy calling her name. Lifting her skirts, she attempted to close the space between them, but felt a harsh tug as Wickham snatched at the back of her gown.

Several feet away, Darcy froze as Harp circled around his feet before racing towards Wickham and letting out a plaintive howl.

Slowly, Darcy lowered the weapon he had drawn from the waistband of his trousers.

"Let her go. Your quarrel is with me, not Elizabeth."

"Ha! Are you daft?" Wickham cried, wrapping his arm around Elizabeth's waist and yanking her backwards until her body was pressed up against the side of his chest. "This is the greatest stroke of luck I've had all year. Now, perhaps you will give me what I want. Unless you wish to see another person you love die in these woods."

Elizabeth watched as her husband blanched, the color

instantly draining from his face. Shifting her gaze, her eyes swept the dense wood, but Lydia was still hidden from view. Despite the odds, a spark of hope ignited within her at the thought that perhaps her sister had gone for help. If she was able to find her way back to the house... But that would take time. Something she was very aware they did not have. Glancing down at her wrist, her heart sank even further as she realized she no longer had possession of her reticule, which held the pistol from the carriage. She must have dropped it when she had gone after Harp.

As if simply thinking the animal's name had captured her attention, the hound let out a low growl as Wickham's grip tightened around Elizabeth's body.

"Shut that beast up, or I shall do it for you," Wickham snarled.

With deadly calm, Darcy once again lifted his own weapon. "Let her go," he repeated, but Wickham only laughed, brushing the tip of his pistol seductively against Elizabeth's cheek.

"Perhaps your lovely wife would like a little taste of what I gave her sister. I always did prefer a woman with a bit more experience..."

Darcy's entire body stiffened, his free hand clenching at his side. Seeing the anguish in his expression, Elizabeth attempted to wriggle free, but Wickham's grip on her was like a steel vice.

Suddenly, a twig snapped in the near distance, and Wickham whipped his head in the direction of the sound.

Taking advantage of his distraction, Elizabeth lifted her knee, stomping on his foot as hard as she could with the heel of her boot. Wickham cursed, momentarily loosening his hold, as Elizabeth jabbed her elbow into the soft flesh of his stomach. Wickham doubled over, gasping for breath, and Elizabeth wrenched free of his grip.

The next three things occurred in such quick succession, Elizabeth scarcely had time to register what was happening.

Wickham lifted his arm, pointing the pistol at Elizabeth as Darcy lurched forward, shielding her with his body. Elizabeth heard the click of a hammer falling into place, just as Harp sprang at Wickham's throat. A second later, there was a deafening explosion, as one shot and then another rang through the air, followed by a sharp canine cry and the agonizing howls of a man in pain.

Elizabeth's heart pounded as she blinked through the smoke to see Wickham lying at her feet, a still heap of glossy brown fur splayed out by his side.

"I've been shot," Wickham cried, gripping his upper thigh. "That bitch shot me!"

Elizabeth's mouth dropped open as she slowly turned in the opposite direction. There, standing several feet away, was her sister, a smoking pistol still clutched in her hand.

Chapter 23

In the next instant, Darcy turned, and Elizabeth flew into his embrace. She could feel his body trembling —or perhaps it was hers. She tightened her arms around his waist as his hands traveled up her arms, caressing her shoulders, her neck, and her hair, before finally landing on her cheeks.

"Are you well? Did he hurt you?" he whispered, pulling back to search her eyes.

Elizabeth shook her head, but her throat was painfully tight, making it difficult to speak.

"Are you certain?" Keeping Elizabeth's back to the clearing, he lowered one hand, placing it reverently on her belly.

"Yes," she murmured. But before she could say more, Wickham let loose with a string of invectives.

"For the love of God, I am the one who was shot!"

Slowly, Darcy shifted his gaze, his eyes like granite as he took in the man writhing on the forest floor. "If you know what is good for you, you will shut your mouth before I finish the job."

Wickham ground out a laugh. "You haven't the guts to shoot me."

With a look of rage the likes of which Elizabeth had

never seen on her husband's face, Darcy whirled around, his weapon drawn. In three long strides he was towering over the prostrate man, who instinctively flinched.

"You would not dare," Wickham yelped. "You would hang for it."

Aiming the pistol, Darcy said evenly, "You held my wife at gunpoint, kidnapped her sister, and shot my dog. I will take my chances."

"I did not kidnap anyone! That hussy came willingly enough."

"One more word," Darcy growled, "and there will be a bullet in your head to match the one in your leg."

Wickham's lips twisted into a mocking grin. "Ah, ever the protective brother. But just like your sweet sister, Lydia Bennet got exactly what she wanted."

There was a hollow click as Darcy cocked the hammer.

Even from several feet away, Elizabeth could see the flash of fear in Wickham's eyes. Quietly, she stepped up to her husband's side, placing her fingers gently on his sleeve.

"Please; do not. He is not worth it."

There was a slight hesitation before Darcy slowly lowered his arm. Disengaging the hammer, he tucked the pistol back into his waistband. But before either of them could speak, the sound of a muffled whimper broke the silence and Darcy returned to the wounded animal lying at their feet. Dropping to his knees, Darcy ran his palm lightly along the dog's silky fur as Elizabeth came to stand by his side.

"She is breathing," he said quietly, "but her heartbeat is weak."

Elizabeth nodded. "We must get her back to the house. And my sister…" Elizabeth turned to look over her shoulder. Lydia stood exactly where she had been when she had pulled the trigger. Her expression was blank, the gun she had used still held loosely in her hand.

Elizabeth immediately rose, hurrying to her sister's side. Carefully extricating the pistol from her sister's grip, Elizabeth tossed it to the ground before enfolding her sister in a tight embrace.

A moment later, Darcy joined them. Retrieving the pistol, he said quietly, "Come. I will take you both up to the house."

Elizabeth slipped her hand in his, keeping her other arm wrapped around her sister's shoulders. But when Darcy attempted to lead them from the clearing, Elizabeth tugged him to a halt.

"What about Harp? We cannot leave her here."

Darcy hesitated. He looked back at the dog, who was breathing heavily now.

"I will come back for her. You and your sister must be my first priority."

Elizabeth opened her mouth to protest, but to her surprise, it was Lydia who spoke.

"No; take her now. Lizzy and I are not injured. And I can ride beside Harp in the back of the phaeton."

"To hell with the dog!" Wickham cried. "What about me?" But no one so much as turned to look at him.

"The phaeton?" Darcy inquired. "You drove here on your own? I did not even think to ask, nor to inquire how you came to be with your sister, though I am relieved to see that she is safe."

"Yes, I will tell you everything on the way back to the house," Elizabeth murmured. "The carriage is waiting at the edge of the woods, near the spot where you tied up your horse."

Darcy looked from her and Lydia to Harp. Elizabeth gave him a small nod and he released her hand.

Making his way to Wickham, Elizabeth watched as he untied his cravat, using it to bind the other man's hands behind his back and then fastening the cloth to a low hanging branch.

"If you are not in this exact same spot when I return, I will hunt you down and kill you," Darcy said simply before stooping to gently lift the injured animal into his arms.

The dog let out a sharp yelp before closing her eyes and resting her head against Darcy's chest. It reminded Elizabeth of the gentle way he had carried her up the stairs at Briarwood when she had been so ill at the ball, and her heart swelled with tenderness. How could she ever have thought him cold and unfeeling? Truly, he was the kindest, most decent man she had ever known.

Choking back a sob, Elizabeth took her sister's arm, and together, the three of them left the clearing.

Several hours later, Darcy stood as Elizabeth entered their bedchamber at Briarwood. He had replaced his neckcloth, but his clothing was rumpled and she could see lines of worry and exhaustion etched upon his features.

"How is your sister?" he asked, and Elizabeth sighed, shutting the door behind her.

"Not very well, I am afraid. She is terrified of going to jail for shooting Wickham, and fears that even if she does not, she is now ruined beyond all redemption. I have tried to reassure her, but she feels incredibly foolish for believing Wickham's lies, and guilty for her part in today's events. The doctor came and gave her a sleeping draught, so hopefully she will be able to get some rest, at least."

Crossing the carpet, she slipped into Darcy's embrace, breathing in her husband's familiar scent as he bent to place a gentle kiss upon her temple. Since returning to the house, she had spent most of her time in her sister's rooms while Darcy had gone with Stratford to fetch the magistrate and retrieve Wickham, so there had been little time for discussion between the two of them until now.

Leading her to a small sofa by the fireplace, Darcy sat, drawing her down beside him. "Lydia will not go to jail," he answered. "I have already given the full story to the magistrate and he is satisfied."

"And... Mr. Wickham?" Elizabeth asked hesitantly.

"A surgeon was sent for, and the bullet has been removed. He will most likely recover, unless the leg becomes infected. Stratford sent for Richard; as luck would have it, he is currently stationed near Nottingham and should arrive by morning. We will meet together with the magistrate to determine what exactly is to be done with Wickham."

Lifting Elizabeth's hand, Darcy placed a tender kiss upon her knuckles before continuing, "But enough about Wickham for tonight. I would much rather talk about you. I have scarcely seen you since we returned to the house, and I have been worried."

Elizabeth smiled, curling into the warmth of his body. "I am well," she said softly, but Darcy pulled back, his eyes searching hers.

"Truly, Fitzwilliam, I am. I never really thought he

would hurt me. I was more concerned for you. I cannot imagine how horrible it was for you to be back in that place again, with Wickham holding you at gunpoint."

To Elizabeth's surprise, Darcy shook his head. "No. I thought it would be, but strangely, it was not as difficult as I feared—until that reprobate put his hands on you. If he had hurt you in any way…"

"Shh. He did not. We are all well, except for poor Harp. How is she?"

Darcy's expression sobered and he released a ragged breath. "Time will tell, but I am optimistic. The surgeon was able to remove the bullet without any difficulty, though it took some coaxing on my part to convince him to oper-ate. I believe Harpocrates was his first patient of the canine persuasion."

Elizabeth smiled. "I am grateful he was willing to work on her, and that Harp was able to withstand the procedure. I am not certain all animals would have been as accom-modating."

Darcy nodded. "She is remarkable. I held her throughout the entire process, but truly, she was exceedingly calm." After a moment, his lips quirked up at the corners. "As for the surgeon's willingness, it did not hurt that I paid him a king's ransom and promised not to hold him responsible if anything went wrong."

Her expression turning serious, Elizabeth reached up, stroking her husband's face.

"I am sorry if I made things worse by coming. It is just that when Lydia turned up, and I realized what was happen-ing, I could not bear to think of you facing something like that alone. Why did you not tell me it was Wickham who sent that note? Especially as it was my sister he was threatening to ruin."

Beside her, Darcy stared down at the carpet before running his fingers through his already tousled hair.

"You are right, I should not have kept it from you. It is just that I was terrified of putting you through that type of anguish when you are carrying our child. I saw firsthand what my mother's grief did to her when she was expecting Georgiana, and I simply could not take that risk."

Elizabeth nodded her understanding, reassuring her husband once again that she was well and strong, and in no danger of losing their child, but Darcy continued to stare across the room, a tormented expression in his eyes.

"This is my fault," he said at length. "If I had dealt with Wickham as I ought to have done after he imposed himself on Georgiana, none of this would have happened. I should have called him out, or had him thrown in debtor's prison. But I have spent my entire adulthood haunted by the memory of Robert's death... and the knowledge that it was Wickham who did the honorable thing in going for help."

His voice trailed off, and Elizabeth gathered him in her arms, holding him as tightly as she could. "Yes, he did a good thing on that one occasion, and he was once a friend to you. It is understandable that you would feel some sense of loyalty towards him. But he is not the hero in this piece, nor are you the villain. He is no longer the boy you played with as a child. He is a man, who has had every opportunity to reform, yet he has only grown more dissolute as the years have gone by. You do not owe him your allegiance."

Darcy was silent, simply allowing Elizabeth to hold him in her arms, until, slowly, she could feel the tension begin to leave his body.

After a while, Darcy sat back, saying carefully, "Eliza-beth, those things Wickham said… about your sister. Did you have a chance to speak further with Lydia about…" His cheeks colored as he continued, "I swear, if he laid so much as a finger upon her without her consent—"

Elizabeth shook her head, cutting him off. "No. I believe that was all bluster meant to provoke you. Lydia did allow him some liberties, but not that. And I am sorry to say everything that transpired was done with my sister's express permission. She truly believed herself in love with him."

Darcy sighed. "Well, I can hardly blame her. She is not the first woman to be taken in by Wickham's dubious charms, as you well know."

Elizabeth was quiet before shifting to look up at her husband. "I am glad she will be safe from the law, but I am afraid we will not be able to contain the story. Once it is known that she eloped with him…" A tear slipped down her cheek, and she shook her head at the unfairness of it all. As much as she censured Lydia for her choices, she did not wish for her to pay for her youthful mistake for the remainder of her life.

Beside her, Darcy rubbed at his jaw, his brow furrowed. "I have been thinking about the situation, and I believe there may be a way to contain the story. From what you told me when we first reached the house, Wickham kept her out of sight during their journey north. By her own admis-sion, the only person Lydia had any interaction with was the maid at the Rose and Crown, and she will not speak out against a member of the Darcy family."

Elizabeth's eyes widened, and Darcy looked at her in confusion.

"Do you disagree? The maid's brother labors for the estate; I cannot imagine she would risk his livelihood."

"No, I do not question your reasoning, I was only surprised that you would consider Lydia a member of your family. Is that truly how you feel?"

Darcy's eyes searched hers, his brow knitted in uncertainty. "Of course. She is my sister, just as Georgiana is yours."

Almost before Darcy had finished speaking, Elizabeth leaned forward, pressing her lips to his.

Darcy returned her kiss with barely repressed ardor, before drawing back to once again study her countenance.

"Elizabeth, forgive me if I have not made this clear before now, but there is nothing I would not do to see you safe and happy, and that includes providing for and protecting those you love. Your family is now mine. So, you may rest assured, whatever it takes to see that your sister emerges from this situation unharmed, it shall be done."

"How are you feeling, Lyddie? Did you sleep at all?"

Elizabeth awoke early the next morning, but knowing Lydia needed her rest, she had waited until midday to make her way to her sister's chambers. She arrived to find Lydia still in her borrowed nightdress, though she was out of bed and curled up on a settee by the window, a tray of cold tea and untouched toast on a small table by her side.

Lydia nodded as Elizabeth claimed the seat across from her before saying, "I am well enough. I just cannot stop thinking about what a fool I was to have believed Wickham's lies. You and Mr. Darcy must think me a total simpleton."

Elizabeth offered her sister a slim smile before gently shaking her head. "No. Mr. Darcy is well aware of the falsehoods Wickham is capable of telling to get what he wants. Nobody blames you for his behavior."

Lydia was silent for a long moment, staring down at the carpet and picking at a loose thread on the sleeve of her nightdress.

"Did… did Mr. Darcy say anything about Wickham?" she finally asked. "He will not die, will he?"

"No, he will not die. At least, not as a direct result of you having shot him. The bullet has been removed, and Fitzwilliam has spoken to the magistrate. You will not be held accountable for what happened."

Across from her, Lydia nodded. "I suppose I am glad. I would not like to go through life knowing I had killed a man, even if he did deserve it."

Suppressing a grin, Elizabeth gently offered, "You were very brave. Still, it must have been a great shock, to have shot someone. I did not even know you knew how to handle a pistol like that! And you were so silent after it happened… I think you must have been exceedingly distressed."

Lydia lifted her gaze, and Elizabeth was relieved to see her eyes were clear, and her expression unaffected.

"Oh, no! I was glad I shot him. He had it coming after those things he said about me, not to mention holding you hostage. My only regret was that I did not quite hit my mark. I was aiming for a slightly different part of his anatomy. I missed by at least six inches."

"Lydia!" A startled laugh burst from Elizabeth's throat,

and Lydia soon joined in. But after a minute, Elizabeth sobered.

"Nevertheless, you were not so unaffected as you claim. You did not move or make a single sound after it happened. If you were not distressed over shooting Wickham, what was it?"

Lydia sighed, her gaze briefly skittering away. "It was... Well, if you must know, it was because of Mr. Darcy."

"Mr. Darcy!"

Lydia jerked her chin up and down in a single nod. "After... after Wickham let you go... I saw the way Mr. Darcy held you, and the way he kissed you... Lizzy, he was crying! And then he was touching your face, and asking you over and over if you were well. I have never seen any man *cry* before. And to think, that it was Mr. Darcy, of all people!"

"Lydia," Elizabeth said gently, "I hope you will not tease him about that. He was very upset, and there were other circumstances at work that are not mine to share."

"Oh, no! You mistake me. I was not mocking his behavior. I was... amazed by it, I suppose. It was like something out of a storybook. Mr. Darcy loves you! I do not think I have ever seen any man look at a woman the way Mr. Darcy looked at you yesterday. And that is when I knew. Wickham never loved me. And I never loved him, not like that. And I want to be loved like that someday, Lizzy."

Without a word, Elizabeth came to sit beside her sister, gathering Lydia in her arms and slowly rocking her back and forth. "I hope you will be," she whispered.

Lydia sniffled. "I suppose it is not likely now. After

what I have done, no decent man will have me." She choked back a sob, but after a moment, she pulled away and her eyes widened in obvious alarm. "Oh, Lizzy! You will not make me marry Wickham, will you? I know I should never have eloped, and that I will be ruined once everyone finds out, but I simply could never marry him now. Not after—"

"Shh," Elizabeth crooned, stopping the flow of her sister's words. "Of course you must not marry him! That would be the last thing in the world I would ever want for you."

Lydia relaxed, breathing a slow sigh of relief. "Thank you," she murmured. "But what about Mr. Darcy? He might not like the idea of having a wife with a ruined sister."

"Mr. Darcy and I are in complete agreement on this. As a matter of fact, he wishes to speak with you about the whole affair, if you are up to it. I told him we would meet him in the sitting room when you were ready."

Instantly, Lydia paled, her face draining of what little color it had left. "Oh, no Lizzy, I could never face him. Please do not make me!"

Elizabeth started at the obvious note of distress in her sister's voice. She had never known her most brazen sister to be this unsettled by anything before, and the sight was rather disconcerting.

"Hush. Of course I will not insist you see him now, if you are not ready. But you must face him eventually. Unless you intend to stay in this bedchamber forever."

Lydia looked away, chewing her lip. "Could... could you not simply send me back to Longbourn? I think I would rather face Papa and total ruination than Mr. Darcy."

Elizabeth laughed. "Unfortunately, I do not believe that is an option. But truly, you have nothing to fear from Fitzwilliam. I think you will find him far more agreeable than you expect."

After a bit more coaxing, Lydia finally consented, and Elizabeth helped her wash her face and dress before escorting her to the parlor at the end of the passageway.

When they arrived, Darcy was already there, and he rose as they entered, offering Lydia a deep bow.

"Miss Lydia. I hope you are feeling better. You look well."

Lydia nodded mutely, allowing Elizabeth to lead her to a long sofa in the center of the room. The two sisters sat, and Darcy took an armchair across from them.

Keeping his attention fixed on Elizabeth's sister, whose gaze was now pinned to the carpet, Darcy continued, "I wanted to let you know that I have just come from the magistrate. Wickham is in custody, where he shall remain until he is fully recovered. It has been decided that at that time he will leave for the West Indies. I have agreed not to press charges in exchange for him removing himself from British soil, permanently. If he returns, I will prosecute him to the fullest extent of the law."

To Darcy's obvious surprise, Lydia's head snapped up, and her eyes grew round. "Oh, no! You cannot do that!" she cried.

Darcy frowned, his gaze shifting briefly to his wife before returning to her sister. "I am afraid I do not understand. Are you saying you still harbor some... affection for Wickham? I thought I understood from Elizabeth..."

Darcy stopped speaking as Lydia laughed, vehemently shaking her head.

"Good heavens, no! He can sail to the ends of the earth for all I care. But… if you force him to leave, that will make him angry, and I shall be the one to pay for it. He will tell everyone I…" Lydia's cheeks grew pink, and she once again lowered her gaze. "Well, he will tell people I eloped with him, and no man will ever have me after that."

Lydia choked back a sob, and Darcy slid forward in his chair.

"Miss Lydia, pray, look at me."

Slowly, Lydia lifted her chin, and her lips trembled as she faced her sister's husband.

"That will not happen. I have made it abundantly clear to Mr. Wickham that if he breathes one word of his involvement with you, he will live to regret it. Let us just say that he knows better than to cross me on this."

Despite Darcy's reassuring words, Lydia's eyes continued to fill with tears. "B-but, even if you are correct and Wickham does not say anything, people will still find out. I have been gone from Brighton above four days. I will have already been missed. People will start asking questions, and eventually everything will come out and there will be a terrible scandal, I just know it."

Darcy stood, pacing several feet away and rubbing the back of his neck before returning to the spot where Lydia sat. "Do you think Wickham told anyone of his plans to elope with you? Anyone in his unit? Or someone in Town?"

After a brief pause, Lydia shook her head. "N-no. I do not think so. He said we must keep it a complete secret. He told Colonel Forster and the other officers he had business to attend to in London, and the colonel granted him leave."

"And did anyone in Brighton see you together on the day you departed?"

"No. Wickham sent a carriage to collect me at the Forster's. I told Mrs. Forster that my father had sent for me. Wickham met me outside of town. We did not want anyone to become suspicious and start searching."

"Good. That is very good. And nobody saw you on your journey? That is, you did not speak to anyone at any of the inns you stopped at along the way?"

Again, Lydia shook her head. "Wickham always went in alone and then came back to take me to the room. The inns were always so crowded, I cannot imagine anyone would have noticed... And we took all our meals inside our chamber."

Darcy nodded. "Wickham said the same, but I wanted to be sure. If what you are telling me is true, I believe we can contain the scandal. We shall say I was the one who sent for you. Elizabeth was homesick for her family, and I arranged for you to come for a visit. You will return to Pemberley with us tomorrow and stay for a fortnight, longer if you wish. I trust you have no objections to that?"

"N-no," Lydia stuttered.

"Good. We shall talk more about that in a moment, but before we do, I have been remiss in not thanking you properly for your service to us yesterday, so pray, allow me to do so now. If you had not acted when you did, what transpired in that clearing might have had an entirely different outcome. Any one of us could have been killed. You acted calmly and heroically, and you have my deepest gratitude."

Lydia stared back at him, her mouth dropped open. "I-I thought you would be angry with me!"

"Angry? You very possibly saved my wife's life. In truth, I owe you a debt I am not certain I can ever repay."

Lydia looked away, her complexion pale. "But Lizzy might never have been in danger in the first place if it were not for me. If I had not agreed to elope with Mr. Wickham, or if I had not come to Pemberley... You must think me a total gull."

"No. I think you are young, with a romantic nature, and an idealized view of the world, but I do not think you foolish. And I am sorry you had to learn the hard way that all that glisters is not gold."

Lydia blinked back at him incredulously as Darcy continued, "But let us not speak any further on that now. Elizabeth and I have been discussing the matter, and I have a proposition for you." Lydia lifted a single brow in an expression so like her sister, it made Darcy smile. Coming to sit beside her, he said, "My sister, Georgiana, is staying with us for a while; however, I have been considering giving up the lease on her house in Town, and having her reside permanently at Pemberley."

Beside him, Elizabeth drew a startled breath. "Truly?" she asked, and Darcy nodded, shifting his attention to her.

"Yes. You were right. I can see how much happier she is. And I am happier having her there with us."

Elizabeth reached for her husband's hand, raising it to her lips before Lydia interrupted the tender moment.

"And what exactly has that to do with me?" she asked, and Darcy reluctantly pulled his gaze away from his wife.

"Georgiana is of an age with you. And although she is content at Pemberley for now, I feel she will miss the companionship of other young ladies eventually. The country can be isolating, especially in the wintertime. I was thinking that if you were to stay on… say, through to next spring…"

Lydia blinked back at him. "You wish me to live with you? At Pemberley?"

"For a time, if that is agreeable to you. However, I must add, if you consent, there will be certain conditions to the arrangement."

Lydia frowned, her eyes narrowed. "What type of conditions?"

"Well, for one, you would no longer be out—"

Lydia gasped, but Darcy continued to speak, "—and you would need to spend at least a portion of each day in a productive manner."

"Egads! Do you mean to say I would have to go back to the school room? No thank you! I should rather return to Longbourn in disgrace!"

Darcy chuckled, darting a quick glance at his wife. "No, not the school room. When I say 'productive' I mean only that. You must find something to do that adds to your self-worth. However, you may elect to spend your days on anything that interests you—so long as it helps to better your mind or improve your character."

"Such as?"

"Well, Georgiana enjoys music and languages and books. But you, I am certain, will have your own pursuits. For example, I believe you are quite an accomplished artist, and Elizabeth tells me you like to dance."

"Dancing?" Lydia asked, her curiosity clearly piqued.

Darcy nodded. "I will hire a dance master, to teach both you and Georgiana the latest figures. And perhaps you would like to study art… or astronomy, or architecture. I will ensure that you have instruction in whatever you like."

Lydia chewed her lip as Elizabeth reached for her hand.

"Oh, say you will stay! I think it would be good for you. And Georgiana is not the only one who would enjoy your company."

"Well... I suppose the dancing does sound rather fun. Do you have a proper ballroom, with crystal chandeliers?"

Darcy nodded, suppressing a grin.

"And will I have to share a bedchamber?"

"No. You will have your own suite of rooms."

Although Lydia was clearly trying to conceal her interest, her eyes had regained some of their usual sparkle.

"Hmm... And, tell me, do you always have those little iced cakes at tea?"

At this, Darcy wrinkled his brow in confusion as Elizabeth laughed. "I believe that can be arranged. Our cook, Mrs. Webb, is quite accomplished, and she has been doing a good deal more baking of late. Not only that, but her turtle soup is simply divine, and she makes a lobster dish that is almost too beautiful to eat."

Lydia's eyes grew round. "And I can return to Longbourn at any time... if I change my mind?"

Darcy nodded. "Any time you wish."

Lydia inclined her head before fixing her brother-in-law with a playful smile. "Very well then, I accept your offer. Pray, tell me, when do we leave?"

The remainder of that summer was one of the happiest Elizabeth could remember.

After their return to Pemberley, Darcy had written to Mr. Bennet, divulging the whole of the story, but the two men had agreed the wisest course of action would be to keep the details solely between themselves. However, Darcy extended an invitation for the entire Bennet family—including Bingley and Jane—to come for a lengthy visit, a suggestion that was met with glee by all concerned.

The weather remained glorious for the duration of their guests' stay, and a great deal of time was spent outdoors. Elizabeth and Darcy took turns driving everyone around the park in the phaeton or the curricle, and the ladies played shuttlecock on the great lawn, while the men fished for trout and pike in the lake.

To Elizabeth's surprise, Darcy even put up an archery target, which resulted in many fierce competitions, of which Lydia was often the victor.

Darcy appeared easier and more carefree than Elizabeth had ever seen him. He laughed readily, smiled frequently, and seemed more amused than put out by the antics of her mother and youngest sisters.

To Elizabeth's great joy, he had also struck up a fast friendship with Mr. Anderson, the architect she had enlisted to build the glasshouse, and the pair were already at work on several other projects: a folly and maze to be built on the far side of the formal gardens, and an orangery that would be connected to the house, so that Elizabeth might have all the citrus fruit she could ever desire.

But by far, the best thing to come out of the visit was the fact that not long after the families' arrival, Darcy had heard of an estate for sale, not ten miles from Pemberley. He and Elizabeth had toured it with Bingley and Jane, and Bingley had made an offer on the spot. The land was fertile, the tenant farms brought in a good income, and the house was large, though in need of some repairs. Luckily, both Darcy and Mr. Anderson were quick to offer their assistance, and it was agreed that Bingley would give up the lease on Netherfield as soon as possible, and he and Jane would reside at Pemberley until their new property was ready for habitation.

So it was that the summer finally drew to a close, and on a cool, crisp evening in mid-September, Elizabeth walked arm in arm with her husband through the gardens, more contented and truly happy than she ever had any expectation of being when she accepted Mr. Darcy's offer of marriage.

Making their way up a small bluff that overlooked Pemberley's lands, the pair took a seat on an iron bench as Harpocrates chased a wood mouse in the distance. To the vast relief of both Darcy and Elizabeth, the hound had made a complete recovery, and seemed none the worse off for her ordeal.

With a contented sigh, Elizabeth turned away from Harp's antics, snuggling into her husband's embrace.

"It seems so quiet here, now that everyone has gone away," she said, and Darcy chuckled.

"It shall not remain that way for long. Remember, we still have Georgiana and Lydia at home, and Bingley and Jane will be back before you know it. Not to mention this little one," he added, placing his hand lightly on the swell of Elizabeth's belly, "who shall be making an appearance this winter."

Looking down at the spread of his fingers, Elizabeth smiled. She had not yet felt the babe quicken, but she could see the subtle changes in her body, and knew that it would not be long before she felt the first stirrings of the life they had created.

"Yes, you are correct, of course. I suppose we should enjoy the peace and quiet while we can." With an arch smile, she added, "Besides, if I am not very much mistaken, I think it likely that there will be two children in the nursery by next spring."

Darcy's eyebrows lifted before a spark of understanding lit his features. "Ah, Jane?" he asked, and Elizabeth nodded.

"She has not said anything, but she confessed to feeling unwell in the mornings, and she could not get away fast enough when Bingley held up the fish he had caught on one of their last days here."

Darcy laughed lightly before saying, "Well, I hope you are correct. It would be a great joy to have our children grow up together. And they will already have two doting aunts in residence to provide them with countless hours of amusement."

At his words, Elizabeth's grin broadened as she shook her head in wonder. It still amazed her that Georgiana and Lydia, despite all odds, had become great friends. Though on the surface, the two had little in common, Georgiana's calm demeanor seemed to quiet some of Lydia's exuberance, while Lydia's more lively disposition had succeeded in drawing the more timid girl from her shell.

To everyone's amazement, Lydia had proved to be far less ungovernable than expected, and even in the short time she had been at Pemberley, the improvement to her character was great. She had begun studying with a drawing master; however instead of working on portraits or landscapes, she had begun sketching fashion plates of her own creation, and had even sold one of her designs to Mrs. McBryde, the local dressmaker.

In fact, it was her relationship with the modiste that had resulted in another major change at Pemberley. Having been introduced to Simon's mother on one of her visits to the estate, Lydia had struck up a friendship of sorts with the young woman, and had soon brokered a deal for Miss Edwards to take up employment with Mrs. McBryde, who was always in need of expert seamstresses.

Simon's mother had given her notice at the dress shop in Sheffield immediately, and come to Pemberley for good. For now, she and Simon were residing with Mrs. Kirk—an arrangement that suited them all admirably—but Elizabeth was certain that it was only a matter of time before Miss Lucy Edwards became Mrs. David Ellis, and the little family moved into a home of their own.

Settling into the curve of her husband's arm, Elizabeth released a contented sigh. Never in her wildest dreams would she have predicted that her life would have taken the direction it had on the day she walked towards her husband at the altar some nine months earlier.

Beside her, Darcy reached out, brushing a curl back from her cheek and tucking it tenderly beneath her bonnet. "What are you thinking, my love?" he asked softly.

"Mmm… Mainly that I am hopelessly in love with my husband," she answered with a smile.

Darcy grinned back at her, but his expression quickly altered when Elizabeth continued, "But I was also thinking about Lady Catherine. I believe I shall write her a letter."

Releasing Elizabeth from his embrace, Darcy straightened his spine, staring back at her with a furrowed brow.

"Lady Catherine? Why on earth would you wish to have anything to do with her? You know very well that I dropped the acquaintance the day she made those disparaging remarks before our wedding. I have not spoken a word to her since, nor do I intend to. If you are thinking to apologize in some way—"

"No, no," Elizabeth interrupted, "nothing like that. I merely wished to thank her for her assistance. You see, contrary to her intent, it was Lady Catherine's visit to Longbourn that led to my acceptance of your offer. For the longest time, I blamed her for forcing my hand, but now I realize she has done me a great service. Had she not abused me so abominably to my face, I might never have retaliated by agreeing to marry you."

Darcy regarded her incredulously before barking out a laugh, and Elizabeth shifted her weight, stretching up to place a kiss upon the curve of his jaw.

As much as she liked to tease, she knew it had been more than Lady Catherine that had brought them together. Despite their faulty first impressions, their hearts had spoken to one another, even when their minds had been too proud and stubborn to listen.

Just then, Harp trotted in their direction, her tail wagging, and Elizabeth smiled up at her husband.

"Come, Mr. Darcy. Let us go home."

Epilogue

J ane entered Pemberley's sunlit parlor, one hand gently rubbing at her lower back. She was growing increasingly uncomfortable in these last few months of her pregnancy, but was grateful she was not so far along as to prevent her from being able to assist her dearest sister with the birth of her niece or nephew.

Across the room, Lydia and Georgiana looked up at her entrance, and the latter quickly stood from her seat to help Jane settle into a chair by the fire.

"How is Elizabeth?" the younger girl asked. "What does the midwife say?"

"The doctor and midwife are both in agreement—the babe will likely be born today, but Lizzy still has many hours left to labor. They sent me away so I could rest a while. They will call for me when we get closer to her time." After a brief pause, she asked, "Have Charles and the colonel returned?"

Georgiana shook her head as Lydia added, "Nor will they any time soon if I had my guess. Did you see Mr. Bingley's face when Lizzy started screaming?"

Jane could not help but smother a smile. She knew Mr. Darcy was happy to have his two closest friends at Pemberley for the birth of his child, but she was equally grateful to Mr. Ellis for volunteering to take the men out on an expedition around the park.

Across from her, Georgiana settled back onto the sofa. "Mrs. Annesley has gone to Mrs. Kirk's, so it is just us for now. Does my brother still sit with Elizabeth?"

"He does. He is determined to be by her side for the whole of it, and to see his son or daughter brought safely into the world. The doctor was clearly dismayed, but the midwife appeared more amused than anything else."

Lydia snorted, lifting her gaze from her sketch pad. "Lord! Imagine having one's husband in the bedchamber to witness all of that! I should forbid such a thing... but then Mr. Darcy has always been irrational where Lizzy is concerned. I have never seen a man so sweet on his wife in all my life!"

Jane laughed, studying her sister. Lydia's eyes sparkled and her pink cheeks glowed with happiness. Even three months after her own relocation to Pemberley, Jane was still struck by the changes in her youngest sister's comportment. Oh, Lydia was still Lydia—brash and bawdy and full of life. But she had learned to temper her behavior in public, and had found an outlet for her energy and creativity with the fashion illustrations she had taken to drawing, which had recently developed into full-fledged clothing designs.

"You are looking very well, Lydia," she said now. "Is that gown you are wearing one of your own creations?"

Instantly, Lydia set her sketchpad aside to stand and twirl before the other ladies. "Yes, do you like it? I only received it back from the dressmaker yesterday. Mrs. McBryde said it was my best design yet. She is making up another just like it to put in the shop window."

"Lydia is exceedingly talented," Georgiana added earnestly. "Mrs. McBryde has already sold several of her designs."

"Indeed, it is very pretty," said Jane.

Snatching up her sketchpad again, Lydia dropped into the chair beside her eldest sister. "Jane, you must see what I am working on now! Is this not the sweetest dress? Oh, I do hope Lizzy's baby is a girl! How I shall love to spoil her."

"Fitzwilliam said he would be elated to have a daughter," replied Georgiana, "but Elizabeth is convinced the babe is a boy."

Lydia wrinkled her nose before saying with a laugh, "Well, I suppose if I can design a gown for a woman nearing her confinement, I can make a pattern for a skeleton suit." Turning to her sister, she continued, "Lizzy loved all the gowns I reworked for her when she was increasing. You must ask if you may borrow some of them, Jane. By the looks of it, you will have need of them soon enough."

Jane blushed as Lydia held her pad up for her sister's inspection, flipping the page. "Here is something I think would do well for Mary. See, there is a built-in fichu in a coordinating color. It is far less dowdy than those high collars she has always favored. Honestly, she will never find a husband if she does not pay some heed to her appearance."

"Lydia!" Jane chided, but her lips were turned up in a smile.

"Well, it is true! And she is the eldest Miss Bennet now, so she should be the next to marry."

At this remarkable statement, Jane's eyebrows lifted. "You did not always feel that way," she said gently. "I believe there was a time when you wished to have a husband before any of your sisters."

"What use have I for a husband?" Lydia replied with a snort of laughter. "Between Mr. Darcy and Papa, I have more than enough pin money. And that is besides the compensation Mrs. McBryde gives me for my designs. Oh! But do not mention that last bit to Papa, for if he knew how handsomely Mrs. McBryde was paying me, he would be sure to cut me off." Setting aside her pad, she collapsed against the cushions before saying, "In any case, I do not intend to marry until I am one and twenty, at least! And that is ages away."

Jane stared back at Lydia with undisguised astonishment. Never in her wildest imaginings would she have thought her most flirtatious sister would be content to spend her days in a rational manner, without even a thought of beaux or matrimony.

Shaking her head in wonder, she said, "And, shall you stay here at Pemberley for all that time? You know you are welcome to come to me and Charles once our estate is in order, if you do not wish to return to Longbourn."

Beside her, Lydia's expression grew pensive. "I have been happy here, but I suppose Lizzy and Mr. Darcy may not want me any longer, now that the babe has come. And soon you shall have a child, too. I suppose I should think about returning to Longbourn. I do miss Mamma and Kitty and my Aunt Philips…" her voice trailed off as Georgiana rushed to her side.

"But you cannot leave! I should be so lonely without you. And I know our brother and sister would not think of asking you to go. Pemberley is your home for as long as you wish it to be."

Lydia's expression instantly brightened and her lips tipped up into a playful smile. "Well then, I suppose I shall stay for a while. Besides, Mr. Darcy promised we could spend the season in Town next year. And someday I wish to go to Paris and study with a real modiste! Perhaps I shall open my own salon in London, and grow impossibly rich, and never marry anyone at all!"

Georgiana giggled. "You could never be a spinster, Lydia!" Turning to Jane she added, "She stared at Richard's friend Captain Wilding a great deal when he came to dinner last month."

"Goodness!" Lydia replied, "I did not say I could no longer appreciate a handsome gentleman in a red coat! But a woman should be able to do for herself. One does not have to marry just to be the center of attention."

Before Georgiana or Jane could comment on such a shocking sentiment, there was a knock at the door to the salon, and a moment later, Elizabeth's lady's maid entered, dropping a brief curtsy.

"Mrs. Bingley, I think you should come now. It looks like the little one is in a greater hurry to be born than any of us imagined!"

~

"He is beautiful, Elizabeth."

Darcy sat on the edge of his wife's bed, his heart near to bursting as he stared down at his newborn son.

He reached out to stroke Elizabeth's hair, and she turned to look up at him, her eyes brimming with tenderness and affection.

"You are not disappointed, then? That he turned out to be a boy and not a girl?"

"Never. He is healthy and perfect, and you are well... that is all I could ever wish for." He paused before saying with a grin, "Besides, I intend to start working on giving him a sister as soon as may be."

Elizabeth laughed, a warm, melodious sound that filled Darcy's heart with joy.

"Well then, I had better get my rest," she teased.

Across the room, Harp yawned noisily, stretching out before the fireplace, and Darcy released a soft chuckle. "I will never forget Dr. Morgan's expression when he arrived. I am not certain if he was more appalled by the presence of a hound or a husband in the birthing room. I was certain he was going to turn tail and run."

Elizabeth smiled up at him. "Well if he had, I am certain we would have managed. The midwife was perfectly capable, and I would not have wished to go through this ordeal without you by my side."

Lifting her hand, Darcy brushed his lips against her wrist before saying softly, "I should probably leave you to get some sleep," he began, but before he had completed his sentence, Elizabeth was shaking her head, her fingers closing around his.

"No, not yet. Besides, we have something of great import to discuss, for we still need to settle on a name for young Master Darcy, here," she said, leaning down to press a soft kiss to the top of their son's head.

Darcy's brow furrowed. "I thought we had agreed on Alexander if it was a boy. Have you changed your mind?"

"No..." Elizabeth answered slowly. "Not exactly.

However, I was thinking... What say you to Robert Alexander Darcy?"

Startled, Darcy blinked back at her, a knot forming in the back of his throat. His mouth opened, then closed again as he struggled to give voice to his emotions.

Obviously misinterpreting his silence, Elizabeth rushed on, "We might still call him Alexander, if referring to him as Robert would be too painful for you. I just thought it might be a fitting tribute, to honor your brother in some way..."

Elizabeth's words trailed off as Darcy quickly shook his head. "I think it a fine idea," he said hoarsely. "To see another Robert Darcy take his rightful place as heir to Pemberley... that would mean a great deal to me. Thank you, Elizabeth."

Elizabeth smiled back at him, reaching up to caress his cheek.

"You are going to be a wonderful father," she murmured as Darcy felt a flush warming his neck.

Once again, Elizabeth squeezed his fingers, but he could see that her eyelids were growing heavy. Reaching out, he gently lifted the babe from her arms before placing a kiss upon her brow.

"Rest now. I will watch over Robert and keep him safe."

Elizabeth looked up at him with a drowsy smile, and Darcy could feel a swell of emotion wash over him as he stared back at the woman he loved beyond all reason, the weight of his son soothing in his arms.

"Elizabeth, I hope you know... That is, I wish I could put into words how much..." His throat tightened, and he shook his head, frustrated now more than ever by his lack of eloquence. But when he gazed into Elizabeth's eyes, he realized it did not matter, for he knew she could see straight through to the recesses of his heart.

"Shh," she whispered. "You need not explain. I find I understand you perfectly now."

The End

THANK YOU

Thank you for reading! I hope you enjoyed this alternate path to Darcy and Elizabeth's happily ever after. If you feel so inclined, the favor of a review would be greatly appreciated.

If you'd like to connect in person, I can be found on Twitter and Facebook at @JAltmanAuthor, or email at Jennifer. Altman.Author@gmail.com.

Until next time,
Jennifer

ALSO BY THE AUTHOR

To Conquer Pride

The course of true love never did run smooth...

When Fitzwilliam Darcy departs Hunsford after his disastrous proposal to Elizabeth Bennet, he does not expect their paths to cross again. Indeed, knowing the lady's true feelings for him, he makes every effort to see that they do not. But when a chance encounter leaves him stranded in an abandoned cottage with the one woman he can never have, Darcy quickly realizes there is more at risk than just Elizabeth's reputation.

Elizabeth Bennet knows Mr. Darcy is the last man in the world whom she could ever be prevailed on to marry. Until the morning he hands her a letter, his countenance as dark and forbidding as the windswept sky. Now, trapped in a snowstorm with the one person she was certain she despised, Elizabeth is startled to discover that her feelings are not at all what she expected.

But is one night alone together enough to alter the course of their future?

Can any man as proud as Mr. Darcy be expected to offer for the same woman a second time?

In this tale of serendipity and second chances, literature's unlikeliest couple must conquer pride, prejudice, and faulty first impressions in the elusive quest for their own happily ever after.

2019 Author Shout Reader Ready Award: Recommended Read

ACKNOWLEDGMENTS

It is a truth universally acknowledged that it takes a village to write a book, and this one was certainly no exception. This novel would not exist in its present state without the generosity and support of the following individuals:

First and foremost, my deepest gratitude goes to Jami Dragan, my first reader. Thank you for reading this book in its rawest form and for encouraging me to keep going. Your positivity and optimism are unrivaled, and I could not have done this without you.

To my editor, Debra Anne Watson: Thank you for taking this project on with very little notice and completing it on an extremely tight timeline. I know I wouldn't have caught half the errors in this manuscript without your help.

To my talented cover designer, Susan Adriani, who is also a gifted writer: Thank you for the countless hours you put into this cover and for never getting frustrated with me, no matter how many changes I asked you to make. You are always a joy to work with.

My heartfelt appreciation goes to my phenomenal beta

readers: Diana Doncaster, Jami Dragan, Susan Ray, Abigail Reynolds, and Joana Starnes, who found lingering typos, offered suggestions, and kept me from embarrassing myself in innumerable ways. Each and every one of you helped to make this a better book, and I am incredibly lucky to have had you in my corner.

To my formatting fairy (you know who you are): Thank you for making this book pretty on the inside, and for saving me untold hours of torment. Your kindness and generosity meant more to me than I can say.

I am also indebted to both Diana Doncaster and Shannon Winslow who assisted in the writing of my book blurb. Thank you for lending me your brilliance and your words.

A very special thank you goes to Melanie Rice, who made a donation to the Jane Austen Variations fundraiser for hurricane relief in 2018 in exchange for a cameo in my next book. I'm so sorry it took nearly three years to get this out, but I hope you're happy with the part you got to play.

My thanks also to my fellow Austen Variations authors for welcoming me into the group, and for your invaluable advice, inspiration, support, and friendship over the past few years.

And to my friends and family, thank you for putting up with me, and for always being there when I need you.

ABOUT THE AUTHOR

Jennifer Altman is a novelist, an anglophile, and a lover of all things Regency. After a long career in the television industry, Jennifer shifted to book publishing in 2016. She currently works in the corporate division of a large publishing company. Jennifer makes her home just outside New York City, where she lives in a compact apartment with a considerable collection of books. When she's not writing, Jennifer can be found reading, watching British period dramas, and not cleaning her house. Her debut novel, *To Conquer Pride*, released in 2018.